Weird Sister

Also by Kate Pullinger

My Life as a Girl in a Men's Prison

The Last Time I Saw Jane

Tiny Lies

When the Monster Dies

Where Does Kissing End?

with Jane Campion

The Piano

Weird Sister

KATE PULLINGER

McArthur & Company
Toronto

First published in Great Britain
in 1999 by Phoenix House
This edition published in 1999 by
McArthur & Company

Canadian Cataloguing in Publication Data

Pullinger, Kate
Weird sister

ISBN 1-55278-085-6

I. Title.

PR6066.U45W44 1999 823 .914 C99-931747-4

Typeset at the Spartan Press Ltd,
Lymington, Hants
Printed in Canada by Transcontinental

McArthur & Company
322 King Street West, Suite 402
Toronto, ON M5V 1J2

10 9 8 7 6 5 4 3 2 1

With thanks to Anne-Marie Casey

And for the books and conversation, thanks to
Catherine Byron, Steph Mastoris,
Rachel Calder, Anne McDermid, Elsbeth Lindner
and Simon Mellor

Then the Judge grew to sentence and asked old Father Samuel what he had to say for himself why judgment of death should not be pronounced on him; whereat he answered that he had nothing to say but 'the Lord have mercy on him'.

Then the Judge asked old Mother Samuel what she had to say for herself to stay judgement; whereat she answered that she was with child, which set all the company on a great laughing . . .

. . . After all this the Judge asked Agnes Samuel the daughter what she had to say why judgment of death should not be given her; at which time there was one (being a prisoner) standing by her that willed her to say that she was also with child. 'Nay,' said she, 'that will I not do; it shall never be said that I was both a witch and whore.'

And so the Judge, after very sound and divine council given severally to them all, proceeded to judgement, which was unto death.

. . . And thus ye have the story of these three witches of Warboys, so plainly and briefly as may be delivered unto you.

From *The Most Strange and Admirable discoverie of the three Witches of Warboys, arraigned, convicted, and executed at the last Assises of Huntingdon, for the bewitching of the five daughters of Robert Throckmorton Esquire, and divers other persons, with sundrie Devillish and grievous torments: And also for the bewitching to death of the Lady Cromwell, the like hath not been heard of in this age.*
London, 1593

Agnes arrives

She has a lot of luggage. It matches. As the taxi stops at the Black Hat the bulb in the streetlamp overhead explodes. A shower of sparks falls over the roof of the black hackney cab, fireworks heralding the arrival of Agnes. The driver doesn't notice; he switches off the engine and climbs out onto the pavement.

The luggage is sleek and heavy and the driver struggles as he unloads it. Rain. She stands beneath her umbrella, expressionless as the driver labours. The narrow pavement is wet and slippery and he is attempting to handle the suitcases carefully; during the long ride from Heathrow – 'what a fare!' he will exclaim to his wife at the end of the day – he has fallen in love with his passenger. A kind of love; he can't quite grasp what is so beguiling about this stranger.

He finishes unloading the cab. 'Do you know where you're going love?' he asks. The streets of Warboys are empty. 'Are people expecting you?'

She doesn't reply to his questions. 'How much do I owe you?'

The driver is embarrassed by the amount. Without blinking, she adds on an enormous tip.

He hands her his card. 'Just ring that number if ever you need a driver. I can come up and take you down to London, sight-seeing, whatever you fancy.' He isn't sure whether or not he is offering these services for free.

'Thank you,' says Agnes, and she holds out her pale hand and smiles.

The driver takes it and is shocked by how cold her fingers feel. 'Get inside, love,' he says, 'get yourself indoors.'

The door of the pub swings open. It's as though the landlord, Jim Drury, has been waiting. Jim looks up, notices that the streetlamp has gone out and feels annoyed. Then he looks back down and sees her. He can hardly breathe.

The taxi driver climbs into his cab, does a U-turn and swings away. He feels full of regret at leaving her in this small, damp village; at the same time he can't wait to get away, back onto the motorway.

Agnes waves as he drives away; he sees her in his rear-view mirror.

Then she turns and offers her cold, cold hand to Jim Drury.

Elizabeth

Agnes Samuel was beautiful, there was no doubt about that. She had the kind of face that you see displayed across the hard shiny pages of one hundred women's magazines, a model's face, symmetrical, perfect, and yet somehow indistinct, malleable. Change of hair, change of make-up and she would look completely different. Completely other. But always lovely. Always. It was a kind of power she had, and it was awesome. You wouldn't want to stand in its way.

I probably kid myself when I say I was in the way, I am perhaps giving myself too much credit.

When Agnes Samuel, and her beauty, came to Warboys, our little village nestled low on the grey fenland, something was bound to happen. It was as though she was too big for us; we were too small. She was American, of course, and that was something to reckon with on its own. We're not on the tourist trail, and so we're not accustomed to strangers. Sometimes when I watch the news on telly I get the feeling that the whole world is on the move, entire populations getting up and shifting, spilling out of boats, straggling over mountains, wedging themselves onto trains. London is full-up with strangers, it's a city of strangers, it has always been that way. Warboys – well, in Warboys we keep to ourselves. Some of us go away from time to time but we nearly always return. Agnes herself was making a return of sorts although we didn't recognize it at the time. I didn't recognize it, although now I see it very clearly.

Agnes was an incredibly angry person. I'm not saying that with hindsight – from the moment she arrived it was evident to me that she was very angry. And she controlled that anger, like she controlled everyone around her, perfectly. In a way her anger was bigger than she was, bigger than all of us. And I think it's what made people love her; her hatred was so complete, so all-encompassing, so passionate. We are all attracted to passion, we don't often think to examine its source. In these muffled times we long for big emotions, it's the big emotions that make our hearts beat. Agnes hated us, and she hated Robert most of all. How could I hope to compete?

Robert

I fell in love with Agnes Samuel because she was beautiful. There was no doubt about that. When I met her I realized that I'd never really been in love before. I'd had girlfriends of course, lots of them, I'd even contemplated getting engaged a couple of times. But it hadn't felt right. It was as though I was waiting for someone and when she came along I knew it. It was her, Agnes. From the moment I met her, I knew.

And despite everything that has happened, I still love her. I know I should not say those words or, at the very least, I should whisper those words under my breath, mumble them to myself in the bathroom late at night, because everyone would be appalled – angry – to hear them. But I say them anyway.

Agnes. My best, my beloved, my girl.

Weird Sister

Some villages are earnest about the past, so earnest they forget about the present day. Forever trotting out the town crier, ladies costumed as milkmaids, blokes in battle dress, arguing about the role their village played in history. Some towns have long memories. Not Warboys. It is as though the village woke up one morning and looked on itself with shame. Grotesque, they said, not worth the telling. Not worth remembering.

They were wrong of course. Awful stories are always the most thrilling.

But people forget. People have forgotten. A few generations on, as little as one in some cases, and the memory stops. As though the events never happened. The Throckmortons of Warboys have forgotten. After all, many generations have passed since they last met Agnes Samuel. Ask them about their family history and Robert might say something about the Gunpowder Plot – wasn't one of their number, from the Warwickshire branch of the family, involved in that? He isn't sure. Perhaps if they'd had more money the family memory would have been better preserved, catalogued, archived. Instead it has been corroded and erased by daily life, left to moulder and brew like the decaying old house in which they live.

But some people do remember. Some never forget. Like Agnes Samuel. In Warboys they say it is as though for her the past lives as vividly as the present. They say it is because of the past that she is here today. And yet decades, generations, centuries, have passed between then and now; it is more than four hundred years since Agnes Samuel last met the Throckmorton family.

Agnes hasn't forgotten.

Robert meets Agnes

Curtains are closed tight against the cold in every window in the village and the icy moon hangs low. The only light for miles radiates from the good pub, the Black Hat. (Around the bend on another corner stands the Marquis of Granby, but it is dark, even when it is full of people it is dark.) In the Black Hat the carpets tend toward the grimy, but the proprietor is forgiven for that, because otherwise the pub is stellar, absolutely gold star, with its wine list full of chardonnays and its Sunday lunch menu of roast lamb and mint sauce and potatoes dauphinoise. In the middle of the village stands the clocktower; on top of it the weathervane swings quietly. No one notices anymore but the weathervane depicts a black witch in a black hat on her black broom. She points north until the wind swings her south, west, east, and everywhere she points, that's where evil goes. This is Warboys, a small village, unsuspecting.

At the Black Hat Mr Drury steps out from behind the bar. He's in a good mood tonight and he feels like a proper and benevolent pub landlord; he always tries to look benevolent but it is all too rare when he actually feels it. He is a small man, tidy, neatly dressed in a white shirt, tie and black trousers, ironed by his wife Lolita – it's a curse, that name, Lolita says, now that she is fifty and having to diet – Jim Drury steps out from behind the bar and slaps Ronald Oxford on the shoulder heartily, laughing at the man's poor attempt at a joke. Ronald Oxford, the village bore, no one likes to end up seated beside him. It's a fact. Jim likes to keep his customers sorted according to what he considers to be their most salient personality trait; at the bar there is Ronald, the village bore, and Geraldine Andley, the village tart (she's not a real tart, the real village tart – if there was one – would drink in the Marquis of Granby, of course). Over by the window is Geoff Henderson, the village athlete, captain of the cricket team. 'Can I get you a drink Geoff?' Jim says. He likes to keep Geoff, and his team, sweet. A loud guffaw resounds behind him and Jim turns to look. It's Graeme Throckmorton, the village bully. The village no-hoper, the village bad guy, Graeme Throckmorton you belong in the Marquis of Granby, although Jim Drury would never say that, no matter how much he longed to.

'I hear your team lost, Geoff,' says Graeme. 'You don't deserve a drink.' He laughs loudly, a joyless laugh.

Jim straightens his tie nervously. All his life he has avoided trouble in the pub, his is the good pub, there is never trouble in his pub, which is why he would love for nothing more than to get rid of Graeme Throckmorton once and for all. But getting rid of Graeme Throckmorton is not in his command.

'It's true,' admits Geoff Henderson, because he is a good bloke, he was born a good bloke and will one day die a good bloke, 'it's true Graeme. My team plays like crap on occasion. On too many occasions.' He laughs and his laugh is genuine and the two women he is sitting with – his wife Marlene and her sister Dora who is visiting from Germany – laugh too. 'Not like,' Geoff says smiling, 'when you played for us.'

Graeme looks down into his drink and Geoff regrets what he said, he meant it kindly, Graeme was once a great player, the best. Geoff worries that when Graeme looks up again he will be bigger, angrier, meaner than before because that's what happens when you rub Graeme the wrong way these days, and it is well near impossible not to rub Graeme the wrong way. And Jim, who still stands between the two tables, gets so rattled he lets the cloth he wipes the tables with fall to the floor.

But just then the door at the bottom of the stairs swings open and the reason why Jim Drury is feeling exceptionally benevolent, the reason why he feels pub landlording is a noble and dignified profession once again, walks through. 'Ah-ha!' says Jim, blushing, bending over and retrieving his cloth with a balletic swoop, 'it's you, love.' And he walks quickly toward the woman standing there.

Everyone in the Black Hat has stopped talking. Everyone is staring. Agnes Samuel heats up the room with her smile. 'I think it's hysterical,' she says, her voice quiet, confidential, 'that everyone calls me love.'

Jim snorts a big laugh and smiles and blushes a deeper red. He takes Agnes by the hand and, before he can stop himself, he bends down and kisses it lightly. He looks up into Agnes's face – he is a small man, after all, and Agnes is a tall American – and he says, 'Let me show you to your table.' Which is ludicrous because this is a pub, not a hotel restaurant with reservations and flowers on the tables, but a pub where you take what you can get and that often means standing-room only. Yet suddenly the table closest to the fire is Agnes's table, the best table, the table with the view of the rest of the pub, the table the rest of the pub can most easily view. Jim leads her over – it's a real fire, wood, and it sparks and crackles at Agnes's approach – and she sits down gracefully. She is wearing high-heeled pumps with her slim trousers and a skinny top with a scooped neck that reveals some of her white, white skin. She has one of those impossible figures at which other women marvel – long legs, narrow hips and a flat belly that runs all the way up to her high, round breasts.

'Miss Samuel,' says Jim to whomever may be listening – everyone is listening – 'is a bed and breakfast guest of the Black Hat. Miss Samuel is in Warboys to seek out her roots.' As he speaks Jim looks into Agnes's eyes and her gaze does not flicker nor flinch. 'And what would you –' his diction is laborious, as though he is suddenly aware of how his English accent must sound to her American ears – 'be drinking?'

'Oh,' she says lightly, 'I'll have a whisky.' And Jim scurries to the bar to fetch it. An out-take of collectively-held breath fills the pub, booze and nicotine, and the noise level gradually begins to build as people return to their conversations, to their gossip and their pub philosophy. These people all know each other, they know each other all too well. Everyone in the room continues to gawp at Agnes, even if with only half an eye or ear. Some with less discretion than others. Some with none at all. Graeme Throckmorton stares at Agnes, he stares and stares, his face gone pale, his eyes electric. Geoff Henderson turns and notices Graeme's expression, and if Graeme had been a different man Geoff would have slapped him on the shoulder and said, 'What's up, mate? You look like you've seen a ghost,' but instead he says nothing and returns to Marlene. Behind the bar Jim Drury is breaking the seal on a bottle of his favourite single malt. His wife disapproves for a moment. 'She's got to learn,' mumbles Jim, 'I said I'd teach her about whisky.' When Lolita looks toward the young woman, she softens. At her table Agnes has shifted in her seat toward the fire and the light cast on her face is very becoming.

Graeme Throckmorton stands suddenly. He takes a step forward, a lurching step, which brings him up short and reminds him to grab his cane. Cane in hand, he walks, a tall straight-backed man with a broad chest and long thick thighs, black unruly hair that hides a scar that runs across the top of his head; Graeme's body is covered with hidden scars – rugby wounds, fist fights, accidents. His right leg stiff as though it has no knee, he swings it round closely like a big club he's trying to hide up his sleeve. He makes his way toward Agnes's table and the noise level in the pub rises again, as though everyone is shouting in an effort to mask how closely they are listening.

Jim arrives with Agnes's whisky. 'Laphroaig,' he says. She smiles at him and takes a sip and is about to speak when Graeme overtakes her.

'What are you doing here?' Spoken harshly as though he knows her intentions.

Agnes turns toward Graeme. 'Excuse me?'

The hub-bub in the pub grows louder still.

'What brings you to Warboys?' As though he thinks he knows what she has in mind.

Later Jim will feel stunned when he remembers how he crossed Graeme Throckmorton that evening. He will wonder how he did it. And, foolishly, he will take credit for saving the situation.

'Graeme,' he says, 'I think you should let the lady drink her whisky in peace.'

Graeme is dragging his stormy gaze away from Agnes, he is turning his attention to Jim. Little Jim Drury, who is in his way. He opens his mouth, he is not going to be polite, when Agnes speaks first. 'Oh Jim,' she says, 'can't you see the man's a cripple?' She smiles benignly at them both. 'Now what was it you wanted to ask me? Love.' With that last word she slides her tongue across her teeth.

Graeme snaps his mouth shut. If he was an animal, he would roar. Furious, he lifts his cane and Jim cringes as though it is coming toward him already. But Graeme uses it to punch the door of the pub open wide and, without pausing, he walks outside. He feels the weight of the pub's scorn on his back and it burns at him, but he does not care. He is used to hatred, it doesn't touch him.

Back inside the pub Jim Drury can't believe his luck. Trouble averted – forgotten – he looks at Agnes and is freshly amazed that a woman like this should happen to come and stay in his pub. He doesn't notice how she stares at the door Graeme Throckmorton has just walked through, how she stares as though she is sending a message. He straightens his tie again and pushes back his hair. 'Madam,' he says and after a moment Agnes looks up at him with her green, green eyes, eyes he could look into forever, 'the drink is on the house.'

Outside the Black Hat Graeme Throckmorton does up the buttons on his black suede jacket. It's a well-made, expensive jacket, he bought it in London, his wife Karen doesn't know how much it cost. He sniffs the night air as he puts on his gloves, the cane standing dormant against his hip. Then he swings out and crosses the street and goes home to where his wife and family are waiting.

Robert Throckmorton does not see his brother leaving as he hurries along the pavement toward the Black Hat. He walks in the same door through which Graeme exited and doesn't notice how people glance up and double-take. He is used to it, and so are they, although the people of Warboys still double-take. Robert looks just like his older brother, only where Graeme is thick and muscley, Robert is lean and taut. Where Graeme is brooding and angry, Robert is calm and quiet. Both men are arrogant, it is a Throckmorton condition, but where Graeme spells it out, Robert keeps it hidden. At least, he thinks he keeps it hidden. Women can see it though, they can see it in his face. They find it appealing.

They all live together, the Warboys Throckmortons, in one big extended family. Robert and Graeme, brothers, Robert thirty-four, Graeme two years his senior. Graeme's wife Karen and their two little boys, Andrew and Francis. Jenny, Robert and Graeme's teenage sister, and Martin, paterfamilias, wheelchair-bound, silent. All together under one roof, one big family. 'Happy?', Robert would say, 'I suppose so. In our way.'

Robert is known in Warboys as the village bachelor, everyone agrees with Jim Drury's private label in this case. The most eligible man for miles around. Robert has dated all the best-looking women in the village and he is feeling a little fed up. When he was a teenager he had secret rendezvous with older women, not all of them unmarried. In his twenties he went through the women his own age as though operating to a system. Now the women he sees are getting younger and younger, even he has begun to notice. He can't follow their conversation anymore, pop stars he's never heard of, movies he wouldn't dream of going to, clubs in distant towns that make him feel like a statesman from another generation. He wouldn't admit it out loud, but Robert is getting tired of being eligible. All this time he has only been looking for love. He is hungry for love.

Robert's evening is going rather badly. He hadn't recognized Lucy Hill, he hadn't seen her since she was about ten years old, and now she is sixteen, the same age as his sister Jenny. Except Lucy Hill doesn't look sixteen, all Wonderbra and tight trousers, or perhaps Robert doesn't know what most sixteen-year-olds look like these days. He was in the Marquis of Granby, the other pub, the pub the upstanding citizenry of Warboys consider to be the bad pub, the topless darts on telly pub, the lager and lime shandy pub, the pub with the mottled red carpets and torn, sodden upholstery.

Drinking there gives Robert a low-life kind of thrill, lets him think he lives dangerously. She'd been standing in the dark corner. 'Hello there,' he said, easing himself out of the banquette, 'can I buy you a drink?'

The girl smiled confidently. 'Sure,' she said, 'G & T.'

'I'm Robert.'

'Lucy.' They began to chat. Robert felt happy.

Later, when Robert stepped up to the bar to refresh Lucy's drink, he found himself next to Derek Hill. Derek Hill is the same age as Robert, they went to school together. Derek was the son of a building labourer and Robert was the son of – a Throckmorton. 'Robert,' Derek says, raising his drink and one eyebrow, 'who's your victim this evening?' People who drink in the Marquis of Granby are used to Robert Throckmorton and his parade of women.

Robert ducks his head and smiles sheepishly, he too is accustomed to – rather fond of – this routine. He fetches the girl, cajoling, arm around her waist. 'Lucy,' he says, showing off to the girl how he can get on with anyone, how anyone can be his friend, no matter how lowly, 'this is Derek'.

Derek grabs Robert by the collar. 'Don't you ever lay your hands on my daughter,' he says. 'Do you hear me?' He gives Robert an acid shake, 'She's sixteen, you filthy beast.'

Robert jerks his shirt away from Derek's grasp. Lucy laughs out loud. Robert is shocked and flustered and he doesn't want to show it. He's an amiable bloke, the kind of fellow who can get on with anybody. He's only looking for love, he didn't set out to be lecherous. That's not me, he says to himself, that's not me. He turns on his heel and leaves the Marquis of Granby without saying another word to anybody.

And makes his pre-occupied way to the Black Hat. How was I to know the girl was Derek Hill's daughter? Jesus Christ, it's not the kind of thing you think to ask. He might as well have had a drink with his old friend – his oldest friend – Elizabeth.

He walks into the Black Hat. At first all he sees is the fire. It is bright and warm after the cold dark of the street. He moves close to the flames, holding out his hands which are reddened and chafed from the cold, this unseasonably cold October evening. He gives a great shiver and allows the muscles in his back to relax, release their tension. Warmth floods through his body and he closes his eyes.

When he opens them he sees a face. She has sea-green eyes and dark wavy hair that shines. Her face is heart-shaped, it starts with a widow's peaked forehead and ends in a chin that is just a tiny bit pointed, and she is smiling at him through red lips, small white teeth.

Robert lowers himself into a chair. 'Hello,' he says, extending his cold hand toward her.

'Hello,' she replies, taking his hand with both of hers. When she touches him he feels it throughout his body. He looks at her and thinks he has known her all his life.

'Agnes,' she says, 'Agnes Samuel.'

'Robert Throckmorton,' he replies.

'Good,' she says, smiling. 'Great.'

From behind the bar Jim Drury observes this meeting. He understands that he is witnessing an important event, an event that will change things in Warboys. He sees the look that passes between Robert and Agnes and he finds himself thinking about when he first fell in love with Lolita. He turns to look for his wife and she is standing right beside him, she is watching Robert and Agnes as well. Jim puts his arms around Lolita's not inconsiderable waist and gives his wife a kiss full of longing and passion. They turn back to watch Robert and Agnes.

'I've had a rotten evening,' Robert speaks slowly and is surprised to hear how rough his voice sounds, as though he's been crying. When he speaks he suddenly realizes how lonely he is, how lonely he has always been. He is tired, so tired, of being lonely.

'Forget about it,' Agnes replies.

'In fact, it hasn't been a great couple of years.'

'Put it behind you.'

'I want to settle down,' Robert speaks without thinking.

'You will get exactly what you've always wanted.'

'I hate being single.'

'You won't have to be what you don't want to be anymore.'

'I don't want to –'

Agnes raises her hand and places it on Robert's cheek, as though in benediction. She strokes his skin with her thumb. 'I'm here now,' she says slowly. 'You won't be lonely with me.'

By now the whole pub is watching. Their noise has dropped away completely, Robert and Agnes speak surrounded by silence. Although their exact words can not be overheard, everyone knows what is taking place and, as Robert and Agnes speak, everyone in the Black Hat begins to feel happy. Happy and happier, deliriously happy. It isn't every day you actually see two people fall in love, it isn't every day you see fate at work in that way. They'll be talking about it in the streets tomorrow, to anyone who will listen, telling it and re-telling it, blow by blow. It isn't every day you witness a *coup de foudre*, right where everyone can see it.

Robert sits back in his chair. He can't take his eyes off Agnes, he can't stop looking at her, he doesn't want to stop looking at her. Agnes is smiling and laughing, her face young and unlined and full of anticipation.

'I knew good things would happen for me in Warboys,' she says. 'I knew I would meet you, Robert Throckmorton. Nothing could stand in my way.'

Robert

It was fantastic when we first met, absolutely incredible. She floored me, she really did, it was like she had taken a broom and swept me right off my feet, I'm sorry to put it that way, but it's true. I would have done anything to be with her. She combined the best qualities of all the women I'd ever met – and more. She was gorgeous and sexy and intelligent and single and American and funny and sporty and . . . well, you see what I mean. She had money, enough not to have to work or worry. And she was interested in me. Me. I'll admit, I was used to women being interested in me, but not that interested, not interested in that way. Agnes was interested in my soul, in my heart, in my mind – in everything about me. That's incredibly seductive. You try getting away from that. Not that I wanted to get away. She had me from the moment we met.

That first night we were both cautious. I didn't want to make her feel like I was rushing things forward, I didn't want to push my luck. And besides, we had Jim Drury to contend with, Jim was so excited, so proud of his pub, so keen to make sure Agnes was having a great time, that she was comfortable, that she would stay for more than one night. I don't think he'd have been too keen on me running upstairs with his prize guest. It seemed important to be gentlemanly, a proper Englishman. And I wanted to get things exactly right. I was afraid that if I did things wrong she would disappear. Just disappear. And we'd all look at each other and wonder if she had ever really existed, if she had been there among us, or was a creature of our collective imaginations.

Could we do that? Could a village, stuck in its ways after hundreds of years of being exactly the same, could a village conjure up the perfect incomer, the perfect injection of fresh blood, new life? Willing itself to open up to a stranger? Well, it was as though that is what Warboys did for Agnes. Warboys was ready. I was ready.

We met at lunchtime the next day. Before parting we had made an arrangement to go for a walk. She was waiting for me outside the Black Hat.

'Hi,' she said, smiling and shivering with the cold. She tucked her arm through mine.

'Hello,' I said, feeling awkward suddenly. 'How did you sleep?'

'All right. Still a little jet-lagged. I found myself wandering around at half past three.'

'Oh no,' I said, 'I hope you brought your slippers.' Where did I unearth that one? I felt even more embarrassed. A woman like Agnes wouldn't wear slippers, would she?

'Yes,' she said laughing, 'I always remember my slippers.' That was what she was like; she put me at ease. We crossed the street.

I'm not that interested in local history and neither, it transpired, was Agnes. Elizabeth would disagree. Elizabeth says Agnes was obsessed with local history, with a particular moment in our local history, but I think she's got that wrong. We didn't look at the church or the graveyard or the houses, we wandered around the village and then took a public footpath leading out to the fens. I know that Jim says Agnes told him she was here to seek out her roots – when things were going very badly he kept repeating that over and over – and I know that Elizabeth used Jim's statement, if you could call it that, to help support her theory, but Agnes never demonstrated the slightest bit of interest in that stuff to me. She was like a lot of Americans that way, to her England itself was historical; to her eyes there was nothing remotely modern about the place. Everything was old and, all too often, decrepit. Agnes liked modern things, it was something she often got homesick for, especially when it was really cold and damp, indoors as well as out, especially when faced with the inadequacies of our house and its plumbing. So I would maintain that Agnes was not interested in history. And I think I knew Agnes, I knew her best. Lots of people now claim to have seen the real Agnes but surely I'm the one to whom they should defer. I was her husband, after all. I knew her best.

We walked for a good two hours. It was a cold day and Agnes's cheeks were healthy and red. She was wearing a big grey sweater with sleek black trousers and a green wool scarf and a black woolly hat and gloves – I remember these details, I found that with Agnes I noticed the details in a way I'd never bothered with before. We enjoyed the cold air and walking fast and warming up, swinging our arms and banging our gloved hands together to keep the circulation going. The sun shone and as we walked it seemed to warm up along with us, the light growing stronger and stronger until it no longer resembled thin English autumn sunshine but felt more southern, Mediterranean, the air warm and soft.

We talked about all kinds of things, including the weather.

'It's cold here,' she said, 'colder than I expected.'

'It's the damp.'

She nodded vigorously, as though it would help her warm up. 'It's the damn damp. Gets into your bones. I feel it. What kind of country is this – hotels advertise they've got central heating as though it's a kind of unexpected bonus.'

'Isn't it warm in the Black Hat?'

'Too warm. The whole building fills up with smoke from the fire and the stink from the ale and the spirits and all the cigarettes – you Brits still smoke a lot – and it gets hotter and hotter until, after closing, Jim and Lolita open the doors and the windows and all the heat and smoke rushes out and the damp clambers in and I'm freezing. I need two hot water bottles just to get through the night.'

'The damn damp,' I said.

'That's right, the damn damp,' she repeated.

It became a running joke between us, Britain and its deficiencies.

It was something we had in common, our complaints. 'Oh,' Agnes would say to me, smiling, 'you're so unpatriotic.'

That afternoon Agnes told me two facts that had a great impact on me, on the way I thought about her, saw her. She told me that both her parents were dead – she didn't say how or when. I'd been talking about my family, she was very interested in my family and so, naturally, I asked about hers.

'My parents?' she said. We had stopped walking and were looking out across the flat field. Although I grew up here I don't particularly care for the landscape. In most seasons the fens resemble an enormous wet car park. Agnes kept her eyes on the horizon. 'They're dead.' She turned to look at me. She had stopped smiling.

'Both of them?'

'Yes.' Her look was calm, as though she was appraising my reaction. I felt like I was trespassing, but at the same time I felt closer to her.

'Dead mothers,' I said, regretting it immediately.

'What?'

'Something we share.' Agnes didn't speak. She stared at me, her gaze unreadable. I felt a bumbling fool. 'I'm sorry,' I said.

'It was a long time ago,' Agnes replied, and she began walking again. For a while neither of us spoke. The ground was soft and covered with fallen leaves. Our shoes were beginning to get muddy. After a while Agnes spoke again.

'I've never really been in love,' she said.

The first confidence had seemed almost ordinary. Not the fact that both her parents were dead, that was terrible, but the fact that she'd told me they were dead. It's normal for two people who are getting to know each other to talk about their families. And her reticence, that seemed normal as well, given the circumstances. But to tell me that she'd never really been in love before – to me that was extraordinary. Call it male pride, but to me it was a kind of challenge. She wasn't coy about it, she didn't lower her eyes and look up at me blinking, as if to say, will you be the lucky boy? She said it in her blunt, disarming, matter-of-fact way, as if she said it all the time, as if Jim Drury, the landlord of the Black Hat, had said 'Would you like a room?' and she had replied, 'I've never really been in love before, but yes, thank you. For at least one night. With central heating.'

I held my breath and struggled to think of something to say. And then it came to me: 'Neither have I.' When I said those words Agnes looked at me sharply. And it was true, it was absolutely true, I was 34-years-old and had never really been in love. Not until I met Agnes Samuel.

So then I was presented with this challenge, this quest: to make Agnes Samuel love me. To make Agnes Samuel stay in Warboys. She might not have seen it that way, but I did. I guess in this instance Jim Drury and I were in league together, he wanted her to stay in residence at his pub, I didn't care where she stayed, I simply wanted her in my village. I needed her in my village.

My village is a funny old place. It's in the middle of nowhere and it doesn't have much to distinguish it. It's too far from London to be in the commuter belt, too far from Cambridge to appeal to rural-looking residents of that city. It consists of an intersection – where the clocktower stands – and several residential streets. There is one shop, Barbara's, which is also the post office, a petrol station, and two pubs. Our house is one of the oldest, if not the oldest. Like I say, I'm not interested in history, but I'm fond of our village. Otherwise, why would I have stayed?

After our walk we went back to the pub, but it was past two o'clock and Jim and Lolita were no longer serving lunch. But an exception was made for Agnes, exceptions were always made for Agnes, it was one of the great things about being with her. So we ate sandwiches – Jim makes a good doorstep – and then I had to get back to the office. At this time of year the estate isn't very busy but if I don't attend to it every day things tend to grind to a halt. We arranged to meet that evening.

'Seven o'clock?' Agnes suggested. Without saying much she made it absolutely clear she wanted to see me again. It was in the way she held my gaze.

'Seven o'clock,' I replied. 'I'll be there.'

My heart pounded for the rest of the afternoon, I'm sure if my pulse had been taken it would have been racing. I actually felt quite peculiar, as though I'd inhaled too much air and it was trapped at the top of my head and between my shoulderblades. I sat in my office, in that cold, cavernous room, working on figures. I knew my father was on the other side of the house, in the sitting room, in his chair in front of the fireplace, a blanket over his knees. I imagined I could hear the steam rising off the cup of tea Karen had taken him, I thought I could hear him breathing. But that couldn't have been possible, there were too many thick walls and corridors between us. I don't know why I suddenly felt so aware of him, of his silent, blank presence. My thoughts flickered back and forth, from my father to Agnes, Agnes to my father, as I stared at the spreadsheet on my computer screen.

That evening I tried to eat what Karen had cooked for dinner but was unable, I was too keyed up. I announced I was going to the pub and when I looked at my watch, I suddenly realized I was going to be late. How could that be? I'd watched the clock so closely all afternoon. Jenny said she wanted to come too, and Graeme said he needed a drink, but I grabbed my coat and rushed out the door, saying I'd see them later. I ran down the drive and out onto the high street, forcing myself to slow to a more acceptable pace.

When I got to the Black Hat it was nearly empty, not many people had come out for the evening yet. Lolita was behind the bar polishing glasses, no sign of Jim. Nor Agnes. Lolita shrugged when I asked if she knew where her guest was, saying 'Lovely girl,' as she pulled my beer, 'lovely. I expect she'll be down later.' She smiled widely, as though she knew this was torture for me.

I sat at the table by the fire, the table where Agnes had been seated the night before. I sipped at my beer and settled down to watch the clock and the door, checking both whenever anyone came in. Gradually the pub began to fill. An hour passed and it was nearly eight o'clock. Jim bustled around the room wiping tables, saying 'lovely girl' whenever anyone asked after Agnes. 'Lovely girl.' Everyone asked after her, and everyone agreed, as though there was nothing unusual about her being here and, equally, nothing unusual about her not being here now. Graeme and Jenny arrived, they stood together at the bar. I got increasingly worked up. Had I misheard the time we were to meet? Had I imagined the whole thing? Was it all a horrible joke cooked up by Graeme?

And then the door opened one more time, and it wasn't Agnes, and I looked at the clock, it was 8:15, and I looked at the window – there was Agnes's face, framed perfectly, hovering at an unnatural height, she must have been standing on her very tip-toes, pale skin, her green eyes staring, but not at me. I grabbed my coat and rushed out the door, but she wasn't there, she wasn't standing on her toes in front of the window, and I thought, damn, I am going crazy, when I heard her voice. She called my name. She was on the other side of the street, by the entrance to the grounds of the church. I went over to her and she gave me a kiss on my left cheek. And we walked again, through the village, around in circles, and all the things – banal and profound – I'd been waiting all my life to say came pushing and stuttering out of me.

What can I say about her? At the time, when it became public knowledge that we were going to be married, I was asked about her several times every day, strange, vague questions that you'd think people might ask of a movie star, not someone flesh and blood, not someone they had sat with at the pub, bumped into on the street. 'What's she like?' they'd say. 'What's she really like, you know, in private?' But the funny thing is that I'd have the same trouble answering that question now, after everything that has happened, as I did then. She was beautiful – but that doesn't tell you anything. Tall – 5'10" – slim, green eyes, black hair – her hair grew very quickly and it fell out a lot, at times it was as though she was moulting. When I'd complain – I did complain I'm afraid, I was forever having to unclog the drains – she'd reply serenely, her tone only very slightly harsher than normal, that it fell out at exactly the same rate as other people's, except her hair was more noticeable because it was long and dark. She smelt fantastic – of perfume, light and floral and, beneath that, something riper, womanly. The profiteroles, one of the young women I'd been dating recently used to say about the way we smell when we are horny. I think she meant pheromones, the sex chemical we are said to release. Agnes smelt of profiteroles. She had the ability to make people feel good; you felt good if you'd been talking to Agnes. When you had Agnes's attention you felt as though the world revolved around you, the universe existed so that you and Agnes could have this conversation. There was nothing better in life than talking with Agnes. 'Yes,' she would say as you spoke, nodding her head, remembering some small detail from a previous conversation, 'what was that like? Tell me.'

Our courtship felt like it lasted a lifetime, but in fact it lasted exactly three weeks. We had a week of lunches and evenings together, long walks, time spent sitting by the fire at the Black Hat. Jim Drury was over the moon, he was so pleased that she was staying, and that she and I had, as he said, 'made friends'. It pained me when Jim used those words to describe my relationship with Agnes and that's when I realized that I had fallen in love with her. And as I have said, it happened when we first met, when I first saw her in front of the fire.

Lunchtime on the eighth day, I went to fetch Agnes for our walk. Jim Drury, rather sheepishly I thought, told me Agnes had asked if I'd go upstairs to her room, she was waiting for me there. I hadn't been to her room before and I'd never had an occasion to go upstairs in the Black Hat. While the pub itself is decorated in classic posh pub style – ornamental shoe horns and rather valuable Toby jugs, logs stacked by the fire, plush and faded velvet curtains, thick, slightly worn upholstery, and lots of gleaming woodwork – from the staircase upward it becomes a different place altogether, a kind of chintz extravaganza, very fussy. Lolita and Jim live on the top floor and on the middle floor there are three extra bedrooms that they let out to bed and breakfast guests, although overnight visitors are pretty rare in Warboys. Agnes was staying in the largest and most heavily decorated room; there was even a ruffle around the sink. 'I don't mind,' she said when I raised my eyebrows. 'It serves my purpose. The bed is comfortable, Robert.' She looked at the bed, and she looked at me.

I'll say only this – a few minutes later Agnes and I got into that bed. We scarcely emerged from it for the next two weeks.

Elizabeth

Agnes's appearance coincided with a very rough patch for me. I was no longer working in London. I'd given up my career as a therapist. It had been my vocation and without my work I didn't know who I was any longer. I'd sold my flat with its stripped wooden floor-boards and yellow walls and those green brocade curtains I bought in John Lewis and I'd come home to the cottage in which I'd grown up. My father had died, and our cottage was there with its sweet-smelling climbing roses and its foxgloves and wild sweet peas. It was as though I'd retired from life, from the world; on very bad days it felt as though I had died and Warboys was the grave I had dug for myself. On those dark days I could picture Agnes looking down at me in my coffin, ready to throw her spadeful of sod.

There was a lot to sort out in the aftermath of my father's death and, as I'd been pre-occupied with work and had left it for some time, it had got rather complicated. I had to sort out his will and transfer his possessions – the cottage, the car, some investments – into my name. The mortgage on the property was completely paid off and I had thought that there was enough money for me to live, if I was careful. But I guess I miscalculated, or perhaps under-estimated the cost of living on my own while unemployed. It was around the time Agnes arrived that I realized I'd have to get a job and that it wouldn't be doing anything I wanted to be doing. I sank very low indeed. And Robert was nowhere to be seen. I tried to ring him, but he was never in, and my messages went unheeded.

Agnes meets the Throckmortons

Although they have seen each other every day and most nights for several weeks, Agnes has not been to the Throckmorton house yet, has not been introduced to the family. Robert feels as though Agnes is his secret, his passionate, dark, consuming secret, even though everyone in the Black Hat – everyone in the village – knows about the affair. Bringing her to the house involves revealing something, an unveiling. He will present her to the family, like a gift, and with this gift they will know more of him as well. He feels ready.

The Throckmorton house stands at the outskirts of the village, tucked behind a dense stand of gone-wild hedgerows and trees, not visible from the high street. A curved gravel drive leads to the front door. On the left is the original sixteenth-century house, grand for its time, small by later standards; in the middle a seventeenth-century, rather larger, addition; on the right a further enlargement, built in the eighteenth century. All these parts give the house a grafted look, like it has sprung up from the earth unnaturally; no attempt to disguise this disunity has ever been made. Inside, most of the rooms have changed their usage half a dozen times as the focus of the house has shifted from left to right to centre. The kitchen is a Victorian addition to the rear of the building. Bathrooms are an even more recent afterthought. The ground floor of the Elizabethan wing now lies empty, as does most of the first floor, empty and waiting for occupancy. It is this, the original house, that was built when the Throckmortons were at their most prominent and confident, their most wealthy; so it is this part of the house that is the grandest and also the most decayed.

The front garden has been overtaken by brambles and sprawling shrubbery, lavateria, forsythia and cistus choking out everything else; the wisteria that once climbed above the front door is dead, the thick vines slowly peeling away from the brickwork, taking the pointing with it. Once a year Robert rakes the gravel drive, pulling up the dandelions and bindweed that spring up despite the cars. The Throckmortons spend no time in this part of the garden; instead they look to the rear, to the field and, in the distance, the cottages. Graeme's wife, Karen, tends the rose garden. There is a lawn framed by massive old yew hedges upon which Graeme practises a mad version of topiary. Standing on the top-most rung of the crooked ladder he shapes and curves the yew with his father's petrol-powered chainsaw; the hedges look like vast dark clouds rolling up the lawn, a dense fogbank between the Throckmortons and the rest of the world. The yew hedges themselves are hollow; they form a long, dark tunnel, tall enough to stand in, where spiders and field mice dwell, hedgehogs and foxes as well, and generations of Throckmorton children have dared each other to hide.

Saturday morning. They've dressed up, Agnes and Robert, they are both wearing suits, Agnes in a narrow skirt. As Robert walks beside her up the drive he can smell her perfume and he worries he has put on too much aftershave. He feels slightly dazed from the almost constant sex they've been having, and at the prospect of introducing Agnes to his family. They enter the house through the infrequently used front door; most of the household traffic comes in and out of the back, through the kitchen. In the entrance hall – too big, given the size of the house, as though they'd worn themselves out building a sumptuous foyer then had no stamina for the rest – they stand below a high empty space where a chandelier once hung, Robert's arm through Agnes's, him squeezing. He feels compelled to giggle and so, as with most things he is feeling these days, Agnes giggles first. She giggles quietly and, for a moment, he wonders what she is seeing, what the house looks like to her. Does it seem too awful, he wonders, will an American be overwhelmed by its layered decrepitude, its battered grandeur? Or will she think it a Hammer Horror house, a haunted house from an old movie? Laughter bursts out of him, echoing up and down the stairway.

'This is where,' he says, pausing for breath, 'I grew up.'

Agnes steps away. With her hands behind her back she walks around the foyer, inspecting the oak panelling, the worn stone-flagged floor with its dips and cracks, the carved and wormy broad wooden staircase, looking up to the elaborate ceiling mouldings, all of it dusty, worn by centuries of people not taking too much notice. The Throckmortons have not employed domestic staff since before the Second World War; one uniting characteristic of the house is that it is filthy. A kind of cosy domestic filth that the people who've created it, who live in it, don't see, the kind of filth that holds things together. The Throckmortons don't notice the dirt, but Agnes does, and Robert notices that.

'It needs some work,' he says, embarrassed yet again.

'It's fabulous,' Agnes says as she perambulates. 'So old. So . . . family.' Her heels click against the stone, are silenced as she steps onto a thin rug, click as she walks on stone again. She stops in front of the painting hanging above the broad mantel of the fireplace.

'They're gone,' he says, 'all the other paintings. That's the only one left. They were sold ages ago. You can tell there were others because of the marks.' He points to a collection of discoloured rectangles on the walls.

Agnes doesn't reply. Robert has informed her about the financial situation, that there isn't any money apart from what he generates on the estate. She has made it clear she doesn't care about that, she doesn't need to be interested in money. 'Who's this?' she asks of the solitary portrait.

'Somebody or other Throckmorton. I don't know. No one knows.'

'It looks an awful lot like you.'

Robert steps forward. 'Do you think?' He peers at the painting and realizes he's never really looked at it before. 'I suppose it does, in a way.' He steps back. The eyes of the man in the portrait follow him. 'Humph,' he snorts, 'creepy.'

'If you're a family with a history . . .'

'Everyone's got a family history. If there's no money left, what's the point?' He laughs again. 'That's my theory, at any rate. My grandfather used to tell people we'd lost all our money in the war. He meant the civil war – the English civil war. He used to say to my father, "We're working class now. We have to work like everyone else." Working class.' Robert shakes his head. He expects Agnes to say something, but she does not. 'Anyway, if there's no money, there's no point in hanging on to the past. And there's no one around who disagrees with me. Except my old friend Elizabeth, she says there might be stories, stories that are worth knowing, worth heeding.'

'She might be right. Maybe you've got some terrible and hidden secret, something so awful it can't be faced, that previous generations have counted on time to bury.'

Robert looks at Agnes; he can't tell if she is teasing. 'Well,' he sighs, 'that would be exciting. But we're not like that. Some old families you hear about – they're obsessed with their own history. They know every brick in the house, every relation who ever lived. It's as though once the money's gone that's all there is left. We're not like that. We might have been grand once but now we're ordinary. We've been ordinary for generations. It's gone. Lost.' He wonders if this disappoints her. 'You've come along about four hundred years too late.'

Agnes looks at him levelly. 'Never too late,' she replies.

Agnes puts her arms around Robert. He realizes then that Agnes doesn't get it, that she doesn't really understand what he's saying. That the Throckmortons have come down in the world, very far down in the world, that they've lost all sense of who they once were, who they are today. We're not impoverished upper class, he thinks, we're not shabby genteel. We're like any other Warboys family.

They stand in front of the unnamed portrait, looking up.

Robert speaks first. 'I should think the only reason Daddy didn't sell that painting is because it's worthless.'

Agnes is silent, gazing at the picture with an intensity that Robert still finds disconcerting.

'Come on,' he says, 'come and let's meet them.'

Without knowing why, or what for, they have gathered in the kitchen. Graeme is standing in front of the open fridge drinking orange juice out of the carton. His wife Karen is at the sink, washing dishes. She is a small dark-haired woman wearing a well-ironed cotton shirt tucked into belted jeans. Trim. Their two children, Andrew and Francis, are playing with toy trucks by the back door. They are scrub-faced and clean like their mother and they wear their dark hair slightly long for little boys; Karen won't let Graeme take them to have their hair cut short. Jenny, the family blonde – where did she get that hair? Robert sometimes thinks, as if it's something she picked up in Peterborough – is standing beside the telephone as if she hopes it might ring, twisting her hair with her fingers. Martin, their father, is in his wheelchair in the corner, a baseball cap on his head, a blanket over his knees. The sun, making a brief appearance, is shining through the back window that overlooks the garden. They are waiting.

'This is Agnes. Agnes Samuel.' Robert makes a flourishy gesture and steps back, leaving Agnes on her own in the middle of the room.

No one speaks for what feels to Robert an age. The collective gaze rests on Agnes and Robert has to stop himself from rushing over to share the burden. This is Agnes's moment: she can make it work, he knows she can.

Everything happens at once. Graeme turns back to the fridge and says loudly, 'Karen, where did you put that bacon?' Karen turns away from the sink, points at Robert's shoes and says, 'You're tracking in mud.' Andrew and Francis knock their heads together as they go back to their play, and both begin to cry. Jenny lowers her hand to the telephone, picks up the handset and puts it down again. She extends the same hand toward Agnes and says, 'It's so nice to meet you.' Agnes is too far away to reciprocate and Jenny lets her hand drop to her side. Martin remains silent, as always, and as Karen glances at him en route to the babies she thinks, with a shock, that his eyes are clear and he is looking straight at Agnes. Karen scoops up Francis the two-year-old and Jenny takes Andrew by the hand. They are standing by the open fridge now, regrouped; they can feel the cool air on their skin.

Robert speaks again. 'We are going to be married. On Saturday. This Saturday. You're all invited. Everyone's invited. I want a big party. I thought we could have it here.'

No one says a word. Their silence is punctuated by little sobs from Francis who can't seem to get his breathing under control. They make a strange family portrait, frozen by the refrigerated air. In the corner, on his own in his wheelchair, Martin wheezes loudly. It is usual for him to gasp occasionally as though he is drawing his last breath. No one, except Agnes, turns to look at him.

Agnes keeps her eyes on Martin's face. She smiles brilliantly and then looks directly into the eyes of each of the Throckmortons, one at a time. Her voice is low and mesmerizing as she speaks.

'I am so pleased to meet you. I've so looked forward to meeting you all.'

She steps toward them, her hands outstretched. She goes from Martin to Karen to the babies (who slip behind Karen's legs) to Jenny and, lastly, takes Graeme's hands into her own. 'I'm hoping we will be happy.' She is speaking to everyone, slowly, deliberately, she has their complete attention. 'Thank you for making me welcome. It means so much to me.'

And with that it is as though she has cast a spell, broken the ice, done whatever it takes, she is in, she is one of them, the Throckmortons take her into their hearts, their house. Even Graeme suddenly feels it is good to see her, to speak to her. Everyone begins to talk. Karen hands Agnes the baby Francis who smiles and reaches out and presses his hand to her lips. He stares at the red lipstick smudged on his fingers as though it is magic. Andrew draws himself together to make an announcement; he says 'I am four.' Agnes tells him she thinks that is wonderful. She draws up a chair next to Martin, Robert's father, and begins to talk to him, her voice smooth, charming.

Karen pauses on her way back to the sink. 'He doesn't speak, you know.'

Agnes looks up expectantly, her face open.

'We're not sure if he hears us either,' Karen continues. 'He will turn the pages of a book, but we are not sure if he reads. We don't actually know how much he can see.' She comes nearer and puts her hand on Martin's head. 'Graeme says he's blind, but I think he sees. I think he saw you Agnes,' she says smiling. 'I really do. I think he looked at you,' she laughs, 'and he likes what he sees.'

While Karen speaks, Agnes takes Martin by the hand. 'He's going to be my friend,' she says, turning to her prospective father-in-law, 'aren't you Mr Throckmorton?' She looks back at Karen, smiling. 'He's going to be my special way in to this family.'

Karen smiles at Agnes uncertainly. She is gazing into Agnes's green, green eyes and for a moment she thinks she sees them go black, as though the pupil eclipses the iris and is restored by a blink. She is startled to see such anger, at least that's what she thinks she sees. She glances at Martin and a look of terror passes over his face, like a spasm, a grotesque facial tic. Then it's gone and what can she do, what can she say? Her skin is prickling. 'Where are you from?' she finds herself asking, thinking – who are you, why are you here?

'Las Vegas,' says Agnes, 'Nevada. The gambling state, although they're making it legal almost everywhere now. Have you been to the US?'

'No. Foreign travel isn't really my kind of thing. Graeme –' she turns to see where her husband is, still standing beside the fridge, although he has closed the door, '– likes his creature comforts. He likes to be at home. He grew up here, in this house – I expect you know that. Robert, too, of course. And Jenny, but their mother died when she was born. Tragic. In childbirth. Things were not good in those days. Mind you, it was only sixteen years ago, hardly the dark ages. She was here, at home. I think labouring women belong in the maternity ward, don't you?' She shakes her head, suddenly worried about the way she is taking up space.

Agnes continues to smile pleasantly and Karen feels as though she might not be listening after all. She makes her way back to the sink.

Agnes pats Martin's hand, leaning closer to whisper in his ear. Robert watches from the other side of the kitchen. He never knows how people will react to his father; sometimes they appear to be afraid of him, most of the time they speak to him slowly and loudly, as if he is a kind of deaf idiot, a large, slow child in a pushchair. Agnes behaves as though Martin is the most important person in the room. Robert wonders if this is an American thing, respect for older people, but he doesn't know. It is probably simply Agnes being herself. He leans against the wall, his arms crossed. Karen at the sink, the little boys playing with their trucks and stealing glances at the new lady, Jenny setting the table; he feels that all is well in the world. Everything is in its place. He is going to marry that woman. He is –

Graeme interrupts his thoughts. 'I want to talk to you about the cottages.'

'The cottages are fine.'

'I think we should be doing more marketing. They're lying empty three quarters of the year.'

'That's an exaggeration. They do all right.'

'All right isn't good enough. They hardly pay for themselves.'

'I –' Robert stops. 'Graeme, I don't want to talk about this now.'

'Oh no?' Graeme's fuse is very short, but Robert doesn't attempt to mollify him. 'When? When will you see fit to discuss it with me?'

'I'm getting married on Saturday, can't you see that this –'

Agnes appears beside Graeme. She moves close to him and slips her arm through his, smiling at Robert. Graeme feels her body pressed to his through layers of cloth. He can feel her breast, heavy and warm against his arm. Robert is stupid with happiness, he thinks.

Agnes speaks as though the incident on her first night at the Black Hat never happened, as though she didn't call Graeme a cripple. 'How can one family produce two such good-looking men?' she asks. She eases herself away and steps lightly over to

Robert's side. She draws his face down and kisses him. Graeme sees a flash of open mouth, tongue.

'Well ma'am,' Graeme speaks in a bad imitation of a Southern US accent, charming and surly at the same time, 'damned if I can tell you the answer to that.' He makes as though to tip a hat and walks away.

Agnes sits next to the teenager, Jenny, at lunch and Jenny feels singled out, pleased. Karen apologizes for the food, mostly leftovers from evening meals of the past few days. 'If I'd known –'

'Don't worry Karen,' Robert speaks sharply. 'It's fine. Agnes is one of us. She's not a guest. She's not a stranger.'

After she has served Robert and Graeme, Karen takes a plate of food over to Martin. Like most household tasks, the care of Martin falls to her, and this is not something she questions. Karen doesn't ask questions – not yet. She puts a large bib apron on over Martin's head and sets the plate on his knees. She places a fork in one of his hands, a knife in the other. She returns to the table and he proceeds to eat rather messily, like a badly programmed automaton. No one watches over him.

During the meal Agnes speaks to Jenny in a confiding tone, as though no one else can hear. 'I'm not sure what to wear for the wedding,' she says. 'I think I need your help. We can go to London together this week.'

Jenny smiles broadly and looks at Graeme and Robert for approval. 'School?' she asks.

Graeme clears his throat but Agnes speaks before he can. 'It's only one day. It can't do any harm. We'll have a good time. We'll go to a museum as well, how about that, that's educational.' She turns to Jenny and says, 'We'll go to the Museum of Fashion.' She winks.

Graeme eats quickly and stands to leave before any of the others are finished, grabbing his cane. 'I'm going to the pub,' he announces. 'Jenny, you should be doing your homework.'

Jenny stands obediently. She goes upstairs. Agnes and Robert help clear the table. Karen thinks for a moment that they might offer to clean up while she sorts out the babies, but they don't. They leave holding hands, Robert saying they are going to inspect the rest of the house.

Now Agnes is one of us, thinks Karen. Then she corrects herself. One of them. A Throckmorton.

Jenny longs for Agnes

Jenny can't believe her new sister-in-law-to-be is real. She's like a creature from another planet, too glamorous and cool for Warboys. Completely unexpected and exciting.

That night, after Agnes has gone back to the Black Hat, Jenny lies in bed chanting her resolutions. She is full of resolutions. Number one: Don't eat. Jenny is tall and thin – a childish thin, she carries her breasts high on her ribcage and keeps her shoulders rounded, turned in, she is hipless, thighless, has no belly – but she is not too thin, and she would like to be too thin. She aspires to anorexia, but she hasn't got the will and looks on this as a failure of sorts. Come mealtime she forgets, and eats what is put in front of her. Jenny is a good girl.

Number two: Blow-dry hair every day. Jenny's hair is blonde and fine with a tendency to curl and frizz and she likes to keep it straight, shiny, and the only way to do this is to mousse it and blow-dry it with a brush every day. She envies Graeme and Robert their dark thick hair; if hers was like that she would wear it short and slicked back like them. But she is a blonde and Graeme tells her that blondes have more fun, all the best girls are blonde, and Karen scowls at him and says not to listen. Sometimes Jenny feels persecuted by her blondeness, as if she can't really be a Throckmorton. Karen tries to help, she supplies Jenny with hair products, but they're never the right kind. I could be a foundling, Jenny reasons, how would anyone know? My mother's dead, and my father, well, he's not saying. I might not belong in this family after all.

Number three: Talk more at school. Jenny never talks at school. When she was younger she was horribly shy; she doesn't feel shy any longer but she hasn't mastered the art of talking. Chatter. The other girls are good at chatter. They will talk about anything – they will say anything – they swear and shout and giggle. Jenny practises swearing as she lies in bed. 'Motherfucker,' she says, 'mothafucka,' raising her voice. She wonders if Agnes says 'Fuck'. She bets she does. Maybe they'll say 'Fuck' together, when Agnes moves in, when Agnes becomes Jenny's fully fledged sister-in-law.

Sister-in-law. Sister. She longs for a sister. Karen's never been like a sister, she's too motherly for that, too tied to the ironing board and sink. Imagine having a sister. Girl-talk. Make-up. Sister things.

Jenny is a lonely girl. Even now, at sixteen, she knows she brings this loneliness upon herself. She's not good at having friends. Robert has noticed this, and Karen, and they've done their best to encourage Jenny to invite people round to the house. She tries – Lolly Senior comes from time to time – but she never remembers. She forgets to be sociable. It's as though there is too much going on in the Throckmorton family, this crowd of people, effectively parentless; Robert and Graeme can't be Jenny's parents, no matter how much they try. Jenny regrets not having parents and this makes her feel disloyal to her father who is, after all, alive.

Resolution number four: Be more outgoing.

She should join something. She's never belonged to anything. Not Brownies or Girl Guides. Not the Drama Club. She's never taken piano lessons or riding lessons or ballet. She doesn't know how to swim. She hasn't got any hobbies. She can't sew – no one sews anymore, she thinks. She doesn't read much – she can't afford magazines. Robert gives her a pound a week, he's given her one pound every week since she was six. She should save her pounds and take up smoking. But Agnes doesn't smoke.

Resolution number five: Be like Agnes.

Elizabeth

They were like a weird family out of a novel, Stephen King perhaps. Not that I've ever read Stephen King, not that any of them would have read Stephen King either, not even Graeme. That was one of the oddest things about that household, as well as one of the things I liked best about it – the complete absence of popular culture. It wasn't that they were particularly high-brow, but more along the lines of no-brow. They weren't interested. They were interested in themselves, in each other. They were absorbed in getting by. They didn't need television or radio or movies or gossip magazines. They didn't watch the news, they didn't buy newspapers. I'd never thought it odd before, it was just, well, a Throckmorton thing.

The person in whom this characteristic, this absence, was most noticeable was, of course, Jenny. The teenager. Teenagers are supposed to be pure popular culture these days, and little else. With Jenny I think that initially it was circumstance that kept her ignorant of boy-bands, girl-bands, block-buster movies, the right kind of shoes to wear. But by the time Agnes arrived it had become more self-conscious, it was what marked her out, what made her different. Not different as a statement, like her friend Lolly who was Different with a capital 'D', but something more profound. Other.

They were all like that. And Agnes fit right in. When she arrived none of that changed. She didn't open the house out, she didn't alter the family in any way, insist on television, videos, CDs. At first I think we were all relieved. It wasn't until later that it began to seem strange.

When Agnes arrived I myself had been back in the village for only six months. Since I returned I'd got used to dropping by the Throckmorton house to see Robert. We'd been friends for a long time, from the day we started school. We always got on well, Robert and I, I don't know why. When we were kids it was unusual for a boy and girl to be friends, but our personalities suited. We were both a little shy, still are. I was an only child and so didn't have a brother; Robert, at that time, didn't have a sister, Jenny came along much later. We were like siblings.

As we grew older, into our later teens and onward, our relationship became a little more incestuous. When we were sixteen we decided we were both tired of being virgins, as though virginity was yet another unnecessary burden, something our parents insisted upon. We did it in the yew hedge at the end of the lawn at the back of the Throckmorton house. I brought a blanket I borrowed from my mother's airing cupboard. Robert brought a bottle of wine he said he'd stolen from the house. Even though it was a bright summer evening it was dark inside that hedge and, as always, a little scary. We drank the wine and had a snog. The act itself took rather longer than I'd thought it might and it felt absolutely fantastic. Afterwards we shook hands and congratulated each other on joining the human race.

Over the years we continued to sleep together occasionally. We'd take advantage of each other when we were desperate or bored or drunk. 'Freelance,' was what Robert used to call our relationship. I think we found it consoling as well as convenient. But it never felt right for us to get together on a more permanent basis. I usually had a boyfriend when Robert was on his own; he usually had a girlfriend when I was single. But we endured. I used to tell myself when all is bleak at least there is Robert, and I imagine he had a similar mantra. It wasn't until it was too late that I realized how much he meant to me.

When we were still in school we saw each other once a week, on Wednesday evenings. Regardless of what else was going on in our lives, Wednesday evenings remained inviolate. We would get together at either his house or mine – usually his, mine was too small to find anywhere private to sit and talk. We'd drink tea, we were both big tea drinkers – PG Tips, we mocked herbal teas. Funny, I'm pretty much a herbal tea person these days. And we'd talk about everything. Serious teenage conversation, about our lives and our dreams. When Robert's mother died while giving birth, we talked about that a lot. Robert was seventeen, Graeme nineteen. Mrs Throckmorton – I knew her as Mrs T – was in the house, Robert and Graeme heard the whole thing. He told me that as it became clear something was going wrong, he and Graeme went upstairs to the old disused part of the house and hid. They stayed in a room full of boxes and crates for a whole night and a day. They huddled together like puppies in one corner of the room, as though they were little boys and not big, nearly-men. No one came looking for them. When they emerged their mother was dead.

We talked and talked after that, about death, about what a hideous thing childbirth must be. For a boy Robert was a very good talker, he would talk about anything. I was always the analyst, even then, the one who tried to figure out what it all might mean, what motivation might lie behind the action. Robert simply enjoyed sharing words and thoughts, ready to explore ideas and feelings, even after his mother died. Talking made him feel better. He's always been that way.

He's more unwilling now. Once Agnes arrived he confided less in me; later he became even more closed. Now there are some topics he will discuss only very reluctantly. There are others that are complete no-go areas. Agnes, of course, and most of what happened with her. Graeme as well. I don't mind, I don't object, I'm happy to pretend Agnes never happened, even though I know it is not healthy. It's a few years since I last practised as a therapist but no matter how firmly I shut the door on that part of my life, it still comes back to me. I think therapy is in my bones, always was, always will be. Robert insists that talking doesn't always make things clearer, that with certain things talking isn't appropriate. He's afraid he'll hurt me with what he has to say.

He still loves her. But that doesn't matter. That's all right.

When I came back to Warboys after losing my job things were a little strained between us. My father had died, my mother passed away a few years before him; they both had heart conditions. I was at a very low ebb and I needed Robert to be my friend. Neither of us had ever needed the other before, at least not since his mother died, but I needed him then. Being needed didn't really suit Robert.

It was my idea to reinstate our Wednesday evenings, but that didn't last for long. Robert was often busy with something to do with the estate. And he was into a heavy pattern of serial monogamy. I couldn't keep up with the string of girlfriends, I couldn't keep track of their names, and none of them were very interesting. I was terribly, incredibly, single and probably rather alarming with it. I'll admit that when I came back to the village one of the thoughts foremost in my mind was that Robert had still not met anyone, Robert was still the village bachelor. Robert was on my mind. And he could tell that. And it turned out to be a problem for him. I was breaking the unwritten rule of our friendship, the precious balance we had maintained all those years.

I guess a central feature of our friendship had been its blokeishness. We were mates and we'd do matey things together; I'd come home from university during holidays, we'd go to the pub and compete to see who could pull first. Occasionally, just occasionally, we would both fail, and we'd drink too much and find ourselves snogging in the tunnel under the yew hedge. Sometimes we'd sneak into his bedroom and spend a few hours pulling off each other's clothes and having sex, but more often than not one of us would push the other away, laughing and saying 'You look ridiculous.' Regardless of what happened, come Wednesday evening we'd be together for the post-mortem, making each other hysterical with our stories of rejection. A funny kind of blokeishness, but you see what I mean.

By the time we were both in our mid-thirties, and I had come back to Warboys for good, that easy familiarity between us had dissipated. We hadn't been to bed together for quite a while, years in fact. Not since Robert's thirtieth, when he'd dared me to do it, even though I was, at the time, engaged to marry someone else.

When I came back to the village sex had come to mean rather more to me and I don't think I could have just jumped into bed with him and out again like it meant nothing. It was as though with age I'd become rather brittle, more breakable, easily hurt. I think Robert felt the same way. At least, he did when it came to me – obviously not when it came to all those other women. And, of course, not when it came to Agnes.

Barbara, who runs the shop, was the first to tell me that Jim Drury had a guest at the Black Hat. I'd gone in to buy a pound of potatoes – I was so broke that was about all I could afford – and I dreaded her asking me why on earth I was buying a couple of potatoes and nothing more, prepared for her litany about how important it was to support the village shop, had I taken to driving over to the supermarket in the next town? But she was full of her news about this new woman.

'An American no less,' she said.

'Is that right?'

'She's called Agnes Samuel. You should see her Elizabeth, she's gorgeous.'

'Is she?' It was unlike Barbara to be so gossipy.

'She's staying at the Black Hat. Robert seems to know her. Are you sure you haven't met her?'

'I'm sure.'

'She's been around for, well, it must be several weeks now.' Barbara gave me a pitying look. I realized then that there must be something between Robert and Agnes Samuel, at least Barbara thought there was. 'I'm sure you'll be introduced,' she continued. 'Lovely, she's just lovely,' an enormous smile on her normally taciturn shopkeeper face. She sent me on my way, refusing to let me pay for the potatoes, which was, in itself, extraordinary.

That evening I put on my red cloche hat and my black dress and a shawl I bought in India and some lipstick that I know becomes me. Perfume on my wrists and in the dip of my neck. I went into the Black Hat and I sat at the table next to the fire. I had a gin and tonic, and another, and there were plenty of people for me to talk to as I hadn't been to the pub for ages. There was no sign of Robert, nor the American stranger. After a while I excused myself to go to the loo.

The women's toilet on the ground floor of the Black Hat is very poky and dimly lit. Over the years I had got into the habit of going up the stairs to the first floor where there is a spacious and bright loo that Jim and Lolita have tarted up for their paying guests. As I reached the top of the stairs I heard Robert's voice coming from one of the bedrooms. It was him, unmistakable. He was moaning. Without thinking I moved across the landing to the door. I placed my hand on the door handle and I heard him again. 'Oh please, Agnes,' he said, his voice thick with passion, 'please, yes, oh . . .' and I stepped away.

I realized it then, I realized it with an awful, doomed sense of my own bad timing: I loved Robert. I'd always loved him and I had left it too late.

I went into the loo, closed the door, and burst into tears. I sat on the toilet and cried. After a while someone tried the door, but I didn't get up or say anything. In the mirror I looked awful, smeared make-up, lipstick caked into the newly forming cracks around my mouth. I washed my face and patched things up, waited until my breathing returned to normal. I opened the door and went downstairs.

Robert and Agnes were at the table by the fire where I had been sitting. They were right, everyone in the village was right, she was beautiful. And – this is what no one ever says, what everyone fails to mention – so is he. I noticed for the first time that night how his dark hair was beginning to grey and how the flecks of white set off his blue eyes. He is tall and straight and wears clothes very well, with a long-limbed elegance that seems very English to me.

I went over to introduce myself, but as I approached they turned to each other with a look of particular intensity. That look struck me like a kind of body blow: Robert is in love, he's in love with this woman, and not with me. I stepped back, I turned and walked unsteadily to the other side of the bar. I sat for a moment with Marlene and Geoff Henderson, Marlene has been a good friend to me. In a kind of daze, I agreed to have dinner with them Friday.

After that I got up and left. Even the shock of the cold October air – it had chilled right down very early that year – did not bring me out of myself. I wandered back to my cottage.

The next few days were the worst I've ever experienced, even worse than when Gillian Collins committed suicide. I wanted to stay in bed and not get up, but I couldn't allow myself that comfort. I found myself going over and over the mistakes I had made in my life. Everything I had ever done wrong. This included coming back to Warboys too late. Coming back to Warboys when it was too late to save Robert, when he was trapped in an endlessly repeating loop of girlfriends and break-ups, when he was ready and waiting for Agnes and her games.

But it was a few days, and that was all. That was all I was allowed. I pulled myself together, I've always pulled myself together, and I got to work on my life. I would get a job, there had to be someone in Warboys who would employ me. And I would get over Agnes, I would get over Robert. If he wasn't going to love me, I could still keep him as a friend. I could have him beside me; we could talk. He didn't see me that night in the pub, he didn't have a chance to tell me his news and see the look on my face. I could embrace him, and his new girlfriend, and continue to be part of the Throckmorton family.

And after all, in the end, in my heart of hearts, I knew he would come back to me.

Agnes makes plans

The last week of October is windy and darkening, great gangs of fallen leaves skittering around the streets like marauding schoolchildren. The wedding is planned for the last Saturday in October – All Hallow's Eve, Hallowe'en. Agnes laughs when Robert tells her the date. 'We'll have to stay home and answer the door to trick-or-treaters all evening,' she says.

'We don't really do that here,' Robert replies, 'although it is catching on in some places, so I'm told. Bonfire Night – Guy Fawkes, November fifth – is the night we celebrate.' He feels absurdly proud of this cultural difference. 'It is quaint, isn't it,' he says, 'American children dressed up as candy-grabbing witches and goblins, Britons torching their terrorist year after year.'

'Cute,' says Agnes, 'sweet.'

Agnes remains in residence at the Black Hat until the day of the wedding. She says it is more seemly, and she laughs because there is nothing seemly about their affair, she and Robert met in a pub and less than a month later they are going to be married. They spend some time in the days before the wedding deciding what to do with the old wing of the house. On the top floor there are three crooked bedrooms with gables and sloping ceilings and a fourth room that was converted to a bathroom in the 1930s. This is the Elizabethan part of the house but that is evident only in the main bedroom – half-timbers showing through the plaster, a big open fireplace, thick outer walls and deeply set windows with lead latticing and bevelled glass – and, downstairs, the large empty room with the ornately carved plaster ceiling that might have once served as a ballroom. The other rooms have had piecemeal work done to them over the years, cheap flock vinyl wallpaper in pink and brown and double-glazing in the 1970s. Robert isn't sure why this work was done, he can't remember anyone occupying this part of the house during his lifetime.

Robert figures they should knock down the wall between the two smaller rooms to create a sitting room, and have the bathroom re-plumbed and decorated. The third room, which will be their bedroom, is filthy with dust and a huge accumulation of dead and disintegrating insects, flies on their backs with their legs in the air, spiders folded and dried, woodlice curled into tight Cs. The room contains decades of Throckmorton junk; Robert will clear it.

He stands in the middle of the floor and surveys. He is alone, Agnes is downstairs. This is the room where he and Graeme hid the night their mother died. These are the crates, the dustsheets, the boxes they crouched behind while she laboured, folding themselves into smaller and smaller spaces. Robert has been in and out of this room many times since – to retrieve things, to store more junk – but the memory of that night waits for him here, hiding behind a shrouded armchair, inside a half-opened box. Clearing the room will be good, he thinks, good for the soul of the house. He'll tell Agnes about what happened, he'll tell her about his mother and that night. She'll understand, she'll listen to him.

Appalled by the standard of British bathrooms, Agnes is insistent about the plumbing. She speaks very firmly; she hasn't made any demands before this so Robert listens carefully. 'I want a shower – separate from the bath – tiled – with steam and heat and power.'

Robert nods. 'Okay –'

She's got her hands on her hips. 'I want a toilet that flushes at first go, a single tap in the sink capable of mixing hot and cold water, a window that actually opens – not one of those disgusting plastic vents that gets very dirty and spins round and round endlessly. Built-in cupboards – not open shelves. A heated towel rack as well as the radiator. A magazine rack, decent lighting. Mirrors.'

Robert kisses her; the sound of her voice – her accent – entrances him. 'I promise the nearest approximation of an American bathroom that England can muster.' Agnes puts her arm around him and passes on the heat of her body. He talks into her hair, 'I am happy to obey.'

'How the fuck do you think we'll pay for that?' Graeme asks when Robert details his plans. Agnes has gone down to London to shop with Jenny.

'There is some money. This is work that needs doing.' Robert is always diligent about keeping Graeme informed, even though they both know full well that what Graeme thinks or says makes no difference to his plans.

'I increased the rent when the farming lease came up three months ago. I told you what I was doing.' These conversations usually fill Robert with dread. This time he's been caught off-guard, his head full of Agnes, he hasn't thought the argument through properly. Graeme has no role in running the estate, there isn't enough work for two people, but they play this game nonetheless. When their father fell ill Robert took on the task of running the house and land; he was about to finish school and wasn't sure what to do next, he hadn't liked school enough to want to go to university. Graeme was already a police constable, working in Peterborough. He and Karen had married as soon as he finished his training; they'd been together since they were fourteen, although Graeme had always played the field. This is how Robert thinks of his brother: Graeme plays the field. So the task of running the house and the land the family still owned came to Robert. It had been his idea to turn part of the collection of outbuildings into holiday cottages, three all together. In an act of supreme bullishness that made him unpopular in both the Black Hat and the Marquis of Granby for a while, he threw the long-standing tenant farmer off the land when the lease lapsed and sold the tenancy to corporate agribusiness. He'd had other business ventures that were less successful; he invested in a new riding stable one year and lost a fair bit of money on that. But on the whole, he makes it work, generating enough cash to support the entire family. And Graeme makes sure that Robert knows he resents him for it. It had been all right when Graeme was working, he couldn't care less what Robert did with the land. But when he lost his job and ended up at home all day every day, it became more difficult. His disability pension doesn't add up to much when it comes to the general cash flow. He is angry – he's always been angry, but now he is permanently enraged.

'The work has to be done,' Robert insists. 'That part of the house is practically falling down. Agnes and I need somewhere to live. I don't want her to move into my old bedroom.' This thought makes him laugh. 'That room has seen rather too much of me.' He turns to Graeme. 'Or would you rather we lived somewhere else?'

Graeme looks away. Robert knows how to shut him up. He can tell that Graeme is pleased that Agnes is moving in; neither of them wants to break up the family, not while Jenny is still in school. That's what they tell themselves. Not while Jenny is in school. Graeme is unable to admit he is pleased that they are staying. And that means that, as usual, Robert has something over him. The work needs doing. Robert will go ahead with his plans regardless of what Graeme thinks. Before his brother can say anything more he picks up the telephone and rings the builder.

Robert

It was a lot of fun, that week before the wedding. We were really excited or, at least, I was. I had a lot to do, what with getting the house ready, making arrangements for the party we were going to have after the ceremony. There was work to catch up on, work I had neglected while I spent my days in bed with Agnes. We still spent a good part of our day in bed, there was no way either of us was going to sacrifice that. I'd go over to the Black Hat at lunch time, or in the evening, say a quick hello to Jim and Lolita, then rush up the stairs to her room. Everyone knew where I was headed, but I didn't care. It wasn't like anything I'd experienced before, with Agnes it was as though all the other women I'd been with didn't count, I had no history, no preconceptions, no idea about how things should or shouldn't be. My life was full of passion. It had never been like that before. Sometimes when Agnes wasn't with me and I was working I'd have to stop what I was doing and press my palms hard against either side of my head, to prevent myself from exploding with happiness.

It was Karen who brought me part way back down to earth. Karen was a quiet woman, a little shy. She and Graeme had been together so long I'd got used to her, she was part of the scenery. She ran the domestic side of the household with incredible efficiency; she took all that work – the boys, Martin, Jenny, the cooking, the cleaning – and rendered it entirely invisible. Later, when it was too late, I realized that all that work had rendered Karen herself invisible as well. But at the time, in the drama of our family, she didn't register much of a presence.

I was helping her with the washing-up. I hadn't talked to Karen about the wedding; I'd assumed she was as excited as everyone else seemed to be. I was drying the dishes and thinking about what I wanted the builder to do upstairs, relieved to have got over the obstacle of telling Graeme about my plans.

'Have you spoken to Elizabeth lately?' Karen asked suddenly.

'Elizabeth,' I said, 'no. Why?' thinking she might have rung with some kind of problem in her cottage. I often helped her out with that kind of thing. I had felt a little uneasy since Elizabeth came back to Warboys. I guess it was a weakness on my behalf, but I didn't like to see her unhappy. I didn't want to be around her if she was unhappy. We weren't as close as we had once been, but I liked to think we had the kind of friendship that could endure long absences and differences of opinion. I hadn't seen as much of her as I should have. I don't know why, but she made me feel guilty.

'Have you told her you're getting married?'

I put away the plate I was drying.

'I just think you should tell her yourself. She's probably heard through the grapevine already. But I think she'd want to hear it from you directly.'

'But I –'

'It's only polite, that's all,' Karen said, as though she was talking to little Andrew. 'I know if I was her I'd want to hear it from you.'

I couldn't really see Karen's point. I knew that if I was happy Elizabeth would be happy for me.

'Just tell her Robert, it's a simple thing.'

So I agreed. Karen didn't often express opinions and I was willing to take her word on this. And now that she had mentioned it, I could hardly wait.

I rang that afternoon. 'Lizzie,' I said.

'Hello Robert.' She sounded cheerful.

'How are you?'

'I'm okay.'

'I'm sorry I haven't been around to see you.'

'That's all right.'

'How are things?' Usually on the telephone we talked easily, but today I felt awkward. Well, it was the first time I'd ever rung her up to announce I was getting married, so I suppose that explained my difficulty.

'Ticking over. Things are ticking over. I'm looking for a job.'

I couldn't wait. I couldn't make small talk. 'Lizzie, I'm getting married.'

There was a small pause. 'Oh, that's great. Who to?'

Her voice was disappointingly flat. I thought she'd be beside herself with excitement. We'd always taken great pleasure in each other's news before. I thought she'd feel like I felt when she got her degree – almost as though I'd done it myself. I know it sounds naive, but it hadn't occurred to me that Lizzie might be jealous. She's admitted as much to me since, but at the time I was surprised.

'Agnes Samuel. I want you to meet her.' This felt important now. 'Before the wedding. You'll love her, Lizzie, she's amazing.'

'That's great, Robert, just great.' Another pause. 'I'm really happy for you.'

Oh come on, I thought, can't you even fake a little excitement? 'Listen –' and this was spur of the moment, I swear that I did not intend to hurt Lizzie – 'will you be my best man or maid of honour or whatever? Please? You're my oldest friend. It's important to me.' The phone was quiet. 'Elizabeth?'

She cleared her throat. I heard her sniff. 'Ahh – no. No, Robert. But thank you.'

'No?'

'I can't. I . . . I'm in mourning. For my father. Still in mourning. I'm sorry. I – it wouldn't feel right. I couldn't stand up in church with you. I couldn't be relied upon. To . . .'

'But Lizzie you –'

'No Robert. Thank you for asking.'

She'd said no. I didn't believe the line about her father. I couldn't understand why she would begrudge me happiness. I didn't want to talk about it anymore. Neither did she. 'What kind of a job?' I asked, pushing the conversation on.

'Oh, anything. Something in the village.'

'I'll keep an eye out for you. Let you know if I hear of anything.'

'Good idea.'

'And I'll bring Agnes round to meet you.'

'You do that.'

'Bye Lizzie.'

'Good-bye.'

I felt let down. Later – much later, after everything had happened and there was no going back – Elizabeth told me that when she hung up she cried so hard she thought her lungs were going to collapse. She cried for the rest of the day. I didn't know that at the time. I don't know how I would have reacted if I had known, if I had been privy to Elizabeth's misery. I was so happy with Agnes, my love for her had such a grip on me, that I probably couldn't have cared less. I probably would have done nothing. I'm not proud of that, but I'm not ashamed to admit it. It just shows how much I loved Agnes, how by then I would have done anything to be with her.

Elizabeth was my great friend. But the fact is, I did not fancy her. Yes, we slept together occasionally over the years. Yes, she knew most of my secrets and I hers. Yes, her opinion mattered to me. And yes, I probably did rely on the fact that she was always there to fall back on – and I probably would have been disappointed myself if she'd got married before me. But I never assumed that we'd end up together. I was very surprised when she came back to Warboys, despite the obvious logic of the move, given her circumstances. She shouldn't have blamed herself so completely for what happened with her client. And she blames herself now for some of the things that have happened here in Warboys. But she shouldn't. What happened was my fault. I take the blame.

Agnes and Jenny go shopping

In London, in Knightsbridge, Agnes is luminescent. Jenny watches her, admiring. They move down the crowded high street and it is as though she flies along the pavement, hovering outside the window displays, darting into shops. Jenny can feel her excitement as the clouds move quickly overhead. It is one of those days when Britain shows its island nature; the weather changes every few minutes, sunshine, rain, wind, hail, warm sunshine again. 'I can't believe it,' Agnes says each time they emerge from a shop and are faced with a new weather front. 'It makes me feel like we've been shopping for days.' She laughs and steps up the pace.

When they go into Harvey Nichols department store, all the women, all the painted ladies, emerge from within their cosmetic flytraps to watch Agnes float by. They beckon to her with their long dark nails, they try to get that lovely face – eyes shining, skin radiant, unmarked by worry or fatigue – to look their way. Jenny and Agnes stop at Clarins, L'Oréal, Lancôme, and MAC as Agnes, credit card flashing, equips Jenny. 'They don't call it a "beauty regime" for nothing,' she says sternly.

Upstairs, they try on clothes. Wedding outfits. Jenny has never been shopping in London before; Elizabeth and Karen usually take her shopping a couple of times a year, and on those trips they go to Peterborough or Cambridge. Jenny has been to London a couple of times on school outings, but those trips were rushed and ordered and she found the city too busy, too quick. Graeme once took her to the theatre in the West End as a birthday treat, but neither of them enjoyed it, they found the play, and the actors, embarrassing. So this, shopping in Knightsbridge with Agnes – this is really something. People – shop assistants, other women – pay attention to them. It is as though they recognize Agnes, as though they know her somehow, except they can't quite place her. It is as though when she smiles at people their hearts melt, even cold London hearts accustomed to beauty and taste and Americans with deep pockets.

'Don't worry about the money,' Agnes says to Jenny, 'don't even think about the money.'

When Jenny finds an outfit, the perfect outfit, she and Agnes exchange a glance in the mirror, there is no need to speak. A soft green shot silk dress with matching swing coat, light with simple lines. Shoes to match, stockings – Jenny can't get over the stockings – the right kind of underwear as well. A hat with a single feather, very chic. It is like an outfit from a dream, a young girl's dream of what she might look like one day. As she stands at the cash desk watching while the dress is packed between careful layers of tissue paper, Jenny realizes that when she was little her Barbie doll had a similar ensemble. She knows she doesn't look like Barbie, she doesn't have the hard boobs or the tanned legs or the tiny swivel waist, but for once, this time, she will do. She will look all right. Jenny is unable to stop grinning.

Agnes can't find anything for herself. She doesn't try on much, she seems more concerned with getting Jenny set up. 'Don't worry,' she says once they have finished, 'I've got plenty of clothes with me in Warboys. I'll find something. You'll see.'

Out on the street it is dark now and raining steadily and all the taxis are taken. They go into the underground. As they are climbing down the last set of stairs to the platform a train rushes in to the station and at the same time they hear a terrible sound, an enormous crippling thud, and people already on the platform begin to shriek and scream. Jenny freezes on the stairs; she is not an experienced underground traveller, but she knows what that sound means, it doesn't take imagination. Agnes keeps going forward, down the stairs. 'Agnes,' Jenny calls out, 'wait.'

Agnes turns around, smiling. 'What's wrong?'

'Didn't you hear that?' she says. 'Didn't you hear that screaming?'

'We're travelling in the other direction. We should just go down, and get on the train.' Agnes walks back up the stairs and takes Jenny by the hand. 'Come on,' she says, 'we'll get the next one.'

They walk to the bottom of the stairs and stand for a moment gazing through to the afflicted train. It has stopped halfway along the platform. Several women are weeping, leaning against the curving wall of the station. Two men are sitting on the ground, their heads bowed. Someone has vomited. London Transport personnel begin to appear, shouting in to their radios. Afterwards Jenny remembers the crackling of their stiff plastic fluorescent jackets as they rush up and down the platform. They look as lost and confused as the passengers. 'He's there,' says a man in a suit, pointing his shaking hand, 'he's down there, under this carriage.'

'Is he alive?' asks the staff member.

'No,' says the man, 'no way.'

The driver stumbles out of his cab.

'Come on,' says Agnes. 'Let's get out of the way.' She puts her arm around Jenny.

'Someone jumped, didn't they?' she asks. 'Someone jumped in front of the train.'

'Looks like it.'

Jenny feels ill. 'God,' she says, 'how awful. You must really want to die to do that.'

'Unless he was pushed,' Agnes says calmly.

Jenny looks at her, looks back through the arch to the other platform. 'Do you think he can have been pushed?'

'You never know. You never know these days. Never take things at face value, Jenny.' Their train is now approaching. 'I hope he was pushed.'

'Why?' asks Jenny, astonished.

'Because if he jumped, he'll never rest. He'll never have any peace.'

'What do you mean?'

'His soul,' Agnes says, and Jenny hears her despite the noise of the train. 'It will be in torment, forever.'

They get on to the train. It is packed and their shopping bags are awkward; everyone is damp and steaming. The doors close and as they pull away from the scene Jenny asks, 'Are you religious?'

'No,' replies Agnes, 'quite the contrary.'

Karen panics

Karen doesn't know what to wear to the wedding. She doesn't have any nice clothes anymore, all she has are mummy clothes, jeans, shirts, stretched old cardigans that she's worn every day for years. There isn't room in her budget, in the money she gets from Graeme, the money they receive from Social Services. When Graeme was working she used to ask him for extra money from time to time, and he'd always looked shocked, and he'd always handed it over, although usually slightly less than what she'd requested. But now she doesn't ask for money for herself and, quite frankly, she can't be bothered. She has ceased to worry about the way she looks. She has other priorities.

Except for now. When Jenny arrives home from her day out with Agnes Karen asks to see what they bought. She is amazed by the quantity of glamour in those shopping bags. 'You'll look fantastic,' she says to Jenny and as the girl blushes, Karen can feel her excitement and pleasure. And that leads her down a narrow bumpy track to the conclusion that she herself will look ugly, she'll look frumpy, she'll look terrible. She'll look short and pear-shaped. Her parents are driving down from Leicester for the day, everyone she knows is coming to the party, and she has nothing to wear.

From time to time, in the past, her brother-in-law Robert has given Karen money. Usually before the boys' birthdays – 'Buy him something from me' – handing her too much cash to spend on a small boy. Between them it is understood that Karen will buy something for herself as well. But she's never actually asked Robert for money, and she's not about to start, especially not now that he's getting married.

That evening, after the children are in bed, Karen goes up to her bedroom. She looks in her closet, hoping to find something she's forgotten, some miraculous item of clothing that has escaped the moths and risen above fashion, but she knows that's wishful thinking. She remembers a box of clothes she brought with her when she and Graeme married; perhaps there might be something in there? This is a dim hope, most unlikely, but she clings to it anyway.

She makes her way through the house, down the stairs, through the sitting room, into the entrance foyer, and up again, into the old part of the house. Robert is there, clearing boxes out of the room that he will share with Agnes. The air smells musty, disturbed. Karen hugs herself. She never likes coming up here, she doesn't know why.

'What's in there?' she asks, pointing hopefully at a box.

'I haven't got a clue,' says Robert. 'Clothes I think. It's quite light. I'm shoving it all into the attic. I haven't got time to go through everything.'

'I'll take it,' says Karen, 'I think it's mine.'

'Help yourself,' Robert says.

Karen lugs the box back through the house and into her bedroom. She finds her sewing scissors and cuts through the packing tape. When she opens it, she recognizes the contents immediately; she is glad she didn't open it in front of Robert, glad that Graeme isn't watching. The box is full of their mother's clothes. Dresses, Mrs Throckmorton was good at wearing dresses; she had an amazing collection of clothes from the 1950s. Seeing them here, neatly folded, tissue paper tucked around them – who did this, Karen wonders, who put these things away so neatly? – brings Sylvia Throckmorton – Mrs T – back to Karen. She died a few months before Graeme and Karen were married. Karen had liked her, admired her, though she wasn't confident Mrs T liked her. She pulls one of the dresses out of the box and holds it up to the light; heavy cotton, wide skirt, cinched-in waist, tailored bustline.

Slightly tatty. Beneath it, half a dozen others like it. Karen can't wear one of these dresses, they're too memorable, too Mrs T, half the people at the wedding would recognize it. She digs down deeper into the box and produces a short navy jacket, boxy with shoulderpads, and matching skirt. Not Karen's kind of thing, really. Not Mrs T's either. But Karen can sew and she can see that if she takes out the shoulderpads and adjusts the skirt – she's not as tall as Mrs T was, not as angular – she might be able to make it work.

Mrs T was unwell throughout that pregnancy, carrying Jenny. She was grey when she was usually pink. Karen remembers feeling uneasy at the time but when she asked, Graeme didn't seem to think anything was amiss. At first she thought he was embarrassed by his hugely pregnant mother, but he wasn't, not in the slightest. He loved his mother and he loved the idea of having a new baby in the family. And Graeme did love Jenny when she was born, despite what happened. They were good at that, Karen recalled, separating the trauma of that loss from the way they felt about Jenny.

Karen shuts the lid of the box, fetches the tape and seals it once again. Carries the box to the bottom of the ladder to the attic. She can hear Robert rummaging around overhead. She leaves the box with the others for him to store away, and sets to work on the suit having resolved not to tell anybody where she got it. Chances are no one, not even Graeme, will ask.

That night, Karen hears Mrs T screaming. The sound is coming through the walls from the other side of the house, as though Jenny is being born and Mrs T is dying once again. Karen was not present the night Graeme's mother died; she and Graeme have never discussed it. Not when it happened, not since. But Karen knows it is Mrs T she is hearing and she knows why she is screaming.

When she sits up in bed, the noise stops. Graeme is beside her, on his back, snoring lightly. She rubs her eyes and gets out of bed. The air is cold, the floor is freezing, but she needs to get to the loo. If she walks down the corridor perhaps she'll shake off that dream. She stops at the window and, without thinking, opens the curtain and looks out at the night.

Across the rose garden stands a Scotch pine, the only one for miles. Karen looks at it and drops the curtain and steps away from the window abruptly. What has she seen? Three bodies, dangling from the tree. Party tricks, she finds herself thinking, Jesus and the thieves. Hanged, not crucified. She is no longer cold but instead is sweating heavily. Three bodies on a gallows.

Then she hears laughter.

She forces herself to open the curtains again. The bodies are gone, but Robert and Agnes are there – what are they doing outside so late? Robert has his arm around his fiancée; they are strolling down the lawn as if it's a summer's day, heading away from the house. Agnes turns her head and looks up, as though she knows Karen is watching. She smiles at her in the grey moonlight. Karen drops the curtain and suppresses an urge to cry out. She suppresses the entire incident in fact, like she blocks out all unpleasant things, something at which she has become adept over the years, a skill that serves her well. Karen walks down the corridor toward the loo and with each step forces away what she has seen and heard. And the next day she will believe nothing odd has happened, nothing amiss. Almost.

Not quite.

Agnes gets married

Agnes is standing in the door of the village church, her arm lightly linked through Jim Drury's. She has spent her last night at the Black Hat, and she has asked the landlord to give her away. They are waiting for the wedding music to begin.

For the first time ever Jim has closed the Black Hat for the day. He is very nervous, about the wedding, and about closing the pub. He tells himself over and over that Robert has invited most of his regulars to the wedding and as he surveys the gathered folk he ticks off a mental list. They're all here, he tells himself, and those who aren't, well, they'll just have to go to the Marquis of Granby for a change. He looks at Agnes, who smiles and squeezes his arm for reassurance. With a surge of confidence he thinks that an evening in the Marquis will make the punters appreciate the Black Hat all the more. And, besides, he and Lolita are doing the catering for the wedding and they stand to make a few bob from that. When Agnes had asked if he would close the pub and come to the wedding Jim agreed without hesitating, without pausing to ask himself – or Lolita – why he would close the pub for Agnes when he had never closed it before. And of course Lolita doesn't mind, Lolita is thrilled – she loves a good wedding.

Jenny is in front of Agnes and Jim clutching a bouquet of lilac and white flowers; she is the bridesmaid and will precede Agnes and Jim down the aisle. She is wearing the pale green dress and coat purchased earlier in the week and although she has spent hours practising walking in her new shoes, they are not comfortable. She feels unaccountably cold. Everyone feels a sudden chill, as though the temperature in the old church dropped several degrees when the wedding party arrived.

Everyone is on their feet, except Martin whose wheelchair is tucked in at the end of the front row. Next to him stand Karen, awkward in the navy suit – she has spent hours unpicking and restitching and now the too-big suit looks crooked, handmade – and the two little boys who are wearing uncomfortable grey wool trousers with matching red waistcoats and white shirts. Elizabeth is beside Andrew, pleased, despite herself, to be included like part of the family. She has assured Karen that she will help make Andrew behave, glad to have a task. Now that they know Agnes has arrived at the back of the church, the boys are clamouring to be picked up so they can see.

On the other side of the aisle the front pew stands empty. None of Agnes's family is here today. Lolita Drury had offered to sit there, she felt that as the landlord's wife she could take the role of surrogate mother. But Agnes said no, thank you, she would prefer it if the seats remained empty. 'It's symbolic to me,' she says, 'of my family. You understand, don't you?' Lolita does understand, and her heart fills with pity for the orphaned Agnes. Agnes had wanted to walk down the aisle alone as well, but that had upset the vicar, so in the end she agreed to take the arm of Jim Drury.

That morning Jenny had a shock when she arrived at the Black Hat loaded down with her wedding outfit, shoes, hat and cosmetics. She and Agnes had planned to get dressed together at the pub, Agnes said it would be fun. 'It will be a good dose of girl-time before I walk down the aisle. Before I lose my freedom.'

Agnes came to the door of her room wearing a white towelling dressing gown, her hair in curlers, a lime-green face-pack smeared across her face. But that wasn't what shocked Jenny, even though they had only an hour to get ready. The shock came when she entered the bedroom and saw the dress that hung from the curtain rail. It was a white dress, a wedding dress that Jenny thought looked antique with long narrow sleeves and a low lace and bone bodice, tiny pearl buttons, a slim, floor-length skirt and a short lace train.

'Where did that come from?' asked Jenny, thinking of their trip to London a few days ago. There'd been no time for shopping since then. Agnes hadn't mentioned that she already had a wedding dress. Would she have arrived in Warboys with one packed in her case? Jenny imagined Agnes issuing more girlie advice: 'Never travel without a wedding dress, *just in case.*'

But Agnes didn't answer Jenny's question. She was across the hall in the bathroom removing the facial. 'Come on,' she called, 'there's not much time. Let's do your make-up.'

Jenny couldn't stop herself, she stepped up to the dress and fingered the fabric, so fine it felt as though it might crumble. She bent closer and realized she could smell Agnes's perfume on the dress.

'Jenny?'

She grabbed her bag of brand-new potions and went across the hall.

'Okay,' said Agnes, 'get started. Remember how I told you to do it?'

Jenny nodded, lining up the cosmetics in a perfect row, as though embarking on ritual magic.

'I'll be back in a couple of minutes to see how you are doing.'

Jenny went through the routine. She had spent three days rehearsing and was able to use the eye-lash curler with a modest amount of success. When she finished – she thought perhaps the make-up was a little heavy, but this was a special occasion – she went back to the bedroom.

Agnes was standing beside the bed. She was wearing Jenny's outfit. The dress and coat looked wonderful, Agnes had angles and curves and points in all the right places. The girl crumbled inwardly. 'I couldn't help it,' Agnes said, and Jenny thought for a moment she heard cruelty in her voice. 'I just wanted to see what it looked like. We're the same size.'

'It looks great,' Jenny replied, thinking it will never look like that on me. I don't know why we bothered to buy it. I might as well wear my jeans.

Agnes was already taking the outfit off. She laid it out on the bed for Jenny. The dress looked flat and uninteresting without her body animating it.

'Okay,' said Agnes, 'not long now.'

Jim Drury was knocking on the door. 'Hurry up ladies,' he said, 'we don't want to be late.'

In the church the music starts. Elizabeth is holding Andrew and he is wriggling with excitement. 'Look at Agnes,' he says, 'look Lizzie.' Elizabeth glances at Agnes but she can't keep her eyes off Robert. She thinks he is incredibly handsome in his hired morning suit, his hair black and shiny. 'Look at your uncle,' she whispers, 'look at him.' Next to Robert stands Graeme, best man since Elizabeth declined the invitation so unceremoniously. She wonders what it would be like to be standing there now, a member of the wedding party. She feels a spike of regret. Graeme looks handsome too, Elizabeth thinks, he has his hair slicked back like Robert's and the shadow of anger his face usually shelters has lifted. The two men look uncannily alike.

Elizabeth has a soundtrack playing in her head, quite separate from the music coming from the church organ. Marlene and Geoff had teased her at dinner last night, Marlene kept singing that old soul song over and over again, 'It should have been me'. Now that melody, those words, runs over and over in Elizabeth's head, it is driving her mad. There is no point in thinking it should have been me, it isn't me, it's Agnes and – doesn't she look lovely.

Agnes and Jim move down the aisle as though on well-oiled wheels. People shiver at the beauty and delicacy. As he watches her come toward him Robert can hardly contain his emotion; he bites his lip and glances upward, begging for control. Even the vicar is struck by the unusual atmosphere; it's so cold that for a moment he thinks the bride's dress is icy, that she has frost dusting her flowers, her lips. Agnes is staring right at him and the vicar finds her gaze unnerving. She stands in front of him, a little too close, and when she blinks the vicar sees her green irises eclipsed by black, as though the pupil has swallowed the colour. He thinks, 'She hates me, why does she hate me?' He blinks once himself, and looks again. It is gone. Her eyes are green. She is the loveliest bride he has ever seen. For a moment he is lost for words, then he embarks on the reassuring and familiar ceremony.

It is over quickly. When Robert kisses his bride the entire congregation feels warmed by their embrace. There is a new Throckmorton in Warboys. Agnes Samuel has found her place. She is here to stay. Robert tightens his grip on her waist.

After the ceremony, the bride and groom lead the congregation on foot through the village in a festive parade. It is the last day of October and the late afternoon sun is fading. Leaves are fast falling, the bare skeletons of the trees showing through. At the Throckmorton house there are fairy lights hanging in the overgrown hedgerows, looping over the heavy branches of the old trees. Inside the entrance hall the fire blazes and they have opened up the big rooms on either side of the house, the Elizabethan ballroom which has not been used in many years and the family sitting room with the double doors that open onto the garden. Each room has an open fire in the grate and outside the sitting room overhead blow-heaters warm the air beneath a white canopy. Around the edge of the lawn, at the base of the massive hedge, wax torches are burning, throwing flickering light over the grass.

Robert has hired Jenny's friend Lolly Senior and three other local teenagers to act as waiters; at the entrance they take coats and hats and give each guest a glass of champagne. Jenny, Graeme, Karen and the little boys are amazed by the transformation of the house; it looks warm and grand and welcoming. As Graeme wheels Martin into the sitting room Agnes bends to kiss him. 'See?' she exclaims, 'he is smiling.' When they look they see his usual blank, clear face but the idea of their father's smile makes them feel happy. They view afresh the ballroom, dripping carved plaster, and the garden with its neglected topiary.

Drink flows, as it always does on such occasions, and with it flows conversation. Round and round, round and round, look at Agnes, isn't she beautiful, aren't they going to be happy? People find themselves in awe of the wedding party, it is a dream wedding. Those who are married can't help but wonder why their own weddings hadn't been like this. Single people pledge that their weddings will be just the same. It is perfect, it is entirely perfect, the bride and groom like the perfect couple in a photograph.

Jenny has never drunk champagne before, she spills a bit on the lapel of her silk coat, but that doesn't matter, nothing matters, she is having a wonderful time, she has forgotten her earlier worries, her vision of Agnes in the green dress. She stands in front of the elaborately layered wedding cake. A little piece of white icing has broken off near the bottom, she licks her finger, picks up it and puts it in her mouth. As it melts on her tongue she peers at the figurines. Robert and Agnes are there on top of the cake. They are tiny, but it is them, holding hands. Agnes is smiling, Jenny can see her green eyes shining. But Robert looks sad, and there is a small tear, a miniature drop tear, rolling down his face. Jenny shakes her head and spins around on the tips of her new shoes once, twice, three times, watching her coat flare out around her knees. When she looks at the figurines again, she knows they will be plastic. Her friend Lolly fetches her another glass of champagne. She has lost her hat with its feather.

At the party Elizabeth sticks close by Marlene and Geoff. Geoff is the kind of man who looks ill-at-ease in a suit, despite the fact that he wears one every day. He squires the two women around and makes sure that their drinks are replenished. Apart from Robert, Marlene is the nearest approximation to a friend that Elizabeth has in Warboys; those she thinks of as her real friends are in London, work colleagues, people she studied with at university. Unlike a lot of the Warboys women with whom Elizabeth grew up, Marlene works; she is the village lawyer. She is German and although she has lived in England for more than a decade, she observes people here with a foreigner's acumen. She always says she is lucky her name is Marlene, people think of her as the glamorous German instead of a Wagnerian Nazi. In the months since Elizabeth came back to Warboys the two women have grown closer.

Elizabeth has not spoken with Marlene about how she feels about Robert, but Marlene knows. Most people in Warboys thought that Robert and Elizabeth would end up together, certainly when they were young, and again once Elizabeth returned to the village. So despite the teasing of the previous evening, when Marlene suggested that Elizabeth should stand up and object when it came to that part of the wedding ceremony, Marlene knows that today is a difficult day for her friend. Outwardly, Elizabeth is doing well. She has made an effort and she looks fine, if a little manly, in a navy trouser suit, shiny patent leather shoes. She has even managed to beat her disobedient hair into submission; Elizabeth has the kind of short hair that looks great the day it is cut and, Marlene muses, somehow backward, wrong way up, the rest of the time. Marlene surveys the sitting room, the garden. If only there was a man for Elizabeth at this party, a single man whom none of them have ever met before. But of course this is Warboys, these are the Throckmortons, and there isn't. Robert was always the single man. So Marlene gets Geoff's attention; he takes his cue and attempts to entertain Elizabeth with stories about houses he has sold recently. As well as being captain of the cricket team, Geoff is an estate agent. He sends his clients to Marlene for conveyancing.

The party is bubbling. In a corner of the sitting room there is a long table heaped with presents, subject of intense scrutiny by the children present. The little girls are excited to be there – no one loves weddings more than little girls – and they are thrilled when Agnes stops near them. She looks like a fairy-tale princess and as she bends low to speak to them they are struck dumb with awe and shyness. Agnes makes her way around the party slowly. She stops and speaks for a moment with every person there. The adults stand around waiting for her to reach them. She flirts with the men and charms the women and, once she has moved on, they spring forward, renewed, into the mêlée of the party. It's as though she sprinkles them with good-time powder.

Karen's parents, Deirdre and Paul, have driven down from Leicester for the wedding. Karen shepherds them around; she is glad to see them. Her parents are both retired now and, in retirement, they have more in common with their daughter. Her mother has never understood why Karen doesn't work.

'Won't he let you work?' They are watching Agnes's progress around the room.

'Who?'

Her mother is annoyed. 'Graeme, of course.'

'It's down to me.'

'But you've been out of the labour market for so long now –'

Karen laughs. 'I was never in the labour market.'

Graeme arrives with a fresh glass of champagne for his mother-in-law. 'So Deirdre,' he says, 'you're looking gorgeous.'

'Thank you,' she says, 'and so are you.'

Karen listens patiently. Graeme leaves.

Deirdre looks at Karen appraisingly. 'You look nice.'

Karen can tell she doesn't mean it.

'But you're such a clever girl . . .' her mother continues.

Karen sighs, looks around for the baby Francis who has his head squeezed between his Uncle Robert's legs.

'Look at John –' says Deirdre; Karen's brother John is a GP in Edinburgh.

'I'm not John,' Karen is calm, cheerful even. She understands her mother needs to say these things. Her parents were both schoolteachers, they both took jobs as Headmasters when they moved back to Leicester. They can't comprehend Karen's lack of ambition, her mother finds it especially difficult.

'Admit it Mum,' says Karen.

'What?'

'You think it's backward not to work, don't you?'

'I never said that –'

'You hated being at home with John and I, didn't you?' Karen turns to her mother with a big smile. 'It doesn't matter,' she says. 'It's all right.' She starts to laugh.

'Why are you laughing?'

'I don't know. The fact is I hated working. I hated school too. I only ever wanted to marry Graeme and play house.'

Deirdre can't resist her daughter, she laughs too. 'That's so weird,' she says, 'that's so peculiar.'

They've had this conversation so many times it's almost a recitation, a dramatic dialogue for two. Deirdre knows Karen is happy; Karen thinks, she knows I'm happy. She watches

Agnes. And then it occurs to her for the first time – I am happy: am I?

Elizabeth is avoiding Robert, so far she has managed nicely. He catches up with her outside the kitchen. He can't contain his happiness.

'We're not going away on a honeymoon,' he says breathlessly.

'No?' says Elizabeth, trying to contain her twin impulses – to stalk away in silence, to scream out her fury. Up till now she hadn't felt fury. It must be the champagne.

'Agnes says that being here is enough of a honeymoon for her. Isn't that wonderful?'

'I myself,' says Elizabeth quickly, 'would prefer the Caribbean.'

Robert's face falls. 'Oh,' he says. 'Is that so?'

Elizabeth moves away.

Graeme and his sister Jenny play with the little boys Andrew and Francis out in the garden. Without regard for the fate of his hired suit, Graeme puts his cane to the side and sits on the cold, damp grass and lets the boys climb all over him while Jenny tickles them and makes them scream. People stand around watching and more than one woman remarks that the thing about Graeme Throckmorton is that he is a very good father, as if they believe that somehow makes up for everything else. Karen picks up Francis and takes Andrew by the hand and says to whomever is listening, 'It might be silly of me, but I'm going to attempt to get them into bed.'

After the boys are gone Graeme and Jenny go inside and sit together for a while. Jenny has had a bit too much to drink. She lays her head on her brother's shoulder.

'You look nice,' Graeme says after a while.

'Agnes bought it for me,' she says smiling. They are both watching Agnes on the other side of the room. 'She's beautiful,' Jenny adds.

'Uh-huh,' says Graeme, nodding.

'Do you wish it was you marrying her?'

Graeme turns abruptly and looks at Jenny, forcing her to sit up. 'What?'

'Well, it's just . . .'

Graeme turns away. 'What a stupid thing to say.'

'I'm sorry – I –'

'Shut up.' Graeme leans back in the seat again.

'Okay.' Jenny rests her head back on his shoulder. They both go back to watching Agnes.

There are unseen children present, children no one notices, except perhaps Agnes. Robert was wrong when he said there was no Hallowe'en in Warboys; there are goblins and witches and ghosts and devils and they flit in and out of the trees.

Once Karen has gone upstairs Graeme starts to drink more seriously. When one of the waiters walks by he relieves him of the bottle of champagne he is carrying. The boy objects and Graeme says, 'It's mine. I'm paying for it.' He tucks the bottle under his arm and goes into the sitting room. His father, Martin, has been parked beside the fire and he stares out at the crowded room blankly. 'Well, dad,' Graeme says, sitting down next to him, 'you've gained a new daughter-in-law today. Somebody else to help around the house.' His mild words are not matched by his expression as he looks around the room at the guests, all these people he has never really liked. Geoff and Marlene Henderson, Elizabeth Hopkins, Jim and Lolita Drury. He looks for his glass but he has misplaced it, so he drinks straight from the bottle instead.

Robert stands in front of him. 'Graeme,' he says, 'can you come and help me in the kitchen? They are having a little trouble getting the food organized.'

Graeme looks up at his brother. 'No,' he says. 'It's your wedding.' He goes back to his bottle, angling his chair so that he can look into the flames.

Graeme doesn't know how much time has passed when he feels warm lips on his ear. He lifts his head expecting Karen but it is Agnes leaning down to him, her hand on his shoulder. 'Don't you think we should move into the ballroom?' she asks, her voice low. 'We should make use of the ballroom; it's so crowded in here.' She straightens and walks away; Graeme picks up his cane and follows.

The ballroom is empty, apart from Agnes who now stands in front of the fireplace. Despite the warmth from the fire, the room is too unused to be welcoming and there is a chill in the air centuries old. The windows, though large, are deep-set and make the room dark on the brightest day, and what remains of the oak panelling on two of the walls darkens it further. In her wedding dress Agnes glows with a white light. Graeme stands near enough to see that there are tiny beads of perspiration strung across her collarbone, like a very fine pearl necklace.

'This room,' she says pausing, 'don't you think this room is strange? I feel very odd when I come in here. This room has seen too much.' She walks away from Graeme, running her hand along the wall. 'If these walls could speak you wouldn't want to hear what they have to say. It wouldn't make for a very nice story.'

Graeme's head feels thick. He's had too much to drink. Ordinarily he would claim to be fond of the feeling.

Agnes walks toward him, stopping only inches away. Her face looms at his, pale. 'Your brother is very sweet to me,' she says. 'I'd like to keep you sweet too.' She moves away, graceful and sinewy in the close-fitting dress. She pauses by the door of the room before leaving. 'We should be friends, you and I, Graeme. Brother-in-law.' She says the last word slowly.

After she is gone Graeme stands on his own in the ballroom. He doesn't notice, but behind him on the floor little mounds of plaster dust are growing steadily. The heavy plaster ceiling has been shifting over the centuries, it has not been restored or stabilized in any way, and the recent building work upstairs has loosened it further. Slabs of plaster work against each other like tectonic plates and dust pours from the ceiling in a quiet steady stream, sand in an egg-timer.

What Agnes said has made Graeme uncommonly angry. His thoughts are inarticulate, contradictory. He shakes off the reverie into which he has fallen and thinks, I don't want to be friends with my sister-in-law, I don't want anyone new to come into this family. I have things the way I want them already, I don't want the family altered. Why couldn't Robert have married that Elizabeth Hopkins woman, she wouldn't make things difficult for me. She knows me. She wouldn't expect to be friends.

He spins round and walks to the back of the room. Agnes's perfume lingers in the air, there is an undertow to it that makes him feel queasy. He wipes his hand across his face in an attempt to rid himself of the smell. He is disturbed by her, and he does not like the feeling. He thinks that friendship is not what she is after. He prods the rotting panelling with his cane.

A group of people have gathered in the entrance foyer. There is confusion over the whereabouts of coats and hats. Robert arrives to sort things out and the group pauses by the front door. Several people look into the ballroom and notice Graeme standing at the far end. There is a sound that they later describe like hearing a rock move, stone scraping against stone, the sarcophagus lid pushing back. A large chunk of carved plaster drops from the ceiling. There is a moment of slow-motion quiet as it falls. Then the plaster crashes down across the back of Graeme's head and shoulders. He pitches forward and, mid-air, turns his body like a dancer, rolling free of the weight of the debris. The air fills with dust and grit. Two men run over. One helps Graeme up and brushes him down while the other searches for his cane. Graeme takes it without a word. He pushes his hair, thick with dirt, from his face and walks out of the room, through the crowd in the foyer, his limp slightly more pronounced than usual. He heads upstairs and does not reappear for the duration of the party. 'He could have been killed,' people murmur to each other, and this moment becomes part of the story, part of the wedding tale.

Elizabeth

I survived the wedding thanks to Marlene. I survived what came afterward thanks to myself. I should have seen what was coming, I should have seen it right away. Everyone fell under her spell. No one escaped from that, except me, and that was because I was already too poisoned against her for even Agnes to be able to bend me to her ways.

At the party after the wedding I got talking to Julia Trevelyan. She wasn't someone I knew well. She and her husband David had moved to the village six or seven years previously. They were IT workers, Warboys' first, and they had their office in their big house along the high street. David worked as an editor for various information technology publications and Julia designed web-sites and commercial on-line information. We were standing next to each other under the canopy, chatting, when Agnes reached us on her tour of duty. Robert hadn't managed to introduce me to Agnes before the wedding; we had a scrambled introduction, one among many, outside the church. And now she remembered my name.

'Elizabeth,' she said, her lips parting over white teeth, 'I'm glad to find you again.' She turned to Julia, 'Can I introduce you?'

Julia laughed. 'Oh no, I know Elizabeth. We all know each other here in Warboys, Agnes. But it's sweet of you to offer.'

'I hear,' Agnes turned back to me, 'that you are looking for work?'

I was surprised that Robert had told her this. I wondered what else he had said. 'Yes, I –'

'And I hear you are looking for an employee,' she said turning to look at Julia.

'Well, that's right, it just so happens that we . . .'

Agnes moved on, leaving Julia and me looking at each other speculatively. 'It's not remotely in your field,' Julia said.

'I'm looking to move on,' I replied. We talked for a while until it became clear that Julia and David Trevelyan had found their new employee. We shook hands, and I said I'd be at their house Monday morning.

I left the party on my own sometime after ten p.m. I walked past the Black Hat but didn't notice anything strange. I had expected to make my way much earlier, but I was so cheered by the idea that I was now gainfully employed that I actually began to enjoy myself. I helped Robert organize the food for supper. I sat outside under the canopy, near one of the blow-heaters. Jenny came and sat beside me. We could see the autumn stars above the hedge at the end of the garden. Jenny dipped her head briefly, laying it on my shoulder for a moment, and I found her presence reassuring. She was not a happy girl and her teenage years were proving especially turbulent. I worried about her. But tonight she radiated charm and confidence.

'You look fabulous,' I said.

'Elizabeth,' she was a little breathless from all the excitement and drink, 'I've got a sister now. Can you believe it? Look at her.' We could see Agnes standing in the garden with a group of people, her figure illuminated by a torch burning near her feet. Her dress shone white against the dark night. 'She's like a beacon,' Jenny whispered, 'blazing away.'

The Black Hat flies off

At three a.m. Robert pushes his father's wheelchair to his bedroom. He lifts him into bed fully clothed, foregoing the nightly ablutions that Karen performs without fail. Robert strokes his father's forehead and says, 'Well dad, Agnes and I are married.' His father makes no response, but Robert doesn't expect him to. Most of the guests are gone, Jenny is asleep on a couch in the sitting room, still wearing her matching dress and coat. Jim and Lolita are labouring in the kitchen, but they have urged Agnes and Robert to go to bed.

Agnes's hair is in a lovely state of disarray. Robert insists on carrying her up the stairs to their new bedroom, cleaned and repainted for the occasion. He helps her get out of the wedding dress and with every button his anticipation mounts. She licks her teeth and looks at him with an open sexual knowing that he finds absolutely compelling. They slide into bed together and begin the gorgeous process of celebrating their marriage.

Elizabeth walked past the pub earlier and she didn't notice. Other people walk past on their way home from the wedding and they don't notice either. There is a low light burning in The Black Hat, but they think nothing of it – perhaps Jim left it on for security. Inside three young men are at work. They wear black puffy jackets and small woollen caps and faded blue jeans and though they are young, their faces are marked and hardened and stern. They look like what they are – thieves. They are inside the Black Hat robbing it clean. They have broken down the back door using crowbars and a large gleaming axe. 'Why did no one hear them?' Jim will wail very early the next morning when he and Lolita make their weary way home. 'How could no one hear them? We weren't *all* at the wedding.'

'This village,' sputters Lolita, 'this village is run through with envy and malice. I swear, they could have knocked us down in the street and no one would have done a thing.'

'Lolita,' says Jim, 'that's not true.' But he hasn't been inside yet.

They have torn down the curtains and smashed the glasses – every glass, not one survives. They have stolen the Toby jugs and taken or drunk or poured out all the booze, holding open the draught taps until the floor is awash with lager and bitter and Guinness and coke. They took an axe to the new computer till and when that yielded nothing, they used the axe on the polished oak bar, the shining counter that has long reflected back the faces of the punters who sit there with their beer. There was no money anywhere in the pub for them to steal, not – as Agnes would say – a single red cent, except the charity box with its pennies. So they have taken their tithe in destruction instead and the Black Hat looks like a wild army of drunken soldiers has vented its war rage on it. Little of its pub beauty survives, the windows, the front door, that's it.

Jim is so heartbroken he is unable to cry.

Lolita becomes a dervish. She fetches the black bin liners from out back and begins to clear the debris.

'Stop,' says Jim, his voice dry and sticky in his throat, 'stop it. We've got to call the police.'

'And let them see the place in this state? No,' she shakes her head.

'I've got to call someone,' says Jim, 'I'll call Robert and Agnes.'

'You will not,' says Lolita, 'and spoil their wedding night?' And with that they hear a noise. They both stiffen and look around. But it is only the cat coming out from where she has been hiding.

'This village,' mutters Lolita, as she bends to her task. And now Jim knows exactly what she means. It is a quiet village, Warboys, they know each other by name, they have flowers in their gardens and there are birds in the trees. It is an oasis of warm people in the cold grey fenland. And if it wasn't for the burglars, it would be perfect. And if it hadn't been for the joy-riders a few years back, it would have been perfect then as well – Jim and Lolita didn't lose their car, but plenty of other people did. You could hardly step out the front door and into the high street without fear of being mowed down. And if it hadn't been for the tricksters and graffitos and those boys who did over the church, and the shop, and the houses along the back.

'This country,' mutters Lolita, as she rights a table, as Jim picks up the dustpan and brush.

In the morning light, Robert wakes. He is very cold, and gripped by an inexplicable fear. He thinks he sees Agnes standing at the end of the bed, dressed in black with a severe black hat, staring at him, her face white with rage. With a sharp movement he turns away from what he sees and finds his wife, Agnes, naked and warm, breathing deeply beside him.

Karen belongs in Warboys

Karen knows she belongs in Warboys. She lies in bed next to Graeme and thinks about the conversation she had with her mother at the wedding. Warboys is Karen's village. She grew up here. This is where she married Graeme, at nineteen. She worked in Peterborough for a while but she knew that was temporary. She didn't much like Peterborough. An in-between kind of place, a too-small city, a too-big village. She was glad when she gave up the commute and took up housekeeping.

Karen couldn't believe it when her parents decided to move back to Leicester. They were in-comers in Warboys, they'd both grown up in the Midlands, and for them the village was temporary. They sold the house where Karen grew up. It was their business, not Karen's – she no longer lived there – but still, it shocked her. Even now when she walks by her old house she has to stop herself from going up the footpath to the front door and walking straight in. And if she did, it wouldn't really matter. Marlene and Geoff Henderson own the house now. Marlene would make Karen a cup of tea and show her around the renovations.

Karen loves the Throckmorton house, with its scabby cracked walls and its broken guttering. She loves it because it is Throckmorton, always has been; they have lived here forever, they are not about to sell up and move away. When things are bad between Karen and Graeme, and things do get bad, the house consoles her. She cleans and scrubs and the house welcomes her ministrations, much like Graeme's father Martin silently accepts her care. The house absorbs her, like it absorbs the noise and thunder of the two little boys. Sometimes she thinks, oh yes, I really am a housewife, the house is my husband, not Graeme, and this thought makes her feel giddy.

Agnes is new to Warboys, Karen reflects on this that night after the wedding. She tries to imagine what it must feel like to leave the place you know – your home, your country – and go live elsewhere. She wouldn't have the courage. She doesn't know how Agnes has the courage. And why, Karen asks herself, why did you come here? What have you left behind?

And then there is Jenny. Karen worries about Jenny. She has always been a little bit unstable, changeable, like a weathervane. Graeme and Robert put it down to the fact that she lost their mother at birth. They do what they can for her but when she was a child they were young men getting on with their lives. Martin did his best for the first few years, until he was no longer able. The Throckmortons are like other people in this regard; they accept their fate and get on with life. There is – has always been – a certain amount of muddling through. Karen has tried to mother Jenny, but Jenny resists, they have never got along particularly well even though Karen has been around all of Jenny's short life. 'Jenny,' Karen asks from time to time, 'is everything all right?' 'Yes,' the girl replies, turning away. She is very close to her brother Graeme and Karen works hard to avoid feeling jealousy. She is not completely successful. And mothering Jenny is complicated by the difficulties she and Graeme had in conceiving their own child.

As soon as Graeme was on full salary with the police force he and Karen got married. Karen quit her job, it was what they had agreed she should do. Stay home and take care of Jenny, keep house for Graeme and Robert and their father. Have a family. But it didn't happen the way they planned. They abandoned contraceptives on their wedding night but months passed and nothing transpired. After five years sex had become well-timed and perfunctory; another year and, despite Graeme's reluctance to involve outsiders, Karen went to the doctor. She embarked on a series of tests that she found degrading and embarrassing; she persisted, there was no alternative. After some months they established that there was absolutely nothing wrong with her, she ovulated regularly, her tubes were clear, everything was the right way up and in its proper place. The GP said Graeme should come and see him; he'd been suggesting that all along, but Karen knew her husband wouldn't agree so she hadn't bothered asking. But now she was gripped by sadness and desperation; she was only twenty-six and she wanted a baby. She wanted a baby in a way that made her ache. And she'd been told there was no reason why she couldn't have one. Her desire overruled her reluctance. She told Graeme he had to go and see the doctor or there was no point in having sex ever again.

Graeme made an appointment, and cancelled it, made another and cancelled that as well. He knew what he was going to be told. One morning after he'd left Karen weeping in the bathroom as she discovered she was menstruating yet again, he drove to London instead of going in to work. He went to a private clinic he'd seen advertised in a magazine and paid for tests. A week later he received a phonecall while on his lunchbreak. He stood at the payphone next to the toilet and insisted on being given the result there and then; the nurse in London informed him that his sperm count was very low. 'How low?' Too low. He did not allow the expression on his face to change. He said, 'Thank you,' and hung up the phone. Later that shift, while making an arrest outside a pub – drunken brawlers – he kicked one of the suspects in the groin. He later claimed the man had been resisting arrest.

It took him six months to tell Karen about the test. During that time he had three affairs with women in Peterborough – a police constable, a secretary who used to work with Karen, and a barmaid from a pub he frequented. With all three women he refused to use contraception and all three allowed him because, for a moment, they fancied having his baby. Karen knew that Graeme was not faithful, although he never confessed and she had never found any evidence. But sometimes, late at night, she thought she deserved to be barren, he deserved it, it was their punishment.

'I think we should go private,' Karen said, one evening. 'I think I should try IVF. I don't want to wait for the NHS.'

'How much will it cost?' Graeme asked. Their room was dark. The wind made the bones of the house creak.

'I don't know. Two or three thousand each time.'

'Each time?'

'It can take several goes.'

They couldn't afford it. There was no way they could afford it on his salary.

'It's my fault,' Graeme said. 'It's down to me.'

Karen thought he was talking about the money. 'I'll ask my dad. Maybe he'll lend us something.'

'I don't mean that, it's –' He shifted in the bed, moving as far away from Karen as possible. 'I haven't got enough.'

'He'll lend us, I've never asked –'

'No,' his voice was raised, angry. He sighed, heavy, sinking down into the bed. 'I haven't got enough sperm. They're dead. There's nothing they can do for me.'

After that, they were silent. Karen had known this must be the case, but she had never allowed herself to think about it before. It was unthinkable. Graeme couldn't do it, he couldn't give her a baby. She knew what he was feeling and there was nothing she could do about it, nothing she could say.

They lay in bed for a long time without touching. Graeme could feel Karen holding her body rigid. After another long while he thought of reaching out for her but by then she was asleep. He heard her breath grow even and deep. He got up, went downstairs and drank all the beer in the fridge. In the morning Karen found him lying asleep on the floor under the kitchen table. She bundled him upstairs and called in sick for him before anyone else got up.

They spent the next week considering their options. Not together, not in deep and confidential discussions, not trying to make each other laugh, not holding each other's hands, but separately, on their own as they went about their duties, hers in the home, his at work. If they couldn't speak to each other, there could be no one else for them to talk to either, and so they kept it to themselves. The options were clear. They could divorce, Karen could find someone else, and Graeme, well, there were plenty of single mothers out there looking for a likely candidate. They could foster, maybe adopt a child, they were young enough, they would probably meet the criteria. They could forget it and Karen could find a job and they could live out their childless lives in the Throckmorton house.

No. None of this was right.

They could use donated sperm. Karen could go down to London and visit a sperm bank, such places existed. But then their children would be strangers to Graeme, the offspring of anonymous men. Graeme wouldn't agree to that.

They came up with the same plan at the same time, the same night as they lay together in bed. They hadn't had sex for months and nor had they spoken about what they had both come to think of as The Problem. From the outside their marriage could look loveless; Graeme treated Karen with an off-hand disdain that other people found painful to observe. And there were his affairs, everyone knew about his affairs. But despite appearances, despite daily realities, there was a way in which Graeme and Karen knew each other thoroughly, completely – and if that's not love, Karen said to herself, what is?

'Robert.' Graeme spoke first.

'Robert,' Karen answered.

They were silent again for some time.

'Do you think he'll agree?' asked Karen.

'He will,' said Graeme. 'I'll make him.'

Robert

The morning after the wedding I woke to the sound of Andrew and Karen whispering on the landing outside our bedroom. Agnes was sound asleep. I felt exhausted, hungover, and too happy for words. I looked over at my wife.

Suddenly I remembered. I hadn't told Agnes about the boys. I guess Andrew had come upstairs to wake us and Karen had caught him before he could get into our room. Andrew woke me most mornings, he woke everyone most mornings, he was our human alarm clock. Four years old and raring to go first thing. I would have to tell Agnes the truth.

I could hear Karen trying to persuade the child to leave us alone. Very intelligent, I thought, for him to remember which room Agnes and I had moved into. Eventually she managed to get him to go downstairs with her. God knows what she had to promise in exchange.

Andrew and Francis don't know that I'm their biological father. Graeme and Karen did not plan to tell them, they didn't think it necessary. As far as I was concerned, Graeme and Karen were the boys' parents and I was their doting uncle. Andrew is a little toughie, he looks more like Graeme than me anyway, and Francis is the image of Karen, the image of Karen transmigrated into a little boy. For me, they are Graeme's boys.

There was nothing I could do about my oversight. I had married Agnes and I had forgotten to tell her about the boys. As the enormity of my mistake began to sink in, the warmth and cosiness of my marriage bed dissipated. When Agnes woke up I would have to tell her. I had no idea how she would respond. How could I forget, how could I not have considered that she might find it difficult to accept this particular information about my family?

I lay awake for ages, rehearsing the speech I would make. There was no good way of telling her.

Eventually she began to stir, pressing her body against mine. She opened her green eyes, smiled and stretched, and moved close to kiss me. But I couldn't let her kiss me, I had to tell her, I had to tell the truth and let her respond. By now I felt sure that ours would be the very briefest of marriages. She would despise me for not telling her this most basic of truths.

'Good morning husband,' she said, but not even that could make me smile. 'What's wrong?' She could read me so well already.

'I –' I started and stopped. I couldn't work out how to tell her. She looked at me, more awake and alert. 'Graeme –' I began again, then paused. 'Graeme can't have children,' I said. 'So the boys, well, biologically they are mine. I was the donor.'

Agnes's green eyes widened slightly, so I assumed she was shocked.

'I know, I know, I should have told you. I should have told you before we were married. But I never think about it. I didn't sleep with Karen, I simply handed . . . it . . . over. I'm not their father, you see, Graeme is. We decided –'

'What a gift,' she said, interrupting me. 'What an amazing gift you have given your brother and his wife.'

I couldn't believe she understood so completely. I thought back to when Graeme had asked if I would do this thing. He was very matter of fact and blunt, as always. 'Karen and I need some assistance,' he said. He had never asked me for a favour and it was only later, as I thought about it, that I could see how much it must have cost him, what a humiliating and pathetic request he was making. I agreed immediately, I didn't have to think about it. I did it for Karen as much as for my brother, I knew her life at home with us would have no meaning otherwise.

'I had a feeling,' said Agnes, 'about the situation. I had a feeling about those boys.' She snuggled up next to me and moved her hand along my chest. 'You are so good,' she said, 'you are such a good man.' She brought her face to mine and began to kiss me.

'We haven't discussed –' I said '– we haven't talked about whether or not we'll have kids –'

'Shh,' Agnes said, 'shh.' And she ran her hand up the inside of my thigh. I turned to her thinking my wife is not only a sex-machine, she's also a saint.

It was awful when we found out what had happened to the Black Hat. Agnes and I stayed in bed for a while after we woke up – as I said, for us bed was a glorious place. When we went down for breakfast it was nearly lunch and Jim Drury had already been by to pick up the glasses and dishes we had used for the party.

'Lucky for them to have left that stuff here,' Graeme informed us. 'Otherwise they'd have lost everything.'

Jenny had promised to make Agnes and me breakfast and she was already at it. Otherwise we would have gone round to the Black Hat right away. Later, after we'd eaten, Agnes was reluctant to go for some reason.

'I know honey,' I said, an American endearment for my American wife, 'it'll be terrible to see the pub – and Jim and Lolita – in such a state.'

'It's not that,' said Agnes – and I thought this was odd even at the time, this proves I wasn't completely blind to some of the strangeness of her ways – 'I live here now. I don't live there anymore.'

Jenny turned at the sink and looked at Agnes.

'But it's our pub,' I said, thinking, another cultural difference? 'Our local.'

'Oh,' said Agnes flatly. 'Okay.'

At the Black Hat it was business as usual. The debris – chairs and tables beyond mending – was pushed into a corner near the fire. The alcohol had been mopped up and drained away, leaving a sticky tide-mark. 'It's a wonder – a shame – they didn't drop a match and incinerate themselves,' said Lolita. Most of the glass had been swept away, the torn curtains taken down, a ruined bench stripped of its upholstery. Geoff Henderson was at work behind the bar and Jim and Lolita were bumping into each other – they hadn't bothered going to bed. Jim greeted us, but his warmth didn't disguise the strain. He took Agnes by the arm. I was surprised to see her body stiffen. She frowned.

Jim didn't notice. 'Well dear,' he said, 'you were a lovely bride. I'd walk you down the aisle any day.' He smiled and winked at me. I was pleased by his magnanimity, given the situation. Agnes didn't respond.

'Thanks Jim,' I said, 'thanks for –'

'It was a great idea for you and Lolita to close the pub,' Agnes interrupted. 'Don't you think?'

'Well, I –' Jim reddened and I saw he couldn't help but glance around at the ruined room.

'If you hadn't closed the pub it wouldn't have been nearly such a wonderful day. Isn't that right, Robert?'

I didn't know what to say. I didn't want to contradict my wife on the first day of our marriage. And she was right in a way, of course, but with what Jim was going through her comments were, well, inappropriate. I searched for words. Jim began to draw away.

And then her face softened, in fact her whole body softened, and she leaned into Jim and her voice took on that husky tone we men loved, and she said, 'You can give me away any time you want, Jim. I'm yours for the giving.' And she kissed him on the cheek. He blushed and smiled and all was forgiven, forgotten, and he ushered us over to Geoff who poured our drinks. Whisky for Agnes, a pint of bitter for me. 'Here's to the happy couple,' Geoff raised his glass in a toast.

'Cheers,' I returned and felt dizzy with lust and happiness as Agnes slipped her arm through mine.

Work was going well in the rooms we had decided to renovate, and the builders were back in on Monday morning. We lived in a world of plaster dust; it got into everything. Restoration work was needed on the carved ceiling in the ballroom downstairs as well now, and that would require specialists. At the instigation of Agnes, we decided to try to find out whether the local council or the National

Trust or Department of Heritage or somebody like that would be able to help us. I had never thought about the house as anything other than our house before, our old house with its cobwebs and dignity. Certainly not a house that warranted the attention of outsiders. Agnes declared she would take on this task, she would sort it out.

We hadn't discussed what she was going to do after the wedding. In fact, as the early days of our marriage progressed it became clear to me just how little we had discussed in the weeks since we met. I knew she had money, that she wasn't going to have to work, and I wouldn't have wanted her to have to work anyway. That sounds so old-fashioned – what I mean is, she could have worked if she had wanted to work but it was great that she didn't have to, that I didn't need her to. Even if she hadn't had her own money our household could have expanded to include supporting her as well. One more person would not have broken the bank. And I suppose I thought she would keep Karen company, lighten her load a little. I know how silly that sounds now, with hindsight. Housework was not Agnes's forte.

I never found out how much money Agnes had, and I never discovered where it had come from. I did ask her once, I asked whether her parents had made their money in Las Vegas, thinking perhaps they'd been gamblers, or casino-owners, or – who knows – perhaps her mum was a show-girl and her dad a croupier. But Agnes laughed at my speculations. She didn't like answering questions about her past. 'I'm here for you now and that's all that matters,' she'd say. And for me it was true, that was all that mattered.

Nothing else concerned me.

Agnes tells Jenny stories

Sometimes at night Agnes tells Jenny stories. She sits on the edge of the bed in Jenny's room, the light dimmed low, and she talks, her voice deep and quiet. Graeme used to read Jenny stories every night when she was small; he stopped when she was thirteen and Karen said she thought it wasn't such a good idea any longer. He misses it though, and so does Jenny, but Andrew came along and Graeme started at the beginning again, back to A A Milne. Agnes doesn't read to Jenny – she talks her stories, she keeps them stored in her memory.

'There is a town, a small town, in the mid-west, a town like any other town. In it lives a girl, her name is Jenny –' the girls are always called Jenny in Agnes's stories '– and she lives with her mother, her parents are divorced. Jenny and her mother don't get on too well, and her father, well, he is a cop and he has a bit of an alcohol problem. Her parents have been divorced for a number of years and her mother is no stranger to the bottle herself.

'Jenny has a group of friends at school, good friends, they watch out for each other. They are in the twelfth grade, which in American high school is called the senior year, they are seniors. There are twelve grades in American high school. Anyway, a group of boys and girls and they are good friends. None of them comes from particularly happy families and it might be this that binds them together. Some of Jenny's best friends have boyfriends and for them the big question is whether or not they should go all the way with these boys, whether or not they should –' Agnes pauses and looks at Jenny knowingly, 'have sex. Jenny's very best friend,

Lolly, decides that yes, she is going to go ahead, she and her boyfriend Ron are going to have sex.

'Jenny has a boyfriend, his name is Tim and Tim would like to sleep with Jenny but she isn't certain. She likes Tim a lot, but she doesn't know if she loves him, and she believes you should love someone if you are going to sleep with them. But Tim is patient, he thinks she will change her mind if he kisses her well enough.'

Jenny interrupts. 'I don't know anyone called Tim.'

'Who says this is about you?' says Agnes. 'You don't live in the American Midwest either, do you?'

Jenny snuggles down.

'Okay?'

'Yes.'

'Around this time, Jenny and her friends start to have the same dream. Jenny dreams that she goes down into the basement of her house, down where the furnace is – American houses are like that, they don't have kitchen boilers, they have furnaces, usually oil-burning, sometimes wood, occasionally both. They always have basements, at least houses in small towns always have basements, basements that are dark and a little bit creepy, houses in the suburbs that have garages and front lawns and backyards and that kind of thing. Creepy.'

'Did you grow up in a house like that?' asks Jenny.

'No,' says Agnes, 'I grew up in an apartment in a hotel.'

'What's Las Vegas like?'

'It's a kind of paradise. The sun shines all year round. It's in the desert, but there is water everywhere. It's a city built on money. Money and chance.'

'Do you miss it?'

'Sometimes,' Agnes says, 'when I'm very cold.' She reconsiders. 'Not really. So anyway, Jenny dreams that she goes down into the basement and the furnace is roaring and she is very, very frightened. She wakes up, she makes herself wake up, and she is covered in sweat, her heart beating fast. One night she has this same dream but this time when she goes down into the basement there is a man there, an evil man. He is living inside the furnace. His face is horribly mutilated and instead of fingers he has fists full of razorblades. He chases her through the basement which suddenly isn't the basement any longer but a kind of factory, an underground industrial factory, windowless, with no exits, and Jenny can't wake up, she can't make herself wake up. And he chases her and chases her and she runs and runs, screaming, until she begins to feel very tired, and he catches up with her. He grabs her and she feels one of the razors sink into her arm – and finally, she wakes up.

'She wakes up in her own bed, in her own room, in her own house, safe and sound. Except when she lifts her hand away from where she is clutching her arm she finds it is soaked in blood. There is a deep cut where the man in her nightmare has sliced her.

'That day when Jenny gets to school she discovers that her best friend Lolly and her boyfriend Ron are dead. Some monster, some psychopath, sliced them both up with knives in Lolly's own bed.'

Jenny interrupts. 'Really?'

'Shh,' says Agnes, 'listen.'

'Jenny and her friends gather together in the school cafeteria. Terrified by what has happened to Lolly and Ron, they begin to talk about their nightmares and, suddenly, they realize they are all having the same nightmare. They know who murdered Ron. The man who lives in their nightmares. The man with knives instead of fingers. He is somehow breaking through the sleep barrier into real life. He is trying to kill them, each and every one one of them.'

Jenny shudders. 'Oh god, Agnes,' she says, heartfelt, 'that's horrible.'

'Are you sure you don't know this story?' Agnes asks. 'I thought everyone knew this story.'

Jenny shakes her head. 'Why? Why is he killing them?'

'Listen,' says Agnes, 'and I'll tell you.'

'One after the other Jenny's friends start to die. They die terrible deaths at the razor-hands of this evil man in his filthy black and red striped sweater and his battered fedora hat. It is always the same. They try to stay awake, they do anything to avoid going to sleep, keep each other talking on the phone, trying to make sure they are safe. They are terrified of falling asleep. But night after night one of them succumbs to sleep, and when they do he is waiting for them. And he gets them, and kills them, he always does.

'The parents in the town are going crazy. There seems to be nothing they can do to stop their children dying. Jenny's mother is hysterical about the situation, Jenny finds she can't talk to her about it at all. Jenny's father, the policeman, is desperately trying to do something. But even though he is armed, he is powerless against this monster, completely ineffectual. At first the adults refuse to believe the children are being murdered by the man from their nightmares but Jenny has a feeling that her own parents know more than they are letting on. She thinks they know the identity of the man in the nightmares but for some reason are unable to face up to it.

'Jenny herself does battle with the razor-fingered man night after night but she always manages to escape although her escape inevitably leads to the death of another one of her friends.'

Jenny is curled up under her blankets. She pulls one over her head.

'Do you want me to stop?'

'No,' she says, muffled.

Agnes continues. 'Jenny confronts her mother. She demands she tell her everything she knows. And so her mother confesses.

'Jenny's mother and father grew up in the same neighbourhood, the very neighbourhood where Jenny and her mum still live. There was a man, an evil man, who worked as a janitor in the school and who got his kicks from molesting children. He was a clever man and the police were unable to pin anything on him, so he kept evading arrest. And he continued to molest children. Jenny's mother herself was one of his victims, she won't say anything more than that.

'One day, the parents in the neighbourhood had had enough. The men – Jenny's grandfather and the other fathers in the area – got together and decided to take the law into their own hands. They went after the man they knew had been molesting their children. They trapped him in the basement of the school and they forced him into the furnace where he burned to death. This is the man who is now killing their own children.'

'He'd come back,' says Jenny, horrified.

'He'd come back to seek his revenge.'

'What happened?'

'Well, armed with this knowledge, Jenny goes to bed that night determined to meet the man and destroy him. He chases her through the endless basement, up ramps and metal stairways, past roaring furnaces, until she can't run any further. Summoning up all her courage and strength, she turns to meet him face to face. They battle for hours, through the night, at great cost to Jenny. But, in the end, she overwhelms him. She is victorious, his evil cannot sully the essential goodness and purity of her character.'

'She wins? Because she is good?'

'Yes. He cannot destroy her. She destroys him.'

'He stops killing?'

'Yes.'

Jenny slumps back down on her pillows. 'Wow,' she giggles nervously. 'That's a horrible story Agnes.'

'I'm fond of it.'

'I've never heard of such a thing.'

Agnes laughs. 'You've led a sheltered life.' She stands to go. 'School tomorrow. Is there anything you'll need help with in the morning?'

'No, I'll be fine. Thanks.'

Agnes nods and goes toward the door. Before she can leave, Jenny speaks again. 'Is he gone forever?'

'Forever?' says Agnes. 'No. Revenge is a powerful thing.'

Elizabeth

I loved Warboys. Even though the sodium lights of London drew me away for a time, I always loved our village. There's something about the fens that I find very beguiling. It's like the low quiet notes that a symphony orchestra plays; most people prefer the loud bits. All that water, the land criss-crossed with canals and drainage ditches; when I was a child my parents used to take me out to the fens to skate in winter. Skating made me love the diluted low-land, the sharp air on my face, my blades scraping against the ice. Of course these days the winters are usually too dreary and mild to force a freeze. But I still love Warboys. I still feel it is my place.

I didn't see Robert and Agnes for nearly a fortnight after the wedding. I wanted to keep away from them, and besides, I was busy. I had started working for Julia and David Trevelyan.

I was the office dogsbody, except that David usually made the coffee. He was very particular about his coffee and had his own espresso machine. I'd arrive around about nine a.m. and open the post while David made me cappuccino. I thought I'd given up coffee but he persuaded me differently. There wasn't that much mail of the old-fashioned variety but there were often faxes and there was a great deal of e-mail. Our computers were networked and Julia and David both received dozens of messages every day. They said they were tired of being enslaved by e-mail and that it was one of their main reasons for hiring somebody; I didn't know enough about computers at the time to know whether they were joking or not. I read the messages and deleted those I considered to be junk-mail, there was an awful lot of that, messages sent ricocheting around the world notifying anyone and everyone about different services, academic research, that kind of thing. The rest I would print out, ridiculous as that might sound in an office devoted to information technology, but I would print the messages out on to paper and sort them into three piles, personal, urgent business and general. That way Julia and David could prioritize them. I answered the phone and, as I became more knowledgeable about the work they did, dealt with a lot of the enquiries myself. I did the banking and the book-keeping, most of it electronically, sent off invoices and reminders, and kept on top of the computer database. It was busy work, not mindless, but not demanding. They paid me by the hour and sometimes I'd be finished by eleven a.m., sometimes I'd be there the entire day. It was an amicable set-up and I think we all benefited from it. I grew accustomed to the hum of computers in the background and came to like the way their blue screens lit up our faces. Most of the work I did had fallen on Julia's shoulders and employing me freed her up for other things, kind of like hiring a cleaner. Except they had one of those already. I felt incredibly relieved that it wasn't me.

Robert and Agnes's wedding had been a big event in Warboys and the buzz from it lasted for weeks. As the weather grew darker and colder it was something people talked about as though to warm themselves, reminiscing, going over the details, what the bride had worn, what music had been played, who had said what to whom at the party. I was sick of hearing about it, I would have been happy if it had happened and never been mentioned again, but that isn't how life works in a small village. Of course I smiled and nodded my head as though I agreed it had been the most beautiful thing I'd ever seen, Agnes the loveliest bride. Barbara, in the shop, was one of the worst offenders, but she was always a bit extreme in her reaction to things. She wasn't a gossip, she wasn't that interested in what the people of the village said or did provided they didn't say or do it in her shop, and so when something was happening you could usually rely on Barbara not to have noticed. But she did feel strongly about certain things. I remember when Princess Diana died she wept for a full two weeks. You couldn't buy a paper from her without coming away with a front page made soggy with tears. Barbara loved Agnes almost as passionately, I think she thought Agnes had stepped out from the pages of her beloved *Hello* magazine.

So it was a couple of weeks before I saw any of the Throckmortons, an achievement given the size of Warboys. Then I ran into Robert in the shop on the way to the Trevelyans one morning. I was picking up milk for the coffee.

'Elizabeth!' he exclaimed, as though surprised to see me alive and in the village, as though he'd forgotten about me completely.

'Robert. How are you? How is Agnes?'

'Oh, we're fine,' he beamed, 'we're very well. You must come round. You've got to come round.' Robert looked red-cheeked and healthy, as though he'd never had a cold, or any kind of ailment, in his life. 'You must see what we are doing to the house.'

I smiled and nodded and hoped his enthusiasm would carry him right out of the shop.

'Come tonight,' he said.

On the day of the wedding I took a decision that I would not allow this marriage to ruin my life, that I would not allow it to affect my behaviour, that I would be steady and even and take everything in my stride. That meant accepting invitations and behaving as though nothing was amiss. Everything was absolutely fine. If I could sustain that lie for long enough, perhaps it would become a truth.

'That would be lovely,' I said.

'I'm sorry it's been so long,' said Robert, and I think for a moment he actually meant it. 'But come tonight and we'll catch up. Come early. Six o'clock.'

Like most households that contain small children, the Throckmorton house ran on a very regular schedule, Agnes's arrival had not altered that. Every day at six the family sat down at the big oak table in the kitchen. I had joined them on many occasions. After the quiet of my cottage, quiet even when my parents were alive, a Throckmorton evening meal was enjoyable for me. Usually Robert and Graeme were arguing about the estate, Graeme and Jenny were arguing about something to do with Jenny's schoolwork, Karen and Graeme were arguing about the boys while Karen tried to feed them and Jenny and Robert got the meal for the adults onto the plates. Andrew and Francis fought with each other and I sat and watched all of it, following the conversation as it wove around the table like one of Martin Scorsese's great tracking shots. (I used to know about cinema, I used to know about the world, I used to love that kind of thing.) After they'd eaten, Andrew and Francis sat on the floor to play and the adults would get on with their meal. But it was never peaceful; Karen would be up and down fetching things, making more salad, Robert would decide that whatever he had cooked was missing an essential ingredient and he'd get up to look for it, Graeme would eat much too quickly before announcing he was off to the pub. Mr Throckmorton would sit in his corner with his plate on his knees.

I was relieved to discover that with Agnes there, none of this had changed. In fact, if anything, she contributed to the chaos, continually leaving off one task to start another, just like everyone else. The builders were in upstairs and so the battle to contain the dust and debris was on, but they took it in their stride. Karen informed me, with a smile, that Agnes had decided to reform her cooking – no more fried food, no more chips, no more red meat. They were eating much more fish, she said, while Graeme put his arm around his wife's waist and made a yuck face, indicating displeasure. I hadn't seen him be so affectionate to Karen in a long time.

Agnes was very friendly toward me, I couldn't fault her there. When I came in through the back door she smiled and gave me a wisp of a kiss on my cheek. She said, 'It's so good to see you,' and she turned to look at Robert. 'I wondered when he was going to invite you round. We've been so busy, what with the renovations.'

I gave her what I hoped was an easy smile. 'I wanted to thank you for what you did at the wedding, introducing me to Julia and David.'

'You knew them already!'

'Yes, but suggesting that they hire me.'

'Did it work out?'

'I'm their new employee.'

Robert came over at that point and clamped his arm around my shoulder. 'Congratulations,' he said. 'Are you giving them 9 to 5 therapy?' His touch made me feel uneasy, self-conscious, and I hoped the colour in my cheeks would not rise too quickly.

'Robert,' Agnes chastised him, 'she's their assistant.'

'I'm the office dogsbody. And it's great. I'm finally part of the Electronic Age.'

'I'm so glad it worked out,' Agnes said. 'I love it when things like that happen.'

'Well, thanks to you Agnes,' I said, but she was gone, across the room to help Karen with the boys.

That evening the Throckmortons were a picture of happiness. They argued, as always, and the boys refused their food and demanded pudding, but that was the way things should be. I would say that no false notes were struck, except it seems to me, with hindsight, that the whole set up was one enormous, loud, false chord. How could it not be? Agnes was biding her time. She was getting everyone where she wanted them. And everyone included me.

After dinner Robert, Agnes and I retired to the sitting room. Graeme had gone off for a drink, Karen was putting the boys to bed, Jenny had gone to her room. The sitting room had been subtly altered, the lighting rearranged so that it was softer, warmer, the curtains not new, but cleaned, an old carpet spruced up and thrown over the back of a sofa where its colours – reds and greens – seemed richer, logs piled in a basket beside the fire.

The Throckmorton house was full of nice old things, worn, comfortable things; there was nothing valuable, nothing that could be classified antique. They were the kind of family who used things up and then moved on; they broke glasses and crockery, they wore out upholstery, they stuffed their junk in the attic and left it to rot.

While Robert fetched a bottle of wine and glasses, Agnes took me on a brief tour upstairs. There the transformation was much more remarkable. The bathroom wasn't finished but I could see that it would be splendid, it would have a hotel gleam. The wall had been brought down between the two smaller rooms and that made a big difference. And their bedroom, well, I could remember playing with Robert in this room when we were young, hide and seek in among the mouldering boxes and crates, but I didn't mention that to Agnes. Now the beams were freshly stained and the walls were very white and the big high bed was luxuriously piled with white pillows, an eyelet cotton spread. She opened the wardrobe and showed me their clothes and shoes jumbled together and it made my breath catch in my throat, this hard evidence of their marriage. It wasn't a game, a trick Robert was playing. It wasn't a dream I was stuck in, night after night.

When she closed the wardrobe I caught sight of myself in the mirror. Agnes noticed. 'That's a great skirt,' she said. I was wearing a long black wool skirt that I had bought when I was working in London.

'Oh thanks,' I said.

'I've always liked wool skirts. I've never lived anywhere cold enough to wear them. It looks great on you. I must stock up.'

I knew what she was doing. She was complimenting me as a way to try to be nice, to get close to me. Women do it all the time.

'We'll have to go shopping,' she said.

'You think?'

'Definitely.'

And so I complimented her taste in return. Downstairs we found Robert pouring us both drinks. Now you've done it, I said to myself, drawing a deep breath, now you've got yourself here and you're going to have to stick with it, a smile stiffening into wrinkles on your face.

We sat and talked for an hour. Agnes was gracious and inclusive and made it clear she thought we were going to be friends. We talked about the Trevelyans, the estate, Christmas, Jim and Lolita Drury and how they'd achieved miracles fixing up the Black Hat since the break-in. Afterward I realized that Agnes had somehow deflected all conversation away from herself onto Robert and me. During the course of the evening I learned nothing about her, nothing that I didn't already know. Her name was Agnes Samuel. She came from Las Vegas. Her parents were both dead. She was beautiful. A few facts, that was all. At the time it didn't occur to me to doubt the truth of the little she had told us. She was one of those people with the highly prized knack of getting others to talk about themselves. Highly prized by those who do the talking. I could see how good she was for Robert's ego. With Agnes there he felt he could do anything.

I was beginning to think about leaving when Graeme returned from the pub. The atmosphere changed. The atmosphere always changed when Graeme entered a room, as though he brought an electric charge with him through the door, it was something we were used to. But when he came into the sitting room that night, the mood changed in a way I hadn't expected – something was going on. I didn't know what it was, just a kind of tension that I hadn't noticed before. It was not coming from Graeme alone, but Agnes as well, I saw it flash across her face. Robert was oblivious to it. I felt very uncomfortable, so I made my excuses and said I needed to get going.

Robert insisted on walking me home. He always used to walk me home, as though danger lurked in night-time Warboys.

'What do you think?' he asked as I knew he would.

'Oh, she's great, Robert, really lovely.'

'She is, isn't she?' He shivered and sighed involuntarily.

'Yes, you've landed on your feet.'

'Lizzie,' he said, his voice full of confidence, 'you'll meet someone, I know you will. You won't have long to wait.'

I hadn't expected that. 'I know. I'm fine.'

'Of course you are.'

I changed the subject. 'How does Agnes get on with Graeme?'

'Well. Really well.'

'That's good,' I said. 'That's great.'

Robert left me at the gate. When I opened the door of the cottage it felt cold though I had left the heating on all evening.

Agnes spurns Graeme

Christmas is approaching, like a splash of crimson spreading on the horizon. It is dark in Warboys, the days are getting shorter and shorter, the sky so low there is scarcely room to stretch. People scurry out to the Black Hat for a quick drink, scurry home to the gas fire once again. The pub has been restored to its former glory, except now everything is new – carpets, curtains, upholstery – and the effect is uncanny; the customers feel slightly ill at ease, like they've walked on to a set, a clever reconstruction of their local. Jim Drury is rather pleased with the way things have turned out and he tries to tempt the punters with mulled wine and hot buttered rum – a drink Agnes taught him to make when she was in residence – but he can't keep them. The curtains are drawn, the lights are dim, every evening feels like a lock-in.

Agnes and Robert are faithful to the Black Hat, although not as faithful as Graeme who appears nightly. Jim Drury is proprietorial toward them, they're his couple, he thinks, he introduced them, because of him they are married. Robert indulges the publican but he finds it a little hard to stomach, he wishes Jim would calm down. Other people have begun to calm down, Agnes isn't quite the movie star she was at the beginning, they are getting used to having her around. Not Jim. The man is besotted, Robert thinks, snorting into his whisky. The man is besotted and, luckily for him, so is his wife, Lolita.

On this Sunday evening Agnes and Robert are in the pub early. Robert is going down to London later tonight, he has a meeting first thing in the morning with the agency responsible for letting out the holiday cottages on the estate. And a meeting with suppliers in the afternoon. He'll stay with Elizabeth's friend Marina and won't be home until tomorrow evening. It will be the first time he and Agnes have been apart. He consoles himself by sitting close to her now, telling himself that in London he'll find time for shopping, he'll buy Agnes something lovely. They spent the afternoon in bed and Robert feels cocooned from the world by their intimacy.

'I'll walk you home before I head off,' he says, looking at his watch.

'No,' says Agnes, 'you go. I want to stay and talk to Lolita. I'll go home with Graeme.' Robert's brother is sitting on the other side of the pub.

'Oh,' says Robert. 'Okay.' He puts on his coat and scarf reluctantly. 'I'll be off then.'

'See you tomorrow.'

He bends to kiss her. 'It's not such a long time.'

And he's away. Agnes surveys the pub. She walks toward Graeme.

At the house, Karen does the washing-up. Over the sink, she thinks back to what happened earlier that day. She'd come into the kitchen carrying Francis and several bags of shopping. Left Francis to play with his trucks, went out to retrieve the rest of the shopping. Put the bags on the floor, dashed upstairs to use the loo. Came back down again. Francis was in the corner, playing with his trucks. No shopping. The bags were not where she had placed them. She looked at Francis.

'Where's the shopping sweetie?'

Francis said, 'Truck,' and made a motor noise. He couldn't have lifted the bags himself anyway. Karen went back out to the car, opened the boot. All the shopping was there. She carried it back in again. Two trips. Am I losing my mind? And when she opened the egg carton it was as though each one of the dozen eggs had been hit by a tiny mallet, their tops pierced, caved-in-concave, tiny perfect circles. Humpty-dumpty. And she turned around and, there at the table, was Agnes. Karen hadn't heard her enter the room. 'Do you ever feel as though you are losing your grip?' she said.

There was no reply. Agnes was gone.

I wonder, Karen thinks now as she rinses a plate, if I am getting enough sleep.

'I don't think much of that agency he uses,' Graeme says to Agnes.

'Why's that?'

'I don't think they're right for our properties. Too down-market.' Graeme's list of grievances is long, and most concern Robert. He is surprised to find Agnes such a sympathetic listener. Despite living under the same roof they have spent very little time together since the wedding. When he looks into her face now he sees her green, green eyes. For a moment he thinks he can tell her anything, then he catches himself, she is my brother's wife, after all. He wonders if Robert has told her about the boys.

'What happened to your leg?' she asks.

Graeme looks at her narrowly. Surely Robert has told her about that. Or somebody else, Jim Drury or Elizabeth. Everyone knows what happened to his leg. Or, at least, everyone thinks they know.

'I got shot. In the line of duty.' Like in an American movie, Graeme thinks. He laughs his bitter laugh.

'Did it hurt?'

Graeme turns to look at his sister-in-law. 'Fucking right it hurt. It hurt like bloody hell.' Part of him hopes he has offended her.

'Fucking right,' Agnes says softly, as though considering. She smiles her smile, seductive and sweet. 'Shall we go home?'

On the street Graeme's long coat flaps open as he walks, his cane emerging from the folds with every stride. A well-cut grey wool coat; sometimes he uses his disability pension to buy clothes in London, spending the whole month's money on one item. He is partial to good coats and leather boots. He thinks Karen doesn't know, but of course Karen knows, and of course he knows Karen knows; marital deception is a multi-layered thing. He is a vain man, he is not ashamed of it, he needs these clothes. He deserves them.

When they get back to the house it is quiet. Robert is long gone, Karen put Martin to bed and retired, so did Jenny. They go into the sitting room where the last embers of the fire are dying. Graeme uses his cane to give the ashes a poke and puts on another log. He asks Agnes if she wants a drink and when she nods, he pours her a shot of whisky. Agnes buys the whisky in this house now; Jim Drury claims to have given her tutelage.

Agnes sits on the big settee, but Graeme can't settle, so he paces up and down in front of the fire. He wants to communicate something to this woman, he isn't sure what. With Robert out of the house he feels liberated, but it is a liberation coupled with urgency. He comes to a stop in front of Agnes and sits down next to her. She rolls the whisky around in her glass and breathes deeply of the fumes.

'I'm not doing what I'm meant to be doing,' he says.

Agnes turns and looks at him coolly.

'I'm not supposed to be stuck like this.' For Graeme this is an enormous admission. It's not something he has articulated before, not even to himself. He examines his hands, large and elegant. 'It's not right. Robert –'

Agnes clears her throat as though she is about to interrupt. Graeme looks at her. He is sitting slumped to one side, leaning in her direction. He can smell her, she smells spicy, gamy even. He puts his hand on her knee, on her tights just below her skirt. He looks into her eyes and thinks that what he sees there is openness, willing. He moves his finger along the hem of her skirt.

'Robert,' he says pausing again, 'Robert is a wimp.' He laughs out loud; he knows he's a little drunk.

Agnes doesn't respond. Her gaze is level. She is letting Graeme set the pace. He moves closer, his body radiates heat. Agnes does not move away. He lowers his face, slowly, slowly, until his lips are brushing against her throat. Her skin is soft, so soft, and pale, he can taste how pale she is. He lets his breath release and it's as though his lungs fill with desire, not air. He begins to kiss her neck again and as he does, he feels her body stiffen, like a cat whose fur has suddenly stood on end. He looks up and sees her eyes are black with anger, real anger, he can feel it. She is edging herself away from his grasp. A moment later she stands and leaves the room without a word.

Graeme is alone on the settee. He sits back, his cane in one hand. He is unsure whether the victory is hers or his. He has been spurned but he is not sure how completely. He raises his glass and toasts the recently departed Agnes. He looks forward to what will happen next, whatever that might be.

Later, after a couple more drinks, he climbs the stairs to Karen. She is accustomed to Graeme coming to bed long after her, she is accustomed to finding him boozy and weary. When he gets into bed tonight he is randy and he wakes her, insistent. They have sex, he is strong and demanding and she responds to his ardour. Afterward he lies beside her and she strokes his back, careful not to touch his leg. She knows that he aches and he likes her to soothe him. She lies awake and thinks.

Karen doesn't know what happens to her days. Time slips by; its pace is dismaying. She feels that she is finally emerging from the baby-fog of the past four years; neither of her boys has been quick to learn to sleep through the night. Sleep deprivation has altered her character; where she was quick she is now rather slow.

It's a challenge to get everything done every day. She has in her mind a vision of the perfect housewife and mother, someone who does everything right, someone who has time to paint pictures and sew baby clothes and bake scones, someone who makes gooseberry jam and elderflower cordial at the weekend, who dispenses love and advice. It's an impossible dream, one she knows is not even of her own making. Instead she is nanny and scullery maid and, for Martin, a nurse. There is no time to do anything well, there is no time to do anything. She wonders how her own mother managed, working full-time as well as everything else. Karen knows she's only just holding on, despite appearances, despite the fact she has chosen to live this way. Last time she baked she burnt Francis's birthday cake. Graeme had to go out and buy one. This felt symbolic of something, Karen isn't sure what.

Elizabeth freaks out

Elizabeth thinks she is calm, she thinks she looks casual, she thinks she's got the situation under control. She has her new job, she has her new life – it's not like her old life but, she says to whomever asks, it will do. Simple. Straight-forward. She doesn't have to listen to other people's trouble all day, she doesn't have to listen to anyone at all. She lives in her parents' cottage. There's a little gate overhung by a rose arbour; a short footpath leads through the tiny overgrown garden, the front door hidden behind a mass of clematis in summer. It's a small house, mid-Victorian, a worker's cottage that – when her parents bought it – was cold and stony and mean, with an outdoor toilet and open coal fires for heating, the bath a tin tub in the kitchen. Her parents moved the plumbing indoors and put in central heating when Elizabeth was a baby. The walls are thick and the windows are small and lead-paned, the original glass bevelled and distorted so that looking outside is like gazing through a film of milky water. Unlike the Throckmortons, her parents were obsessive collectors and the house bristles with features, both original and fake, impossible to tell which is which – picture rails, tiled fireplaces with cast-iron surrounds in every room, open oak beams on some ceilings, mouldings and rosettes on others, a gas-powered Aga in the kitchen, cubby-holes and nooks in unexpected places – and it is stuffed to the gills with stuff, furniture, china, pictures, tea services, silver toast racks, porcelain bed warmers. Downstairs, two rooms, a sitting room and a dining room, a kitchen in the back extension her parents added, upstairs two bedrooms, the bathroom. Compact, charming and a little damp, the house so laden with climbing vines that from the street it looks as though it is sinking beneath the weight of prettiness, so much quaintness.

All this belongs to Elizabeth now. And none of it feels like it is hers.

Tonight she rattles around the sitting room, picking up objects – the fire poker, the tea cosy, the newspaper – and putting them back down again. There is a terrible restlessness in her. She lifts the bottle of red wine she opened earlier and takes a big swig, not bothering with a glass. She puts it down, rattles around some more, comes back for another drink. It's a good red wine, strong-smelling, thick. Elizabeth knows a bit about wine. I'm a woman who knows about fine wine, she tells herself, good wine, not the crap Barbara sells in her shop, not the crap they drink down the pub. She rattles around thinking, what's missing, what's missing?

She stops in front of the CD player, one of the few things she imported into the cottage. There's an old favourite of hers lying out on top, she bought it in London, an old band that's been through several revivals of late: Hot Chocolate. She puts it on. Errol Brown's voice is black and creamy. She starts to sing.

The song makes her think of Robert. She can't help it, there's no connection between him and the song, but she can't keep him away from her thoughts. Errol Brown sings on but Elizabeth stops hearing. She sits down and takes hold of the bottle of wine. Her heart is breaking. It is breaking.

She's going to keep up her public façade of stoicism and generosity and getting on with things. She knows she can do it, she can do the stiff upper lip thing. I will survive. But behind closed doors the going is rough. It's when she is alone that it hits her. And she is often alone, too often, she thinks no one should have to be alone as much as she is. It should have been me; her mind is a morass of old songs now, Errol Brown started it. It should have been me.

Now that he's gone, she sees what she has lost. Before, she had assumed he'd be around. He'd be there, he always was. She hadn't thought it through properly – she laughs at that, me, a therapist, not thinking things through – but now she knows she had assumed they would end up together. It was inevitable. It was right. Ten weeks ago if you had asked her how she felt about Robert, how she really felt, she would not have said, it's a great and blinding passion. If I can't have him I will surely die. There is no one else on this planet for me. But now that's exactly what she would say. A great passion. It was meant to be. These are the words that Elizabeth mouths as she slumps on her parents' furniture and drinks a bottle of wine from the cellar that her father laid down over the years. When she went through the house after her father died she found four cases of champagne and she knew, without asking – there was no one to ask – that he had been collecting them for her wedding. They had never discussed marriage, weddings, but now she thinks on it – yes – they must have assumed it as well. Elizabeth will marry Robert. It was always going to be that way.

She sniffs the wine and swills it around her mouth like the expert on TV. Her heart is broken and this cosmic shift has produced an excess of energy. What's she going to do, what's Elizabeth going to do, how is she going to stay sane?

She goes out through the kitchen and into the back garden for some fresh December night air. The garden is small and old-fashioned with a hedge and, in summer, dahlias, columbine and drooping poppies. The houses nearby crowd in, warm light spilling out of their windows; there are people in there, Elizabeth thinks, families, and they are happy.

I'm out here, aren't I?

A great and blinding passion. It should have been me.

This she says out loud, waving the bottle over her head. Drops of red wine escape and rain onto her hair. She knows her neighbours, but they are acquaintances, not friends. I maintain a firm distinction between the two, I think it is important. I hate people who meet you once and then refer to you as a friend, as if they've known you for years.

She is babbling now, she is saying all this and more, out loud.

Next door they are watching TV, next door on the other side they are doing the same. Two doors along, a different programme, three doors, they have satellite. No one is listening to the night sounds. No one hears Elizabeth talking.

Elizabeth screams.

It's a small scream, but it is profound and satisfying.

She screams again, warming up. The noise that escapes from her mouth is surprising. Her throat hurts a little. She swigs the wine. Glug, glug, glug, goes the wine down her throat.

Elizabeth screams and she screams and she screams and she screams. And then she stops and goes inside.

The neighbours pick up their remotes and lower the sound. 'What was that?' they say to each other. They listen. One goes so far as to turn off her TV and stand by the window, peering out. But there is silence. Nothing moves.

In her bedroom Elizabeth takes off her clothes and stands in front of the mirror. Look at me, she says, look at my body. He doesn't want me, she thinks. He does not want me. Before she knows it, she is weeping.

Robert

The problems started with the renovations.

Workmen stomped through the house day after day. Work upstairs was scheduled to take four weeks, which I knew was optimistic. After four weeks both the bathroom and the new sitting room still looked devastated. With every step forward the builders discovered something else that needed to be done. Work on the ceiling revealed a leak in the roof. Work on the flooring revealed dry rot in the joists. Work on the plumbing revealed lead piping throughout the wing. Costs escalated. Every day involved more decisions, more money. Only our bedroom was finished, the work on it cosmetic. At night after Agnes and I had made love and she had fallen asleep, I stared at the walls, at the ceiling, and wondered what lay behind them, what the careful paintwork concealed. Sometimes I worried that if I leaned against the wall it would crumble to powder beneath my weight; if I knocked in a nail to hang a picture the whole structure would collapse. It was as if this part of the house, this oldest part of the house, neglected for so long, had decided to give up the ghost. As if it couldn't stand the thought of the twenty-first century, coming as it does from the sixteenth.

I was struggling to meet the costs. I know now that I'd taken on too much, spurred on by my desire to make things nice for Agnes, good enough for Agnes. I thought it was a case of juggling payments, when in reality, we were beginning to get into trouble. But I wasn't ready to accept the truth.

The real nightmare was the room below, the small ballroom with the carved plaster ceiling, a section of which collapsed on Graeme's head the day of the wedding. Finding the solution for this room was Agnes's job. She arranged for a man from the National Trust to come and look. When he arrived he was very dour and as he inspected the house he gasped and muttered under his breath, 'Oh no, oh dear, oh dear me.' In the ballroom he stood on a stepladder and stuck a thermometer into the patch where the plaster came down. He looked at it, shook his head and clucked. He looked at me over the rim of his spectacles, pointed upward and said 'Lime and goat's hair, that's what's up there, lime-and-goat's-hair and wooden lathes. Original. Late sixteenth century, early seventeenth.'

'We know that,' I said, 'we know the dates.'

'I would say,' said the man from the National Trust, 'I would say it is almost too late.' He continued his progress around the house, reacting with alarm when I took him upstairs to view the renovations. 'You've got to be careful,' he said, 'with a house this old. You've got to treat it with care, like you would a very old lady.'

'It's only a house,' said Agnes reasonably, 'people have to live here.'

'Only a house,' said the man over his spectacles. 'American, did you say?' Then he left without telling us when he'd be in touch again.

I'd had a few complaints from the workmen about other matters. I knew that both Agnes and Graeme had taken to popping upstairs to see how things were going; the men were more than happy to entertain Agnes from time to time but I hadn't realized that Graeme had taken it upon himself to become unofficial overseer. He'd been a policeman, you'd think he'd have known how to get on with the lads. But no, not Graeme. The foreman was polite, perhaps deferring to Graeme's disability, but I could tell he'd have liked to have taken away Graeme's cane and given him a good whack over the head with it.

'I'll have a word with him,' I promised.

'What the fuck?' Graeme was, predictably, outraged.

'Just let them get on with the work.'

'The lazy bastards, with their tea-breaks and their fag-breaks and their –'

'They're doing good work.'

'How do you know that? You don't know the first thing about building work.'

'They're getting on with it.'

Graeme glared at me. I turned away. He'd leave them alone now, I could tell. He'd have to find someone else to plague.

Elizabeth

Later, when things began to go wrong, people used to ask me what Agnes was really like. It was as though she was in our midst but none of us could really see her. Or what we saw differed so dramatically from one person to the next that you wouldn't think we were describing one person, but many.

This is what I saw: Agnes Samuel, anywhere from twenty-eight to thirty-five, although she could have been one of those impossible forty-year-olds who are lithe and strong and glossy. I think she was probably thirty. I never asked her how old she was, it wasn't the kind of thing one asked of Agnes. When I asked Robert – later, much later – he didn't know either. That surprised him. That made him sad.

She was about 5′10″, tall, but not too tall, the perfect height for Robert who is 6′2″. Robert and Graeme are the same height, they were always the tall boys in the village. Jenny was tall as well, maybe even a little taller than Agnes, and I think at first it was very good for Jenny to have another woman her size around, an example, a role model. Karen was little, 5′3″, and I'm not much bigger. I used to buy Jenny clothes for her birthday, Christmas, but I could never get it quite right. Once Agnes arrived the way Jenny looked and dressed improved dramatically.

Agnes had shiny dark hair that fell to her shoulders with a wave that she straightened or exaggerated, depending on the look she was after. She always had a look. She didn't wear a lot of make-up but what she did wear was perfect and expensive; maybe a fine face powder or cream, a little eye shadow, mascara and beautifully outlined and coloured-in lips. She must have had a very steady hand, I could never get make-up on that straight. She smelled faintly of perfume, nothing heavy, flowers and apples perhaps. She had that kind of undeniable femininity that few women achieve, bogged down as we are by other things.

Her clothes were just right. Elegant, close-fitting, showing off the slim long lines of her body. She wore a lot of black, metropolitan black, much more than any of the other women in the village, even Marlene who was probably her closest rival in the glamour stakes. Not that Marlene has any sense of competition in that sense. Agnes was partial to velvet and fine wool. She wore designer shoes, usually with high spiky heels, and everything in her wardrobe was well taken care of, dry-cleaned and carefully pressed. She looked easeful, as though she dressed this way without a great deal of effort. Expensive, but not ostentatious. I noticed that when she played with the boys she wore her hair pinned up, tendrils escaping; she would get down on the floor with them and play hard and when she had finished her face would have a lovely healthy glow and she'd brush the dust off her hands and knees casually, as if it didn't worry her. Her voice was low and sometimes a little throaty, if it was late at night or early in the morning. Her laugh was low too, immediate and thrilling. Conspiratorial.

When Robert looked at Agnes Samuel I don't know what he saw. Love, I guess, love itself, his own love reflected back at him. More than enough to keep him going. More than enough at the time.

Toward the end of November I went round for a meal. I was determined to continue to be casual and friendly, how I felt at home late at night was nobody's business but mine. Robert invited me, so I went. As I was getting ready to leave, Agnes gave me a bright smile.

'Have you got your Christmas shopping done yet?' she asked.

'No,' I said, 'I'm afraid I haven't even thought about it.'

'Let's go together – how about Saturday?'

'I . . .'

'Cambridge. I think we should go to Cambridge. I hear the stores are good there.' She seemed determined that we should go shopping, as if she believed that's what women do best together.

The thing about Agnes was that you always found yourself agreeing with her, no matter how you actually felt. Cambridge is not my town of choice when it comes to shopping. It is a long drive across country to get there, the traffic is terrible in the town centre and there is nowhere to park. But I made the mistaken assumption that Agnes, as a tourist in this country, wanted to look around the colleges as well as shop, so I agreed.

I picked her up first thing in the morning. Even then, so soon after the wedding, I couldn't stop myself liking her, enjoying being with her. Liking her confused me, I felt I was being disloyal to Robert, disloyal to myself somehow. She was an extravagant and decisive shopper and that appealed to me. And as I've said before she was very good at getting people to talk about themselves. She worked her magic on me despite my resistance. As we wove in and out of the shops she asked me a series of questions and I found myself telling her my life story. I left out the bits that included Robert, like the time we went to Greece together when we were twenty. Robert could tell her what he wanted about me, about us.

She appeared to find my life fascinating and, of course, that is very seductive. We went to a pub at lunchtime. Before I knew what was happening I was telling her everything.

'I had finished my psychology degree and was taking some training and working as a counsellor. I hadn't embarked on my psychoanalytic training yet – that came later. Therapists – at least the kind of therapist I was – do endless training. I was in therapy myself, of course; I'd been in therapy since my first year in university.'

'Why?' asked Agnes.

'Why? Well, didn't you find leaving home and going off to university a little traumatic?'

'I didn't go to university.'

I suddenly felt embarassed, as though I'd been bragging about my own erudition.

'Tell me what happened,' Agnes said.

'Like I said, I was doing some work as a counsellor. I had a few clients – students, for the most part, at the university – and my work with them was supervised; I didn't have someone sitting in on the sessions but I would report in detail on each client to my supervisor. Have you ever been in therapy?'

Agnes raised one eyebrow and shook her head. There are some people who would never go in for therapy. Agnes was one of them.

'One of my clients was a young woman, a university student – Elaine Warner.'

I swallowed hard. I'd told Agnes the client's name. I had never breached confidentiality before, not once. And yet I'd done it now, without thinking. Yet another indication of how disconnected I'd become from my profession, my previous life.

'She was nineteen. Elaine was not eating, not going to lectures, not really doing anything much. Classic symptoms,' I paused.

'Of what?'

'Depression. I found her fascinating. She was like something out of a textbook. Some days she would come to me too depressed to speak, but still, she came, twice a week. That gave me faith, I suppose, that she could get it together to come and see me. I felt it was a very positive sign and I told her so.'

Agnes leaned back in her chair and took a sip of her drink. She nodded encouragingly.

'One day she didn't turn up. She hadn't rung to say she wouldn't be coming – for all Elaine's troubles she was a responsible and thoughtful young woman – and so I started to worry. But I was busy myself, trying to find my way, and I didn't do anything about it. She didn't show up for our second session that week either. That galvanized me into action, finally, and I tried to ring her.' I paused again. Agnes had on her listening face – that's the only way to describe how she looked. It was perfect. I kept talking. 'But I was too late.' Too late, I thought, always too late. 'She had hanged herself that morning. Her flatmate came home after a lecture to pick up some books. She found her.'

'Oh, how sad,' said Agnes, heartfelt. 'It's so sad when young people die.'

'I should have known she was at risk, I should have recognized the signs. I should have done something immediately, at the beginning of the week.'

'You were inexperienced.'

'That's right. I was inexperienced and I was a little too interested in the way that she fit the symptoms for clinical depression so nicely. I should have taken much more action – any action. I should have done something for her.'

'But you didn't. She was beyond you. You couldn't save her. You didn't.'

'I didn't. And she died. And I got over it. My supervisor was very sympathetic – something similar had happened to her when she was my age. She told me that sometimes when people decide to die there is nothing we can do to stop them. We're therapists, not policemen, not social workers, not paramedics. We can call on the services of those professionals, but we aren't in the business of rescuing people, not literally. I listened carefully to what my supervisor had to say, I talked to my own therapist, and I put what had happened to me, to Elaine Warner, I mean, behind me.'

'Did it make you a better therapist?'

'Yes, I think it did. A little hyper-sensitive to the risks of suicide, for the first few years at any rate. I worked primarily with students and I was forever informing the university when I thought they were at risk.'

'Did it work?'

'Maybe. None of them killed themselves. My clients survived their therapy.'

'That's good, isn't it?'

'Yes. And the years went by, and I became more confident, and I went to work for a clinic and embarked on psychoanalytic training. And began to take on private clients. I converted the extra room in my flat into a therapy room . . .'

'What was it like?' Agnes interrupted.

'There was a big couch for clients to sit – or lie – on and a desk against the opposite wall; I had a swivel chair so I could turn to look at clients and take notes at the same time.' I could picture it clearly. I loved that room. Lots of books, a thick carpet, and a big window, free of curtains, with a view of an oak tree and the sky, and I made sure I always had fresh flowers in the vase. 'I had a cleaner –' I laughed, '– those were the days – and one of her duties was to dust the houseplants in my office. It was a nice room. People were comfortable in it.'

'Sounds lovely.'

'When I lived in London I came to believe in things in a way I no longer do – can no longer afford to. Material things.'

'What do you mean?'

'I thought it was important to possess well designed good-looking things. A kettle wasn't simply a thing to boil water in, it had to look smart, it had to come from the right place.'

'Fashion,' said Agnes.

'Of a sort. I was never any good at clothes. Am still no good at clothes,' I felt myself blushing.

'It doesn't matter.'

'No?' I wondered why Agnes would say this when it was clearly important to her.

'Of course not. That's not what counts.'

'Maybe –'

'What happened?'

'My parents died and I inherited their cottage –'

'No,' Agnes said, abruptly. 'In London. To your job. To your life.'

This rattled me. I was the one who thought my life was over. Other people were meant to disagree.

'Why aren't you a therapist any longer?' she persisted.

'Why did you leave the US?'

Agnes folded her arms and pursed her lips, mock-annoyed. 'We're not talking about me. I'm boring. We're talking about you, Elizabeth.'

'Well,' I said, suddenly resigned to telling Agnes the whole of my story, 'then my therapist left me.'

'What do you mean?'

'My therapist, whom I'd been seeing for years – she left the profession.'

'Why?'

'I don't know why.'

'Did that matter?'

A non-therapy person like Agnes would never understand the significance of this. Losing Christine was like losing my mother. Except worse somehow, in some ways. It was like losing my voice. But I wasn't about to try to explain that to Agnes.

'Yes. It mattered.' I paused. 'And then it happened again.'

'What?'

'I lost a client. "Lost" – listen to me. Another suicide. Another client killed herself.' I spoke calmly, quietly, in fact the words came easily. Too easily. As if they had lost their power, their true meaning. Telling these stories made me feel dead inside. Was I dead before Robert got married? Or had I been dead for a long time?

'Was the client another woman?'

'Most of my clients were women. Another young woman; she was twenty-three. Gillian Collins. I'd been seeing her for more than a year. Again, she was seriously depressed, but I didn't think she needed to be hospitalized. She wasn't on any medication, I didn't think she needed it. She seemed, I don't know, she seemed okay to me. Making progress. But when I looked back at my notes, well, it was quite stark really. Her deterioration. The signs were there. I didn't see them. Or couldn't see them. Couldn't be bothered to see them –'

'I'm sure that's not the case.'

'Are you? Her parents weren't so easily reassured.' I could see Gillian's mother clearly. I went to the funeral; I was so surprised to be invited I thought I had better go. The mother resembled her daughter, they were both petite blondes. I felt my eyes begin to tear as I remembered. 'Why didn't you call us?' her mother asked when

I introduced myself. I didn't know how to reply. I stood there like an idiot, smiling.

'Did you get into trouble?'

'Trouble? No. Not professionally. She left a suicide note that specifically absolved me, among others, of blame. Not that I found that reassuring.'

'This must happen to therapists all the time.'

'It happens. It happened to me. Or rather, my client. Clients. Two of them. It happened twice. And with Christine – my therapist – gone as well . . .' I sat and stared into my drink. I had run out of words, out of steam. I swallowed my tears, my dismay.

'What did you do after Gillian Collins died?' Agnes asked calmly.

'I quit. I gave notice to my clients – I had left the clinic a while back. I had a substantial roster of private clients.'

'You were popular.'

'Popular? I guess. In a way. I was in demand.'

'So you gave it all up.'

'I did.'

'And you came back to Warboys.'

'Yes.'

'You exiled yourself from everything you'd earned, everything you'd gained.'

'I felt I no longer deserved it.'

'No one was blaming you for her death,' said Agnes.

'A bit of blame might not have been such a bad thing. I could have fought against it then. Sometimes I feel that I've gone unpunished, that some kind of reckoning would have enabled me to put the whole episode behind me.'

'Elizabeth,' said Agnes, 'that's just too masochistic for words.' She shook her head. 'You've given up your career. Isn't that punishment enough?'

I looked at Agnes. 'The strange thing is – the thing that bothers me now . . . I can't figure out why she did it. Gillian Collins. I don't understand why she wanted to die.'

'Oh,' said Agnes, 'that's simple. Punishment. For some reason she needed to punish people.'

'She did?' I thought Agnes over-confident about what she was saying. She'd never met Gillian Collins.

'That's what suicide is, isn't it? A punitive act?'

'I don't know. Punishing oneself?' I asked. I used to be able to speak authoritatively about these things. No longer.

'Punishing everyone who knows you. You'll never know why she did it. It's got nothing to do with you.'

I knew that I should have said it had everything to do with me, but I couldn't. I no longer had the energy. Agnes's explanation was sensible, if a little bald. It made me feel better.

We stopped talking and went back out onto the streets of Cambridge. I felt a kind of relief after telling my story, as if in the telling its impact had been lessened. I offered to give Agnes a tour of the colleges, I knew my way around. But she wasn't interested.

'King's College Chapel?' I suggested. 'It's amazing.'

'I don't like chapels,' said Agnes. 'I don't much like old things.'

Agnes makes a move

It is the week before Christmas and Robert is away again for the night. Another meeting in London, and he is panicking about Christmas shopping, panicking about money. He leaves in the car on Wednesday lunchtime.

Agnes is working in Robert's office when Jenny comes home from school. She is sitting in front of the computer. Jenny comes in, drops her books and sits down opposite her.

'It's cold in here.'

Agnes looks up. 'It's not too bad. I wear layers. I take them off and put them on as I move from room to room.'

'Was it cold in your house in America?'

'I didn't have a house in America, you know that Jenny.'

'Did it ever get cold in Las Vegas?'

'Briefly. December, January, the temperature drops, especially at night. Sometimes there's a little snow. But even then the sun is very strong.'

'How hot can it get?'

'Forty degrees Celsius or more is pretty common in the summer. It's not that far from Death Valley where it gets incredibly hot.' Agnes stretches as though the mere mention of heat warms her.

'Why did you come to England?'

Agnes looks at Jenny sharply.

'Why would anyone come here when you could stay in America?'

'Had a bad day at school?'

'That's where I want to go. Do you think they'd let me emigrate more easily because I have an American sister-in-law?'

'No,' Agnes says, 'no. It's hard to get in to the US.'

'I've heard that. God, that's depressing.'

Agnes looks at Jenny again. 'I might be able to help you though,' she says.

Jenny sits up straight. 'Yeah? How?'

'I'll look into it. I know some people.'

'Great,' says Jenny. She picks up her books and leaves the room.

The evening passes; dinner, the boys to bed, Martin wheeled into his room, Graeme off to the pub. Karen comes back downstairs after Andrew and Francis are asleep and finds Agnes on her own in the sitting room, reading a magazine. No one has bothered to light the fire. Karen suddenly feels uncomfortable, like an intruder in her own house.

'Can I get you a drink?' Agnes offers.

'Thanks. I'll have a glass of white wine.'

Agnes returns with the drinks and sits next to Karen on the settee. 'How was Martin this evening?' she asks.

'Fine.'

'He's a charmer, isn't he?'

'Martin?' says Karen, thinking, you must mean Andrew. Or Francis. Or even Graeme.

'Yes. Charming.' Agnes sips her drink.

Karen feels a little bewildered. What can Agnes mean? She changes the subject. 'Christmas. I'm never ready on time,' Karen says.

'No?' says Agnes, leafing through the magazine.

'I don't much like it. Too much work, too much drinking, too much too much.'

'I don't like it either,' Agnes says, turning to face Karen. 'It reminds me of my family.' Agnes blinks and Karen thinks she sees her green eyes turn to black; she blinks again and her eyes are normal. For a moment Karen feels frightened. Agnes is angry, she thinks, Agnes hates me, then she pushes that thought away. She chastises herself and takes another drink. She has never heard Agnes talk about her family.

'Were you very close?'

'Yes. We stuck by each other. We had to, in the end.' Agnes returns to her magazine.

Karen can't think of any other questions to ask that won't sound too prodding. 'Like the Throckmortons,' she says.

'No,' says Agnes, now her eyes are glinting, 'not like them at all.'

Us, Karen thinks, but she doesn't correct her out loud. Karen would like to pursue this line of conversation, it occurs to her now that she and Agnes could be natural allies, both outsiders in the family. Perhaps Agnes finds marriage and the Throckmortons different – less easy – than she had anticipated. Karen is trying to think of what to say next when Andrew appears in the doorway. He is crying, he has had a bad dream. She lifts him, gives him a hug and carries him upstairs to his bed. Once she has calmed him down and tucked him in she feels too tired to go back down, back to Agnes and her drink. She goes to bed.

Graeme comes in at eleven-thirty; he's been at the Black Hat until closing. He and Agnes have been perfectly civil to each other in the month since their encounter on the settee. Robert is away again for the night and Graeme has stayed out late, hoping to avoid his sister-in-law. But she is there when he comes in.

'Hello Graeme,' she says, and she stands and walks toward him. 'Let me take your coat.' She moves behind him and he feels her hands on his shoulders. 'It's cold, isn't it?'

'Yes,' he says, he has had quite a bit to drink and his tongue feels thick in his mouth.

'It's a beautiful coat,' she says as she peels it away from his back. 'Did you get it in London?'

He nods, turning to face her. His cane is leaning against the wall next to the door. Agnes steps close. She reaches up and pushes Graeme's hair away from his eyes. She moves her hand down his cheek, her fingers lightly touching his lips. He swallows, and feels dazzled and tired and ready.

'It's an ideal situation,' she says.

'What?'

'Us, you and I, here in this house. No one would know. I have my husband, you have your wife. He's away, she's asleep.'

Graeme pulls himself together. I have been waiting for this, he thinks. I have been biding my time. He takes a step toward Agnes, backing her up against the wall. There is no fire, the central heating has gone off, and the curtains on the big windows are thin. He feels a chill that makes him want to touch her more than ever, makes him want to feel her warmth. He looks into her face and her green green eyes and he thinks he sees openness, willing. He puts his hand on her breast and tries to kiss her. She turns her face away and, at the same time, puts her hand on the zipper of his trousers.

They have sex there, standing, in the sitting room, the cold December night around them. Graeme pushes inside her, against the wall, and she lets him, she urges him on. They keep on their clothes and bare only the necessary flesh. He tries to look into her face, tries to kiss her, but she won't let him. Her face is turned away, buried in his shirt, looking away from him, over his shoulder. Her breathing is strong, his laboured, and they aren't locked together for very long before Graeme feels himself start to slide into orgasm. He tries to find her lips once again, but she won't allow him, so he lets what has begun happen. He pushes deep, hard, and shudders and gasps, and then withers.

When he steps away from her she looks at him. Her lips are dry and she licks them. And she smiles, she smiles her lovely smile, and Graeme thinks he has died and gone to heaven. Very slowly, quietly, she adjusts her tights. Moments later, she leaves the room as though nothing has happened. Graeme does up his trousers and goes to bed.

The sharp smell of his sweat lingers on in the sitting room until the next morning. Karen wrinkles her nose as she opens the window and lets fresh air fill the room.

Graeme goes shopping

Several days later Graeme drives down to London and parks his car near Holborn underground station. He hasn't told Karen where he is going. He walks through the back streets to Covent Garden. He knows his way, he has been before, many times; he is heading for Armani. He has on his black suede jacket and he walks along like a big man, like an elegant man with a cane. Then, up ahead, he sees Agnes, her dark hair swinging as she walks. She stops and turns and – there – she sees him and smiles. Agnes! How brilliant to see her. They will spend the day together, they will look at beautiful things, he can ask her opinion, he can buy her something. He goes quickly toward her.

Agnes raises her hand, gives a little wave,. and steps into a hair salon. Graeme catches up, pushes through the door. In the salon – very chic – everyone looks at him. Agnes isn't there, of course she isn't there, it was his imagination, she's in Warboys. He runs his hand through his hair, disappointment pulling hard at him, and leaves. He makes his sorry way along the pavement.

At Armani the doors are open to him, the blond wood floors and glass display cases gleam, the air is hushed, and as he passes the shop assistants bow slightly, one by one, slim and solemn. Here no one knows he lives on a disability pension, no one knows his wife is a drudge and he is fucking his sister-in-law Agnes. He is wearing an expensive jacket and possesses a credit card and nothing else matters. The day is redeemed.

He fingers the fabric of a suit.

A young man stands to one side. 'Would you like to try it on sir?' He lifts it off the rail and holds it up. Nehru collar, no lapels.

Graeme takes a look. 'The cut's too fashionable,' he says. 'I like things to look more – classic.'

'How about this?' The shop assistant holds up another.

'Black,' says Graeme, 'I want it in black.'

Graeme spends one hour and nine hundred pounds in the shop, the equivalent of weeks and weeks of the income he and his family receive from the state. He tries on stiff white cotton shirts and pale silk ties and cashmere sweaters. He tries on overcoats and raincoats and a sharp black tuxedo. The shop assistant fetches and carries.

The suit he buys is a thing of beauty, in its cut, in its fabric. In the changing room when he looks at himself in the mirror, his pleasure is intense. It's a suit he could wear out in the evening with Agnes, it's a suit he could be buried in. He buys it without hesitating.

Agnes tells a story

Jenny is having problems at school. She has never done particularly well, although each year she excels at something, the next year something else. Last year she did well in art class, she began to paint. Still life: collections of things, a vase of cut flowers, an open book, a human skull, odd juxtapositions, strange angles. Skull and sausages, flowers and knives. This year she has been doing well in English Literature. She is reading *Macbeth* and enjoying the gore. In general, teachers despair of her, they sense a clever mind masked by insecurity. But, despite that, they like her, they find her intriguing. And they like her two brother/guardians, Robert and Graeme, who take it in turns to appear on parents' night to charm the women teachers.

Jenny doesn't have many friends. The boys she knows are tongue-tied and clumsy, confused about girls, a little afraid. Girls her own age find her aloof. However there is one girl Jenny gets on with, Lolly Senior. Lolly shares her name – Lolita – with the pub landlord's wife and she is permanently annoyed by this coincidence. She has read Nabokov and she's disgusted. She has a stutter which, after hours of speech therapy, she has almost mastered; it gets the better of her when she is angry or embarrassed and because she is sixteen this is much of the time. Lolly has ways of making herself feel better though, she has a little game she plays. Lolly pretends she is a witch. She tells people she is a witch. D-Don't c-come near me, she'll say, I'll cast a sp-sp-spell on you. And everyone laughs, including Lolly. Oh that Lolly, they say, she thinks she's a witch.

Lolly takes her hobby seriously. She has a large collection of books about witchcraft and she has rented every video, every horror movie, that might feature witches. Lolly prefers satanic witches, she isn't interested in Wicca, or white witchery. Her mother, an ageing hippie called Doris, has tried to get her involved with crystals and covens and that kind of thing, but it doesn't work for Lolly. She likes her witches to be in league with the devil, destructive forces, nothing good or New Age, nothing old-fashioned-feminist.

Lolly takes it upon herself to befriend weird people, she likes the weird people of this world. She herself is quite popular, but she is not interested in the smooth girls, in the good-looking boys; she likes the specky nerd who knows too much about computers, the strange girl who goes cross-eyed when you say her name. She likes Jenny.

Lolly is very happy to be studying *Macbeth.*

On their way home from school this cold December day a mist has risen off the fen. Lolly chants loudly,

Fair is foul, and foul is fair:
Hover through the fog and filthy air.

At the moment this is all she can remember. 'I've got to go home and have another look at that play,' she says. She is calm, no stuttering. They walk along the side of the road, there is no pavement. 'There's a story about this village, did you know that Jenny?'

'In the play?'

'No, idiot – a real story.'

'What kind of story?' Jenny is used to Lolly's stories.

'About witches. Real witches. They were burned at the stake!' Lolly lets loose a hideous scream. She clutches her throat and whirls round in a circle, gravel flying from under her feet.

Jenny laughs. 'You see witches everywhere.'

'No, it's true. Look at that.' She points at the village clocktower. It stands at the intersection and around it clusters Warboys.

'Four o'clock,' says Jenny, 'the witching hour?'

'No, look on top, cretin.'

Jenny looks up. The weathervane is a blackened witch riding on her broom.

'North, south, west, east,' Lolly chants, 'everywhere she points, that's where evil goes.'

'What's the story?' Jenny asks. She has looked up to the weathervane before, so often she has forgotten it, but she has never heard of a story.

'I don't know,' says Lolly, 'but I'm going to find out.' And she gallops off down the street toward her house. In her enthusiasm she forgets she is sixteen and behaves like a nine-year-old. This is a trait in Lolly of which everyone is fond.

That night Agnes puts Jenny to bed. They have begun to develop a night-time ritual. While Jenny soaks in a bath full of rose-scented bubbles, Agnes closes the lid of the toilet and sits down. They talk. Agnes shows Jenny her copy of 'Vogue' and they discuss the clothes. Agnes knows a lot about fashion, the designers, the houses, as well as fashion history. She tells Jenny fashion is art. This is news to Jenny; she is eager for it.

The bathroom Jenny uses – everyone uses while the renovations are on-going – is in the Georgian part of the house along the corridor where Jenny, Graeme and Karen, and Andrew and Francis have their bedrooms, and it is draughty. The wind rattles the thin glass of the window in its frame, whooshes across the tiles and under the door. Agnes wears a pullover and a cardigan and wool trousers and still looks a little cold. Jenny feels sorry for her, her sister-in-law from the sunny desert.

Agnes shivers and frowns. 'It's so fucking cold in this place.' This is part of their private ritual – Agnes swears in front of Jenny. They've established that Jenny doesn't swear when she's with Agnes – she swears when she's with Lolly – but she enjoys Agnes's bad language and the knowledge that Agnes thinks she is old enough to hear it.

'How was your day?' Agnes asks.

'Okay. English – I like it. I like Mr McKay,' she says, a little dreamily.

'Talk to any boys?'

'No boys.'

'Which ones do you like?'

'None of them.'

'Ask them about sport, it always works. Football. Ask them who they support, ask how their team is doing. Guaranteed.'

Agnes holds up a towel and turns her face away to protect Jenny's modesty.

'Who do you support – no, whom do you support – and how are they doing?' Jenny repeats as she climbs out of the bath.

'That's right.'

'Guaranteed.'

They leave the bathroom and go into Jenny's bedroom. She puts on her flannel night-gown and gets into bed. 'They'll be begging for it,' she says.

'That's right.'

'Guaranteed.'

They giggle. Agnes kisses Jenny and gets up to go. 'Tell me a story Agnes.' Every night Jenny says the same thing. Some nights Agnes does stay, other nights she smiles and leaves. Tonight she stays.

'Okay. Let me think.' She arranges herself in a chair. When she's ready, she begins. 'A group of friends – five – two boys and two girls and the brother of one of the girls – he's confined to a wheelchair –'

'Like Daddy,' says Jenny.

'Except this is a young guy,' says Agnes. 'He's fine, apart from being in a wheelchair.'

'Why is he in a wheelchair?'

'I don't know. He was born that way. Okay?'

Jenny nods.

Agnes continues. 'They are travelling around in their beat-up old van. One of the girls, Jenny, and her brother – the one in the wheelchair – think that the house their father grew up in is somewhere nearby. They drive past the slaughterhouse where their daddy used to work. Later, along an empty road, they pick up a hitchhiker. This young man is a bit scary, nervous and weird. Jenny's brother tries to humour him. But the hitchhiker pulls out a knife – to their horror, he cuts himself on the hand. It's as though he doesn't feel any pain.'

Jenny looks repelled. Agnes continues.

'Then the hitchhiker turns nasty. He tries to cut Jenny's brother with the knife. They drive the van to the side of the road and wrestle him out on to the gravel shoulder. Then they pull away, free of him. Before long they are happy again, travelling along without a care. They stop at a gas station, but the old guy who runs it tells them he is out of gas. They push on.

'Not long after that, they come to the place where Jenny's father used to live. They pull off the highway and find the house. It's a lovely afternoon. Birds are singing, the grass is long, the sun is shining. It's a struggle to push the wheelchair over the rough ground, but they manage.

'The house is semi-derelict, abandoned. They have a look around; Jenny and her brother can remember coming to visit. There is a swimming hole down the hill. The other boy and girl decide to go for a swim. Jenny stays behind with her boyfriend and her brother. Her brother can't do much in his wheelchair; he is hot and bored.

'When the other boy and girl find the swimming hole all that is left of it is a dry gulch – the water is long gone. Through the trees they can see another house and they decide to go explore. As they get closer they hear the sound of a generator. Hoping they might be able to buy some gas, they approach the house. But it looks like no one is home. The girl waits in the front yard on the swinging bench while the boy knocks. The front door is open – he decides to go inside.

'The house is quiet and dusty. Through the passage ahead the boy can see a collection of skulls and skins on a red wall. He goes toward the door. Suddenly, an enormous man appears; he is wearing a torn leather face-mask and wielding a mallet. He hits the boy over the head and drags him along the passage.

'Outside, all the girl can hear is the noise from the generator. Impatient to leave, she goes to the front door, sees that it is ajar, and enters the house, calling her boyfriend's name. All of a sudden, the man with the leather face appears once again. He grabs the girl. She screams and tries to get away, but he catches her and drags her into the kitchen. She screams and screams when she sees her boyfriend lying dead on a butcher's block. The man with the leather face hangs her on a meathook. He picks up a chainsaw and pulls the cord on the throttle. It roars to life.'

'Ugh,' says Jenny.

'Had enough?' asks Agnes.

'Enough?' Jenny shakes her head.

'Back at her father's old house, Jenny and her boyfriend wonder where their friends have got to. It's time to leave. The boyfriend says he'll go down to the swimming hole and get them. Once there, he sees the other house through the trees and hears the generator, like the others before him. He makes his way to the house, finds his way into the kitchen. The butcher's block is awash with blood. Against one wall there is a large freezer. He feels compelled to open it. Inside is the girl. In her death throes, she sits up and flings herself forward. Just then the man with the leather face-mask appears, wielding his chainsaw. He kills Jenny's boyfriend.

'Now it is getting very late. Jenny and her brother don't know what to do. They honk the horn and call out for the others. There isn't enough gas in the van to go for help. Jenny decides to go and find them. But her brother won't let her leave him on his own. After arguing, she agrees to push his chair over the rough ground, through the grass and tumbleweed, down to the dry swimming hole.

'Of course there is no one there. But beyond the trees they can see a light. They go toward it, they can hear the generator. As they near the front porch, the door is flung open by an enormous man wielding a chainsaw and wearing a leather face-mask. He attacks and kills Jenny's brother in his wheelchair.

'Jenny tries to run away. The man with the chainsaw comes after her. She tries to run through the trees, but her hair keeps getting caught on the thorns and tangled undergrowth. She runs and runs, the man with the chainsaw right after her. She runs, screaming for help, but there is no one to hear. Finally, she finds herself at the gas station where they stopped earlier. She pounds on the door. The gas station attendant opens the door and lets her in. He calms her down and says he will drive her to safety.'

'Oh thank God,' says Jenny.

'Well,' says Agnes, 'just wait. The gas station man is actually the father of the man with the leather face.'

'What?' says Jenny.

Agnes nods grimly. 'He ties her up and takes her back to the house.'

'Oh no,' says Jenny.

'I know,' says Agnes, 'awful, isn't it? When they arrive the hitchhiker is there as well. '"So," he says, "you've met my father."'

'Oh, he does not say that,' objects Jenny.

'Be quiet,' replies Agnes. 'Do you want to hear this story?'

Jenny nods obediently.

'So Jenny is taken prisoner in this terrible house, this house of madness. They tie her to a chair at the dining table. When they remove the gag from her mouth all she does is scream, so they put it back on her.

'At dinner there is the hitchhiker, the man with the leather face, and their father, the man from the gas station. He whacks his son the hitchhiker across the head with the back of his hand whenever the son tries to say anything. The grandfather sits at the head of the table, the hitchhiker and the man with the leather face carry him there. He can't speak or move and Jenny thinks he might be dead. He looks as though he is mummified.'

'Kind of like Daddy,' says Jenny.

'Your father?'

Jenny nods.

'Kind of. Not really. The hitchhiker serves the meal. Jenny can't bring herself to look at the meat on the plates, she thinks it might be her boyfriend. This is a family of insane cannibals. Country folk. People like you might find in Warboys.'

Agnes smiles. She looks at Jenny. 'You know the end, don't you?'

Jenny licks her lips, her throat is dry, she feels a little nauseated. 'Somehow, after a lot of screaming, she gets away.'

'You always know the end.'

'These stories tend to end the same way,' Jenny says.

'That one is a particular favourite of mine.'

'You always say that.'

'It's true. The moral of this story is – what do you think it is?'

'What? I don't know. Don't eat meat.'

Agnes laughs. 'Madness has a tendency to run in families. Don't pick up hitchhikers. Never trust a man with a chainsaw.'

'Except Graeme,' says Jenny.

'What?'

'He has a chainsaw. You know. He does the topiary.'

'Except Graeme.'

'Okay,' says Jenny, 'I'll take that advice.'

'Okay,' says Agnes. 'Guaranteed.'

She turns out the lamp beside Jenny's bed. Before she leaves, she holds the door cracked open and looks back in at Jenny. 'Do you want to know what it's really about?'

'Okay,' says Jenny.

'The comedy of senseless violence. The pleasure of running amok.'

She closes the door and walks away. Jenny hears her footsteps along the corridor, down the stairs. As Agnes leaves, Jenny thinks about the story. This time Agnes kept it brief, cut herself off mid-flow, as though she had second thoughts – it was too much, too gruesome. Even so, images from the tale stick with Jenny. For a moment she thinks she can hear the chainsaw starting up, the generator rattling. She feels the walls of her bedroom press in toward her. The black night threatens to swallow her whole. It is as though she is being taken over, as though Agnes's stories are taking possession of her somehow, leaving less room for Jenny, letting in the unknown. When she falls asleep she dreams that when she looks in the mirror she doesn't know her own face.

The next day at school Jenny faints during a class. She slumps down in her seat and it is Lolly who notices eventually. They have no idea how long she's been unconscious. When she comes round she says to the school nurse 'I could hear my own heart beating. My heart was beating so loudly that everything else disappeared.'

Christmas arrives and with it bad moods and temper tantrums. This year Robert hopes that Christmas will be wonderful, a dream Christmas with fairy lights and cosy rooms and everyone dressed up and wonderful presents piled under a beautiful tree. They put the tree in the ballroom, because the ceiling is higher and the room less cluttered. The bits of plaster that came down have been salvaged and are piled up in one corner. On Christmas Eve they light a fire and sit around the tree, but the room is cold and uncomfortable, derelict and dusty, they keep glancing nervously at the ceiling. One by one they gravitate toward the sitting room, until Robert and Agnes are left on their own. Robert opens the last of the champagne left over from the wedding and pours two glasses. He asks Agnes if she will dance with him; she slides into his arms. There is no music, the Throckmorton house has no music, but that doesn't matter. Beneath her shawl she is wearing a long black satin shift dress with spaghetti straps that slip off her shoulders as they move around the room. He touches her skin and finds it very cold but when he begins to speak she puts her finger on his lips and says, 'Shh. It's all right.' They dance slowly and Robert holds her close. He feels a little dizzy; he's been drinking steadily all afternoon, the champagne has sent his head spinning. He looks around the room and it is as though fine mist is seeping through the cracks in the panelling. The ballroom fills with spectral dancing forms. Again he tries to speak and Agnes puts her finger to his lips, 'They are joining us,' she says, 'don't worry.' The moment is lost to him and he thinks she's referring to Graeme and Karen. As he looks into her eyes he sees the black pupils eclipse the irises, but she blinks and he is swamped by the green greenness of her eyes.

Afterwards they sit in front of the fire. Robert puts his arm around Agnes and his head on her shoulder. They look into the fire and he thinks of perfect Christmas Eves, and soon he is asleep.

Agnes slips away. She goes into the kitchen. Karen is making hot milk to take up to Andrew and Francis in an attempt to subdue them; Andrew is too excited to sleep and Francis is taking his cue from his brother. Jenny is in her room wrapping presents, this year Agnes gave Jenny money for her Christmas shopping. Now Jenny is fretting over the wool scarf she bought for Agnes – is it good enough, will she like it, does it matter that Agnes paid for it herself? Graeme is sitting at the table. Once Karen leaves the room Agnes stands behind him. She begins to play with his hair, pulling the curls at the nape of his neck straight, letting them pass through her fingers. Graeme finds her touch shocking. They have not stepped near each other since that night. Suddenly he is full of the most intense longing.

'Let's go outside,' she says.

He follows her out the back door. Two of the holiday cottages are occupied for the Christmas week, smoke puffs from their chimneys. As they cross the field – Agnes in her dress and her shawl, Graeme stumbling behind – he looks up and sees that the cottages are like something out of a fairy tale, like Hansel and Gretel gingerbread houses, like the house where Grandmother waits for the little girl with the red riding hood. Agnes holds up the key for the third cottage.

Inside it is cold. The heating is off and in the bedroom the bed has been stripped, the sheets, pillows and duvets stuffed into bin liners to keep away the damp. Agnes turns and beckons Graeme. 'Here,' she says, 'warm me up.'

They are there for less than a half hour. When they finish Graeme finds himself lying on top of Agnes. He props himself up on one elbow and pushes his hair out of his face and looks down at her. She smiles, and he feels a pleasure as dense as any orgasm. 'Don't move,' she says, 'you're keeping me warm.'

He looks down at her face, her lovely heart-shaped face, her lips that this time she allowed him to kiss, and he thinks, this is it, my marriage is over, I want Agnes, I do, to the exclusion of all others, I will have her, she will be mine. Even if I have to get rid of my brother, I want her, she will be mine. In that moment something inside him hardens, his black heart turns to lead. There is no going back.

They move apart. Agnes sits up and begins to dress, turning away. Graeme lies on the bare mattress, steaming. 'Come here,' he says, his hand on her hip.

'We have to go back,' she replies. 'We don't want them to notice we are missing.'

Graeme pulls himself together. She is right, of course, like she said before, it's the ideal situation. She is married to Robert, he is married to Karen, they live in the same house. There is nothing to stop them from doing exactly as they please.

Elizabeth

I never intended to become friends with Agnes. I didn't have it in me to be that generous. I think she knew from the start that I was in love with Robert and that she had usurped what I – and a lot of other people – saw as my rightful place. And I also believe that, at the beginning, she felt genuine empathy with me. Agnes's version of empathy. Either that or she was the most splendid faker. But, like I said, she had a strange ability to get me talking. And keep me talking. Afterwards, I hated myself.

'Elizabeth,' she said one evening in the new year, 'why is it that a lovely woman like yourself has never been married?'

I looked at her aghast.

She laughed. 'Oh Christ, I'm sorry, what a question. Just the kind of thing people used to ask me. Please forgive me. I'll shut up now.'

We were sitting on our own in front of the fire. After dinner Robert had discovered there was nothing to drink in the house. He'd gone to the pub to buy us a bottle of wine.

I stretched my feet toward the fire. Before she arrived I had always loved to spend time in that room. Being in that room, in front of the fire, always made me feel expansive. Or perhaps it was something else, I don't know, some spell that Agnes had cast. I looked at her and, before I knew what was happening, my tongue was loosened.

'I did almost get married,' I said. 'A few years ago. When I was twenty-nine.'

'Okay,' she said, pulling her shawl around her shoulders. She had a glamorous collection of scarves and shawls in dark colours. 'What happened?'

There is great pleasure to be found in confessing. As a therapist I saw how profoundly people enjoy talking about themselves, even when dealing with painful things, or when they know they have done wrong. I knew the thrill well from my own therapy, the euphoric gratification that comes with spilling the beans. As I told Agnes what had happened, I began to feel like the wife-killer who walks into the police station and tells all; it was a tremendous relief.

'I met him on holiday. In Greece. I know it's a cliché but at least he wasn't a Greek golddigger or a professional holiday gigolo or something like that. He was English. I'd gone with my friend Marina – you know, the woman Robert stays with sometimes in London.'

'Oh yes,' Agnes said speculatively. 'I've often wondered about the mysterious Marina.'

'Agnes – you don't think that –'

'No,' she laughed. 'I make sure he's worn out before I send him off to stay with Marina.'

I didn't much like what that conjured so I got on with my story. 'We were in Crete, in Agios Nicolaus, a little town on the coast that really only exists for the tourist trade, although it pre-dates tourism, of course. Restaurants, cheesy night-clubs, dangerous rental mopeds, that kind of thing.'

'I've never been to Greece.'

'No? Well I wouldn't recommend this particular place. Marina and I met Michael and his friend Alan in a restaurant one evening. Our tables were next to each other and we got talking. They were both charming and clearly in need of company, they'd run out of things to say to each other. There was something fantastically adolescent about the whole thing – I remember that after we'd eaten and were getting ready to go off to a night-club together, Marina leaned over to me and said she'd take the tall one. That left me with Michael, which was fine. He suited me. We went dancing and drank far too much and after the club closed, had a moonlit walk beside the sea.'

Agnes sighed, closed her eyes and smiled.

'Spent the rest of the fortnight together. We got on brilliantly. Well, Marina and Alan got on well enough, Marina said she was relieved to be getting it regularly. She hadn't been out with anyone for ages. She's like that, usually single with these very intense, often rather inappropriate, involvements from time to time. Nowadays her boyfriends are usually married.'

'That's not very reassuring,' Agnes laughed.

'Oh,' I said, suddenly worried, 'I'm sorry.'

'Back to the moonlight.'

'Well, it was great. He lived in London and I lived in London and before the end of the fortnight we had a long talk and decided we would keep seeing each other when we got home, even though we both knew that not being on holiday – ordinary life – might alter our relationship. And so we did. He worked for an insurance company – he was an accountant, although he wouldn't have called himself that. He owned a flat –'

'What would he call himself?'

'He'd say he was a manager – in financial management. Which he was. Accounting. He lived in Battersea and I lived in Islington, quite far apart, but we both had cars so that was fine. It was very nice. We slotted in together, as if we'd both had enough with being single and decided that this was it.

'Did you love him?' asked Agnes.

'No.'

She frowned sympathetically.

'But that didn't seem to matter somehow. I liked him a lot, we had a good time, he treated me well. I don't know. We were on course.'

'What was the sex like?'

'The sex. Ahh,' I said, 'a Marina-type question.'

'Hmm,' said Agnes, 'that Marina.'

'Yes. Fine, I suppose – fine. Good. Great sometimes. Fine.' I wasn't used to talking about sex. I know I'm supposed to be – that's our generation, isn't it? I talk – talked – about it endlessly with my clients. But I never got used to talking about myself that way. I try to bluff it, but I'm no good. 'He was handsome. He had this amazing line of hair which ran from his navel down to – well, you know. That line of hair was a thing of beauty.'

Agnes smiled. 'What happened?'

It was vivid to me still. I could remember his words precisely. 'He asked me to marry him. "We'll get married, shall we?" That's what he said. Just like that. Those were his words. "We'll get married, shall we?" We were lying in bed.'

'Was it romantic?'

'No. Not really. It felt parental somehow, like something my father might have said – "We'll have lunch here, shall we?" when he would just as soon have lunch elsewhere.'

'You know Elizabeth,' Agnes said, 'you've never really told me much about your parents.'

'Haven't I?' I found this an odd comment, coming as it did in the middle of my story. 'Well, what do you want to know?' I didn't quite know what to say. I'd got started on Michael and didn't want to stop.

'Did they like him?'

Relief. Back on track. 'They loved him. He used to fix things around the house – my father was useless at that. It transpired that Michael could fix anything. I didn't know about that side of him, nothing in London ever needed fixing, unlike the cottage where virtually everything was broken all the time.'

'What did you say?'

'I said yes. No one had ever asked me to marry them before. Unlike Marina. People used to ask her to marry them all the time.' I looked at Agnes. 'I'll bet you've had a few proposals.'

She smiled. 'A few proposals in my time.'

'You'll have to tell me.'

She nodded. I knew she would never tell me. 'So what happened?'

'We planned to get married in the spring. We'd both be thirty – our birthdays were within a few days of each other.' I suddenly began to feel reluctant about telling the rest of the story. Remembering it – what I'd done – was making me feel ill.

'And . . .?'

'And we made the arrangements, booked the registry office, booked a restaurant for a party – both sets of parents offered to help pay. We didn't have engagement rings, we thought they were – I don't know – silly.' I knew I had to finish the story now. I had been enjoying telling it, but no longer. I drew a breath. 'And I changed my mind.'

'You changed your mind,' Agnes said simply, nodding as though it was perfectly understandable behaviour. 'That was that.'

'Well, yes. Michael was away for a couple of nights on business and I called in sick, cancelled my private clients, stayed in my flat and had a long dark night of the soul.'

I paused. Recalling that time now – forty-eight hours, no more – made me ache inside. It was too hard – life was too hard for me. Michael . . . and here I was looking at Agnes. Who had married Robert. And I realized suddenly that I'd rather be here in Warboys, miserable as hell, than married to Michael.

'What?' said Agnes.

She wanted me to tell her what I was thinking. I rallied round, for the sake of the story if nothing else. 'I stayed in bed mostly and foraged for sweet things in my cupboards, except there weren't any. I took a number of hot baths. I stared out the window. I listened to *Gardeners' Question Time.*'

'How did you tell him?'

'Well, I . . .' I could see his face. I hurt him terribly. 'We had arranged to have dinner once he got back. We met in a restaurant near me, our favourite, the one we'd booked for our reception. We ordered a bottle of wine and, once he'd had a glass, I told him. I said, "I don't want to marry you Michael."'

I took a sip of the tea that Agnes had made me earlier. Robert was taking a long time to get back from the Black Hat. He must have stopped for a drink. Maybe they'd planned it. You pump her for information, Robert said, she's never told me what happened. Nonsense, of course. Robert didn't care about the time I almost got married. Not then. He didn't care.

'What did he say?'

'He said, "What?" like people do when they don't want to believe what they've heard. So I said it again, "I don't want to marry you Michael." I couldn't come up with any excuses, I didn't want to lie to him, so I told him the plain truth. And I think I needed to make him hate me. I wanted him to hate me. It would make me feel better if he hated me. I deserved it.'

'You're always looking for punishment,' Agnes said.

I didn't answer.

'Did he hate you?'

'I don't know.'

'What do you mean?'

'I don't know. I never saw him again.' I remembered how he looked that evening. As soon as what I was saying registered properly he stood up, took his coat down from where it was hanging and left the restaurant. 'I never heard from him, nor spoke to him again. I thought he might ring me. I wasn't about to ring him. But he didn't.'

'A clean break.'

'It didn't feel clean.'

Robert came into the sitting room with the bottle of wine and the glasses. I sat up straight, buttoned my cardigan, blew my nose. I hadn't started to cry, but I was close, and I did not want him to see me. 'It's freezing,' Robert said emphatically, before running up to the loo. While he was gone I turned once more to Agnes.

'Pretty screwed up,' I said, 'for a therapist.'

She shook her head and poured the wine. 'Just because we do something for others, doesn't mean we can do it for ourselves.' She shrugged. 'Besides we have more than one chance for happiness.'

'More than one?' I asked. 'How many?'

'As many as we make.'

'Listen,' I said, 'don't tell Robert. I've never told him.'

'I won't,' she said. A promise. Not that I had any idea how much a promise from Agnes was worth.

Robert came back into the room. He leant down to kiss Agnes

and somehow I felt shocked by that, as though I'd forgotten that he belonged to her, not me. I let Michael go because of Robert. I hadn't known it at the time, but I knew it now. I knew it all too well.

I hadn't told Agnes the whole truth about Michael and me. I left out the bit about Robert. The previous weekend – before our big scene – I'd been home to Warboys for Robert's birthday. I didn't invite Michael; I wanted to go on my own and, besides, he was away. Robert had organized a party in the Black Hat. We got very drunk – everyone got very drunk – and I rescued him from a tussle with Geraldine Andley. I didn't notice what was happening until Jim Drury spoke to me.

'Save him Elizabeth,' he whispered.

'What?'

'Save him from that tart.' He looked down the bar meaningfully. Robert had his arm around Geraldine. She was looking up at him lustfully.

As far as village tarts go Geraldine Andley is a poor excuse. But that's Warboys. She'd had a reputation for as long as I could remember but no one I knew had ever slept with her, or at least no one admitted to sleeping with her. Given the chance, she'd go on at you about her past lives. She was into anything vaguely New Age; she shared this interest with Doris Senior, Lolly's mother, but not even Doris was able to get on with Geraldine.

Over the years I had tried to be her friend. Occasionally I offered to buy her a drink. She always accepted, but we found we had nothing to talk about. I think she thought I was trying to chat her up. She was a good ten years older than us, she wore – still does – very short skirts and too much make-up. She wasn't a prostitute but she was supposed to be easy. Horrible thought. I'm sure she'd always had her eye on Robert, probably does to this day.

I walked the length of the bar and squeezed myself between them. I gave Robert a great suggestive kiss in the hope that he'd turn his attention to me. He did. We had sex in the tunnel under the yew hedge behind the house – a favourite location. I'd completely forgotten about Michael that evening. When I woke up – alone – the next day I knew I couldn't marry him.

Agnes discusses Elizabeth

'She's a funny one, isn't she?' Agnes and Robert are in bed. Robert is caressing Agnes's breast. It is round and full and the nipple points straight upwards and Robert thinks it's miraculous. Agnes is staring at the ceiling.

'Who? Aren't all the women round here funny?'

Agnes frowns, shifts away. 'Your friend Elizabeth.'

'Oh,' says Robert. 'Her.' He feels a tiny pang of disloyalty.

'There is nothing very deeply felt about her.'

'What do you mean?'

'She hasn't really lived through anything.'

'I don't know about that. She's had – she's got – her life. There was her professional trouble. And her parents are dead. She's like you that way.'

'She seems shallow to me. I can't see into her. Perhaps there is nothing to see.'

'Agnes, that's so harsh.'

'I know but –' She turns to her husband and slips her hand under the covers, between his legs. Robert trembles. 'Why didn't you marry her?' She is stroking him.

His voice is thick, his throat a little constricted. 'I married you.'

'Before.'

He sighs with pleasure, and weariness at having to reply. 'She wasn't – it never – oh Agnes, you've just told me what she's like.'

Agnes giggles and Robert finds her subtle malice thrilling. Where he grew up everyone pretended to be nice.

Robert

Things were going from bad to worse with the renovations – lead piping, dodgy wiring, wet rot, dry rot, decrepit boiler. I was getting into a real mess over the payments; the foreman had begun to lose his patience and that morning we'd had a shouting match. For every bill I paid, there were three or four I couldn't pay. January was a very quiet time of year for the estate and our income was low, perilously low. I was at my desk, punching numbers into the calculator, almost in tears. Agnes came into the room. She pulled up a chair and sat close beside me. Her hair was wet, she must have come straight from the shower. She often took a shower before lunch, after she'd been out walking.

'How's tricks?' she asked.

I looked at her, I looked into her eyes. Ask, I thought. Ask her for money. But I couldn't. We were too happy. I'd find a way through. She gave me a kiss and her brow creased when I didn't respond. At least tell her there's a problem, I thought. Just say it. But I couldn't do that either. She raised her skirt and straddled my lap.

Agnes could always make me forget my worries.

Graeme tells Agnes everything

Agnes and Graeme are fucking. At least once a week, usually before lunch. Robert is in his office working, Agnes tells him she is going out for her walk. Jenny is at school. Karen is busy in the house – Karen is always busy in the house, as Agnes observes one day, 'Karen is basically our maid. Except we don't have to pay her.'

'It's not true,' Robert objects.

'Yes it is,' she replies and he knows she is right.

Graeme is doing what Graeme usually does – he is unaccounted for. He goes upstairs to his room and gets out his new suit; he keeps it shrouded in drycleaner's plastic at the back of the wardrobe where he thinks Karen won't find it. He puts it on with a clean white shirt and a tie, his good shoes, then throws his suede jacket on over it. He limps out to the holiday cottages, swinging his cane, keeping clear of the mud. He doesn't care who sees him heading that way. Agnes is altogether more discreet, she goes the back way, through the woods.

The cottages are always very cold, unless they are lucky and one has been let recently. But in winter this is rare. Usually the radiators haven't been on for weeks. The mattress is bare, slightly damp – clammy. Graeme and Agnes add their stains to the ones already present.

It is rough, their sex. Graeme doesn't love Agnes, he wants her. Agnes enjoys his wanting her. She taunts him, his limp, his cane, his leg, and flaunts herself before him. She knows he finds this powerfully erotic. They are both unembarrassed – they like doing this thing.

'Nice suit,' she says.

'Thank you,' returns Graeme, full of purchased grace.

She brushes something off his shoulder, straightens his tie. These wifely gestures make Graeme wince. He grabs her hand and lowers it.

Their sex doesn't take long, and it is bruising. Sometimes, later in the afternoon, Graeme finds himself wondering how Agnes withstands his assaults on her body. He dips his head in something approaching shame. Fucking his sister-in-law, penetrating her body; it is as sensual as it is corrosive. He stifles his dim conscience by telling himself it's not his fault. She asked for it. She is bewitching.

During their sessions in the cottages – Agnes refers to it as 'cottaging', a little joke that Graeme hates – they rarely speak to each other beyond issuing carnal instructions. But this afternoon Graeme can't help himself. He has orgasmed deep inside her and now he is drifting. He feels compelled to explain to her how he got his cane. That's how he thinks of it – how I got my cane, as if the cane is a kind of trophy – not how he injured his leg. Not how he came to be unemployed, leaving behind what was once, however briefly, his vocation.

'I shot a man in Peterborough one evening,' he says, unprompted. 'An unarmed man.' And he tells Agnes his story. She is silent throughout. From time to time she nods encouragingly.

'I had been a cop for more than a dozen years. I had a reputation in the force for being mean in both senses of the word – stingy as well as cruel.' He laughs. 'They used to say I would dodge my round of drinks in the pub and kick a man when he was down. And it was true. As the years went by and I was passed over for promotion, I got meaner still. I was a good policeman, I got results, I could be relied upon. But that didn't add up to my fellow officers liking me. And they did not,' he boasts.

Andrew is four months old when it happens, Francis has not yet been conceived. The baby is not sleeping at night, waking every few hours for feeding. Karen is drawn and exhausted, still carrying much of the weight she put on during the pregnancy. Lactating and tearful, her baggy clothes spotted with baby milk and baby sick, Karen knows that Graeme finds her completely unattractive. There are other women once again, and she knows that as well. But she is stoic, uncomplaining and completely in love with the baby, so she gets on with things.

Graeme and another officer are out on their rounds. It is a warm summer evening, after midnight, and they have walked through one of the city's rougher housing estates. The area is quiet. Now they are on a leafy street, large brick houses with gardens and new mock-Victorian garages, when PC Carl Dodgson, the other officer, thinks he sees a light flash on and off in a house that is otherwise dark. They stand behind a car on the opposite side of the street and watch for a moment and, indeed, a light sweeps around the sitting room. Someone inside the house draws the sitting room curtains. A burglary in progress. Carl radios in to the station and they go to investigate.

The back door of the house is ajar, the pane of glass above the handle smashed. Carl enters first and Graeme follows. They stand inside the dark kitchen and listen. Voices are coming from the sitting room around the corner; two men are having an argument. Torchlight jumps around the room like a little demon.

'You fucking cunt, leave that crap behind, we don't want it.'

'They've got great movies! Look at this, *Gone with the Wind*, *Lawrence of Arabia* – it's great stuff.'

'Leave it! We've fucking got enough to carry anyway.'

'If we'd borrowed your sister's car like you said we were going to do . . .'

'She had to take her wee lad swimming. What was I supposed to say – "oh that's okay, I don't need it 'til midnight". Now come on. They'll be fucking coming home soon.'

There is a pause and the sound of furniture being shifted. Graeme and Carl look at each other. Carl begins to move toward the sitting room.

'That would be funny, wouldn't it.'

'What?'

'If they came home while we were in the middle of this.'

'Funny?'

'Yeah, like in a movie,' he begins to giggle. Graeme thinks they sound stoned. 'A mad-cap caper movie.'

'Yeah, right, we'd fucking have to kill them, wouldn't we? Now that would be funny.'

'Trust you, Greg, killer instinct.'

By now Carl is at the entrance to the sitting room. Graeme is directly behind him. He can hear a heart pounding, he isn't sure if it is his. Carl hits the light switch on the wall, expecting the room to flood with light. A small lava lamp comes on in the corner near where the two burglars are standing. It casts enough wobbly orange light for Graeme to see a gun lying on the side table next to him. Carl shouts 'You're under arrest!' at the same time as the man called Greg heaves the video recorder he is holding in their direction. Graeme picks up the gun, pulls off the safety, and shoots Greg in the chest.

Graeme has used guns in training and at target practice but has never been on armed detail. He is unfamiliar with this particular type of handgun. The recoil from the shot he fired is so strong that it pushes him backward, off his feet, and onto the floor. He drops the gun and it clatters forward. The other burglar throws himself down and grabs it. He lets out a scream and shoots Graeme in the leg.

Carl dives across the room, landing on top of the gunman. 'Fuck, you fucking fuck –' their obscenities get tangled. Carl wrestles the gun away. Graeme, propped up on one elbow, clutches his leg above where the bullet entered. There is a small hole in the trousers of his uniform, a neat hole that gives no indication of the pain caused by the smashed and seared flesh and bone below. He allows himself a whimper.

Graeme looks at the burglar called Greg, the man he shot. Greg is dying, blood pumping directly from his heart onto the carpet. He stares solemnly back at Graeme. Outside a back-up car arrives, lights flashing.

Graeme is in the hospital for weeks recovering from the shotgun wound; the upper femur in his thigh is completely shattered. They keep him on his back, the leg in traction, later operating to pin the knee together. He is placed on a slow programme of rehabilitation.

PC Carl Dodgson tells his Commander himself that he isn't sure why Graeme shot the burglar. He says, 'I don't think he meant to kill him.' He pauses. 'Did he?' The Commander, over-worked himself, pleased to have an arrest, decides that Graeme's explanation – self-defence – will do. Besides, the dead man's family is too messed up to make a formal complaint. The other burglar is charged with attempted burglary and attempted murder; he has a lousy solicitor, pleads guilty, and is sent down for a long time. The case does not attract attention from the national papers.

As far as the Commander is concerned there is no question about Graeme's future; he will not be allowed to return to work in any capacity. Graeme tells Agnes the Commander had never liked him, and had been trying to get him to transfer for years. Despite Graeme's vehement objections the force retires him on disability. The Commander makes it clear there is no alternative; if Graeme registers a complaint or tries to appeal, the circumstances of the suspect's death will be investigated. And Graeme doesn't want that, does he?

So there is Graeme, jobless and crippled, aged thirty-three. He makes a good recovery, refusing to use a wheelchair, he says there isn't room for two wheelchairs in one family. His leg will always be stiff, the knee not flexible more than a few degrees. It will always cause him considerable pain, and on cold nights he can feel the metal pins under his skin, piercing his bones.

He rubs his leg, shifts, looks toward Agnes and finds her stare unnerving. She sniffs once, yawns, and speaks. 'Why?' she asks. 'Why did you kill him?'

Graeme doesn't know why he shot the burglar that night, and no one, not even Carl Dodgson, especially not Carl, has ever asked him to explain. The gun was there, it seemed a good idea to use it. He replies slowly. 'I joined the force expecting action but really the job was dead dull. Paperwork, endless training, community liaising, the last one the most fucking boring of all. Maybe I wanted out,' he pauses. 'Maybe I joined the force in the first place so that I could kill someone. And I did. Now people can whisper "Graeme Throckmorton, he killed a man, didn't he?"' Graeme laughs, takes hold of Agnes's breast, squeezes. He has never felt any guilt, only a mild surprise that someone could die so easily.

Sometimes he wishes that the circumstances of the incident had been a little more heroic. Undercover work, informers, corrupt local politicians, a high-speed chase, something like that. But it wasn't to be. Instead it was sordid and small, a little event that was visited upon him and then went away again.

As well as the physical ache in his leg, Graeme finds not working painful, more so than he could have guessed. He doesn't tell Agnes this. He hates spending so much time around the house and yet it doesn't occur to him to do anything else. Now he has Agnes to occupy him.

Karen gets uppity

Karen and Graeme are in bed. Down the hall Francis starts to scream. Karen throws on her dressing gown and rushes to him. He is dreaming. When she asks what is wrong he sits up and says 'Jenn' – his name for his aunt Jenny, '– bad. No.' He shakes his head vehemently. He points at the window. Karen takes him onto her lap and quietens him. She sings 'Twinkle, twinkle little star.' He says, 'Again.' So she sings it over and over. After a while, he sleeps.

Karen returns to bed. She slides under the cover and lies there in silence, unable to get back to sleep. She can tell that Graeme is awake as well.

'What are you thinking about?' she asks after a while, ever hopeful.

'Nothing,' he replies. 'Sleep. Why can't I?'

'Me too,' she says. She hesitates, and then she says it, the thing that has been bothering her. 'Don't you think there is something a little odd about Agnes?'

Graeme controls his reaction carefully. 'What do you mean?'

'I don't know. I just find her a little – strange.'

Graeme doesn't reply.

'I know she makes Robert happy and she's been living with us for all this time now but . . . I find her cold. And there's something odd about her eyes.'

'Her eyes? That's ridiculous.'

Karen knows it's ridiculous. She wishes she hadn't said it. But, still, she pursues her point. 'I think she hates me. I think she hates all of us.'

'That's the stupidest thing you've ever said.'

'She makes me uncomfortable. In my own home.'

Graeme's heard enough. He turns over. They both continue to lie awake, and they both continue to think about Agnes. In different ways. For different reasons.

Jenny misses Graeme

In his bluff, baleful way, Graeme is a good friend to his sister Jenny. He's always taken her as she is, he's never placed expectations on her that she feels she can't meet, they've always had an easy, unspoken allegiance to one another, ever since Jenny was a small child. Robert asks things of Jenny, he wants her to do better at school, he wants her to be better behaved, he wants her to go out in the world and accomplish things – he wants her to do things that he himself isn't capable of doing. In a way, Jenny is thankful that Agnes has appeared because now less of Robert's attention swings her way. Less and less, in fact, until some days Jenny feels that Robert no longer sees her at all, so intense is his focus on Agnes. She is grateful and jealous at the same time.

But Graeme, the drift in Graeme's attentiveness is unexplained. Why does he no longer sit with Jenny of an afternoon? Why doesn't he walk her home from school? Why does he no longer come into her room after he's been down to the Black Hat, to lie on her bed and talk about things? They used to gossip, Graeme and Jenny, about the good and upstanding citizenry of Warboys, and Jenny enjoyed her brother's bitterness, his sharp tongue; she understood from an early age that he saw things differently from other people. She was his audience and she was appreciated. She was prepared to listen to what he had to say, and she was allowed to not take him seriously.

'Shall we go into Peterborough tomorrow?' Jenny asks him one Friday evening.

'What for?' asks Graeme. He is wolfing down his dinner, sitting at the table hunched and shifty.

'I need to do some shopping.' As if she does that kind of thing, as if she and Graeme do that kind of thing together.

Graeme looks at Jenny, as though he is tempted. 'What for?'

'Oh, things. I need some trousers.'

Agnes stands up and begins to remove the plates. Graeme looks across the table at her and Jenny can tell his mind is suddenly elsewhere, not on this conversation.

'Graeme?' demands Jenny.

'Oh,' he says, returning to her, 'I don't think so.'

'Why not?' she asks, angry and hurt, showing her age.

'Don't pout,' he frowns. 'It's unattractive.'

Jenny gets up abruptly. She walks over to the sink and starts to help Karen clear up. Robert glances at his father, sees his baseball hat has slipped down over his eyes, goes over and straightens it. 'All right Dad?' he says. Graeme continues to watch Agnes move around the kitchen.

Agnes puts her arm around Jenny. 'How are you feeling?'

'I'm all right.' Jenny fights her urge to lean into Agnes, to let Agnes's arms envelop her completely, to rest against her shoulder and sigh.

'You haven't felt faint again?'

Jenny shakes her head.

'I still think you should have gone to the doctor.'

'That's not how we do things in this country,' Karen interjects, irritated suddenly. 'We don't go to the doctor for every little thing.'

'You don't?'

Karen is embarrassed now, she feels she's been rude. She shakes her head. 'It's not that kind of culture.' She doesn't know anything about Americans and their doctors, she doesn't know why she is saying these things, it's not even true.

'Well, when I was in the doctor's office the other day –' and everyone looks up at this, why would Agnes have been visiting the doctor's surgery? – 'they had a whole lot of posters on the walls of the waiting room telling people that they should only visit the doctor if they really feel they must. As if you are a nation of hypochondriac time wasters.'

'That's just the NHS trying to save money.'

'Oh,' says Agnes, raising her eyebrows to show she's not convinced, 'okay.'

'Why were you at the doctor's?' asks Jenny. Everyone is relieved, glad someone else did the asking.

'Just a check-up,' Agnes says dismissively, surveying the room. Robert looks anxious, is my beloved unwell? Graeme's face has darkened; he can't bear the idea of the doctor touching Agnes, the doctor giving Agnes a physical examination. He feels ill himself at the thought. 'Anyway,' she continues, 'how are you feeling?'

'I'm fine,' says Jenny. 'I don't know what happened. The school nurse said it might have been because I was having a heavy period.' The two men blanch slightly and look away. Robert stands and bangs his knee on the table. Agnes laughs out loud and Jenny feels pleased with herself. 'She said I should take it easy.'

'Why don't we do something together tomorrow? Just you and me,' says Agnes. Everyone in the room looks at Agnes expectantly. 'Why don't we go to Peterborough.'

Now Graeme looks openly miserable. He doesn't say a thing. Karen feels very tired, she can't remember the last time she got away from the house on her own. Ordinarily this doesn't bother her, she loves being with her boys, small and big. She works hard and, in the evenings, she contemplates the assault on the domestic world she will carry out the next day. But now she feels that there is nothing she would rather do than wander the streets of Peterborough. Buy a dress. Some shoes. Get her hair cut. What bliss. What freedom.

Robert folds his newspaper, clears his throat. He speaks manfully. 'Sounds like a great idea. I'm sure you both could do with an outing. Go ahead, don't worry about me.'

Agnes gives him a cool look. 'I wasn't planning on it,' she replies.

He smirks and shrugs boyishly. Graeme leaves the room, not concealing his disgust. Karen returns to the washing-up.

Robert

The builders quit. They walked off the job. I had given a lot of work to that firm over the years – they did all the work on the cottages and most of the other jobs that have come up around the place – and as soon as problems arise, they're off. They were in the habit of packing up their tools at the end of the week – I think most of them worked elsewhere on weekends – and come Monday they simply didn't arrive. We were used to them coming and going and so it was lunchtime before we noticed that no one had turned up. I'd become so accustomed to the noise that I no longer noticed whether there was any or not.

I was making Andrew and Francis and myself sandwiches. Karen brought the boys in – she'd been to pick up Andrew from nursery – and she said, 'Are none of the big men here?' We'd adopted Andrew's habit of calling the builders 'the big men'. I put down the jar of mayonnaise I was holding and went through the house to the foot of the stairs. Up top there was silence, no dust, no hammering. I checked in our bedroom to see if Agnes was there, but she was not. I stood at the door of what was to be our bathroom. All the floorboards had been taken up and several of the joists were missing. Much of the plaster had been chipped off the walls, exposing the fretwork of wattle and daub. All of the plumbing had been removed, apart from the old bathtub which balanced precariously on remnants of the floor. They'd taken away the old radiator and sealed off the pipes. The window had been taken out and not replaced – at night across the hall Agnes and I barricaded our room with draught excluders on the floor and a heavy curtain over the door, burying ourselves under two duvets – and wiring dangled loose from what had been the overhead light and its switch. There was a weird pattern of mould covering what was left of the ceiling.

I walked across the hall to the two smaller rooms that were being converted to a sitting room. Patches of the flooring had been removed here as well. The wall between the two rooms had been brought down and much of the resulting rubble taken away. The plaster on the remaining walls was intact; this room had had most of its ceiling removed and several beams afflicted with wet rot excised. The room was open to the crawl-space overhead and the draught that moved through from above was heavy with an attic smell of old birds' nests. There was a small hole in the roof and, on the floor directly below, a bucket half-full of stagnant rain water. It looked like a photograph of a London house during the Blitz.

There were no tools left behind, not even the ladder. Usually a battered old radio sat on the window-ledge in the sitting room; that was gone as well. I could tell they weren't coming back.

I went to my office – where was Agnes? – and tried to track down the contractor. I soon gave up on that and phoned Derek Hill instead. His daughter, Lucy, whom I had attempted to chat up in the Marquis of Granby the night I met Agnes, answered.

'It's Robert, Lucy, Robert Throckmorton.'

She didn't reply.

'Is your father around?'

'Why do you want to speak to him?' Suspicious.

'I've got some work he might be interested in.'

'Oh. Well he's not here. You can get him on his mobile.' She gave me the number.

'Thanks. What are you up to –' She put the phone down. I felt incredibly relieved that I was married.

I went into the kitchen and Agnes was there, helping Karen give the boys lunch. I ate the sandwich I had made earlier. The kitchen was full of Andrew and Francis's conversation – they liked to shout and interrupt each other – and no one mentioned the builders. I asked Agnes to bring me up to date on what was happening about the ceiling of the ballroom.

'Ah,' she said, 'thanks for reminding me. I'll get on to it.' I was a little surprised that she hadn't done anything, but at least if she hadn't engaged anyone, no one could quit.

Derek came round after lunch; his crew was building a house elsewhere in the village. I took him upstairs. 'Christ almighty,' he said as he looked around. He went back and forth between the rooms several times. 'Jesus Christ.' He turned to me with a pity-filled and mocking smile on his face. Derek Hill had never like me and he liked me even less since that episode with Lucy. 'It'll cost you,' he said.

'Just give me a quote. I need someone reliable.' He agreed to get back to me within the week. I didn't want to think about the money.

As I said, Agnes and I had to make a lot of effort to ensure that we didn't freeze to death at night. Despite the cold, and the dust, we enjoyed the privacy of being on our own in this part of the house, away from everyone else – we could make as much noise as we wanted during sex. But it was an epic journey to and from the nearest bathroom. Sometimes Agnes got up to go to the loo in the middle of the night; I'd fall asleep and wake up, fall asleep and wake up, and it would feel as though hours had passed before she returned.

That night we went to bed early. I felt depressed about the house. I told Agnes the builders had walked off and, to my relief, she didn't ask why. She said she was going to cheer me up. She climbed under the duvet and went to work on my body. Soon I could think of nothing but her mouth. She left me feeling drowsy, longing to hold her, saying she wouldn't be gone more than a minute.

It was while she was away that night that I first heard the noises. The noises that the house started to make.

Agnes sits with Martin

Agnes sits with Martin, by the oven in the kitchen, by the fire in the sitting room. She sits with him for hours at a time. She takes his hand from where it rests on the blanket across his knees and holds it in her own lap. She leans close to him, her lips to his ear, and she whispers. None of the others can hear a word of what she says. Karen moves in and out of the room and watches, sometimes she stands right next to them as she works at the sink. But she can't hear a word of what Agnes says, no matter how she concentrates. Agnes has not taken on any of Martin's care, that labour remains Karen's responsibility, but this talking goes on and on, and Karen tries to convince herself it is a good thing. She watches Martin's face as she sits at the table helping Andrew learn to read. He is blank and placid, as always, although occasionally Karen thinks she sees something else pass across her father-in-law's face. He grimaces. He blinks heavily. Is he distressed? Or is he happy to be whispered to in this way?

It is mid-afternoon, dark outside, Karen deposits the boys in the sitting room. Graeme is in there, she leaves them to play. Karen carries the shopping into the kitchen. She glances at Agnes and Martin in the corner, puts down the bags, and notices an odd, familiar smell. She looks around the kitchen, toward the window which someone has propped wide open. She realizes that Martin has got a cigarette dangling from one corner of his mouth.

Karen stares as Agnes removes the cigarette carefully and places it between her own lips. She drags on it, exhales smoke through her nose into Martin's grey face. She puts the cigarette between his lips again. The gesture is intimate and controlled, as though part of a well-worn routine.

Karen straightens her back. She speaks quickly. 'What do you think you are doing?'

Agnes looks up. She smiles pleasantly. 'He wanted a smoke.'

'He can't smoke,' Karen says. 'Some days he can hardly breathe.'

'It's the little pleasures that make life worth living,' says Agnes. She looks at Martin. 'Isn't that right, darling?'

Karen moves away from the sink abruptly. She goes into the sitting room. 'Graeme.' Her voice is too shrill so she starts again, 'Graeme,' more softly.

He doesn't look up. Both the boys look at their mother expectantly.

'Agnes is in the kitchen with Martin. They are smoking.'

The little boys' eyes widen. They stand up. Andrew makes a bee-line for the kitchen with Francis following right behind. Graeme lowers his paper. 'They're what?'

'Agnes is force-feeding your father a fag.'

Graeme takes hold of his cane and hauls himself out of his chair. 'This I've got to see.'

He stops in the doorway of the kitchen. Karen stands on her toes and peers around his shoulders. Andrew has pulled out the kitchen drawers to form a set of steps and is climbing toward the jar of biscuits. Francis waits patiently. Martin is sitting on his own next to the cooker. The window is still wide open, the room smells of damp fenland air. There is no cigarette, no tell-tale odour, no ash dropped on the stone tiles. Agnes has disappeared.

'Karen,' says Graeme and she hears a whine in his voice. She knows he is thinking, you stupid bitch, and he'd say it if the boys weren't here. He doesn't believe her story, thinks she is mad, a mad woman. She looks at Martin, around the kitchen, and feels the muscles in her neck knot. Defend me Martin, she thinks, but of course he does not. Why should Graeme believe anything I say? Why would anyone believe me?

Jenny tells Lolly a story

Agnes continues to tell Jenny stories. Strange stories, brief, violent and gory. They are not like anything Jenny has read or seen, but she leads a sheltered life. The Throckmortons do not own a video player; Graeme and Robert watch sport on the old 14″ colour television occasionally, half-heartedly, but otherwise, it's not often on. They have no objections to telly, they simply aren't in the habit of watching. And it's not because they are bookish or musical or absorbed in hobbies – they are not. Jenny used to try and watch *Top of the Pops* but she was always forgetting when it was on, always switching on the set as the programme was finishing. Now she doesn't care, she's got used to being resolutely uninformed about popular culture, the stuff that other kids at school live and breathe. It is part of what makes Jenny weird and everyone, including Jenny, is used to it.

She is lying on her bed with Lolly. They are sharing a bar of chocolate. Lolly is wearing a black fright-wig she bought with her allowance last week, her black Glastonbury dress, and a ring with an enormous black stone that her mother gave her for Christmas.

'I love your house,' says Lolly.

'You do?'

'It's so . . . gothic. Creepy.'

Jenny isn't sure she knows what Lolly means. 'Thanks.'

'And this room,' she indicates the windows on three sides – Jenny's room is long and thin, at the end of the corridor, and from it she can view not only the front drive and the back garden, but over the field toward the cottages as well – 'all these windows, it's like a castle watchtower. It's fantastic.'

Jenny rolls over and looks around. 'I'm the Queen of all my Domain.'

'Don't you think Nigel Ross is cute?'

Jenny is reluctant. 'He's all right.'

'Just all right? I'm going to sleep with him. I'm going to roger him stupid. Fuck his brains out.'

Jenny laughs. Lolly's always announcing who her next conquest will be; as far as Jenny knows her talk is fiction.

'What do you bet that he's a cherry?' asks Lolly. She is fond of American slang.

'Yes,' says Jenny. 'Definitely.' She lies back on the pillow. 'Shall I tell you a story?'

'Okay,' says Lolly, a little reluctant. Usually she is the teller of tales.

'Once upon a time, there was a young woman called Jenny Throckmorton –'

Lolly snorts.

'– who comes home one evening to find that her flat-mate and her flat-mate's boyfriend have been murdered by someone who – it turns out – was trying to kill Jenny. He's killed two other women that evening and they are both called Jenny Throckmorton.'

'Ugh,' says Lolly, 'gross. I didn't know it was that common a name.'

'Shut up,' says Jenny. 'Anyway, this person obviously intended to kill her. She must get away. She calls the police from a crowded bar – they tell her to stay where she is, they will come and find her. There are only three Jenny Throckmortons in the phone book. Just then a man comes crashing through the bar toward her. Jenny runs and finds herself hemmed in by him. She is terrified, but this guy turns out to be on her side. He is trying to help her. He has been sent from the future to protect her. He tells her that one day Jenny is going to have a baby and that that baby boy will be a great leader – in the future – and that the man trying to kill her has come from the future as well. There are people who don't want the baby to ever be born –'

Lolly interrupts. '*The Terminator*.'

'What?'

'That's the plot of *The Terminator*.'

'It is?'

'Haven't you . . . oh yeah, I forgot, you haven't seen a movie since *The Wizard of Oz*.'

Jenny is looking at Lolly. 'The plot of a movie?'

'Yes.' Lolly feigns annoyance. 'Let me think. She and the guy go on the run with the big guy – that's Arnie – following them wherever they try to hide and they fall in love and fuck and then they destroy the big guy in an epic battle involving a burning lorry and a machine factory and the guy helping her gets killed but she is pregnant with his baby and that's the baby who is going to be the future leader after the apocalypse or whatever.'

'That's right,' says Jenny, subdued now.

'It's fantastic!' says Lolly with sudden enthusiasm. 'I love that movie. I'd like to watch it right now. Let's go rent it – Barbara will have it. We can watch it at my house.' She springs up from the bed, her wig askew.

'No,' says Jenny, shaking her head.

'Why not?'

'I don't know. I wouldn't like it.'

'Oh come on Jenny . . .'

'No. Shut up.'

Lolly shuts up.

That evening Agnes comes into Jenny's room after Lolly is gone. 'Do you want a story?' she asks.

Jenny is in bed. She turns her face toward the wall; she feels petulant, self-righteous and betrayed. 'No,' she says. 'No thank you.'

Agnes stops and stares at Jenny's huddled shape. After a moment a smile spreads across her face. She turns and walks down the hallway.

Into her pillow Jenny mutters: 'Go away.'

Agnes hears her.

Robert

The night noises were very strange. A kind of low wailing, a weeping. I'll admit that it scared me. It never failed to scare the shit out of me.

At first all I could hear was an indiscriminate moaning. It was like the wind, except with a human twist at the end of each dying rise, like a sob catching in someone's throat. I told myself it was the wind. After all, that part of the house was full of holes and missing windows. And the wind can sweep through Warboys, it runs straight off the North Sea and across the fens without mercy, especially in winter.

It took me a while to realize it, but the noise would always start once Agnes was no longer in the room. I see the pattern clearly now. Most nights at some point she'd get up to go to the loo and her movement away from the bed would invariably wake me. She'd go without turning on any lights and once she was gone the darkness would enclose me. And the noises would start. Sometimes it was as though they had been there all along but it wasn't until Agnes had left that I would hear them. Other times it seemed more deliberate – Agnes closed the door and, moments later, they began. I say 'they' because that's what it sounded like, several voices intertwined. Three voices. I don't know why I thought that, why that was what I began to hear. I can be quite specific about those voices: an old man, an old woman, and a young woman. Often you can tell the age of a person by the timbre of their voice, especially if they are very old, or young, and that was how it was with these. It got so I would almost expect them. And I'd grow more and more frightened and I'd attempt to control my breathing and my heart-rate, stop myself from spiralling way out by trying to trace the pattern of each voice except that wouldn't work and I'd get more and more frightened until, finally, it was as though they overwhelmed me, and I'd sink into the bed as though I was dying, as though I had died. The next thing I would wake up, and it would be morning, and Agnes would be sleeping beside me.

One morning I mentioned the voices to Agnes.

'Oh,' she said, 'it's probably me you are hearing.'

'I don't think so –'

'I hum a little. I walk down the corridor and I sing.'

'You do?'

'It's the middle of the night. I've got to do something to keep myself company.'

I realized that she was teasing me. 'Well,' I said, 'you should take up humming professionally. It is humming of exceptional quality.'

'Thank you,' said Agnes, and she kissed me.

But the voices did not go away.

Graeme loves Agnes

Graeme loves Agnes. Love has come over him, like the flu. It isn't what he intended, and he hates himself for his weakness. He has an urge to talk about it, he wants to tell people, and this is how he knows this affair is different from the others. But he can't tell anyone, of course not. Except Agnes. And telling her is out of the question. At least, that's what he thinks before today. But he surprises himself.

'I want to play golf.'

'Why?' asks Agnes, amazed.

'I always thought that when I got older I'd play golf. I'd belong to an exclusive club somewhere and every Saturday afternoon I'd sling my clubs into the boot of the car and head off, leave everything else behind.' Graeme likes to tell Agnes about his dreams and aspirations. She opens something up in him, something that is usually closed, locked up tight.

'Golf's for faggots,' says Agnes.

'What?'

'Only men who don't like women play golf.'

'Lots of women golf.'

'They're all dykes.'

Graeme laughs.

'Really,' says Agnes. 'Believe me.'

Graeme strokes her hair, tries to stick his tongue in her ear. She flinches and moves away.

'I hate it here.'

'What?' Graeme is alarmed. Two o'clock in the afternoon. They are lying together on the stripped down bed in the cottage. 'In Warboys?'

'No. Warboys is fine. This bed, this cottage.'

Graeme feels as though she has dealt him a mortal blow. He loves their cottage. 'Why?' He tries not to whine and instead sounds very gruff.

'It's fucking freezing. It's hard to stay warm anywhere, but out here it's ridiculous.'

Graeme moves closer to her.

'Look at you,' she says, 'you're turning blue.'

Graeme looks down along his own body. He is naked, she has kept most of her clothes on. He doesn't feel the cold, he feels desire. He realizes with a shock that, since the accident, Agnes is the only woman he has undressed in front of, apart from Karen. He fucked the others with his trousers on. And he doesn't want his wife to look at his leg, he doesn't want to have to look at it himself, he insists on lights out in their bedroom at night. But with Agnes – he lets Agnes touch him. He allows Agnes to run her hand along the twisted muscle, into the hollow along his thigh where the bullet blasted through. He lets her feel the pins that hold his knee together, he lets her see how they are visible just beneath his skin. She caresses him with tenderness, with openness and curiosity; it's a kind of enchantment. She's not squeamish. She's not polite.

He pulls her down to him, ready to have her once again. Despite the temperature, he feels very warm, his body is suffused with light and pleasure. She touches him and he gets goosebumps. He speaks without thinking. 'Agnes,' he says, 'I love you.'

'No you don't,' she says, kissing him.

'I do,' he objects.

'No you don't. You love to fuck me.'

'But I –'

'Shut up,' she says. 'I'm your sister-in-law.'

'Robert doesn't –'

'Robert gets this every night.'

Graeme doesn't know what to say. He can't see her face; her hair has fallen across it.

'I'm just stopping by.'

'What do you mean?'

'You're temporary. That's not to say I don't appreciate it – you. But really Graeme,' she pauses, moves her hand down along his belly. 'Let's get on with it.'

Elizabeth

Life progressed at an even, uneventful pace for a time. I got on with work at the Trevelyans, I spent time with Marlene and Geoff, I visited the Throckmorton household at least once a week. I tried to inhabit my cottage more fully. I changed things around, sold some of my parents' heavy old furniture, cleared the rooms of their tat. I moved the sitting room into their bedroom and my bedroom into what had always been the sitting room, but it was too confusing. At night I felt like a migrating bison from a nature programme, stumbling across a new motorway. I moved it all back again.

Since I started working for the Trevelyans I had become obsessed with coffee. I used to drink coffee, ages ago, but I could take it or leave it, and I gave it up around the same time that I stopped smoking and joined a gym. But after David Trevelyan showed me how to use the cappuccino machine I became hooked almost immediately. In the morning I had to have my coffee hit, and not just any coffee; it had to have a milky froth. It had to have a splash of chocolate on top. I took it with sugar. Some days I would have one cup and then, later, I would have a second. David and I spent as much time anticipating as drinking. The task of cleaning the white enamelled Italian coffee machine fell to me; I took it on willingly.

But the weekends were hell. There was nowhere else in Warboys with an espresso machine. I'd tried to persuade Jim and Lolita to buy one for the Black Hat, I told them all the groovy pubs and bars in London had one, but they were happy with their glass jugs of filter coffee that they allowed to sit and brew on the hot plate all day. It was clear I would have to buy one for myself. David had a mail-order catalogue; he helped me order it. We had a little inaugural ceremony at my cottage the day it arrived.

I tried not to think of my relationship with my coffee machine as a sign of encroaching spinster madness. And, truth be told, although it was lovely, it didn't take the sorrow out of my days. Lack of coffee hadn't been the only reason the weekends were hard. My machine did not make the time pass easily.

I wanted to know where Agnes' money came from. To put it bluntly, I couldn't stand the fact that she had money, that she had beautiful clothes, lovely things, that it wasn't an issue for her. From my new rather impoverished perspective the issue was particularly pressing. Where did the money come from? Exactly how much was there? I couldn't ask Robert, I knew a question like that from me would annoy him and, besides, I had a feeling he didn't know. Perhaps I simply should have asked her. But I did not. Instead I spent a fair amount of my spare time speculating.

As winter progressed, I began to worry about Jenny. It seemed to me that Agnes's influence was not entirely benign. I didn't like the way she looked. At first I had been relieved that Agnes had taken over shopping with Jenny but now her clothes were often inappropriate, too adult, too revealing – very short skirts and very tight tops – too much make-up, nail polish. I tried to speak to Robert about it one evening when Agnes was not within hearing, but he was dismissive. As substitute parents he and Graeme were an odd mix, too lenient on some things, far too strict on others – Jenny wasn't allowed out enough, for a teenager she led an inordinately home-bound existence. Now that Agnes was around I felt less able to intervene, to take Jenny under my wing. I knew they did things together from time to time but I thought that wasn't enough.

'I could teach her to drive,' I suggested to Robert one evening.

'What? Jenny – drive a car? She's far too dreamy.'

'You ought to take her into town more, to London, on holiday.'

Robert looked at me like I was crazy.

'At least let me take her out. I'll take her for lunch in Peterborough.' Agnes had come back into the room and I felt he was no longer listening. 'Robert? Toward the end of next week. I'll call her.' It didn't matter if he wasn't listening. This was between Jenny and me.

A storm in Warboys

The wind that resides in the attic of the house is whipping itself up, whirling up and down the fen and back again, gathering speed and strength. A storm is on the way; the wind makes ready to meet it. Robert is down in London at his annual tourism conference, two days and nights. His colleagues look upon it as a chance to drink and shag and swill about the night-clubs of London, but not Robert. He phones home and Agnes tells him that she and Graeme are nailing shut the doors of the unfinished rooms upstairs in order to keep out the gale. He is alarmed – he thinks of water cascading through the holes in the roof and what further damage that will do – but she calms him. 'The rain is coming down so heavily we are worried the house will float away. Like the ark,' she says lightly. 'Graeme will paddle with his cane.' Robert laughs and tells her how much he loves her. He puts down the phone and turns on the TV.

In Warboys the citizenry are worried. Lolita Drury runs up and down the stairs of the Black Hat, securing the window locks, pulling the curtains shut, closing the fireplaces. Jim is outside, beneath the cellar doors, taking a late beer delivery. The driver and his helper throw down the kegs and Jim's arms feel the strain. Jim has felt tired – terribly tired – in the months since the pub got vandalized. Sometimes he finds himself wishing that he was still playing host to Agnes upstairs. He thinks if she was staying with him – if she hadn't married Robert Throckmorton – everything would be all right.

Marlene Henderson calls Geoff on his mobile. He is in another village showing a client a house; she wants him to come home.

When the wind comes off the fen she longs for her parents' sturdy house in northern Germany, a thick blanket of snow covering everything. Marlene is not an anxious person but at the moment she is changed. She's a lawyer, a successful professional, confident, articulate and skilled, but at the moment, she feels superstitious and fearful. She is pregnant – just ten weeks – and she wants Geoff near her, safe.

Karen is frantic, the meal is late as though the weather got in the way, and the little boys are fractious, as if the wind is whipping up them as well. Francis smacks Andrew and Andrew tips his brother's pudding into his lap. Both boys scream with frustration and glee. Graeme rises up from the table like a monster from the deep. He raises his hand as well as his voice. He has been casting dark glances at Agnes all evening – he went to the cottages before lunch today and she didn't arrive. He is worried that she is tiring of their meetings. 'Get down from the table,' he shouts, and the adults wonder if he means them as well as the boys, but it is only Andrew and Francis who slide off their seats. Karen puts her own body between her husband's and the boys thinking, he would never hit them. He would never hit them, would he?

Jenny sits next to Agnes at supper. She has been avoiding her sister-in-law of late – since discovering Agnes's stories were fraudulent, the plots of tacky movies – but now that the storm is coming she needs her reassurance, wants to be near her. She is contrite and solicitous toward Agnes, asking if she can get her anything, offering the salt, the pepper, a clean plate. Agnes accepts her overtures graciously and Jenny wonders why she ever doubted her, how she could have been avoiding her, when she is so elegant and serene. So what if the stories weren't 'real' stories, what does 'real' mean?

While they are eating, Martin's wheelchair moves toward the table suddenly, away from the corner where he is sitting. Everyone looks up. Graeme stands, wheels him back toward the fire. A few minutes later the chair rolls forward quickly, as though the wind has given it a heave. Martin's face is expressionless.

'Perhaps he's trying to tell us something,' says Agnes.

'Oh yes,' says Graeme, 'and what might that be?' He gets up and pushes his father back to his place, tucks his blanket around his knees.

After dinner, Karen wrestles the boys into the bath. Sometimes their physical strength amazes her; it's as though their little bodies are made of solid muscle as they flip and twist away from her like freshly netted fish. They fight with her as though there is no love between them and it is all she can do to stop herself from pushing their heads under the water, one at a time. She dries them off and gets them into their pyjamas and they are clean little angels with spiky damp hair. A story, and a cuddle, and a kiss, and they are off to bed.

The kitchen is a mess. No one has bothered to clean up. Jenny has gone to her room. Agnes and Graeme are in the sitting room, drinking whisky. The fire remains unlit, because of the wind. After putting Martin to bed – tonight she devotes more time than usual to him, she keeps thinking of his wheelchair swinging forward – Karen begins to clear the dishes, then looks in on Agnes and Graeme and thinks better of it. She joins them for a glass of wine.

Graeme roams around the room, restless. He taps the floor with his cane as though testing the floorboards. Agnes sits by the window, holding open the curtain. She is watching the trees as they bend and sweep. Karen stares into her drink and shivers with the cold.

'I should be at this conference as well as Robert.'

Karen looks at her husband. Agnes doesn't shift.

'I don't see how I can be expected to just sit back while Robert continues to fuck things up with the estate. He underestimates me.' Robert has not told Graeme about the state of their finances; as far as Graeme is concerned the builders walked off in a fit of petulance.

He rants on. 'We could expand so easily. Tennis courts. Swimming pool. Angling.'

Karen wonders whom Graeme is addressing. Not me, she thinks.

Agnes turns away from the window. 'A shooting range,' she says acidly.

Karen is shocked. Graeme laughs. 'Great idea! A rifle range. We could hire the locals as targets. I could give lessons.' He laughs again. Neither of the women responds. He continues to pace, keeping his thoughts to himself for the time being.

Karen finishes her wine. The windows rattle in their frames. Suddenly she longs for sleep. 'Well,' she says, 'I can hear my bed calling me.' She smiles at no one, for no reason.

Agnes turns away from the window again. 'You work so hard Karen. You take such good care of those boys. You're a wonderful mother.'

Karen is surprised, and Agnes's words give her pleasure. She smiles and finds herself moving toward her sister-in-law. She leans down and kisses her soft cheek.

Graeme and Agnes sit in silence for a time, a noisy silence – the storm is well underway. Rain scrapes against the house like paint stripper, coming back up through the ground, streaming down through the fissures, cracks and holes in the roof. Thunder. They look up warily. There is lightning far off, moving closer. Graeme stands and takes a step toward Agnes. The curtains are drawn tight, there is only one lamp burning. The empty wing of the house groans and creaks and drips. Graeme moves forward until he is standing directly in front of Agnes where she sits on the settee. She puts her hand up and unzips his fly. Later, he gets on top of her and the awkward angle of his stiff leg on the settee makes him angry, impatient. He pushes into her without caution.

Jenny has fallen asleep sitting up. Her desk light is burning her hand with its heat and thunder jolts her awake. She pushes the lamp away, alarmed, but her skin is unharmed. The thunder sounds very close. She can hear gabbling voices. She puts her dressing gown on over her clothes and ventures downstairs to see who else is awake.

In the sitting room Graeme is fucking Agnes. When Jenny walks in they are displayed in front of her like an intricate tableau, an oil painting. The colours are very rich – the yellow walls, the red rug on the floor, the dark green sweater her brother is wearing, lit by warm golden lamp light. They are fully clothed, no flesh exposed except Agnes's right breast whose nipple Graeme has been sucking.

Graeme is grunting and muttering obscenities and he does not hear his sister enter the room. But Agnes opens her eyes and stares at Jenny, her face expressionless, showing neither pleasure nor dismay. Graeme continues humping. For a long moment Jenny is transfixed. Then she turns and flees.

That night it takes Jenny a long time to fall back asleep. She gets into bed and she can't help herself – she doesn't want to do it, she hates doing it, it makes her feel dirty, she can't stop herself – she masturbates. Her brother's stiff leg, her sister-in-law's bare breast. Fucking on the settee. All those stories Agnes told her and none of them were . . . true? She knew none of them were true – none of them were . . . none of them belonged to Agnes. Now none of them belong to Jenny.

She falls into a fitful sleep and is woken by a noise from outside, a loud banging. She goes to her window and opens the curtain a fraction. Outside she can see the wind has bent the curly willow so low it is hitting the wall, over and over again, knocking itself senseless. She watches, half-asleep, mesmerized. She hears something else – footsteps on the gravel. Agnes has walked out of the front door of the house. She is standing in the drive, light from the doorway falls on her. She is looking up at Jenny, stern, her arms crossed. Her face changes, softens, and she smiles and slowly rises off the ground without moving her arms or her feet. Jenny is horrified. Agnes's skirt flaps gently around her legs and she rises and rises through the air until she is directly outside Jenny's window. Her face nears the glass. Jenny wants to close the curtain and scream but is unable. Agnes is speaking in a low voice, Jenny can hear her. She says, 'Don't you tell anyone, Jenny Throckmorton, don't you tell anyone what you have seen.'

The next day in school Jenny has dark rings under her eyes and she doesn't respond to teachers or friends, not even Lolly. In her English class Mr McKay speaks to her directly. 'What is the significance of the green light at the end of the pier Jenny?' They are discussing *The Great Gatsby*. Jenny loves *The Great Gatsby* but she doesn't hear the question. 'Jenny?' The teacher repeats himself.

Again, no response. He walks down the aisle to Jenny's desk. 'Jenny,' he says in a firm, teacherly voice.

Jenny turns her head slowly and looks up at him. Her vision is a little blurred, she has a headache. 'Fuck you,' she says.

The class takes a collective gasp and begins to giggle. Lolly looks around the room proudly, as though to claim Jenny as her friend.

'Jennifer, you –'

No one ever calls Jenny Jennifer. She interrupts the teacher. 'Fuck you, Mr McKay.' She looks at him for a moment, considering. 'Who are you fucking these days? How do you like it? Do you do it every night?'

Mr McKay takes a step backwards. The class is now too shocked to laugh. Mr McKay stands stunned for a moment and then leaves the room. Twenty pupils sit in silence, staring at Jenny. He returns moments later with the Headteacher. 'Jenny Throckmorton,' says the Head. 'Wait for me in my office.'

Jenny sits on her own in the office. She stares at the collection of diplomas on the wall. After a while the Head arrives, very composed, steely.

'Jenny, we are issuing you with a formal written warning, by-passing the verbal warnings we usually give. The severity of the situation warrants this. Have you any explanation for your behaviour?'

Jenny doesn't speak, doesn't nod or shake her head. The Headteacher has thin lips and matching thin lines across her forehead.

'I am calling your parents – your brothers – to come and pick you up. I will inform them of what has happened and you will return to school tomorrow. Mr McKay is expecting a written apology. You will catch up with your classwork tomorrow.'

Jenny does not respond. She stares at the diplomas. She can think of nothing apart from Agnes and Graeme.

Elizabeth

It was pure luck that I happened to be standing beside the phone when the school rang. I'd dropped round to see Robert. The storm had brought down a tree across the footpath in my garden and I wanted to ask if he could come over with the chainsaw to help get rid of it. And I wanted to find out how the house had fared last night – the wind had been so strong that I lay awake imagining that their roof would come off. As soon as I arrived I remembered that Robert was away and there didn't seem to be anyone else at home, except Martin on his own in the sitting room. As always the back door was unlocked.

I answered the phone and agreed to go to the school to fetch Jenny. She was lucky it was me who answered – God knows how Graeme might have reacted and I can't imagine that either Karen or Agnes would have been much use in this kind of situation.

I drove to the school. I would take Jenny out for lunch in Peterborough – she could tell me her side of events.

She was very quiet during the journey. I let her choose where we ate – a pizza restaurant. After we ordered I asked how she was feeling.

'Agnes is a witch,' she said calmly.

I laughed. 'She's not that bad,' I said but Jenny wasn't smiling. I decided it might be wise to confide in her myself, to let her know that I was on her side. 'I don't much like her either.'

She frowned. Had I made a mistake? 'She's a witch,' she said, 'and she can fly.' Jenny looked away, across the restaurant. The tips of her fingers were raw – she'd been biting her nails.

'What do you mean?' She didn't reply. I decided to change the subject. Neither of us liked Agnes, now we both knew. 'How are you getting on with Robert these days? How is he?'

'He's a wimp. And a fool.'

I was astonished by her anger. I didn't like hearing her speak of Robert that way. But it wouldn't be of any use to show how I felt. 'Why do you think that?'

'I don't know.'

Where could I go with this? If she'd been a client – but she wasn't. 'Are you getting on with Graeme?'

'All he thinks about is sex.'

My heart flipped in my chest. 'What?'

'All he thinks about is sex and fucking. He can't do anything else. He's disgusting.'

I tried to stay cool. What was Jenny saying? What was going on in that house? Was Jenny disclosing some kind of abuse to me? I was no longer a therapist and, well, I had misunderstood people before this. But I couldn't let her – it – slip by without comment. I had to find a way through to her.

'Do you want to talk about it?'

'Not particularly.'

'Would it help if I found you someone else to talk to about it?'

She looked at me as though it had just dawned on her who I was, to whom she was speaking. 'No,' she said vehemently. 'No way.' She shook her head. 'He's disgusting.'

At that moment I could see all kinds of clues I might have missed. Clue after clue, over the years. Jenny and Graeme were close – too close perhaps – and their household had such a strange hothouse environment. Sixteen-year-old girls can be terribly provocative and I wasn't sure Graeme had the strength of character required in the situation.

But, as I kept reminding myself I had got things wrong before. I didn't have good judgement – I'd proved that in London. And Jenny was not making any outright allegations; teenagers – children – often don't. I decided I had better bite my tongue and wait.

'He's disgusting,' she repeated. 'But she's the bad one. Agnes is a witch.'

Now I felt completely confused. Perhaps Jenny was jealous of Robert and Agnes, jealous and confused to find such an exclusive and powerful love affair happening right in front of her. Watching your surrogate parent fall in love, not something any teenager wants to witness. I was pretty certain that Jenny hadn't been involved with boys – Graeme wouldn't allow it. That was it right there – Graeme wouldn't allow it. I felt horror rise up inside me once again.

The waitress brought our pizzas and Jenny ate the first few mouthfuls as though she was starving and then pushed the rest away. I tried to think of other things we could talk about, more neutral topics, but all I could think of was the weather, last night's storm, the current freeze. Jenny didn't want to talk about that. I decided to blunder on.

'What happened in the classroom today? What was that about?'

Jenny looked at me. 'Do you know anything about witches?'

'Witches?'

'Yes. Do you believe they exist?'

'Well, I . . .'

'Lolly knows about witches. Not white witches, not spangly fangly New Age witches – that's what Lolly's mum is into – but real witches. Evil witches. Who cast spells and change people and kill babies and . . .'

'No,' I said, taking a deep breath, 'no, I don't think I do believe in witches.'

'Why not?' Jenny looked up at me and I noticed how her black mascara was blotchy on her lashes, pooling in the corner of her right eye, next to her tearduct. Before Agnes arrived Jenny hadn't worn make-up. 'Do you have proof that they don't exist?'

'No, I –'

'Lolly says they do exist. They exist if we want them to. Like anything we choose to believe in. Father Christmas. The bogey man. God.' At this last word she looked at me defiantly but I wasn't about to argue with her about religion. I didn't believe in witches;

at that time I didn't believe in anything beyond what was scientifically proven.

'Okay,' I said, 'so they do exist. What then?'

'Agnes is here for a specific reason.' Jenny lowered her voice and leaned across the table toward me. If she hadn't been so alarming she would have been funny. 'I don't know what that reason is yet, but I'll find out.' She sat back in her seat. 'I can't tell you much more than that.'

'You can't?'

'No. I can't.'

I didn't know what to make of what she was saying. Why would Jenny suddenly turn on her beloved sister-in-law? Why would she despise her brother Graeme? Call Robert a wimp and a fool? What was going on in that house? I had noticed peculiar tensions between Agnes and Graeme on more than one occasion. Graeme and sex. Agnes. Could Graeme and Agnes be having an affair? I chastised myself, it was wishful thinking. I wondered what Jenny knew, what she had seen. I tried to steer the conversation back in that direction, but Jenny wouldn't have it. She had closed the door on the topic. She wanted to talk about witchcraft. That or nothing. She finished her lunch in surly silence.

When I got Jenny home, Karen was in the sitting room with the boys; they greeted Jenny enthusiastically, immediately involving her in their play. Karen went into the kitchen to get started on their tea and I followed. I gave her the letter of warning that the Headmistress had asked me to pass on and told her what had happened. She was bewildered and distraught.

'She never uses that kind of language.'

'I know. The school was as dismayed as you are.' We kept our voices low.

'What's wrong with her? What are we going to do?' Karen was tearful. As I had anticipated, her reaction wasn't very helpful. I should have waited and told Robert first – but he was away. Or Graeme. It would be good to tell him myself, see what I could learn from his reaction.

'Where's Graeme?' I asked.

'Out at the cottages. We've had a last minute booking. He's out there getting it ready. They're arriving tonight.'

I headed along the track instead of taking the short cut across the field. The lights were on in the first cottage. I knocked.

Agnes answered. I struggled not to show my surprise. 'Hello Elizabeth,' she said, smiling. She seemed completely unfazed to see me and did not behave as though anything untoward was taking place. 'Come in, come in –' she took me by the arm '– although it's not much warmer in here than out there. We're in the bedroom, making the bed.'

Graeme gave me a quick look before returning to the sheets. The work was awkward for him, with his leg. 'Elizabeth,' he said, concentrating on the corner tuck, 'what brings you out here?'

I told them what had happened. I tried to remember exactly what the Headteacher had told me. 'She used foul language. She asked her teacher – Mr McKay – who he was fucking.'

Agnes laughed loudly. 'This is a small place, isn't it?'

'What do you mean?'

'Well, where I come from – a little bad language – you would praise the student for showing initiative. They should thank their lucky stars that their worst problem is a little swearing.'

Graeme was scowling. 'Shut up.' He spoke sharply. I looked at Agnes, but her face remained open, smiling. 'It's not funny. They've issued a written warning. I'm going to –' he interrupted himself. 'You finish here.' He pointed at me.

'Me?'

'Yes.' He took his coat from the chair, as did Agnes. 'The bathroom needs doing,' he said. And they were off.

I did what they told me. I cleaned the bathroom. I did it for Robert, not for Graeme, nor Agnes.

Graeme lashes out

Graeme goes straight into the sitting-room, straight into Jenny. He grabs her by the arm and hauls her up off the floor where she is playing with Andrew and Francis. His grip on her is fierce; he is hurting her. The little boys scatter. Jenny keeps her body curved, away from Graeme. His other hand is raised.

'What do you think you are doing?' His voice is vicious, full of contempt. Jenny looks at him and then sees Agnes standing behind him, in the doorway. It is as though Jenny's entire body gains sudden strength. She straightens her back, draws herself to her full height and faces Graeme. She makes a sound in the back of her throat and spits in his face.

Graeme pauses for a moment, completely stunned. His sister's phlegm drips off his cheek onto his jacket. He doesn't know that Jenny has seen him with Agnes, all he can think is that she's a bitch.

He hits her. He slaps her face, a big open-handed slap, allowing his arm full swing, full strength. Jenny crumples to the floor, her bravery wiped away. Graeme pauses over her and, for a moment, it looks as though he is going to kick her, but he turns away. He leaves through the front door of the house, heading for the Marquis of Granby.

Agnes gathers the girl in her arms. Jenny clings to her, despite hating her; she wants to kick and punch but she can't. She begins to cry, she wants to be held. Martin is in his chair by the fire, his rug over his knees, his face turned toward them, blank and calm as always. Agnes helps the sobbing girl over to her father. She seats her on the floor next to him, puts her arms around his knees, and places one of Martin's hands on Jenny's head, the other on her shoulder. She calls Andrew and Francis and they crawl out from behind the settee and climb into Jenny's lap, wrap their arms around her neck, cooing, offering her kisses, they never like to see a grown-up upset. Agnes goes into the kitchen where Karen is working, the radio on rather too loudly – she hasn't heard a thing. 'Graeme's gone out to the pub,' Agnes announces. Karen sighs. The two women chop vegetables.

Elizabeth is burning

Elizabeth is burning with the knowledge she carries, her suspicions flare out from a well-fanned flame. She can't wait to talk to Robert; he is due back this morning. At the Trevelyans she keeps her eye on the street and when she sees Robert's car pass before lunch she gets up from her desk and rushes out. She reaches Robert as he is parking.

'Jenny has got into a bit of trouble,' she says, catching her breath.

'What?'

'I took the call.' She suggests that they walk to the Black Hat for a drink – she wants to talk, to find a way to air her worries – but Robert refuses. He hasn't seen Agnes for forty-eight hours and he doesn't welcome another delay.

So Elizabeth tells him what the school told her. She adds that she took Jenny for lunch in Peterborough so they could talk about what happened. 'I didn't get far with her. She seems very angry. Angry at Graeme, angry at Agnes, angry at everyone.'

'Agnes?' says Robert. He takes a step away from Elizabeth, waves his hand across his shoulder as though brushing dandruff away. 'There must be some explanation. That's not like Jenny.' He sees his wife standing in the window of the sitting room, watching. She looks as though she has been there for some time. He lifts his hand in greeting but Agnes doesn't react; it's as though she stares beyond and through him. Distracted, he turns back to Elizabeth who has been trying to find a way to voice her suspicions. Of course she can't do it, there is no way she can say to Robert what she thinks. She feels bowed by the weight of what she is not saying.

'Robert, I – I don't know what you think, but Graeme . . . Agnes and Graeme . . .'

'Oh Christ, does Graeme know about this? I can just imagine how he must have reacted.' He grabs his bag from the backseat and heads toward the house.

'Robert,' says Elizabeth, 'I think we had better . . .'

Robert turns abruptly, annoyed. He starts to speak, thinks better of it. He clears his throat. 'Thank you for your help Elizabeth. It was good of you to pick up Jenny from school and take her out for lunch. I'm back now. I'll deal with it. It's my family.' As he walks toward the house the door swings open. Elizabeth, who hasn't quite given up yet, glimpses Agnes's face, sees Robert's pace quicken. She stays for long enough to see them embrace.

Robert buries his face in his wife's neck and breathes in deeply. 'Oh God,' he says, 'it's been torture. I hate being away.'

Agnes takes his hand and places it on her breast. Robert's love for her fills the house, it doesn't leave room for anyone else, not even Jenny. 'Let's go upstairs,' Agnes says and she turns and moves quickly. Robert chases after her, happy.

In their bedroom there are two new galvanized steel buckets on the floor, catching the drips. Robert swears when he sees them. Agnes shrugs. 'Derek Hill,' says Robert, 'our saviour Derek Hill is starting work on Monday.'

As they take off their clothes they can both see their breath on the chill air of the afternoon. 'Come here,' says Robert, pulling Agnes to him, 'let me show you how much I love you.' Agnes smiles and they are away.

They resurface an hour later. Robert feels restored, as though he's got his head back on straight. He can deal with whatever comes his way. 'Tell me what happened.' His voice is steady.

'I'm not sure. Some kind of trouble – Jenny swore at a teacher. Apparently the school phoned and Elizabeth answered. I don't know what she was doing here – none of us were in the house at the time.'

'The back door is always open.'

'Yes but –' Agnes gives Robert a hard look. 'She took it upon herself to go to the school and get Jenny. She brought her home several hours later, at the end of the afternoon – we were completely unaware of what had happened. Graeme and I were out at the cottages – Elizabeth came and found us. Graeme didn't react well to the news. I think Elizabeth's involvement made it worse for him. He didn't handle Jenny particularly well.'

'He didn't?'

'No. He hit her.'

'Oh shit.' Robert sighs. He rises from the bed and begins to dress. 'He didn't ask to hear her side of the story.'

'It's not the first time.'

'What do you mean?'

'Well, he has a short fuse. It's what he does. You know what he's like. He lashes out. He takes things very hard, and he lashes out. It's unusual for it to happen with Jenny, but we've all been subject to it at some time or another. I expect you will be eventually.'

Agnes snorts. 'He wouldn't hit me.'

Robert considers. 'No, I expect you're right. He's just – well, I don't want to make excuses for him, but – how did Jenny react?'

'How do you think? He hit her. She was devastated. I'm worried about her Robert. I think she –' Agnes pauses. 'It seems to me that she's in the grip of all kinds of delusions – god knows what she'll come out with next.'

'She's a teenager.'

'And that makes it all right?'

'No, of course not, but she's not an adult. I think sometimes we expect too much of her. She's just a child, really.'

'She's obsessed with sex.'

'What do you mean?'

'She sees everything and everyone in terms of sex. She thinks I'm having an affair with Graeme.'

'What?' Robert stops typing his shoelace. Agnes is standing in front of the mirror running her hands through her hair. She speaks to Robert's reflection.

'I'm guessing. But it was something she said to me yesterday. She seems to have got it into her head that Graeme and I are sleeping together.'

Robert stands. 'How did she get that idea?'

Agnes turns. 'I know, it's ludicrous, but it's the kind of thing she's been coming out with lately.'

'God,' says Robert, 'that's – well – sick.'

'I know,' says Agnes, 'revolting. And I'm unhappy about Elizabeth – about Elizabeth's influence on Jenny.' Agnes moves toward Robert and puts her arms around him. With a kiss she dispels the picture forming in his mind – Agnes and Graeme.

'What should we do?' he asks.

'We should be patient with her. We should be nice to her. We should let her get out with her friends a bit more.'

Robert strokes Agnes's glossy hair. 'You're right. You're absolutely right. I guess I've been neglecting her lately – it's easy to assume she's fine. I'll make more of an effort.'

'And tell Graeme to keep his hands to himself.'

'What?'

'Tell Graeme that next time he wants to hit her, he should pick on someone his own size.'

'Like me?'

Agnes laughs. 'Yeah, like you.'

That night Robert stands outside Jenny's door. It's nine o'clock, Jenny had refused to come down for dinner earlier. He wants to check on her. He knocks. No answer. Knocks more loudly. Still no reply. He grabs the handle and opens the door. It is dark. He turns on the light.

Jenny is in front of the window, her back to Robert. The curtains are open, her head lists to one side at a peculiar angle, her arms dangle lifelessly. Robert realizes she is too high up, her feet can't be touching the floor. My god, he thinks, she's hung herself. He rushes forward into the room.

She turns and looks at him. Now he can see that she is standing on a stool, looking down into the garden. 'Christ Jenny,' he says 'what are you doing?'

'Have you come to tell me off as well?' She steps down.

'No, no, of course not. I meant what are you doing standing like that in front of the window?'

Jenny gives Robert a long look, he feels her appraising him. 'Watching,' she says.

'Watching for what?'

She shakes her head. 'Nothing.' Jenny steps forward, gives her brother a hug. She has decided she can't tell him she saw Graeme and Agnes. She doesn't want to have to be the one to tell him, not yet. She thinks he probably wouldn't believe her anyway.

Robert rumples Jenny's hair. 'If there's anything I can do,' he says, 'just come and talk to me.'

'Okay.'

'Are you all right?'

'Yes,' she says, 'I'm fine. Really.'

At school, Jenny does what is required of her. She gives a written apology to Mr McKay. He thanks her but he still feels hurt; he went out and got drunk last night and his head is pounding. Jenny's words hit home; he hasn't had a girlfriend for ages. Jenny apologizes to the Headteacher, she catches up with the work she missed, she is polite, she is meek. The other students watch her warily, half-hoping for another outburst. They look around the classroom, speculating. What will happen next, they wonder, if anything?

Robert is back home, working, Martin is in his chair, Karen is off doing the food shopping with Francis while Andrew is at nursery. Graeme tracks down Agnes in the house. She has watched him approach, trekking in from the field. She knows he is heading her way.

He opens the bedroom door. Agnes is seated in front of the mirror, waiting for her nail polish to dry.

Graeme sits down on the bed.

After a while, Agnes, her hands raised, her fingers spread limply, turns to face him. 'Yes?' she says.

Graeme stands without speaking. He walks toward her and stops right in front of her.

'Yes?'

He grabs her by the wrist and pulls her up. He pushes her against the table, knocking over pots of cream, bottles of perfume. The nail polish, cap off, tips and begins to spread. He fumbles with one hand, his trousers, hers; she doesn't help him, she keeps her hands in the air, her fingers relaxed and spread. He releases the buttons and zippers and cloth, pushing. He mumbles, 'Oh Christ, I want you so much, I want you, I want you.' While he is at it, Agnes looks at her nails. He knows she isn't into it – that frustrates him and makes him even more excited.

Graeme takes his pleasure quickly. Agnes's nails are shiny and dark. When he finishes he pulls away, breathing heavily, leaning hard on his cane. Agnes slides down off the table, adjusting her clothes. She can smell the spilt polish, she knows it has leaked onto her trousers, her skin. She doesn't do anything about it for the time being. Graeme is looking at her, his eyes wide, slightly watery, he is overcome by a spasm of post-coital gratitude, guilt and grief. Agnes snarls, she snarls, and he sees her eyes flash black before returning, in a blink, to green. With one neat movement she kicks away Graeme's cane. His face registers surprise as his leg buckles and he falls massively to the floor.

She stands over him. He looks up and thinks she's like the Wicked Witch of the West.

'That's it,' she says calmly. 'You aren't getting any more. Get up,' she says, and she points at the door.

Graeme's heart seizes up; he stops breathing. In that moment he feels lost, utterly lost, as though his life has ended, is no longer worth living. And he's been waiting, he knows he's been waiting for this to happen, for Agnes to say these words. He's lying on the floor and his knee and hip are aching and his humiliation is complete, Agnes has completed it for him.

She moves away and leaves the room without saying anything more. He rolls over and draws himself up onto his hands and knees. Grabs his cane and uses the end of the bed to lever himself up to standing. As he walks his leg drags badly. Downstairs he can hear Agnes in the kitchen with Karen and Francis, they are laughing as they unpack the shopping. He slips out the front door of the house, closing it quietly.

'You stink of nail polish,' says Karen.

'Do I?' asks Agnes, blandly. 'Must have spilt it on myself.' She smiles. 'Did you know that Graeme hit Jenny the other day? When he found out what had happened in school.'

'He did? No one tells me anything.'

'I'm telling you now. It was very brutal of him.' With that, Agnes walks out the back door. Karen sits down abruptly. Francis demands a biscuit; she hands one over without thinking. He runs out of the room before she can change her mind.

Karen talks to Jenny

That evening Karen knocks on the door of Jenny's room. Softly at first, then more loudly when, as usual, there is no reply.

Jenny could tell it was Karen coming along the corridor, she recognizes her soft step; she thinks, Karen's got her sneakers on, she never wears high heels, not like Agnes. She no longer knows how to feel about this – is it good that Karen wears canvas sneakers that she buys in Woolworth's in Peterborough, not kitten heels from Gucci? She glances at the small pile of *Vogue* she has stacked beside her bed, gifts from Agnes. Suddenly she feels nauseated.

'Hello?' she says, when Karen knocks again.

'It's me.'

I know that, thinks Jenny.

'Can I come in?'

'All right,' Jenny sighs, world-weary.

Karen sticks her head round the door and smiles nervously. She comes in and closes the door behind her. She stands awkwardly, waiting.

Jenny is surprised to see Karen looking so unsteady. 'Are you okay?' she asks, suddenly concerned.

Karen laughs. 'That what I was going to ask you.' She comes over and sits next to Jenny on the bed.

'Oh,' says Jenny, sullen again, 'of course I'm all right. I'm fine. Why does everyone want to know if I'm all right?'

'Well, you –'

'I know what I did. I don't want to talk about it.'

'Okay.'

They sit in silence.

Karen speaks. 'Graeme didn't mean to hit you.'

'What?' Jenny gives Karen a look of contempt, then turns away. She gets up and looks out the window, into the night.

'He didn't mean –'

'Why are you making excuses for him?'

'I'm not – I –'

'Of course he meant it.' Jenny turns around, glaring. 'And so what? I don't care if he hits me. He hits everyone. That's what he's like. I don't know why you stay married to him.' It dawns on Jenny now that she could tell Karen what she knows, she could tell Karen what she saw.

'I love him,' Karen says.

'Yes,' says Jenny, and she feels as though she sees her sister-in-law for the first time. Karen loves Graeme; it's pathetic. Jenny knows now that she won't say it, she won't tell Karen, like she didn't tell Robert. She can't. 'You can go now,' Jenny says, heavy with knowledge. Karen stands slowly, as though she has more to say but can't find the words, and suddenly Jenny is full of regret, looking at Karen, wishing they were closer, that they could confide in one another. And Karen looks at Jenny and feels that same regret, tinged with guilt; Karen thinks, I haven't been anything like a mother to her.

'Good-night Jenny,' says Karen.

'Good-night,' replies Jenny.

Martin talks to Agnes

Graeme doesn't go to the pub, he spends the evening wandering the estate. He careers through the dark from cottage to wood to field, boiling. He tells himself he is glad it has ended with Agnes; part of him wanted to end the deceit. Although he is used to lying to Karen, to cutting away from her without explanation, there is a part of him that longs to stop. And he is always about to stop, he is always about to make good. Tomorrow. Or the next day. But with Agnes he has had no thought of finishing, no thought of reining himself in, no thought of Karen and what she might think. So now that Agnes has ended it, he tries to conjure up a feeling of blunt satisfaction. He tries to convince himself he engineered the break. It isn't working. She has got him; he feels as though she has taken his soul away.

There are guests staying in one of the cottages, Graeme remembers just as he is about to try the door. He was opposed to these holiday cottages when Robert first came up with the idea but now he is glad they are there. Somewhere for him to escape to, at least in the low season, somewhere for him to be on his own. Somewhere for him to be with Agnes. Well, he says to himself, we won't be coming out here anymore. Not Agnes. Not me. He thinks these words, he runs them by, but he can't catch their meaning.

He walks up and down in front of the cottages until he becomes aware of someone watching him through the curtains. He gives a jaunty wave and hares off once again, over the field.

He tramps across the gravel on his way up the drive, on his way to the pub. Light flows out from the sitting room and he stops short.

Agnes is sitting in the window. Next to her is Martin in his wheelchair. Agnes is talking with great animation, using her hands, gesticulating, smiling. Graeme stares at her. Her hair frames her pale face; she is lovely. She is talking, and she is laughing. Then Graeme notices Martin. His father is responding. His father, who hasn't spoken for years, he is talking to Agnes, he is smiling, he raises his hand to make a point – a forgotten and familiar gesture – and he is laughing. He is laughing. They are both laughing and smiling.

Graeme spins across the drive to the house, lurching through the front door. He moves as quickly as his leg will take him, across the dark foyer to the door of the sitting room. He puts his hand on the doorknob and it feels hot and he twists it and flings the door open. Martin sits alone in the window, alone in his wheelchair, blanket over his knees. There is no sign of Agnes. Graeme rushes across the room. 'Daddy,' he says, 'daddy,' and he drops his cane and bends down awkwardly and takes Martin by the hands. 'Talk to me. Talk to me.' Martin stays as he is, his face blank, his gaze directed somewhere to the left of Graeme's shoulder. He does not respond to his son's entreaties. His hands are cool and he is perfectly still, as always. Graeme knows now that he hasn't spoken, won't speak, but he persists. 'Tell me what she was saying. What was Agnes saying? What were you talking about? Daddy?'

Karen is in the doorway. 'Graeme?'

He stands abruptly, his voice catching in his throat. 'I saw him talking to Agnes.'

'She's always talking to him, god knows what she finds to say –'

'No. I saw him talking to her, he was laughing, he was smiling, he was –'

Karen moves across the room swiftly and draws Graeme near to her. 'Sweetheart,' she says, drawing his head down to her shoulder.

'All these years,' Graeme whispers, 'all these years without speaking. Where has he gone, Karen? Where is he?'

'Graeme, shh, shh, be quiet. You know he doesn't . . . you know he can't . . .' She walks him over to the settee. 'Come here,' Karen says, and she takes him into her arms like a child.

'Karen,' Graeme whispers, his head on her breast, his voice catching. He feels everything narrowing in on him. 'I'm sorry.'

'It's all right, shh, it's okay.' Karen thinks he's apologizing for his outburst. She hoards these shards of Graeme and his troubles, as though once she finds all the pieces she'll be able to mend something, put it back together again. She turns and looks at Martin, he is looking at them, staring, but she knows that's a trick of the light.

Later, in the night, Karen is jolted awake. She is thinking about Agnes and Martin. Agnes with a cigarette in her mouth, passing it to Martin. Martin and Agnes in the sitting room talking. Martin . . . Just then, Graeme rolls over. He's asleep, but he's talking. 'Agnes,' he says, loudly and clearly, 'Agnes.' In a flash Karen knows about Graeme and Agnes, in a flash she sees what has been happening.

Elizabeth

I knew Robert didn't want to talk to me. I knew he was beginning to feel my involvement with his family had moved beyond interested and toward meddling. But I couldn't stop myself. I had to talk to him. I told myself that if my suspicions were correct, I had to do something to prevent him from being hurt. I knew my motives were questionable. I didn't care.

The next day I left work early and went round to the Throckmorton house. I let myself in through the back door. Robert was in his office, catching up with paperwork. I was relieved to find him alone.

'Listen,' I said, full of purpose. 'How are you – how are you and Agnes getting on these days?'

'What?' Robert was annoyed again. I could hear it. He didn't want to see me. 'Thank you for picking up Jenny the other day,' he said, forcing a smile. 'I'm dealing with it.'

'I'm not worried about that,' I said, 'about school. I'm worried about you.'

'Me?'

'Yes, you.' I took a breath. I knew there was a good chance I'd humiliate myself, whatever I said. 'Graeme –'

Robert interrupted. 'So his reaction was a little harsh. Jenny knows how to take him, we all do. We find ignoring him works best.'

'That's just it. What if he relies on that? What if . . .' I looked around for somewhere to sit, feeling defeated before I'd even begun.

'Come on Elizabeth, I can't read your mind.'

'It's something that Jenny said the other day when I took her out for lunch. She told me that she finds Graeme disgusting, that all he ever thinks about is sex. And fucking. That's what she said. Sex and fucking.'

'Really?' Robert put down his pen. At last I had his attention.

'I thought it was odd. I thought, well, I thought it was inappropriate. It made me wonder, it made me wonder if perhaps, well, something . . . something wrong was happening with Graeme . . .'

'Something wrong?'

'Yes, if Graeme and Agnes . . .'

Robert started to laugh.

'What?' I asked, 'what's so funny?'

'I see,' he said nodding, 'okay. This makes sense now. You've got it completely wrong.'

'What?'

'Jenny thinks that Agnes and Graeme are having an affair.' Robert laughed again. 'Agnes told me.'

'Oh,' I said, and I felt like I'd been pushed back in my seat. It wasn't true then.

'Yes, it's silly, well, not silly. But that would explain what she said to you, wouldn't it? If she thinks that Graeme's the kind of dirty dog who would have it off with his own sister-in-law, well, no wonder she's disgusted.' Robert laughed once more, and stopped abruptly. 'It's the kind of thing I might have imagined when I was her age.' He gave me a look that made me think about what we had been like as teenagers. Jenny was a paragon of good behaviour. Into witchcraft perhaps, paranoid about her new sister-in-law, but nothing more sinister – or adventurous – than that.

'You should stop worrying,' Robert said. 'She'll be fine.'

And maybe he was right. Standing there next to him I wanted to believe him. For a long moment I did.

Robert

When I came home from London it was as though everything had changed. I couldn't say exactly what was different, there was nothing definite, apart from what had happened to Jenny, and I found that inexplicable, along with her allegations about Graeme and Agnes. I was completely baffled. Agnes was the same, if anything things were even better with her than before, sharper, sexier. But she had hardened her dislike of Elizabeth; she felt my old friend was prying. So did I, really. And Graeme, well, Graeme seemed to be having some kind of brain fever, he was all over the place. At the time I couldn't understand what was happening to him and even thinking back now, I still find it difficult. And Karen was lost. Karen was lost to us already.

But Jenny . . . I see now that it was Jenny I was failing. I found it hard to be her parent and her brother at the same time; I guess I wanted her to be grown-up, to take care of herself like Graeme and I did after our mother died. From the time our father was disabled it had fallen on us to be her parents. Karen was living with us by then and I suppose I assumed that Karen would mother Jenny, although truth be told, I didn't think about it all that much. I was confident we could stay together as a family, in the house, as though the house itself would parent us. And we did stay together, and we did get by, and we were a happy household. And Agnes only added to my joy.

But after Elizabeth paid her call and told me her suspicions about Graeme and Agnes I was cross with Jenny. And her stories. I laughed it off in front of Elizabeth, but I was angry. When my sister came home from school I cornered her outside her bedroom.

'Agnes and Elizabeth tell me you've been telling stories,' I said.

'What?' Her eyes narrowed.

'Agnes tells me that you've accused her and Graeme of having an affair. Elizabeth says you said virtually the same thing to her.'

'She is.' I could see Jenny's hands were clenched into fists. Colour was rising in her cheeks.

'She is what?'

'Having an aff–' She stumbled over the words.

'Yes?' I said, attempting to be patient, understanding.

'I wasn't going to tell you. I saw –'

'You saw nothing. Out of the blue you accuse Agnes of having it off with Graeme. You've got no right to –'

'I did not.' Jenny was angry. 'I never accused Agnes of anything.'

'Oh, so now you deny it. It's not true then?'

'I saw them,' Jenny said coldly. I could see she was trying to salvage her dignity. 'She's only saying it because she knows I saw them fucking.'

I was shocked. I tried not to show it. 'I don't believe you.'

'Fine. Don't believe me then. See if I care.' Jenny turned and walked away, leaving me standing in the hallway.

And I didn't believe her. Agnes would never do that to me. Graeme would not do that to me. They would not. What had got into Jenny?

When the builder Derek Hill finally turned up on the following Monday morning he declared our house a disaster site. He wasn't joking – he threatened to call in Health and Safety. He said that the whole structural fabric of the old wing of the house had been undermined, primarily by neglect, although the work of the last set of builders hadn't helped any. I'd been hoping that his crew would simply move in and take over where the last lot had left off and that Agnes and I would finally get our own bathroom and sitting room. But according to him the costs had sky-rocketed well beyond all previous estimates. The wing needed a new roof, all the structural supports – joists, beams – should be replaced, new wiring, new plumbing . . . he said it would be best if we could think of that part of the house as just a shell. It would have to be taken apart and put back together again, including what was left of the precious plaster ceiling in the room downstairs.

He gave me a quote. There was no way that we could afford it, especially not this time of year. I was still paying off the previous workmen; I'd had to struggle to prevent them from suing. I could pay Derek Hill to shore things up and prevent the wing from collapsing, but that was it. He said Agnes and I had to move out of our room, it was too dangerous, both the roof and the floor could go at any time. I would have ignored him but, as though to demonstrate, half the ceiling in our bedroom collapsed that evening while we were downstairs eating.

So Agnes and I moved into what was my old bedroom, back on the same side of the house as everyone else. There wasn't time to redecorate. In my old bedroom I felt like a boy again; contrary to how that might sound, it was not a good feeling. And Agnes wasn't happy. She didn't show it, she hid it well, but I could tell she was dismayed.

Lolly makes a discovery

Lolly is doing a research project for History. T-top-secret, she tells everybody. She has got permission from the Headteacher to use the university library at Cambridge to do her research. Her mother drives her in after school once a week.

'Lolly,' Jenny whispers during class. 'What are you doing?'

'I'm not telling.'

'Come on,' Jenny wheedles, 'you can tell me. You owe me one.'

Lolly looks at Jenny, unaware of owing her anything. Then she thinks of Jenny's confrontation with Mr McKay, a highlight in recent school memory. 'Okay,' she says. 'Remember I told you there was a story, a really terrible story, somehow connected to this village?'

Jenny pales. Her face shuts down. Her eyes flicker. 'You mean witches?' Jenny hasn't told Lolly about seeing Agnes fly, even though she knows it's the thing Lolly would most love to hear. It's too much, she thinks, it will sound daft, like she's making it up. She can't tell anybody.

'Yeah. That's what I'm researching.'

'Oh,' says Jenny. She blinks. 'Witches and Warboys.'

'You got it,' says Lolly. 'That's right. I'll tell you about it later.'

After school Lolly waits for Jenny behind a tree. When Jenny walks by, Lolly leaps out, screeching. Jenny screams herself rigid, and they both laugh hysterically. Lolly links her arm through Jenny's. 'Guess what,' she says.

'What?' Jenny expects news about some boy or another Lolly is pursuing.

'I found out what happened. You won't believe it. It's so cool.'

'What?' asks Jenny, suddenly frightened.

'Your aunt – Agnes –'

'She's not my aunt. She's my sister-in-law.'

'Oh yeah. Anyway, she's called Agnes Samuel, isn't she?'

'Yes,' Jenny thinks she doesn't want to hear what Lolly has to say.

'Well, four hundred years ago more or less – 1593 – three people from Warboys were hung for witchcraft. An entire family, mum, dad, and their daughter. Guess what their names were.'

'What?' Jenny speaks sharply. She doesn't want to guess.

'Alice Samuel. John Samuel. And Agnes Samuel.' Lolly looks at Jenny. Jenny doesn't react. 'Agnes Samuel was their daughter. They were accused of witchcraft by – get this – Robert Throckmorton.' Lolly claps her hands together and jumps in the air with glee. 'That's right! Robert Throckmorton! Isn't that amazing?'

'Why were they accused?' Jenny has stopped walking.

'Why? For bewitching his children, that's why. For causing his children to have terrible fits. The Samuels were hung – hanged,' she shakes her head, 'and their bodies were stripped naked for public viewing!'

Jenny closes her eyes. She skips a beat. 'So what,' she says, hedging, defensive.

'So what? So your sister-in-law is descended from a witch, that's what. And she's married the man descended from her accuser and –'

'She can't be descended from them. They're all dead. There was no one to be descended from.'

'Oh,' says Lolly, taken aback by Jenny's logic. 'Oh. Well then,' she pauses, and almost levitates with excitement as she works it out, 'Well then, she IS a witch. She must be! She's come back. She's come back from the dead, from an unmarked grave, to get her revenge.'

'Lolly,' says Jenny, fear in her voice, 'shut up.'

'But it's fantastic!' says Lolly.

'Just shut up, will you, just fucking shut up.'

'Oh,' says Lolly, wounded. 'O – okay. I j–just thought –' but Jenny has fled.

Jenny runs all the way home and up to her room. She locks the door and refuses dinner. She lies on her bed and stares at the ceiling. She thinks about her mother, tries to conjure her from photographs, but she can't see her. She's never been able to see her. Why are you dead, she asks, why did you leave me?

That night she sleeps fitfully. She wakes around midnight and can hear the voices of Robert and Agnes in her brother's old bedroom on the other side of the wall. Later still she wakes again, to the sound of banging and moaning. She gets up and looks out the window, alarmed. Then she realizes that what she is hearing is Robert and Agnes having sex, the bedstead, or someone's head, rhythmically hitting the wall. It's as though she can smell it – them. She sees Agnes and Graeme on the couch and is overwhelmed by disgust. She climbs back into bed and pulls the cover over her head, jamming her fists over her ears.

Karen opens the closet

Evening. The boys are asleep. Graeme is nowhere. Agnes and Robert are at the Black Hat. Jenny is in her room studying. Martin lies on his back in bed, his eyes open. Karen is tidying the bedroom she shares with Graeme, the bedroom she has shared with Graeme since she was nineteen. Since her revelation about Graeme and Agnes she has done nothing, said nothing. She stands at the far end of the bed straightening the patchwork quilt Mrs T. made for Graeme years ago. She plumps the pillows, opens the wardrobe, puts the shoes in the shoe rack one at a time. Footles about looking for her old trainers. Her hand moves against the dry-cleaner's plastic hanging there.

She empties Graeme's side of the closet onto the bed. Jackets, trousers, shirts, these are clothes she knows, clothes she has laundered. She hauls out the dry-cleaning bag, lifts the plastic away from the shoulders of the suit.

Karen knows Graeme splashes out from time to time, she knows he needs to, he needs to have beautiful things. She remembers how, a long time ago, he used to take great pride in his uniform, always after her to polish his shoes, starch his shirts. She knows he buys things they can't afford and she turns a blind eye – it makes him happy, he is so rarely happy these days. They can handle the debt, they always handle the debt somehow.

But this suit is different. She can tell right away. She can see it is well-made. She notices the label. When she lifts the suit to examine it more closely, a waft of perfume drifts up. Karen sniffs the cloth – Agnes.

She sits down on the bed, dry-eyed, breathing evenly. Everyone has something to hide, she thinks. Robert is the father of my children; we all pretend that's not the case. Agnes hates us but she convinces us of her love. And Graeme? Well, my husband hides a lot – his failed career, his infertility, his infidelity, his designer suit. It keeps him very busy.

And me. Karen sighs and brushes her hair away from her face. I hide from the fact that I no longer love Graeme. I hide from the fact that my marriage is a dead and rotting thing.

Elizabeth

I was in the Black Hat on my own one evening. I had gone in hope of finding Marlene and Geoff – they hadn't been at home when I rang earlier. Marlene was nearly four months pregnant and she and Geoff had vowed to see every movie ever made before the baby arrived, and so I wasn't surprised when they weren't at the pub either. I sat at the bar on my own for a little while, talking to Lolita. I moved to a table by the fire. After a while the door opened, and Karen came in.

It was very unusual to see Karen Throckmorton in the Black Hat, and even more unusual to see her there on her own. I'd known her for years but when she walked in that evening I realized I didn't know her at all. We'd never had a proper conversation – on our own, without the commotion of her household surrounding us. I resolved to try and change this; perhaps Karen could be my Throckmorton ally, my friend. She was probably not all that keen on Agnes herself, even if she didn't suspect the affair. I beckoned her over and offered to buy her a drink. It was silly of me to imagine I could make up for all those years in one evening.

'Agnes and Robert are at home with the children,' she said, apologetically. 'I thought I'd get out for a while.' She looked harassed, nervous.

'It's good to see you.'

'Thanks. Cheers.' She raised her glass.

'How are the boys?'

'Oh, they're fine.' She gave a fond and trampled smile.

'And yourself? Graeme?'

She looked at me, around the pub, evaluating the situation. 'You know us pretty well, don't you Elizabeth.'

'I guess . . . I –'

'You've been Robert's friend for a long time, haven't you?'

'Yes.'

She took a long swallow of her drink. 'I always thought he'd marry you.'

I turned toward the fire.

'He should have married you.'

I wasn't comfortable with the conversation. And yet, when I think on it now, there was little else I'd rather have discussed with Karen. 'I don't know, he seems happy –'

She leaned forward, silencing me. 'I should never have married Graeme.' With that, she got up and fetched another drink for herself, trading pleasantries with Jim Drury. She sat down again – she was still wearing her coat – and carried on from where she'd left off. 'I should never have married Graeme Throckmorton. That's what my mother said. But, it was like . . . I don't know, it was like we were fated. I couldn't avoid it – him. I couldn't alter the path we were taking. I loved him.'

I couldn't believe she was saying this to me; I don't think she could quite believe it herself. Her cheeks were very red.

'Are you having . . . difficulties?' I knew about Graeme's previous affairs, everyone did. He had hit on every woman in Warboys, even me. And suddenly, I wanted Karen to be concerned with that alone; I didn't want her to suspect Agnes and Graeme. I wanted her to be spared.

'Difficulties?' she said. 'No, not really. It's quite straightforward. Graeme's having an affair with Agnes.'

For a moment I thought I hadn't heard her properly and must have looked that way. She repeated what she had said.

'How do you know?'

'I just know.'

It had to be true. I wanted it to be true. It meant I was right and that Robert should not have married Agnes. She was like a curse. It set on me then, like I'd stuck my heart in a deep-freeze; I hated Agnes

Samuel. I hated her and everything about her. I hated what she was doing to this family, what she was doing to Robert and Karen.

'What will you do?'

'I don't know,' said Karen, 'I don't know. The terrible thing is that I don't think she even likes him.'

'Does Robert know?'

'Robert?' She looked at me. 'No. I don't think so. Not yet.'

We didn't talk much after that. We sat and looked into the fire. Karen drank steadily. I know it was her life that was devastated, not mine, but I couldn't stop thinking about Robert. About what this would mean to him. And I'll admit that I felt a little hope spring up, a little hope for my own future. Perhaps Robert would leave Agnes. Perhaps Robert would be free.

After Karen left – I could see she was drunk and feeling it – I sat on my own for a while. Then Geraldine Andley approached me. We hadn't spoken for a long time. On the street and in the pub we exchanged greetings but nothing more than that. I hoped she wasn't harbouring a grudge left over from Robert's thirtieth. I was pleased that she made an overture toward me; tonight was a night for overtures. Until I heard what she had to say.

'What do you think of her then?' Geraldine looked around furtively.

'Who, Karen?'

'No. That Agnes. Agnes Samuel.'

No one ever called Agnes by her married name.

'Robert's happy.'

'You're avoiding my question.'

I didn't want to talk about this with Geraldine. 'She's lovely.'

Geraldine frowned. 'I feel that I know her.'

'Well, she can be very personable.'

'No, not like that. I mean really know her. We've met before.'

'When?'

'In the past.'

Ah. Geraldine's 'other' lives. I nodded. I didn't want to encourage her, but I wasn't ready to go home yet, back to my chilly, silent cottage.

'Agnes Samuel. It rings a bell. I don't know. I've got to do some more –' She paused, unsure of her words.

'Some more what, Geraldine?'

'I'll find it – her,' she said. 'Just wait.'

Karen drinks as much as Graeme

Graeme is drinking. He is at home, in the sitting room, drinking. Agnes and Robert are putting the boys to bed – his own sons – Agnes and Robert are taking care of them. Karen asked them to baby-sit, not him, as if he can't be relied upon to take care of his own boys. Karen said she wanted to go out for a drink, alone.

Graeme gets another beer out of the fridge. The kitchen is a mess, dirty dishes, pots and pans left out after dinner. Martin sits next to the window, Graeme speaks to him gently. 'Come on dad,' he says, 'let's get you into bed.' It's been a long time since he has put Martin to bed and he is gentle and loving as though to prove to himself he can be, as though providing insurance against what might come next.

His father in his pyjamas, tucked up, his face turned toward the wall, Graeme goes back to his beer. He gets out the whiskey and pours himself a glass. Before he drinks it he goes upstairs to check on the boys. The nightlight illuminates their room eerily, the stuffed animals cast dark awkward shadows. They are both sleeping soundly, Andrew small in his big boy's bed, Francis spread-eagled in his cot.

Graeme pauses by the window. He looks out into the moonless black night. Across the fields are the frozen fens, flat and low all the way to Norfolk. As always, he can hear the wind. He can hear other sounds as well, after a few moments he recognizes the voices – Agnes and Robert. Murmuring, talking, warm and excluding. He stops outside Robert's old bedroom and leans his body against the wall, his forehead touching the cool paintwork. He decides that what he hears is the sound of love-making and he presses himself against the wall with a surge of passion and frustration. He pushes his hand down into his trousers and takes hold of himself. His breath is speedy and laboured and beads of beery sweat break out across his forehead.

The door opens suddenly and Agnes steps out of the room. She is fully dressed. She looks at Graeme calmly, she sees what he is doing, she is unsurprised and uninterested. She shuts the door behind herself and goes down the corridor to the bathroom.

Graeme slumps against the wall. He removes his hand from his trousers and draws a deep breath. He walks toward the stairs. As he passes the bathroom he hears Agnes say, 'Good-night Graeme. Sweet dreams.'

Back in the sitting room, he goes to work on the whisky.

Karen is coming home, she is weaving down the lane, she feels giddy and hilarious and tearful. Marlene and Geoff drive by, catching her in their headlights, and Karen glimpses Marlene's face. 'Hello,' she calls out when the car is already well past, 'Good-bye.' She is glad to have told Elizabeth about Graeme and Agnes and she is sorry that Elizabeth now knows. She wants to tell everyone, she wants no one to know; she wants to hide and display her humiliation.

She stands in the drive and feels inspired to sing her favourite song. 'It's a little bit funny . . .' She sings loudly and badly and makes herself laugh, she hasn't done anything like this for so long. She starts over. 'It's a little bit funny . . .' Her singing wakes Andrew in his bedroom upstairs. He sits up and rubs his eyes.

Karen enters the house through the front door and goes straight into the sitting room. Graeme is sitting in the half-light. He has not lit the fire, he is alone with the bottle of whisky, Agnes's bottle of whisky.

'You've been gone a long time,' he says.

'Graeme,' says Karen, 'it's a little bit funny –'

'You've been drinking.'

'I've been to the fucking pub, haven't I? What else do you expect me to do there?' Karen never swears. Graeme gets to his feet.

'You've had a lot to drink.'

'Yes, well, I've had a lot to think about.'

Graeme walks toward Karen slowly. Karen backs toward the fireplace at the same pace.

'I've been thinking about you,' she says, her tone still aggressive.

'Oh yeah?'

'I've been thinking about our marriage.'

'Yes?' Graeme comes forward, Karen backs away.

'You've been –' she pauses, licks her lips, her mouth has gone dry. She wants to stop moving backward, but she doesn't want Graeme too near. She takes a breath, she knows what she's going to say. 'You've been screwing Agnes, haven't you?'

'Screwing? Karen,' he chides, shaking his head, 'not me.'

'Stop lying,' her voice is sliding up the scale.

'Lying?'

'You've been having an affair with Agnes,' she says.

'Not me.'

'You bastard,' she is shouting now, high-pitched, 'why can't you just admit it? Do you have to lie as well as be unfaithful?' She is backing up, she is nearing the hearth of the fireplace. Graeme is moving closer and closer. 'You're fucking your own sister-in-law,' she flings the words at him.

'I am NOT,' he roars, and he raises his hands and, throwing his weight – six foot two inches, two hundred pounds – gives Karen a heavy, hard shove.

Karen grunts on impact, air forced from her lungs. Her heel strikes the hearth. She loses her balance and, unable to grab hold of anything, falls backward. Graeme lurches forward, to catch her or push her again, he isn't sure. His fist dislodges the big ceramic vase from where it stands on the mantelpiece.

Karen hits her head on the pitiless marble surround and crumples to one side of the hearth, away from Graeme who is reaching down to her, to strike her or help her, she isn't sure. The vase is falling from the mantelpiece, neither of them sees it, it falls and falls and then it hits Karen on the head, crack, and her skull smacks the stone hearth. There is a terrible shattering. Her head, her neck.

Graeme is on his knees. He brushes the broken pieces of ceramic away from Karen's face, slowly, carefully, like an archaeologist at a dig. He gathers his wife into his arms, one limb at a time. She is limp and bleeding. It takes him a moment to realize that she is dead.

Andrew is standing in the door of the sitting room. He has seen Mummy fall and Daddy go forward. He is silent, as if he recognizes the enormity of what is happening. Agnes is directly behind him. She puts her hands on his shoulders and turns him and as she moves Graeme looks up and their eyes meet. Her expression is odd, she is wearing a little half-smile. She leads Andrew away.

Graeme starts to wail.

Robert

Karen's death was calamitous for us all, but especially Andrew and Francis. They couldn't understand why she was gone, why she wasn't there with them, she had always been there with them.

I was in bed, asleep. Agnes told me later that when she got Andrew into bed he went back to sleep immediately, as though he'd been sleep-walking. She came into our room, woke me and told me to call the police. 'Graeme's pushed her,' she said, 'Karen's dead.' From the moment I heard her words I felt like I knew what had happened; it suddenly felt so inevitable that I was surprised it hadn't happened already. Agnes got into the bed as I got out of it. She smiled at me, lay back, closed her eyes and turned away.

I went down to the sitting room. Graeme was sitting on the settee holding Karen in his arms. She looked small and young in her shirt and jeans; her head was bloody, her hair plastered to her forehead. He was rocking back and forth, a tiny movement, barely perceptible.

Graeme didn't notice I'd come into the room until I was standing right in front of him. 'She died,' he said, 'just like that. People shouldn't die so easily.' He looked down at Karen, pushed a bloody strand of hair away from her eyes.

I didn't cry, in fact I'm ashamed to admit I didn't feel much of anything. It was as though Agnes was occupying my emotions so fully that there wasn't room for anything else. I rang the police, I said there had been an accident. I felt like we were in some dreadful movie. Agnes stayed upstairs; she told me later she had taken a nap. At the time I thought this perfectly normal. She came back down when the police arrived. In her statement she said that she had heard them arguing as she came down the stairs, that she saw him push her, that the vase had been knocked over accidentally. Graeme knew the officers who came to the house, he'd worked with one of them. He told them that they'd had a row, that he had pushed her, that it had been an accident, a terrible mistake.

No charges were laid. At the inquiry her death was ruled accidental. None of us mentioned that Andrew had been a witness to the scene.

Jenny slept through everything. After the police were gone I went upstairs to tell her what had happened. I bent close to her face to wake her up; her breath was sweet like a baby's. She opened her eyes.

'Karen is dead,' I said, immediately regretting my blunt words. 'Karen has passed away.'

The colour drained from Jenny's face. Looking at her made me feel the cold, my fatigue. 'Agnes did it,' she whispered, 'didn't she?'

'No,' I said, annoyed. 'Graeme pushed her. They were arguing. She fell against the mantelpiece. He didn't mean to harm her – he didn't mean for her to fall so hard. He'd –'

She looked at me with wide incomprehension.

'I don't want to be in this house anymore,' she said. 'It isn't safe.'

'What do you mean?' I felt the hair on the back of my neck rise.

'Agnes – it isn't safe, none of us are safe.'

I asked her what she was talking about and she began to blather, nothing she said made any sense. Eventually I got cross and told her she had to listen to me.

'They'd both been drinking. Graeme and Karen. Agnes had nothing to do with it.'

'Is that supposed to explain it?'

'No,' I said, 'listen, I wanted –'

Jenny began to cry. I felt incredibly relieved. At last someone was responding in a way that was normal. I took her in my arms and cried as well. We cried together, Jenny and me, for Karen, for what was happening to our family.

Martin

Martin knows who Agnes is.

Martin knows

Martin Throckmorton has known who Agnes is from the beginning. He recognized her name. Of course he didn't say anything about it – how could he?

He sits there, day in and day out, wheeled first this way, then that way. He doesn't walk, doesn't speak, doesn't give any clues about how he is feeling or thinking, if he is feeling or thinking. They've got used to it, the Throckmortons are used to it, as a family they pride themselves on getting used to it, they can get used to anything. He is part of their lives, Daddy with his blanket on his knees, a benevolent presence, someone to love unquestioningly. His care is onerous, but they shoulder it, Karen shouldered the bulk of it. She is gone now.

No one knows what he sees and doesn't see. No one asks. The doctors are absent, their visits are rare, and he is an old man, even though, in real time, he is in his mid-sixties. No one takes him on directly, confronts him, challenges, teases. They don't dare. It would be cruel. No one knows what he thinks.

Except Agnes. She knows he knows who she is. It's their little secret. He's not telling.

Agnes is a witch and a whore

They are at the church burying Karen; Andrew and Francis throw clods of dirt down onto her coffin and Francis tries to pick up another and turn it into a game. His levity makes everyone feel worse. Robert looks up at the sky; he feels as though the old church is leaning heavily toward him, as though it might collapse and crush him – crush them all – under its stony weight. Agnes slips her arm through his, he is momentarily reassured. Graeme stands behind his two sons, controlled, impenetrable. For a moment Robert thinks his brother looks like a bouncer at a suburban night-club, dark overcoat and puffed up chest. Someone should puncture that man, he thinks angrily. Graeme turns and looks at him and Robert sees his eyes are rimmed with red. He softens. His brother's wife is dead.

Robert has arranged everything; Graeme is incapable. He went through Karen's clothes himself, to try to find something to bury her in. Karen's clothes – Karen didn't have any clothes to speak of. Discovering this, Robert feels a tremendous sense of failure, as though Karen's shabby life was his responsibility. In the end he settles on a dark suit – an ill-fitting suit that he recalls Karen wearing to the wedding. The undertaker has done his best but, in death, Karen looks as neglected as she was in life.

The post-funeral reception at the Throckmorton house is an uncanny recreation of the wedding. Same guests, same vicar, same use of the house and garden. Lolita and Jim Drury provide a scaled down version of the catering, sausage rolls instead of smoked salmon, cheese and biscuits instead of crab vol au vents; they bring the food in before Lolita goes back to open the pub for lunch. There is no marquee and the door of the ballroom is locked, the room unsafe. No teenage waiters, no champagne. Robert lights the fire in the sitting room. Everyone is draped in black. It is a bleak February day.

Graeme is wearing a black suit, a white shirt, a black tie, his hair thick with gel, the lines in his face accentuated, deepening. Marlene Henderson leans on her husband Geoff as she looks at Graeme; she is offended by his handsomeness, it doesn't seem right. She thinks he should take his face away from this place. She is not feeling well and when Elizabeth sheers up to her, hoping to gain a little warmth, wanting her friend's good and sensible company, she prevents her from speaking so that she can speak first.

'I lost the baby,' she says.

'What?'

'I lost the baby.' Geoff Henderson bites his lip and looks away, he doesn't want to hear this conversation. 'We saw Karen walking down the road – I'd been in hospital. I miscarried.'

Elizabeth pulls Marlene to her and hugs her fast. 'Oh Marlene,' she says. She takes Geoff's hand too and makes him look at her. 'I'm so sorry.' She speaks to both of them.

'It – she – it was a little life, not like Karen, but a life . . .' Marlene stops talking. She stares beyond Elizabeth, at the window. Elizabeth turns. Agnes is there, outside the window, staring into the crowded sitting room. Her face – high, at an unnatural height – is framed by the window, that's all that can be seen of her in the dark afternoon. Elizabeth looks at Marlene, and back at the window. That's it – Agnes is gone.

'Did you see her?' asks Elizabeth.

'Who?' says Marlene, but her face is white and full of fear.

Graeme stalks the reception like the uninvited guest. He has scarcely spoken since that night, stayed drunk mostly, leaving Agnes and Robert and Jenny to care for the boys and Martin. Today he is blanched and sober, his brooding over, as though he's been through the options and worked it out. People offer their condolences timidly and he accepts their handshakes. He knows they think he killed her. He stands stiffly beside Karen's parents who can't bring themselves to look at him. Her mother asked to take the children and was upset when Graeme said that they were fine where they were. She thinks that Graeme killed her daughter. She never liked him. She repeats to her husband under her breath, 'I told you so. I told you this would happen. She should not have married him. She should have gone out to work.'

Jenny clings to Robert. She avoids Agnes, she avoids Elizabeth. Part way through the afternoon her friend Lolly arrives, resplendent in black dress and rings, her clothes suitable for once. Jenny draws Robert to one side – he is happy to be drawn, he is tired of mouthing the same phrases over and over, 'It was a shock. A terrible accident. She was a good person. We will make sure the boys are all right. Thank you. Thank you for your offer. Thank you.'

'I'm going upstairs to my room with Lolly. Is that okay?'

Robert is pleased to be asked. He says that's fine.

Andrew and Francis sit under the table where the food is piled. They are wearing their suits, which they find uncomfortable, too small, they have both grown since the wedding. There are no other children present. Their father is busy. They can't find their mummy.

Geraldine Andley is there, Elizabeth wonders if she was invited. She follows Elizabeth around the room, giving off the scent of patchouli. When Elizabeth stops at the drinks table, Geraldine bumps into her.

'I've remembered,' she hisses, low, making sure no one else can hear.

'What?' says Elizabeth.

'I've remembered where I met Agnes Samuel. Before.'

Elizabeth turns, ready to walk away.

'I was at her execution. I saw her hanged.'

Elizabeth's heart drops drown into her belly. 'What?'

'My past life. I was there. Mistress Andley they called me.'

'This is nonsense,' says Elizabeth. 'You're talking rubbish.'

'Witchcraft,' whispers Geraldine, 'witchcraft. She's very dangerous.'

Elizabeth feels angry now and she is shocked at what she feels, unsure who she is protecting, Agnes or Robert. And she is panicked by this allegation; what kind of a world is it where women we don't like are called witches? 'You're jealous,' she says, and it's an effort to keep her voice down. 'You're jealous of Robert and Agnes.'

'It's not me who's jealous,' returns Geraldine. 'I thought I should tell you. I thought you'd want to know. You can ignore what I say. It's your funeral.'

Elizabeth is glad to see Geraldine has the grace to be embarrassed by her turn of phrase.

'What I mean is, I'd watch out for your beloved Robert.' She purses her lips. 'I've nothing more to say.'

Elizabeth turns her back on Geraldine. When she looks around, moments later, she is gone.

Agnes moves from kitchen to sitting room to garden and back again. She doesn't stand still, she doesn't converse with anyone. She dispenses sad smiles and takes people by the arm. They are still warmed by her touch, they are still thrilled by her presence, but now they find her unnerving. There's something strange in her eyes. Her black dress is a little too low-cut, her shawl a little too slinky. The men find her attractive and are suddenly awkward with that. She's American, foreign, too young, too bright, they love her and hate her at the same time. Even Jim Drury finds himself shifting from foot to foot as Agnes passes by. He feels sad, terribly upset, and it isn't until later that he realizes it isn't because of Karen.

Graeme launches himself across the room when he sees Agnes go by, as if he's had enough and has to act. He follows her into the garden. She keeps walking, across the lawn, down to where Karen's rose garden begins.

'Agnes,' he says. From his first word it is clear he has decided to plead. 'Agnes, I need you.'

She keeps walking.

'Don't turn away. Don't – Agnes. I want you. Don't you see? We can be together now. I want you. Don't you see?' He follows behind her, stumbling, his cane catching on the wet grass, sliding, not noticing that they've come full circle and are approaching the house once again. He hadn't realized this was what he was going to say.

Agnes stops abruptly and turns to face him. There are people dotted around the garden, inside the French doors, around the sitting room – they have an audience. Everyone watches Agnes, always, without thinking, they can't help themselves.

Upstairs Jenny and Lolly are chanting. It's a simple chant, something Lolly invented. 'Out out, damn witch, go on, go on; Out out, damn witch, go on, go on . . .' Candles burn, the girls are lying side by side on the floor, feet touching.

'I want you Agnes.' Outside, Graeme is begging. With every 'I' his voice gets louder. 'I love you. I need you.'

Agnes speaks, her voice low but loud enough to carry. 'You're disgusting,' she says, 'you disgust me. You killed her. You killed your wife.'

The party falls silent. The watchers are listening. Robert, who has been talking to Karen's mother, steps toward the French doors to see what is happening.

Graeme has never grovelled before. 'You mustn't push me away, you mustn't –' his voice doubles in volume, trebles.

'You can't tell me what to do,' Agnes says in a near-whisper. 'You killed her,' she says, 'you killed Karen.'

'You don't mourn her,' he says, growing angry, 'you wanted her out of the way. For us . . . for . . .' He tries to take Agnes by the hand.

'Don't touch me,' she hisses.

He snatches her wrist. Infuriated, Agnes attempts to wrench her arm away but he tightens his grip, squeezing. With his other arm he grabs her around the waist. He pulls her body to his in a frantic embrace. 'Agnes,' he shouts angrily, 'Agnes – I –'

Robert springs forward from inside the house, overtaken by fury. He grabs Graeme's shoulder and, as his brother turns toward him, punches him in the face. Immediately Robert grips his own knuckles, his hand stinging. Graeme is stunned. Robert shakes the bones of his hand loose, pulls back, and punches his brother again. Graeme lets go of Agnes. He draws himself together, then hurls himself at Robert, as if liberated by the violence, as if he's been waiting for it to reclaim him. They fall, punching and kicking, onto the grass which quickly becomes mud. In the mêlée it is hard to tell one man from the other.

Agnes watches, composed and static. The guests stay rooted, mesmerized.

Graeme shouts as he fields punches. 'She seduced me. That whore –' With a new fury Robert flips his brother onto his stomach and pushes his face into the mud, silencing him. Graeme struggles to raise his head. He reaches out toward Agnes, snatching at her ankles. She steps away lightly. Robert traps his hand. 'She let me fuck her,' Graeme shouts, his face coated in mud, 'she wanted it.' Robert shoves his face down into the muck again. Graeme bucks as he struggles to breathe. Robert lifts his head up by the hair. 'She fucked me,' Graeme says, looking up at Agnes. In the light cast from the sitting room he sees her eyes go from green to black and back again. 'She's a witch,' he bellows with all his strength. 'I know she is.'

Robert is enraged. He yells 'Shut the fuck up,' and he grinds his brother's face into the dirt once again, using all his weight. Graeme jerks and kicks like an animal.

Suddenly, the brothers stop fighting. Robert allows Graeme to lift his head and take a breath. They stare upward, at the window on the first floor. Jenny is looking down at them, tapping her fingers on the glass, her lips moving. A moment passes. Then she puts her fist through the window; the glass fragments and scatters like confetti. Now they can hear her screaming, 'She's a witch, she's a witch, I know she is, I've seen her.'

Both men look at Agnes. The funeral guests have crowded forward, they have gathered at the French doors, they are spilling out into the garden. Marlene clutches Geoff, the Trevelyans stand together, Jim wishes Lolita had stayed. Elizabeth is on her own, spell-bound. No one speaks.

Agnes pauses. She sighs. She steps confidently toward Robert and helps him to his feet, drawing him to her. She wipes the dirt off his knuckles and lifts his hand to her lips, smearing blood and muck across her cheek. She smiles and touches his face. His look is one of love and that love is palpable, everyone present feels it. 'Agnes,' he says, his voice full of grief, 'Agnes.' She kisses him, and leads him away.

People find their coats and their hats. They begin to leave, no one shows them out, no one thanks them for coming.

Andrew and Francis are under the table.

Martin sits on his own by the fire.

Graeme stays face down in the mud and the cold and the night, as though he too has been buried.

Robert

Of course I didn't believe what Graeme said to me at Karen's funeral. Karen was dead. Graeme was distraught. Agnes was not a whore. Graeme had never slept with her. He was blaming her – he needed someone to blame. I was sure of it then, and I'm sure of it now.

Graeme and I fought, more violently than ever before; we hadn't had a knock-down fight like that since we were boys. We both sustained wounds which were, luckily, minor. He didn't apologize – I knew he wouldn't apologize. But, despite that, despite his terrible accusations, Agnes forgave him. She did not harbour a grudge, was not capable of harbouring a grudge. She forgave him. And so I followed her lead.

And thank God I did, because of what came next.

Talk happens

They can't help themselves, the people of Warboys, they can't stop themselves from gossiping. Everyone, everywhere. In their homes, in the pubs, in the village shop, even in the winter street. Have you heard, they say, Graeme killed Karen. Graeme and Agnes were having an affair, Karen told Elizabeth *the very night she died*. It's not clear from where they get their information, but they get it. Have you heard, they say, I know it's none of my business but have you heard what everyone is saying?

No one mentions anything about a witch. It is as though the very thought is too malevolent. But one morning as Jim Drury is opening the Black Hat he glances down the high street toward the clocktower. He looks up and sees the weathervane; a black witch in a black hat on a black broom. It catches the wind and swings round to point at him. Jim Drury scuttles inside.

Marlene Henderson is sunk deep into her own sadness. She stays at home, nursing herself back to well-being. But it isn't working, she isn't feeling any better, and she dwells on what happened. She is looking to lay blame for the miscarriage. It can't be Geoff's fault, he is too open and loving. It isn't her fault, although she has been betrayed by her own body. Marlene knows that where she comes from – the deep woods of northern Europe – they would have an explanation. When an unborn baby dies something unnatural is afoot. In her dreams Marlene returns over and over to Karen's funeral. She sees Agnes's face as it hovers outside the window. She sees Agnes's ill will cast over the village.

Marlene is the first to repeat the word witch. She says it in the shop to Barbara, the shop-keeper. 'Agnes is a witch,' she says, wild-eyed over the under-ripe tomatoes, her accent thickening. 'Agnes killed my baby.'

Barbara is shocked, she comes out from behind her counter and puts her arm around Marlene. 'There, there,' she says, patting her shoulder, 'never mind.'

But the words have been let loose, Marlene has freed them. Barbara repeats them, she whispers to her customers as she hands over their stripy carrier bags. The words are in the air that hangs over Warboys, flapping in the fenland wind, growing louder. The village resists; everyone loves Agnes, Agnes is their girl. But that resistance is shrivelling, it is being blown away, it is slowly vanishing.

Robert and Agnes are happy

Robert and Agnes take good care of the boys. Robert bathes them and wipes their bottoms and makes sure they have three meals a day. At night Agnes reads to them – she's been banished from Jenny's room, although she hasn't mentioned this to Robert and he hasn't noticed. The boys get Agnes's stories now, but she doesn't tell tall tales, she reads to them from their little library. She has a knack for finding just the right thing: Grimm tales about evil stepmothers, Struwwelpeter, shock-headed because he refused to comb his hair or cut his nails, James James Morrison Morrison Weatherby George Dupree whose mother goes down to the end of the town and is never seen again. Agnes is there for them, always, morning, noon and night, but she is not like Karen, she doesn't try to be like Karen, she isn't mummy. With her own money she hires a cleaner who comes in every other day, and she buys a dishwasher, a tumble dryer, a microwave; the new appliances perch in the big kitchen, awkward in-comers, gleaming.

Robert does the laundry and most of the cooking. When the boys cry, they go to him. He sees to Martin, shaves him, bathes him, changes him, all the things that Karen once did. None of these tasks are new to Robert but he's never had to attempt to manage them single-handed, and it's the weight of them, the extraordinary bulk of inescapable duty, that threatens to unbalance him now. It's as if the teetering house itself has taken over their lives.

Graeme isn't around. Robert doesn't notice – he's too busy – but his brother isn't there.

Neither is Jenny.

They have skulked off, but not together. Jenny spends a lot of time in her room. She goes to school; Mr McKay and the Headteacher are pleased with her, she seems her quiet old self, despite the bereavement. In class people keep a respectful distance. Lolly is her bodyguard, her guide. After school, they go home together. Lolly encourages Jenny to go through her collection of books; Jenny is reading up on witchcraft lore. They tell each other they are arming themselves for battle. There is a witch among us, she must be cut out. She must be made to leave. Yet, even as they say it, they giggle with pleasure; and even as she giggles, Jenny is afraid.

And she misses Karen. She misses Karen dreadfully. Before she was gone Jenny hardly saw Karen, but now every time she enters the kitchen she thinks, where's Karen? After school, first thing in the morning. Where's Karen? Of course there's a big change in the household, there's so much work to do, so much to organize, Jenny knows that Robert is struggling to keep the house functioning. But quite apart from that, apart from the laundry and the cooking and the boys and Martin, Jenny misses having Karen in the house, having someone there who was, well, ordinary.

In Jenny's bedroom, she and Lolly whisper about Agnes.

'She said she would help me emigrate.'

'Where to?' asks Lolly.

'The US, of course, where else? She said she knows people.'

'America?'

Jenny nods.

'What would you want to go there for?' asks Lolly, amazed.

'I don't know,' says Jenny. 'I'd get a job. Get a life.'

Lolly cackles fiendishly, Jenny joins her. 'You could work in one of those casinos. You could be a cigarette girl!' They laugh and whoop and then stifle themselves when they realize how much noise they are making. 'Did she do it?' Lolly asks. 'Have you got your green card yet?'

'Of course not,' says Jenny. 'She was lying. She's always lying.'

After Lolly is gone Jenny reads and reads, and studies. She gets up to the boys at night if she hears them cry – Robert and Agnes never seem to hear them crying. She gets up and goes down the hall and gets into bed with whomever is upset, sometimes both of them. All three crowd into Andrew's little bed and Jenny holds them, a boy on either side. Andrew and Francis love their auntie, they love both their aunties, Aunt Jenny and Auntie Agnes.

Graeme is spinning around and around in circles. All day, everyday. In his head, around and around, over and over, his thoughts repeating themselves. He sees Karen's face as he pushes her, as she falls again and again. How did it happen? he wonders. He can't quite remember how it happened. What did she say? What was she saying?

When he looks at his sons, his boys, it's as though he is seeing them from a very great height. He looks down and they are tiny and he is very far from them. They are safe; he is safe; they are safe from each other. They are not really his boys. This thought gouges at him like a blunt table knife. They are Karen's boys. Oh, but he loves them, he loves them so much he can smell it, he can feel it in his guts, in his brain. They are all that there is for him, they are all that he has made of his life, they are all that is left of Karen. And they're not mine – he pushes those words away. And they're not mine. They are Robert's.

He spends his time in the Marquis of Granby and if not there, the last cottage at the end of the field. He hasn't gone back to their bedroom since the night Karen died. He has made a nest in the cottage, a pile of dirty laundry stolen from the house. A couple of shirts and a pair of jeans that belonged to Karen, an old shirt of Robert's, Francis's pyjamas, Andrew's jumper, Jenny's old dressing gown with the belt missing, a pile of his own things. A pair of knickers belonging to Agnes. Her trousers. A bra. He nestles in and the smelly clothes are reassuring.

Elizabeth

The scene between Robert and Graeme at the funeral was extraordinary, no one was about to forget it quickly. And the intervention from Jenny . . . well, everyone was alarmed and concerned. I felt like I knew what was going on because of the knowledge I possessed – about Agnes and Graeme – about what Karen had told me the night she died. But I also felt frightened.

I was frightened of Graeme. I realized for the first time that I had been frightened of Graeme since we were children. He'd always been a bully and he had never liked me. Nothing that Graeme said about Agnes at the funeral seemed to make any impact on Robert. It was as though her touch wiped everything away. In Robert's eyes she was blameless, the affair had never taken place. I wanted to shake him. I wanted to slap him and bring him to his senses. But I suppose in a way that's what Graeme tried to do. He failed, spectacularly.

And of course I was afraid of Agnes. It is appalling to watch someone walk into your life and commandeer a situation, a whole set of people, an entire family, that you thought was in some way your own. It chills the soul – it chilled my soul. And Agnes herself was frightening. She invoked in me a horrible mish-mash of emotions that I've since spent much time trying to sort out. I admired her, on some level I think we all admire good-looking people. I envied her confidence and poise, the way that men found her seductive and women found her charming. I was jealous of her marriage, of course, and I loathed the way she relied upon her – what else can I call it? – feminine wiles to get her way. I was a little in awe of her Americanness, we are all in awe of Americans these days, we despise them and we long to be Californian. I was disconcerted by the way she had no discernible interests outside her marriage, her new family, the village, and I longed to be able to know my own mind in the way that she seemed to know hers. I wanted to be like her while knowing I never could be. I hated her and I found that frightening.

A couple of days after the funeral I saw Marlene. I had finished work at the Trevelyans before lunch and, walking home, I was surprised to see her in her garden. I had assumed she would be back at work. She invited me in for a cup of tea.

'I'm having some time off,' she said, 'a couple of weeks.'

'A couple of weeks?' I said, not meaning to sound surprised.

'Yes. I told you Elizabeth, I lost the baby.'

'I know, I –'

'I don't think you do.' She made herself soften her tone. 'Just some time to myself. To think about things.'

I hesitated before speaking. I didn't want to say the wrong thing, to upset her further. 'I'm sorry Marlene.'

'It's all right,' she said. 'It's not your fault.' She looked out the window. She repeated herself, 'It's not *your* fault.'

'Whose fault is it then?'

'You heard what she said at the funeral.'

'Who?'

'Jenny Throckmorton. She's a mad girl –'

'Jenny's not mad –'

'But still, she said it. As did Graeme. Graeme said it too.'

'What?'

'Agnes. She's a witch.' Marlene folded her hands across her empty belly. 'Geoff and I have been trying to conceive a baby for years.' She looked at me. 'Years and years. I've been giving myself hormone shots. I take a big syringe –' she held up her hand, miming '– and I inject myself in the bum.' She stared at me so intensely it was all I could do to keep from turning away. 'I'm 39 years old.'

'I know, but you've conceived once now, you'll do it again –'

She shook her head. 'Not while she is in Warboys. It's Agnes. Don't look at me that way Lizzie, you know it's true, everyone knows. She's a witch. She killed my baby.'

Marlene Henderson is a lawyer. She is bright and articulate and well-informed about politics and history. She reads and considers and Geoff takes her to London to the Royal Opera on her birthday. She wears expensive clothes and their house is lovely. Geoff is the captain of the cricket team. Marlene thinks Agnes Samuel is a witch, she said it and she believed it, I could tell. I was horrified. Accusations like this were no good; it wasn't going to help anybody. There was a problem with Agnes – she'd been having an affair with her brother-in-law who, in turn, accidentally, tragically, killed his wife. It had nothing to do with witchcraft, nothing to do with the supernatural. At least that's what I believed at the time.

'What are you going to do about it?' I asked.

'Spread the word,' she said. 'Warn everybody.

I decided I needed to talk to Robert; we needed to talk things through. I wanted to find out what he was thinking, how he was coping in the aftermath of Karen's death. I had been trying to get to see him – I was always trying to see him – but every time I dropped round to the house he was with Agnes. She was always there, at his side, in the office, in the kitchen. It was as though recent events had drawn them closer to each other, as though as time passed Robert was ever more deeply ensnared.

One day when I went round they were both in the office, Robert at his computer, Agnes sitting reading by the fire. They looked – she looked – so ordinary at that moment, happy, content, that I wavered. No one could take the charges seriously, whatever form they took: witchcraft, adultery.

'I've come to see Jenny,' I said, lying.

Robert glanced at his watch, annoyed. He was perpetually annoyed with me these days. 'She's still at school.'

'Of course,' I slapped my palm on my forehead as if to excuse my stupidity. I was getting used to looking stupid. 'Anybody fancy a drink?'

Now they both looked at me as though I was the village idiot.

'Thanks Lizzie,' Robert spoke for them both, 'but we're busy. I've got to see to the cottages.'

I smiled and shrugged and said I was off to the pub. As I left I could feel Agnes staring at me. She'd understood why I was there. I left via the back door, uncertain of what to do next.

I walked down the garden and went into the tunnel under the vast yew hedge. I hadn't been in the tunnel for ages. As a child I had found it too gloomy, I had tripped over bare roots and clutched at handfuls of needles too many times. The branches overhead were dense enough to keep out the rain, but that had not made it a good place to play. As my eyes adjusted to the black, I waited for Robert to leave the house and go out to the cottages. I didn't hear Agnes enter the tunnel behind me. She was very light on her feet.

'Elizabeth?' she said.

I tried to turn and fell over, scraping my hand against bark. Agnes was smiling. She didn't look cross, or even bemused at finding me there.

'I was waiting for Robert.'

'Have you arranged to meet?'

'No.' I got up off the cold ground. 'I wanted to surprise him.'

She smiled again. I could tell she was laughing at me. 'Here he comes now,' she said and, indeed, there he was, heading out toward the field. She called to him, stepping through the gap in the hedge. 'Robert,' she said when he reached us, 'Elizabeth wants to see you. I found her here in the tunnel. I think she was hiding from me.'

Robert looked at me as though I truly had gone crazy. I didn't try to deny what Agnes had said. 'I wanted to have a word with you.'

'All right Lizzie.' He turned to Agnes. 'Let's go out to the cottages.'

'I'll come out later,' said Agnes, to my relief.

We trudged across the frost-burned field without speaking. Inside the cottage Robert lit the gas fire and we both stood in front of it, warming our hands. I couldn't think where to begin.

'Let's have it,' Robert said. There was no warmth in his voice.

'The night she died – Karen – I . . . we . . . I saw her in the Black Hat. She came in on her own. We sat together for a while. She was very upset.'

Robert's face changed; the annoyance he felt with me fell away. 'She was upset?'

'Yes.' I paused before continuing. Robert looked miserable.

'Oh Lizzie, I can't believe she's dead. The boys – it's so hard, Andrew's confused and Francis, well, he hardly seems to notice somehow and that's almost as upsetting.'

'They're young.'

'They are. Babies.'

I thought of Marlene. 'Karen said something quite extraordinary to me that night. She said she knew that Graeme was having an affair.'

'An affair?' He sounded uncertain for a moment but then his tone became bitter, 'Well, there's nothing new about that. I never understood why she put up with it.'

'This was different.'

'How could it be different? My brother would follow his dick anywhere.'

'It was Agnes.' I didn't want to say it, but I had to.

'What?'

'Karen said he was having an affair with Agnes.'

'Oh,' replied Robert, his voice soft. He did up the buttons on his jacket, shivered involuntarily. 'That again.'

'That's what she said. She said she knew it was true.'

'Well, it isn't. Karen might have believed it, but it's not true. How could it be? She must have got the idea off Jenny. Really Lizzie,' he turned to me, 'you are determined to pry.'

There was no point in defending myself. There was no point in continuing our conversation. He would not, could not, believe the allegation. I couldn't keep on abasing myself. I know I should have persevered; if I had convinced him of the truth perhaps none of what followed would have taken place. And I can just imagine what his response would have been if I had told him about Marlene's accusation. My pride got in the way – I was amazed to find I had any left, but I did. Robert didn't believe me. He thought I was saying these things because I was after him for myself. I imagine part of him enjoyed it, the spectacle of two women struggling over his heart and soul. Except I was the only one struggling.

I let myself out of the cottage. I left him standing in front of the fire, happy in his ignorance.

Happy families

It is the summer before Agnes arrives: Graeme and Karen take Andrew and Francis on a picnic to celebrate Francis's second birthday. Karen has made a chocolate cake in the shape of a bunny, Graeme packs crisps and smarties and cans of Coca-Cola into the hamper alongside Karen's boiled eggs and carrot sticks. They don't go far – to the end of the garden – but for the boys it is a tremendous treat to have both parents there, together, willing. They play football, Graeme running like a madman every time Francis gives the ball a good kick in the wrong direction. The boys force their father to give them horsy rides on his back and they scream with pleasure when he bucks and throws them. Karen tickles them, Karen sings to them; they are happy. After lunch Graeme lies on the grass with the sun in his face; he falls asleep.

He dreams.

He dreams it is thirty years ago – more than thirty. He is playing with Robert at the end of the garden; he looks up, here comes Mummy and Daddy. Daddy is tall and straight in a white shirt with rolled up sleeves; he wears his dark hair slicked back. Mummy has on the dress that Graeme likes best, yellow cotton with tiny flowers all over. She is carrying a hamper, Daddy kicks a ball. The boys tumble, they shout happily. Graeme doesn't want the afternoon to end, he is afraid of it ending.

Robert

After Karen's death my brother began receding, I can see now we were losing sight of him. It was as though he was standing on the deck of a great ship, we were on the dock, and we were having a prolonged leave-taking. My arm ached from waving, my face hurt from smiling. When would the boat pull away? I got so used to saying good-bye that when he disappeared for real I didn't notice. I was otherwise engaged.

I thought that Agnes and I were managing. It was hard work, but I thought our household was fully functional, that we'd been wounded but we were recovering. Everyone was quiet, low to the ground, that was only natural. We had to find a new way of living and I naively imagined that we had found it. Agnes was contributing more of her own money toward running the house – she paid for the cleaner, the dishwasher – and I felt fine about that. I needed her help and she gave it freely. The Elizabethan wing of the house had sucked up all my money, though I hadn't actually told Agnes; as always, she just knew. Jenny was back at school, calm, the boys were okay, as okay as could be expected, Andrew at nursery and we'd found a childminder for Francis, Agnes paid for that as well. Dad had his blanket on his knees. Managing the house without Karen was difficult but we were doing it, we were fine. Graeme was there, somewhere, fading away, and that was fine with me. I didn't want to see him since we had had our fight at the funeral, I wanted to forget what had happened.

And Agnes, oh Christ, she made me so happy. When the February days after Karen died were long and dark and arduous she took me into our bed at night and showed me new ways to love her. And during the day – I don't know, it was as though we had some kind of bug, we were both desperate for it. A way of making ourselves feel alive, a way of showing that Karen might be dead but we were *alive*. We had sex all over the house. Whenever we thought we wouldn't be noticed, in the kitchen, in the sitting room, in the bathroom, outside, wherever we could find. We fucked on the floor in our old bedroom despite the danger, in the ballroom against the dirty steel scaffolding that Derek Hill's crew had put in to shore up the house, in amongst the dust and debris. When I came I heard the voices, the singing moaning voices that I used to fear at night, but now I loved them, they were beautiful. She opened herself to me and urged me on. Maybe we stank of it, perhaps everyone knew, I didn't care and I don't care to this day.

And it was not only the sex. That was merely the physical manifestation – the excess energy, the sparks off the top – of a connection that ran very deep. It probably seems strange to say it, after what happened, masochistic perhaps, but it was as though Agnes and I were made for each other, created for each other. I lived so that Agnes could tell her story through me. I had her and she had me; I know there is some kind of truth in what we had together, there has to be. It wouldn't have happened otherwise.

Agnes turns it on

Agnes is in her bedroom, except it's not her bedroom in the way it should be, it's Robert's old bedroom. She doesn't much like it and neither does Robert. It smells of teenage boys.

Agnes is getting dressed. She is slipping into her sharply pressed wool trousers, her leather belt, her cashmere polo neck, her leather boots with the cuban heels. She applies her make-up slowly, carefully, dabs perfume behind her ears, on her wrists. She brushes her hair and looks in the mirror. Fine. She looks good.

She is going to the Black Hat for a drink. Robert will join her once he has put his father to bed. Downstairs by the door she puts on her heavy coat, her velvet hat and scarf, her calf-skin gloves. She checks herself over in the mirror by the doorway, and leaves.

From her room Jenny watches Agnes go. She sighs and flops down onto her bed. There is nothing about her sister-in-law that is really all that witchy. She has gleaned what she can from Lolly's books – as far as she knows Agnes has no supernumerary nipple, there are no pets who could pass as animal familiar. Jenny did see Agnes fly, Agnes raised herself to the level of Jenny's bedroom window, but sometimes, late at night, Jenny wonders if that was a dream. She always has such strange, unhappy dreams. She knows she saw Agnes with Graeme – that was no dream or nightmare – but she can tell the affair is over now, it's been over for a while, and that in itself is no proof of witchcraft. Jenny feels weary, too grown up too soon. She needs proof, proof enough to impress more than just Lolly. More than the compelling historical coincidence of Agnes Samuel's name.

After a while she hears another set of feet crunching across the gravel drive. She pops up and looks out the window. Robert, off to join Agnes at the pub. I knew they were going out, she thinks, Robert asked if I would baby-sit. Now they are gone, they are both out of the house. The boys are asleep, Father is in his bed, Graeme isn't around and if he is he won't bother me. Jenny puts on her slippers and her favourite old sweater and passes along the corridor to Agnes and Robert's bedroom, running her hand along the wall. She puts her hand on the doorknob, it feels hot, she turns it quickly and slips inside. There's no one home, she tells herself. She turns on the light.

The room is crammed with too much furniture, furniture intended for a larger room, a traffic jam of furniture. Two wardrobes, a wide chest of drawers, and a vanity table with a long mirror. The bed is neatly made and there is no clutter, clothes and shoes have been put away. Robert's old posters, from when he was Jenny's age have been taken down but their shapes remain on the otherwise bare walls; in their hasty retreat from the other side of the house, Agnes and Robert did not have time to redecorate. There is a single candle in a cut-glass candlestick on the bedside table – domestic, romantic. Jenny hears them having sex all the time. She goes through the drawers. She looks under the bed and inside the wardrobes. She feels for hidden panels, secret partitions, false bottoms. She finds nothing. She finds an abundance of beautiful clothes and the textures – satin, silk, devore, mohair – fill her with longing. She wishes for a mother, she wishes she had a mother who dressed like this, this is not how her dead mother dressed. Agnes's scent is everywhere.

Jenny stops looking, she knows she won't find anything. Her sister-in-law has many sides; she is unfaithful, closed, cruel, beautiful, clever, seductive, charming. Jenny knows these things, she just doesn't know – can't prove – if Agnes is a witch.

In the Black Hat the patrons are warm and settled. It's a bitter night; last week's hints of spring have gone to ground again. Agnes comes in on her own. People look up from their drinks and smile. She's here, they think, Agnes has arrived. She goes to the bar and speaks lightly to Jim Drury.

'It's quiet tonight.'

Jim is polishing glasses. There's a couple of French tourists down the other end of the bar, Lolita is in the back making their supper. Jim nods their way. 'Do you speak French?' he asks Agnes.

Agnes looks at the tourists. She laughs. 'Are you kidding?'

Jim smiles when she laughs, he can't help himself. He has heard what Marlene is saying and he witnessed the fight at the funeral. He has heard that Agnes and Graeme were having an affair. Barbara says that Karen told Elizabeth who told Marlene. Jim knows this is gossip but in Warboys gossip usually tends to be true. He's got a bad feeling about Agnes now and he wants it to go away. He wants to feel like he used to do about her. 'They're staying upstairs.'

'In my room?' she asks, mock indignant.

'Yes, your room.' Jim apologizes. 'But you're welcome back here any time. Just say the word.' Jim blushes; he doesn't mean to imply that Agnes might leave Robert.

Agnes ignores his gaffe. She leans forward, conspiratorial. 'But what would we do with Lolita?'

Jim swallows hard, turns toward the glasses and pretends not to get the joke. 'Lolita? She's in the back cooking these people a meal.'

Agnes stops smiling. Jim won't play. She asks for a Bush Mills – she drinks Irish whiskey to wind him up – and goes to sit by the fire.

Geoff Henderson is in tonight with David Trevelyan, they've come out together for a drink. Geoff has left Marlene at home with a hot-water bottle in front of the TV. He knows what his wife has been saying about Agnes; he's worried, but he thinks she'll get better soon. She's being German, and she'll get over it. Geoff was frightened at the idea of his wife bearing a child – he remembers all too well when Mrs Throckmorton died labouring with Jenny, he was at school with Robert and Graeme at the time – and a deep unspoken part of him was relieved when Marlene lost the baby. This relief has soured his grieving and makes him feel ashamed.

Marlene can say whatever she wants as far as he is concerned, she can blame Agnes, she can blame the Prime Minister and the Pope if she likes; he is glad to have her in one piece.

He excuses himself from David for a moment and crosses the pub to Agnes.

'Hello,' he says and gives her his dependable smile.

Agnes is staring at the fire. She sits with her legs crossed and her back straight. Her hair is black and glossy and it's as though Geoff Henderson can see the flames reflected in every strand. 'Hello,' she says without looking up.

Geoff pulls over a stool and sits down beside her. 'How's Graeme?'

'Who?' says Agnes and he sees the effort she has to make to pull herself away from the fire.

'Graeme?' says Geoff, thinking she must have misheard him. He too has heard the rumour about Agnes and Graeme but he has decided to ignore it. Idle talk.

'Oh,' says Agnes. 'He's fine.'

Jim Drury watches from behind the bar. He can smell Lolita's lasagne as the oven exhales in the kitchen. He feels guilty for dismissing Agnes earlier, he doesn't know why he didn't want to be seduced. He wants to be near her, he wants to sit beside her like Geoff Henderson is doing, he wants to take her by the hand and talk, really talk. He knows she isn't like what people are saying. He has seen how much Robert loves her, he knows she wouldn't betray him. He was at the wedding, he has seen how happy they are.

Agnes turns her attention from the fire to Geoff. 'How is Marlene?' she asks, solicitous.

Geoff feels a pang of guilt for leaving his wife at home on her own. 'She's okay. It's tough. She's a little . . . unstable, she's –' He stops himself mid-sentence. He can't believe he has said this of his wife. He is appalled at his own small act of betrayal.

'She'll be fine,' Agnes says simply. 'You both will be.'

'Yes,' says Geoff, 'I know you're right.'

Agnes shifts the mood again. 'When are you boys going to start playing cricket? I have yet to see a single cricket game on that field.'

'Match,' corrects Geoff apologetically. 'It's a cricket match. And it's a pitch, we play on a pitch. We'll start playing again in the spring, when it's a bit drier.'

'You must explain it to me.'

'Really?' Geoff doesn't believe she is interested but she questions him brightly nonetheless. He finds himself explaining the game. Agnes listens attentively. Her eyes glisten and Geoff enjoys himself; he talks away.

After a while Robert comes into the Black Hat. He stamps his feet to knock out the cold and asks Agnes and Geoff if they want a drink before he goes up to the bar. When he returns Geoff is standing. 'You must come round for dinner sometime,' Geoff says. 'It would be great.' He has completely forgotten his wife's allegations.

'That would be nice,' says Robert.

'Yes,' says Agnes. 'Give my regards to Marlene.'

He remembers then, and he blushes a deep red as he makes his way back to his drink.

'Everything okay?' Agnes asks Robert, meaning back home, at the house.

'Yes,' he says and he begins to tell her his plans, his new scheme to promote the cottages. 'We've got to be more assertive,' he says, 'we've got to sell ourselves upmarket, throughout the year.'

Agnes stares into the fire once more. She is listening and not listening, one of her talents. In the fire she sees herself, she sees the Throckmorton family. She sees Jenny in Robert's bedroom, searching through her things. She looks up at Robert and interrupts him.

'People don't like outsiders,' she says.

'No.' Robert is immediately overwhelmed by worry. 'But you've been welcomed here, haven't you? You feel welcome.'

'That's changing. It was only skin-deep.'

'What do you mean, love?'

'You'll see.' She takes Robert's hands in hers. His are warm, hers are cold, he moves his hands round hers. 'People enjoy rumours, they enjoy speculation,' she says. 'They like to be nasty. Even the nice ones; everyone gives in to the nasty, the mean spirit. You mustn't listen to them, Robert.'

He is afraid to ask her what she means. He is reassuring instead. 'I won't listen, Agnes, I won't.'

'They don't like outsiders,' she says, 'even though this is where I belong.' Agnes shifts the mood once more. 'Although I despair of the perfect bathroom.'

'I know, I –'

'I hate that bathroom,' she laughs. 'The water's never hot enough, there's no shower, the toilet is . . . ornery, there's nowhere to hang the towels, there's no room to put anything in fact . . .'

Robert is laughing too, back on safe territory. This riff is comfortable, happy.

Elizabeth is failing

Elizabeth has stopped dropping in on the Throckmorton household. My skin isn't thick enough, she thinks. She is resigned to not seeing Robert, but she worries about Jenny. She speculates that perhaps Lolly Senior is a bad influence, except she's always liked Lolly. She wants to see Jenny. And if she sees her she might see Robert as well. Am I using Jenny as a kind of round-about way to get to Robert? she wonders. No. I want to see Jenny.

She picks up the phone and dials the Throckmorton number. Agnes answers.

'Can I speak to Jenny?' Elizabeth asks after exchanging faint pleasantries. She can hear Robert in the background.

'I'll get her,' says Agnes.

The girl comes on the line. Her voice is sullen. 'What do you want?'

'I'd like to see you Jenny. Can I take you out for lunch at the weekend?'

'I don't know. I'm pretty busy with schoolwork.' Elizabeth hears Robert hissing parentally. Jenny speaks again, louder this time. 'Why don't you come round here?' (Jenny turns and sticks her tongue out at Robert, who frowns and makes a face.)

'All right. When's a good time?'

'I'm in most evenings.' As if there is anywhere for me else to go, she thinks.

'Okay,' Elizabeth says, 'That would be nice.'

Elizabeth arrives on the Throckmortons' doorstep two days later.

She carries a bunch of freesias that she picked up earlier from Barbara's. She knocks this time, no longer feeling able to open the door and walk straight in. Agnes appears.

'Elizabeth!' she says, smiling widely. 'I haven't seen you since – the other week.'

Elizabeth recalls the tunnel incident. She feels her colour rise. 'Is Jenny around?'

Agnes's smile fades. 'No, she's out with Robert. They've gone to Peterborough. But come in. Come in and have a drink.'

Elizabeth finds herself escorted through to the sitting room. She gives Agnes the flowers, reluctantly. Martin is parked beside the fire, there is an open bottle of wine on the side table. The lights are low and there's the warm glow that Elizabeth associates with long evenings spent in this room. Agnes settles into the big armchair. After greeting Martin, touching his hand, Elizabeth lowers herself onto the settee.

'So,' says Agnes, her voice relaxed, even, 'what is Marlene Henderson saying about me?'

'Marlene?' says Elizabeth, taken aback. She glances at Martin. He stares at the floor.

'Marlene Henderson,' Agnes replies sharply, 'German. About 36. Good-looking woman. Your friend?'

'Yes. She's – she's not been very well.'

'There's always that excuse.'

'She's –'

'Have you heard what she's saying? She lost her baby. Okay, I'll allow for the torture of that. But really – in this day and age –'

'I don't know what she's thinking . . .' Elizabeth finds herself shaking. 'Of course it's ridiculous, I know that.'

'It's like something a child would say, like something Andrew would come up with to explain her poor behaviour.'

'Look,' says Elizabeth, 'don't be too harsh. Marlene's not . . .' Elizabeth attempts to explain her friend.

Jenny is not in Peterborough with Robert. She is upstairs in her bedroom with Lolly. They are burning candles and reading. Lolly has done some more research. Earlier today in the library in Cambridge she found a little book. It has a long title:

> *The Most Strange and Admirable discoverie of the three Witches of Warboys, arraigned, convicted, and executed at the last Assises of Huntingdon, for the bewitching of the five daughters of Robert Throckmorton Esquire, and divers other persons, with sundrie Devillish and grievous torments: And also for the bewitching to death of the Lady Cromwell, the like hath not been heard of in this age.*

Lolly took the book out of the library, although it was not available for loan; she stole it, temporarily. She brings it into the Throckmorton house, gives it to Jenny.

'1593,' she says, gleefully pointing out the date on the title page. '1593.' To her the book's age gives it authority.

Jenny handles the book cautiously. It is small and, for its size, extraordinarily heavy. She feels her heart sink down through her gut, like a stone dropped into turbid water. 'What is it?' she asks.

'Look!' says Lolly. 'It's about Mother Samuel, Father Samuel, and their daughter Agnes. It's all there, exactly what happened. It's written down.' She takes the book away from Jenny who has failed to open it, she finds a page where the names are listed plainly. 'Look.' She pushes the book at Jenny. 'They were hanged.'

But Jenny isn't looking, she won't look. She stares toward the window. 'She had a wedding dress with her when she arrived,' she murmurs. She turns to look at Lolly. 'She brought an old wedding dress with her to Warboys.'

Robert walks into the sitting room. Elizabeth looks at him, wide-eyed, then back at Agnes. She'd said he'd gone to Peterborough.

'How are they?' asks Agnes of him. 'Are they happy?'

'Yes,' says Robert wearily. 'They're fine.' He turns to Elizabeth. 'Trouble with some guests. They couldn't get the gas fire working. They were freezing out there. I almost invited them back here.'

'Oh,' says Agnes, 'don't do that.'

'They complained about Graeme. They thought he was a tramp.'

Agnes laughs.

'Don't worry,' says Robert. 'They're sorted. What brings you out Elizabeth?'

'I came to see Jenny.'

'Right,' he says, uninterested, relieved, already heading for the kitchen. 'Anyone like a cup of tea?'

Once Robert has left the room Elizabeth gets up, retrieves her coat and goes toward the door without offering any excuses. Agnes watches from her armchair, doesn't object, doesn't say anything. Why did you tell me he was in Peterborough? Elizabeth is filling with unasked questions, it's all she can do to stop herself overflowing. Why did you tell me he wasn't here? Why did you invite me in?

At the last moment, as Elizabeth nears the door, Agnes rises from her armchair. She moves smoothly across the room, Elizabeth blinks hard, it's as though she hovers above the floor, as though she glides on a thin cushion of air. She stops very close, puts her arm around Elizabeth's waist, gives her a soft, warm squeeze. 'You're looking lovely,' Agnes whispers in her ear, 'Robert will be pleased. Let's get together,' she smiles, 'soon.'

Elizabeth is in the foyer of the house; she never uses the front door but she will today. She catches a glimpse of herself in the mirror. She stops dead, her face has gone white. As she pauses she hears a sound filter through from upstairs – girls' voices – and realizes that, of course, Jenny has been here all along as well. Elizabeth is through the door quickly and out onto the drive. She turns and sees Agnes standing in the sitting room window, very straight, very still. Elizabeth – she can't stop herself – gives in to her impulse to run up the drive.

Upstairs Lolly is imagining herself a High Priestess. Of what she isn't sure, it doesn't matter. She is thrilled by her find. The little book is amazing. She doesn't notice what is happening to Jenny.

Something has happened to Jenny. Inside her head a door is opening, the handle comes away in her hand. The door swings back and falls off its hinges. There is nothing between Jenny and what's out there. There is nothing stopping Jenny.

Lolly looks at her friend. She thinks she has fallen asleep. She gets up off the floor and drapes a blanket over her where she leans against the bed. She puts the book on Jenny's pillow. She pulls on her coat and tiptoes out of the room. In the corridor she hears Robert and Agnes talking in their bedroom. She creeps through the house and away.

Outside the Warboys moon is high in the sky. It is a clear night, a spirit night, frosty. Out on the fens there is a stirring and Agnes hears it, even as she pleasures Robert, she hears it. There is no avoiding it; it is coming this way.

Jenny tells Agnes a story

Jenny finishes the last page of the little book. She places it under her pillow and falls asleep.

Then in the middle of the night, Jenny wakes up. Agnes is standing at the foot of her bed. She is dressed all in black, like a cat burglar, black slim trousers, black roll-neck top. 'Hello Jenny,' she says.

Jenny sits up, rubs her eyes, stretches. She is relaxed, she's been waiting for this. Now she possesses knowledge – the facts – and she feels calm, in control, and rather pleased. She wishes Lolly could see her. 'Hello,' she says to Agnes, 'have a seat.' She indicates the end of the bed. 'Let me tell you a story.'

Agnes settles on the bed and nods as though she is ready to listen to what Jenny has to say.

'Once upon a time,' starts Jenny, 'there was a family called Throckmorton; Robert Throckmorton, his wife, their five young daughters and one small son. They lived in a tiny village called Warboys on the edge of the fens in Cambridgeshire. They were the wealthiest family in the village and also the most powerful. Their grand house with its beautiful ballroom and intricately worked plaster ceiling was famous throughout the region.' Jenny stares at Agnes as she speaks and Agnes returns her gaze. It's a long story.

'The Throckmortons lived next door to the Samuels. Alice and John Samuel were an elderly couple with only one child, a young woman called Agnes. They were poor people, they owned no land. It was said that John Samuel was lazy. Alice Samuel – Mother Samuel – was a frequent visitor to the Throckmorton house, often taking on small bits of paid work – sewing, some laundry, caring for the children.

'One day Jenny Throckmorton, who was ten years old, fell into a strange kind of sickness. Sometimes she would sneeze without stopping for half an hour. Other times she would fall into a trance from which her parents were unable to wake her. Her body would become completely rigid, her arms and legs unbending. Sometimes one leg would shake uncontrollably, then the other. Or an arm. Sometimes her head would shake violently, as if she had some kind of palsy, her eyes rolling back in their sockets.

'One day, during one of these fits, Mother Samuel came to visit. She was taken in to see the sick child. Suddenly, Jenny sat up on her bed and pointed at the old woman and said, "Look at the old witch. Did you ever see one more like a witch than she is? Take off her black cap, for I cannot abide to look at her." Jenny's mother rebuked the child for her rudeness, apologizing to Mother Samuel.

'The illness continued and the family became increasingly worried. When not even their family friend, the respected Dr Barrow from Cambridge, could begin to understand what was making her sick, they called in a second doctor. But he was unable to discover what was wrong with the girl. And not long after that, two more of the girls, both older than Jenny, also fell into fits and prolonged bouts of shaking. The next time Mother Samuel entered the house, they cried out, "Take her away, look where she stands, there in her black cap. It is she that has bewitched us and she will kill us if you do not take her away."

'Robert Throckmorton and his wife found their daughters' accusations deeply shocking. They were new to Warboys and had no knowledge of the village and whether it had a history of witchcraft. They prayed that the girls were mistaken. But soon the two remaining daughters in the family also fell ill; the oldest girl, Joan, most seriously of all. She would sneeze and screech and groan fearfully, sometimes she was shaken by convulsions so strong that her body would bounce across the bed she lay in, or almost break the chair in which she sat.

'It seemed that nothing could be done. During these fits the girls were unable to see, hear, or feel anything or anyone; all they could do was cry out "Mother Samuel, take her away! For God's sake, take her away in her black cap and burn her or we shall all be killed." Sometimes these fits lasted an hour, sometimes the day and they caused the whole family, indeed the whole village, great anxiety. Experts were brought in, from Cambridge and further afield.

'Soon the sense of the girls' allegations became inescapable: it was witchcraft, it had to be. Mother Samuel was responsible for the illness afflicting the Throckmorton children.

'The fits continued. In desperation, the Throckmortons took their daughters to another village, in the hope that they might recuperate. And, indeed, whenever they were not in Warboys, the children stopped having convulsions as abruptly as they had started. And when they returned, the fits returned with them. The sickness did not require the presence of Mother Samuel, but the children blamed her, they blamed Mother Samuel. "Burn her or we shall all be killed!"

'Time passed, and this dreadful pattern repeated itself over and over again. The children's uncle, Gerald Pickering, came to visit and, appalled by the state of the household, decided to bring Mother Samuel into the house to test out the allegations. Mother Samuel refused to enter, she said she knew what they intended to do to her: they wanted to submit her to the test of scratching. She was right, this was what they wanted to do, scratching might bring the children some relief.

'It was said that if you scratched a witch, and let her blood, you would recover from her spell, and in doing so, prove her a witch. The demon she had let loose would come out of your body to suck on the blood of its mistress.

'They brought Mother Samuel into the house, and the children immediately fell into violent fits, Jenny the worst of all. It took several men to wrestle the writhing child onto her bed; she was blinded and she could not hear. In her trance she began to scratch the cover of her bed, saying "Oh that I had her! Oh, that I had her!" So Master Pickering put his hand before the child in order to test her but, her eyes still closed, she would not touch his hand. Other people present put their hand in front of the child but she would not touch them either. Then Master Pickering told Mother Samuel to give her hand to the child. She refused. So Master Pickering took hold of Mother Samuel's hand himself and thrust it to the child, who no sooner felt it than began to scratch with such vehemence that her nails broke into bloody splinters with the force. While the child was scratching Master Pickering forced his own hand forward, but Jenny would not scratch it, only Mother Samuel, who was by now weeping with the pain of the blood-letting.

'Then the other girls began to clamour "Oh, that I had her! Oh, that I had her!" and when allowed to touch Mother Samuel who was forced near them, they too began to scratch.

'Mother Samuel was taken away and the children were as though fully recovered.

'But not long after that the convulsions grew worse. The children were afflicted at night as well as in the day, at the house as well as outdoors, even on the Sabbath.

'Lady Cromwell, a friend of the family, came to visit the children and comfort their parents. She had Mother Samuel brought to the house and, tiring of listening to the old woman's protestations of innocence, snatched Mother Samuel's kerchief from her head and clipped a lock of her hair and gave it to Mistress Throckmorton to burn. That night Lady Cromwell dreamt that Mother Samuel came to her as a cat and tried to pluck off all the skin and flesh from her body. The next day Lady Cromwell fell into an illness, from which she never recovered, languishing until she died.

'The learned men in the village took every opportunity to confront Mother Samuel and question her about what she was doing. But Mother Samuel would not answer their questions and, instead, claimed that the children were wanton and that if they were her own she would have punished them long ago.'

'Jenny,' Agnes speaks, suddenly impatient. Throughout Jenny's narration she has sat at the end of the bed, collected, unastonished. Now she is agitated. 'We both know this story. You tell it well. But get on with it.'

'You know the ending, don't you?'

'You can't tell a story without telling the ending.'

'All right.' Jenny still feels very calm, she finds the sound of her own voice reassuring, she feels safe in the muffled quiet of the house. 'The fits continued. The situation grew worse. The children began to see evil spirits – they were called Blue and Catch and Pluck – and these spirits bartered and fought over possession of the Throckmorton souls. Over and over again, Mother Samuel refused to acknowledge the truth in the allegations of witchcraft. The Throckmortons came to realize that the force of evil in Mother Samuel was so great that her daughter, Agnes, and her husband John, must have been witches as well. When Agnes was brought into the house one of the daughters, Elizabeth, fell upon her, scratching ferociously, exhorting her to amend her evil ways. Jenny scratched Agnes on her left cheek, and then on her right, causing her to bleed copiously.

'All three Samuels stood accused.' Jenny's tone becomes flat now, she has lost her momentum. 'None of their defences were accepted and, in the end, they confessed. They were, indeed, witches, all three. There was a trial with a judge and jury at which the confessions were read. The Samuels were sentenced to hang.'

Agnes looks at Jenny evenly. 'Top marks,' she says. 'Ten out of ten. And did they hang?'

For the first time that night, Jenny feels afraid. 'Yes,' says Jenny, 'yes they did. And from that day forward the children were in perfect health.'

'Perfect health,' says Agnes. 'I love a happy ending.' She gets up off the bed. 'Well, thank you Jenny. I knew I could count on you. Thank you for that lovely story.'

Jenny doesn't reply. She is hot; she feels the molten heat of Agnes's anger. 'Don't go,' she says in a small voice. 'Don't leave me.'

'I'm already gone,' says Agnes. And she closes the door and walks away.

Jenny lies awake for a long time. How long can one night last? she wonders. She hears the voices, the moaning voices that sing every night like a chorus of grim fallen angels. After a while she gets up. She makes her bed. Then she sits down at her desk to read the book, *The Most Strange and Admirable Discoverie of the Three Witches of Warboys* . . . as if reading it again will help her understand what it might mean.

Jenny's no tomorrow

Graeme crashes into the house at daybreak. He has risen from his nest and come into the kitchen to forage. He fumbles around in the cupboards, the fridge; everything in the house feels different, everything has changed. Nothing is in the right place. He is full of agitated energy, the lethargy of the past few weeks gone. He eats two bowls of cereal and a quantity of toast. He can hear sounds emerging from upstairs, the voices of Andrew and Francis. He will see the little boys, he will see them and he will know whether they are still his, whether they have gone from him permanently.

They rush into the kitchen shouting 'Daddy, Daddy,' and attempt to scale his legs. He lifts them up and gives them kisses, crumby kisses, coating them with butter and honey, filling up with their embrace. He sits them at the table and makes them breakfast and they talk at him, Andrew single-mindedly interrupting Francis until the smaller boy shouts with frustration. They make him feel needed, his little boys.

Robert comes in, wearing pyjamas, rubbing his eyes. 'Oh hello there,' he says, surprised to see Graeme, surprised to feel pleased to see Graeme.

'Brother dear.' Graeme ruffles Robert's hair like he used to do when they were kids.

'Stop it,' says Robert, laughing, mock-aggrieved. 'I'll go get Dad.' He pauses. 'He'll be glad to see you.'

'I'll get him,' says Graeme and he stands and stretches hugely, roaring with it to amuse the boys. He goes into his father's bedroom.

Martin's eyes are open, he is staring at the ceiling. Graeme leans over him, sliding into his line of vision. 'Morning Dad,' he says. 'Come on. Let's get you up.' He can smell his father's nappy, it needs to be changed. Graeme fills a bowl with warm water from the sink in the corner. He lifts the night-shirt over his father's head, takes down the nappy and cleans his father's bottom, his genitals, and gives the rest of his bony body a sponge bath, turning him over, gently massaging his limbs, following the intimate routine. New nappy, fresh set of clothes, the old man like a big and placid baby. Karen used to perform these tasks every day, Graeme thinks, and he wonders for a moment who does it now, this as well as all the other things, but this thought doesn't stay with him for long. Martin stares at Graeme throughout, Graeme smiles and chats amiably. He slips his arm around his father's waist, the other under his knees, and lifts him into his wheelchair. He wheels him to the sink, ties a towel around his neck and gives him a careful shave. His skin is like paper leaves, the shed coins of an honesty tree. As Graeme works he remembers how his father used to look before he was invalided. 'Just like me,' he mutters under his breath, 'you used to look just like I do now.'

Graeme wheels Martin through to the kitchen and parks him next to the fire, his usual place. The two boys are mucking about on the floor, Robert is drinking a mug of tea. There is no sign of Agnes. Graeme is relieved. 'Jenny up yet?' he asks.

'No,' replies Robert.

So Graeme bounds up the stairs. He knocks on Jenny's door, softly at first, then more loudly. 'Jenn?' he says. 'Wake up. Jenny?' No sound. He pushes the door, it swings back easily.

Jenny is hanging from the curtain rail.

She is absolutely still. Graeme notices several things: the noose is fashioned out of the belt from Jenny's old dressing gown, the one he has out in the cottage. Her bed has been neatly made. The curtains are open. She is wearing her night gown and her hair hangs down over her face. When did your blonde hair get so long, Graeme wonders. When did your blonde hair get so long?

He drops his cane and goes toward her, her name stuck in his throat. His eyes fill and begin to sting. He puts his arms around her body and lifts her so that she is no longer hanging. He raises one hand to bring down the noose. Her body flops over his shoulder. She is cold. He looks out the window.

Agnes is standing in the gravel drive, staring upward. When she sees Graeme she waves.

Warboys is in overdrive

Robert hears Graeme wail, a long and pitiful cry. He runs to the stairs to find his brother falling down shouting, 'She's dead, she's dead,' in his harsh man's voice.

Robert halts. Everything stops moving. After a long moment, Robert says, 'I'll call the police.' It's the only thing he can think to do.

'No,' says Graeme. 'Don't.'

'We'd better.'

'No,' says Graeme, 'what's the point?' The last thing he wants is his ex-colleagues here again, looking him over, looking the house over, looking them all over. Looking at Jenny.

'I'm ringing them,' says Robert, stepping toward the phone. He hasn't seen his sister's body, he doesn't need to, he sees her – it – every detail – in his brother's face.

Andrew and Francis scramble across the room, they take hold of Graeme's legs. Graeme walks forward, dragging the boys with him. He intercepts Robert, grabbing his arm. 'Jenny's dead,' he says, 'don't you understand?'

Robert doesn't understand. 'No,' he says, 'how can that be?'

'She's dead,' he says, and if he has to, he'll repeat it, over and over again.

Agnes comes in to the kitchen. Her entrance distracts both men. The little boys go to her, she picks them up, one under either arm.

'What were you doing out there in the drive?' Graeme bellows at her.

'Walking,' Agnes says calmly. 'I was out for my walk.' She carries the boys out of the kitchen and closes the door.

'She was out there, looking at Jenny,' Graeme splutters.

'What do you mean?' asks Robert.

'She knew what Jenny had done. She was out there checking, making sure.' Graeme stares hard at Robert, his expression changing rapidly as he thinks it through. 'She did it,' he shouts. 'She's responsible.'

Graeme rushes into the sitting room. Robert follows close behind him. 'That's nonsense,' Robert says, 'You know that can't be true. Agnes loves Jenny, Graeme, like a sister, like she loves you and me.'

Agnes is sitting on the settee as though nothing is amiss. She is reading to the boys. She looks at Graeme, closing the book. 'Go to your daddy,' she says, 'give him a hug.' The boys climb down and go toward their father uncertainly. 'I've already called the police,' she adds.

Graeme clutches his sons to him, scowling. He wants to throttle Agnes but he controls himself. He is calm now, suddenly he is very calm, and he thinks he sees things clearly. Jenny is dead, Agnes is responsible, and Graeme is strong with this knowledge.

Robert and Graeme are pacing off the kitchen as though it's a boxing ring. Agnes is gone, Robert has persuaded Graeme to let her take the boys to Francis's childminder. 'We don't want them here today,' he says. 'They'll be fine,' he tries to placate his brother. 'You know Agnes couldn't harm them.'

'Like she harmed Jenny?' Graeme says.

'What are you talking about? Agnes didn't harm Jenny. She spent the night with me.' As he says this he recalls Agnes getting out of bed like she does every night, to visit the loo. He keeps this to himself. 'You can't just hang someone. Don't you think we would have heard something?'

Graeme stops walking. 'How do you know she hanged herself? You haven't seen her.'

Robert is shocked. It's true, he hasn't been upstairs. But he has seen her, he knows he has. Through Graeme? In his dream? 'Agnes told me,' he says, convincing himself, 'Agnes told me.'

'Do you think Jenny – our Jenny, our little sister –' says Graeme, 'would kill herself? Would commit suicide?'

'Well, no,' says Robert and, suddenly, he begins to shake. He is thinking, trying to think. He changes his mind. 'Yes,' he says. 'What else could have happened? We have no way of knowing what goes on in other people's heads. Not even our sister, Graeme. Not even family,' he says, now shaking uncontrollably.

Two policemen arrive at the back door. 'Graeme?' says PC Shorter. Robert and Graeme both know him, he's a Warboys man like them.

They stop pacing and stare at the policeman. PC Shorter is disconcerted, he's never noticed how alike Graeme and Robert Throckmorton are. He frowns. 'Someone reported a murder?'

'A murder?' Robert asks. His knees weaken. He sits down heavily and puts his head in his hands.

'Someone called it in,' says Shorter.

'It's Jenny,' says Graeme. 'She's hanged herself. I cut her down.'

'You should know better than to tamper with a scene,' says Shorter.

'Shut the fuck up, Shorty,' replies Graeme as he leads him to the stairs. 'It's not a "scene". She's my sister.'

'I don't want to see her,' says Robert, speaking quietly. 'I don't want to have to see her.'

'That's all right, Mr Throckmorton,' says the other, younger, constable. 'You don't need to go up there. Shorty will handle it. Shorty will take care of everything.'

Agnes comes into the kitchen, back from delivering the boys. She stands behind Robert in his chair and he leans against her, pressing the back of his head into her abdomen. 'Two down,' she says.

'What?' Robert thinks he's misheard her. He has pulled out his handkerchief and is blowing his nose. His eyes feel puffy and sore, as though in anticipation of weeping.

'Two Throckmortons dead. First Karen, now Jenny.'

'I can't think about it. Jenny.'

'It's my fault,' Agnes says, her voice even.

'What do you mean?'

'It's my fault. We meet, we marry, we are both so happy – and look what it brings us. Look what I've brought to this family.'

The young constable wants to make himself small in this moment, although that doesn't stop him from listening. He thinks Agnes is gorgeous.

'Oh Agnes, don't say that,' says Robert. 'Without you I couldn't cope. Without you, I couldn't go on.'

'It's my fault.'

'Don't say that.' Robert spins round in his seat. He takes Agnes's hands, pressing them tightly to his bruised lips. 'Don't even think it.'

'It's what they'll be saying.'

'Who?'

'Just wait. It's what they'll be saying. Soon.'

Robert stands, drawing himself up straight, taking Agnes in his arms, holding her. 'I've got you,' he says, 'you've got me.'

'I think we should go upstairs,' says Agnes. 'I think we should see her.'

'You do?'

Agnes nods.

Robert is silent for a moment. 'All right,' he says. He draws a deep breath.

They leave the room and the constable can't help but think this scene was for his benefit.

Upstairs Jenny is laid out where Graeme lowered her, on her bed. She could be asleep except for the fact that she only ever slept buried under blankets and duvets, even in summer. 'She'll be cold,' Robert says, and Shorty prevents him from stepping nearer. 'She was always cold at night.' Her flannel night-gown comes down to her ankles and she has on her slippers and, so covered, she looks very young and chaste. Her face is a little blue and there are red marks around her neck but the light is low enough for the onlookers not to have to dwell on that.

Her bedroom is tidy, apart from an array of unlit candles all at different stages of their burning. 'She likes candles,' Robert says, now standing at the foot of the bed. 'She's always asking me to get them for her. There's a shop in London – I –' he turns to the officer and stops speaking. Agnes holds him.

'What do you want us to do?' Shorty asks Graeme, his tone respectful.

'I don't know,' says Graeme, shaking his head.

'We'll have to have an autopsy . . . the coroner . . . you know.'

'I know,' says Graeme. 'I know.'

Elizabeth

That evening, the very day they found Jenny, I opened the door of my cottage to Agnes. It was raining hard, it had been raining since lunchtime, and she was standing beneath a large black umbrella wearing a hat and a scarf and a beautifully cut raincoat. It was made of navy blue rubberized cotton and it must have cost a lot of money. I stood there without speaking, as if the sight of the coat had ruled out plain conversation.

'Elizabeth,' Agnes said, business-like. 'May I come in?'

I had heard from Marlene that there had been a police car and an ambulance at the Throckmortons' that morning, she had rung the Trevelyans to tell me. My first instinct had been to go round to see what was wrong, to see if I could help, but we'd gone beyond that, the Throckmortons and me. I kept my head down all day; if word of what had happened was out in the village I didn't want to hear it that way. I couldn't say I was glad to see Agnes, but I was surprised.

We went into the sitting room. That weekend I had had another round of attempting to re-arrange the furniture but the room still looked out-of-sorts. Agnes stood in the doorway and took it in, without saying a word. I felt she breathed disapproval, pity even, at my attempt at interior decoration. But she took me by the hand. 'Let's sit over here, shall we?' she said, directing me toward the settee.

Her hand was warm and soft, she stroked my skin lightly with her thumb. 'I've got some bad news.'

'What?' I said. I felt annoyed.

'It's Jenny.'

'What?' I said again. 'Tell me. Tell me quickly.'

Agnes looked into my eyes. She held me with her gaze. 'Jenny is dead. She's hanged herself. Graeme found her in her room this morning.'

I'll say it now and get it over with; my first thought on hearing the news was about myself. I hadn't done enough. I had failed once again. I hadn't seen it coming and now she – Jenny – was dead. I thought of those other young women, Elaine Warner and Gillian Collins. How could I get things so wrong, over and over again? I looked at Agnes. She was waiting for me to say something. 'I should have tried harder to help her.'

'It's got nothing to do with you.' She spoke sharply.

'You're right,' I said, embarrassed, 'of course.'

'I thought you should know. Robert asked me to come and tell you.'

'That was good of him. He must be devastated.' Why is it that the words we use at times like these seem so inappropriate?

'Yes.'

'The boys? Are the boys all right?' I thought of them, their little heads, their little hands and feet.

'They are going to stay with Karen's mother. Graeme's agreed they should go away for a while. I think it's best if they are kept safe.'

'Safe?'

'Away from Graeme.'

'Graeme?'

'You've had your own suspicions about Graeme, haven't you Elizabeth?'

'Yes, but –'

'He killed Karen.'

'She –'

'He pushed her and she fell and she is dead.'

I couldn't tell what Agnes was getting at. Either Jenny hanged herself or she did not and someone did it for her. But Graeme, Graeme couldn't be capable of such a thing. Karen, well, she was his wife and he'd been having an affair and she was angry – that doesn't mean she deserved it, but these things have a way of happening. Men kill their wives and girlfriends. But Jenny, not Jenny, his little sister.

'I'd better get back.' Agnes got up to leave.

'No,' I said, 'wait a minute.' I took a breath. I don't know where I got the courage to ask this question, it came from somewhere deep inside me. 'Can you tell me, please tell me Agnes – are you and Graeme having an affair?'

Agnes gave me a terrible, cold look.

'It's just that, well, that's what Karen told me the night she died.'

Agnes sighed. 'You wouldn't have thought Karen was a jealous woman, would you?' She took my hand again. 'Elizabeth, who is your most prized friend in the world?'

I tried to draw my hand away. She wouldn't let me. 'You know the answer to that Agnes.'

She nodded. 'Say it.'

'Robert,' I said, 'Robert. Your husband.'

'You know him, and you know what he's like, don't you?'

'Yes.'

'And do you think that I could cheat on him?'

I looked at her. I thought she was mad. She had hold of my hand and she was staring hard at me, concentrating, as though willing me to believe her, as though if she held on to me for long enough I would have to believe her. Determined, not desperate. My pulse picked up its pace. I took a deep breath and pulled my hand away from her grasp. 'I don't know, Agnes.'

She turned abruptly toward the door. Looking back at me, her eyes flashed black and green and black. Then she was composed, yet again. She retrieved her umbrella. 'We will let you know when the funeral will take place.' And she left.

I don't know why Agnes wanted me to believe her that night. It had been demonstrated to me very clearly – by Agnes, by Robert, by Jenny – that what I thought about that family didn't matter one bit. I suppose it was good of her to come out to tell me what had happened, but I didn't feel grateful at the time. And I didn't believe that she couldn't cheat on Robert; I knew that she'd been having an affair with Graeme, Karen's words and then her death convinced me of that. It was almost as though Agnes came to me hoping for my support, hoping to prove to herself that, despite everything, I was her friend. But at the same time I couldn't believe that she would care one way or the other.

Once she was gone I moved back into my sitting room. I sat down on my parents' settee. Oh Jenny, I thought, Jenny. What happened? What should I have done to help you? And Gillian Collins. And Elaine Warner. What should I have done?

About an hour later – it was nine o'clock, I was about to watch the news, I couldn't think what else to do with myself, I was in a state of shock, torn between wanting to go to Robert and knowing I could not – there was a knock at my door. I almost didn't hear it, it was so tentative, one faint clack of the knocker. I got up and looked out the window, but couldn't see anything. I picked up the poker from beside the fire. I stood beside the door and spoke loudly, 'Who is it?'

'It's Lolly, Elizabeth, Lolly Senior.'

I opened the door. There was Lolly, black mascara streaked down her face. She rushed in and with her brought the cold night air. She stood in the door to my sitting room, hugging herself in her great black coat, a beret pulled down over her ears.

'Have you h–heard,' she asked, her voice cracking, 'h–have you heard what's happened?

I nodded and stepped toward her.

She recoiled. 'No one b–believes me,' her voice was uneven and raw, 'no one will listen to what I have to say. I thought you m–might – I thought – I know that you cared about Jenny, that you . . . I couldn't go to her family. I n–need to tell someone, I can't go to the police, they won't believe me, no one believes me . . .'

I put my arm around her and squeezed hard, as though that might cut off the stuttering words. It did.

I took Lolly upstairs to the bathroom. I sat her down, got out my face cream and some cotton wool and cleaned her face. I gave her a warm damp flannel which she twisted around and around in her hands. Neither of us spoke. I gave her a towel. We went back downstairs and I made her a cup of tea. We sat in the kitchen. I suddenly felt wary of taking her to the room where Agnes had been, as though she might have left something behind, something malevolent, something that could see and hear what Lolly had to say.

'It's Agnes,' Lolly said, calm now, ready to speak steadily. 'It's because of Agnes.'

'I know,' I said. I wanted her to see that I was ready to believe her. And I was, I was ready to believe.

'She's a witch,' said Lolly, 'I can show you. I found a book in the library at Cambridge. 1593 – that's the date it was published. It's a kind of, I don't know, a testament or something, it's a record of what happened in the village – our village, in Warboys. Right here. Three people were hanged for witchcraft – three people. A family. A mother, a father, and their daughter. The Samuels. That was their name. And the daughter, she was called Agnes. Agnes Samuel. You see? She's come back.'

I took a sip of my tea and found it had gone cold. I got up and pulled the blind down on the window over the sink. I wanted to stay calm. 'What did this book say?'

'The old woman, the mother, she bewitched her neighbour's children – the Throckmortons, Robert Throckmorton, that was the father's name.'

I was getting very cold. My back was beginning to feel stiff. 'Robert Throckmorton?' I said. I felt as though Lolly's story might overwhelm me.

'Yes. And they were all hanged – the mother, the father, and the daughter Agnes.' Lolly looked at me, her eyes wide with appeal, 'Don't you see? She's come back. She's come back to take her revenge. Why else would she return? Why else would she come all the way from America? I took the book from the library,' she lowered her eyes, 'I needed it. I'll take it back. I showed it to Jenny.'

I tried to think what this could mean. 'It could be a rather odd – horrible – coincidence. Couldn't it? The names.' I wanted it to be a coincidence.

Lolly's shoulders fell and she became an unhappy teenager suddenly. 'It could be.'

'But then again –' I didn't want to lose her.

'My friend is dead. She's hanged herself.'

Hanged. The word swung back and forth in front of me. 'Where is the book?'

'I left it with Jenny. I gave it to her. I don't know, it seemed serious to me, and we were scared, but we were sort of enjoying it as well. It was fun. We'd discovered something. It was a secret. We –'

'We'll go and get it.'

'What do you mean?'

'We'll go round to the Throckmorton house and get the book.' I wanted to see it. I wanted to keep it from Agnes. I hoped it wasn't too late.

'Okay,' Lolly stood, nodding in agreement, relieved to be taking action.

'Not tonight. It's too soon. Robert would – Robert would be angry. We'll go tomorrow. After school. Come here and fetch me. We'll go together. I'll help you. I'll help you Lolly.'

After she left I locked the door. I went from room to room in my little cottage and pulled the curtains shut, keeping my face turned away from the window, too afraid to look out into the darkness, too afraid of what – who – I might see.

Elizabeth and Lolly investigate

A pall hangs over the Throckmorton house, a death pall that won't blow away. Inside, it is very quiet. The boys are gone, and with them their human spirit. Graeme is nowhere, again. Martin sits in his chair, the blanket slips off his knees, it keeps slipping off his knees. Robert hovers near to Agnes, he cannot bear to be alone.

Robert has arranged for Jenny to lie in an open casket in the old ballroom. The room is festooned with Derek Hill's scaffolding and the steel pins his workmen hammered into the plaster ceiling are, inexplicably, rusting, stains veining slowly outward. Robert spends the night sweeping. He pushes the dust and debris to the far end of the room and covers it with a tarpaulin. The coroner has released the body and when the undertaker arrives with her in the morning the room is presentable. It is an unusual practice these days, an open coffin in the home, but Robert assures the undertaker that people will want to come and visit, people will want to view the body before the funeral. The undertaker and his assistant surround the coffin with lilies; their heavy scent drifts through the house like a languid ghost.

The day is quiet. After the undertaker leaves there are no other visitors. Robert goes into the ballroom from time to time, he worries that his sister is lonely. He sees her still, white face and realizes yet again that she is gone from him, she is dead. He leaves the room in haste and goes looking for Agnes and when he finds her, clings to her like a child.

Toward the end of the afternoon, twilight, Elizabeth and Lolly arrive at the Throckmorton house. They knock at the front door like strangers. Robert is in the kitchen staring at the sink. He hears the knock and, for a moment, can't imagine what the sound might be. He goes forward – a visitor – at last someone has come to see Jenny.

'She looks fine,' he says, before they can speak. 'I'm so glad that you've come to see her.' He takes both women by the hand, Elizabeth on the left, Lolly on the right, and draws them into the house. 'Come,' he says, 'you'll see.'

Elizabeth thinks the look on his face is quite strange. His eyes are ringed from lack of sleep, the skin beneath them purpling. As he draws them toward the ballroom, Lolly staring at Robert as though mesmerized, Elizabeth realizes what he is doing. She pulls her hand away and takes Lolly by the arm. 'No Robert,' she says softly, 'that's not why Lolly has come.'

Robert looks from Lolly to Elizabeth, uncomprehending. He continues backing into the ballroom. Now Lolly is stretched between Elizabeth and Robert, who each have her by the hand.

'No Robert,' Elizabeth says more firmly. Lolly jerks her hand sharply away from his grasp. Robert is left holding her glove, he looks at it stupidly for a moment, hands it back. 'Lolly left some homework in Jenny's room the other night,' Elizabeth continues. 'She needs it for school. I realize it's not a good time, but she must get it.'

'Oh,' says Robert as though he doesn't quite understand, 'oh.'

'We'll go up to her room. We'll go together. Lolly is upset.'

'Of course,' says Robert, stepping aside. 'Make yourself at home.'

With that, Lolly and Elizabeth rush up the stairs. At the top they meet Agnes. Lolly stifles a scream only partially successfully.

'Hello,' says Elizabeth, with a big smile. She decides to brave it. 'I've brought Lolly. To see Jenny.' Before Agnes can speak Elizabeth embraces her. 'It's terrible for you and for Robert and for Graeme –' over Agnes's shoulder she nods at Lolly to continue along the corridor toward Jenny's room '– coming so soon after Karen.'

Agnes stands impassively while Elizabeth hugs her. Elizabeth can feel her shoulderbones, her ribs, beneath her clothes and finds herself thinking, oh, she's too skinny. They both hear Lolly open the door to Jenny's room. They turn and watch Lolly slip inside.

'She's come to retrieve some school-books,' Elizabeth explains. 'She left them here the other night.' She lowers her voice. 'I think she wanted to see Jenny's room once more, I think she feels it's a way to get close to her friend. Let's leave her to it, shall we?'

'Yes,' says Agnes, smiling. Elizabeth thinks her smile is inappropriate. 'Poor Lolly.'

Elizabeth nods in agreement. 'Poor Lolly.'

Lolly is relieved to find Jenny's room is much the same, except neater than usual. There are no signs of Jenny's death, of what took place. The room is cold but that was always the case. Lolly stands without moving for a moment. She wonders where in the room Jenny died, and wondering that makes her frightened. She thinks perhaps if she holds her breath and shuts her eyes when she lets go and opens them Jenny will be there. She tries but her friend does not appear. Jenny is not there.

Lolly works her way through the room quickly and systematically.

Elizabeth is viewing the body. There was no way around it, Robert insisted. Elizabeth feels a little queasy upon seeing Jenny's face, doll-like in death as she never was in life.

'The funeral is the day after tomorrow. Three o'clock. You must come,' Robert says.

'Of course,' says Elizabeth. 'I'll be there.'

'No wake, no reception. We had that for Karen. We can't face it again.'

'That sounds wise.'

'Just a funeral. In the church. At three.'

Robert is nervous, agitated. Elizabeth watches him and thinks, for the first time ever, I have no idea how he is feeling. What could he be feeling?

After a while Lolly appears in the doorway. 'I found it,' she says, holding up a science textbook. She doesn't come forward into the room.

'Oh good,' says Robert, walking over to give the girl an awkward hug. 'Thanks Lolly,' he says, 'thanks for coming.'

Lolly and Elizabeth don't speak until they are up the drive and halfway through the village. Elizabeth can't wait any longer.

'Did you find it?'

'No,' says Lolly, 'it wasn't there. I looked everywhere. It's gone. Agnes has taken it.' She bursts into tears.

Elizabeth grabs her hand, slows their pace, puts her arm around Lolly's shoulder. 'It's okay. We'll be okay without it, you'll see.' She wonders what she means.

'Did you see her?'

'Yes.'

'What did she look like?'

'She looked – okay. You know Jenny's face. She looked calm. She looked like she wasn't there anymore.'

'Why did she do it, Elizabeth?' Lolly's grief is powerful and damaging.

'I don't know – I –'

'I should never have brought her that book. It was Agnes.' Lolly stops walking. 'Do you think it was Agnes?'

Elizabeth closes her eyes. Her head is pounding. How could it be?

'The book is gone, Elizabeth, I left it there with her that night.'

'We'll find the book. I want to see the book.'

'How?'

'We'll go to London. There'll be a copy in the British Library.'

Doors close in Warboys

After Jenny's death the temperature in Warboys falls several degrees. The air smells of ice and frozen peat. In nearby canals and streams the water flows very slowly as if at any moment it might freeze. It is March, but the crocuses and daffodils show no sign of emerging.

With Jenny's death, the village stops talking. The gossip and malice grind to a halt. Marlene Henderson has returned to work, she works long days and at night cooks Geoff heavy German meals. The Black Hat is quiet, the few people who venture forth talk about anything else, anything that comes to mind, apart from the Throckmortons, apart from Agnes and Karen and Jenny. Jim and Lolita busy themselves, they are finally redecorating the downstairs ladies' loo, they talk of tiles, of colours, of basins and ventilation, they ask opinions, compare prices.

At night the blue light from the village's televisions seeps past the sitting room curtains and illuminates the Warboys sky dully. The citizenry is in retreat. There will be no village uprising, no public accusations, no collectively hurled abuse, no stoning. The village backs down, as if they hope that because the gossip has stopped, the stories will go away. If no one speaks of it, it cannot be true.

The good people of Warboys abandon the Throckmortons; they leave the Throckmorton family to find its own way. Like they abandoned the Samuels a long time ago.

Except Elizabeth. And Lolly.

Graeme is in London

Graeme drives down to London. He goes south of the river because he thinks they might have what he wants there. He has connections in Peterborough but he doesn't want to use them, he doesn't want anyone to know what he's doing. He goes into the street market with its yams and its breadfruit and its music.

He stops the first man he thinks looks likely. 'I want to buy a gun.'

'What?' says the man, 'who are you asking?'

Graeme says, 'You,' and the man laughs and brushes Graeme's hand away from his arm lightly.

'I want to buy a gun,' Graeme steps out again toward another black man in a leather jacket.

'Are you crazy? What makes you think you should ask me?'

Graeme keeps going, keeps asking, he'll either find what he's after or get beaten up. He spends the whole night being led astray, traipsing up urine-sprayed steps on rotten council estates. He roams around in his car, on foot with his cane as his companion. White boys offer to sell him drugs. He tells them to fuck themselves and limps down the stairs and away. It's as though he is protected by naiveté.

And he gets it. He gets what he's after. He hands over the cash he withdrew from Karen's account. He drives back to Warboys with the handgun on the passenger seat and his mood lightens with every mile until he's rocking with laughter. He hasn't laughed so hard in ages.

Elizabeth and Lolly go to London

Elizabeth takes Lolly out of school for the day; getting permission was easy given the circumstances, recent events. She picks her up and they drive fast, unaware that, across country, they journey in tandem with Graeme. At St Pancras they walk through the entrance of the library. Elizabeth kept her pass from her London days; she requests the book and while they wait they wander through the reading room, gazing at the other readers. The book arrives and they are on it like cats to a meal.

They sit side by side and begin to read. Later Lolly says she's going to go outside and wait. Elizabeth nods, continues to read. She is hooked. The book has her in its grip.

One hundred thin scripted pages. The ink from one side shows through on the other, sometimes rendering the words blurry and blackened. Arcane spellings, unfamiliar diction and grammar, but the pages drip with the atmosphere of Warboys, recognizable somehow, even now. Elizabeth is riveted; she keeps forgetting to breath. 'Look at where the old witch sits. Did you ever see one more like a witch than she?' It is a chronicle of accusation, a poisoned text fully convinced of its own self-righteous truth. 'Take her away. It is she that hath bewitched us and she will kill us if you do not take her away.' Ordinarily Elizabeth would view the book with scepticism – not its authenticity as a document, but its sixteenth-century assumptions about the supernatural, about death and disease. Witchcraft. Mass hysteria. The document is gruesome and compelling. Pain all around – the bewitched children with their uncontrollable fits, the accused witches subjected to cruel tests, scratched and battered and humiliated. And the names. Robert Throckmorton. Jenny Throckmorton. Agnes Samuel. Agnes Samuel. Elizabeth turns the pages until she has finished, until Mother Samuel, Father Samuel and their daughter Agnes are condemned to death. Hanged.

She turns the last page and sits staring out the window. Elizabeth does not know what to do with her knowledge. What can this little book possibly mean? What can this chronicle represent to Warboys now, in our so different century? Who is Agnes Samuel?

Elizabeth drives Lolly home. They are silent much of the way. 'Why?' says Elizabeth when she can stand it no longer, 'did Jenny think – did you and Jenny –' She stops. 'Did you try to use witchcraft yourself?'

'N–no miss,' says Lolly quickly, as though she's in trouble at school. 'I m–mean Elizabeth.'

Elizabeth shoots her a look. 'Are you sure? It may be important.'

Lolly fidgets, unwilling to speak. 'Well,' she says, 'we did a b–b–bit of chanting, lit a few c–candles, read up on spells – that k–kind of thing. But it was just fun, that's all. Fun.'

'Did Jenny think that she was a witch?'

'Agnes?'

'No, Jenny – Jenny herself.'

'Oh,' says Lolly, shocked. 'No. N–not Jenny. It's something I,' she paused, 'p–p–play at. But not . . . seriously.'

'But Agnes . . .?'

'Yes.' Her stutter eases. 'It was like a kind of weird game. Sometimes Jenny seemed to believe it, sometimes not. Until I found the book.'

'What do you think about Agnes now Lolly?' Elizabeth asks.

'I think she is evil,' Lolly answers evenly, staring straight ahead at the road.

Elizabeth drops the girl off at her house and waits until she is safely indoors. The journey has helped Elizabeth compose herself. She drives over to the Throckmorton house.

The old house is full of absences now. During the day Robert pushes his father's chair from room to room. He misses the little boys. Robert and Agnes are on their own, they are always on their own these days. They've given up the supper hour – there is no one to feed except Martin – they go upstairs to their bed. Robert feels guilty as he lies with his wife. How can it be right to take pleasure when Jenny is not yet buried, when she is laid out downstairs? How can she be dead? Agnes is sitting astride him, naked, moving back and forth.

The doorbell rings.

They stop. Agnes lies down, smiling, lips wet. She says she'll wait for him. Robert puts on his dressing gown and goes down the stairs. He opens the front door and, for a moment, can see no one. Then Elizabeth steps forward, out of the dark night.

'Robert,' she says, 'we need to talk.'

Robert sighs. Lizzie always wants to talk, he can feel her heavy and pressing need. He is tired of talking. That's why he loves Agnes, he thinks, she doesn't want to talk. She wants to fuck, she wants to live, she wants to get to it. Without delay. He is about to speak harshly, but stops himself. He feels Jenny, she is in the ballroom behind him. He can smell the lilies.

'All right,' he says. 'I'll get dressed.'

He leaves Elizabeth standing in the open door. She pauses for a moment and considers whether or not to go in the ballroom and look at Jenny once again. She walks forward, toward the coffin. There she is, Jenny. She lays her hand on her cold brow. 'We'll sort it out,' she whispers. 'Don't worry.' Then she turns to leave.

She is shocked to see Agnes standing by the door. Elizabeth thinks she looks taller, thinner, altogether sharper, more extreme. They move into the entrance foyer, away from Jenny.

Agnes speaks slowly. 'So,' she says, 'have you come to tell me a story?'

'You know about the book.'

Agnes laughs. 'The world is full of stories.'

Elizabeth realizes she is breathing very quickly, she slows herself down. She decides to try out a theory; it develops as she speaks. 'I don't know if Agnes Samuel is your real name. You think you are a witch, but you are not, you can't be. You have internalized the story. I don't know why but –' Elizabeth speaks quickly.

A smile is spreading across Agnes's lovely face.

Elizabeth wants to get it all out in the open, she is dying to get it all out. 'Witches don't exist. The Throckmortons were rich, the Samuels poor. They had no way of mounting a defence. The children were hysterical. No one understood about these things.'

Agnes takes a step toward Elizabeth.

Elizabeth holds her ground. 'The accusations were false, but at that time people believed they were true. The girls' symptoms were real enough. The trial couldn't possibly –'

'Shut up,' hisses Agnes, drawing close. 'Shut up.' Her voice is full of loathing. Elizabeth backs up until she is against the fireplace. Agnes draws nearer. 'All you do is talk, you can't stop talking.' Her nails are long, her face bony, too thin, it is as though she is changing as she speaks. She points her finger at Elizabeth's chest. 'You are jealous of my marriage. You have always been jealous of my marriage. It clouds your judgement.'

'That might be,' says Elizabeth, the mantel pressing into her back. She leans her head back, nudging the painting that hangs over the fireplace. 'I'll admit it. I am jealous. I wish you had never come here, I wish you did not exist. I've seen the book. I've read it. I know what happened to that other Agnes Samuel. I know what you –'

'Look at that,' says Agnes, pointing above Elizabeth's head.

'What?' Elizabeth doesn't dare look, she's afraid it's a trick.

'Look at the painting.'

Elizabeth turns. It's the only painting still hanging in the entrance foyer, a portrait of a man, the glaze yellow and cracked.

'It's Robert Throckmorton,' says Agnes. 'Did you know that? Robert doesn't know that. But I do. His namesake.'

'Agnes, it's not –'

'Shut up,' Agnes says, loudly this time.

'Agnes, you've got to tell me what you –'

Agnes slaps Elizabeth across the face. 'Stop it,' she says, 'stop talking.' Her eyes go black, the pupils eclipsing the irises.

Elizabeth is terrified, her face stinging. She's never been hit before. She thinks of Jenny, she wonders if Jenny saw this face the night she died. She starts again, determined – 'I –'

Agnes slaps her hard this time. Her eyes are still black, they have not returned to green. She is about to speak. The room is full of hissing.

Robert enters. Agnes falls away from Elizabeth. She is immediately smooth. 'Oh there you are sweetheart,' she says, her voice light, dreamy. 'Elizabeth,' she smiles, showing her white, neat teeth, 'can I make you a cup of tea?'

Elizabeth is breathless. She tries to hold her fear inside. She wants to be as charming as Agnes. 'No thank you,' she says, straining.

'What is it you want to discuss, Lizzie?' Robert is calm, at ease, benevolent even, as though he gave himself a pep talk while he got dressed. Be kind to those less fortunate than ourselves.

'Well,' she tries to think, '– I wanted to make sure you want me to come to the funeral tomorrow. I thought you might have decided to keep it quiet, just family.'

'Oh no,' says Robert, looking glum again, 'Jenny would want you to be there. She'd want us all to be there.'

'All right. I'm sorry Robert, I'm sorry to disturb you.'

'That's all right Lizzie.' Robert crosses to her. He puts his arms around his old friend, gives her a hug. Elizabeth closes her eyes tight so she doesn't have to look at Agnes. She breathes deeply of Robert, willing him not to release her.

A row of solemn teenagers

Jenny had often thought about her own funeral. Having gone so far as to plan it on occasion, she might have found the real thing uncomfortably close to her fantasy. Or perhaps she would have been pleased. There is a row of solemn teenagers dressed in black, leaning into the wind, Lolly at their head. Her family in a tight knot around Martin in his wheelchair – Robert, Agnes. Graeme is there, he stands slightly apart, his hands shoved deep into his pockets. Weeping into the collar of his coat, trying to hide his distress. Karen's mother has brought the little boys home to Warboys for the day so that they can attend, she stands as far away from Graeme as possible. Mr McKay from school, with the Headteacher. Elizabeth. The vicar says his prayers and speaks of Jenny's good character. Robert and Graeme each heave a shovel full of dirt; Lolly drops a red rose on top of the coffin. And it begins to rain.

Afterwards, Elizabeth follows the Throckmortons back to their house, she doubts she is welcome but she can't stay away. Robert is friendly to her, welcoming, as though grateful for the distraction. She takes it upon herself to build a fire in the grate in the sitting room. She wheels Martin in his chair next to the fire, tucks the blanket around him fondly. 'There you go Mr T,' she says, 'there you are.' Robert bustles about making drinks. The little boys have left already and he feels their absence keenly.

'There's a book,' Elizabeth begins. She's on her knees in front of the fire, next to Martin. She's not sure where Agnes is; this is not the right time but she thinks it will never be the right time. 'Lolly came across it. She was doing some research into the history of Warboys.'

'Is Lolly here?' Robert asks, looking around the room suddenly.

'No, she –'

'I should have asked her back. She's a nice girl.'

'Yes she is. She found this book Robert, this strange little book,' Elizabeth can see it on the library desk, lit from within, glowing.

Agnes enters the room. She is wearing a black velvet scarf around her neck, as she moves it flashes scarlet lining. As she crosses the room Martin's eyes follow her.

'Here's your whisky, my love,' Robert hands Agnes a drink. 'What will you have, Lizzie?'

Just then the front door swings open and wind tears through the house. The fire gutters and backs up in the grate. The door slams shut and in walks Graeme. He is soaked through from the rain. He stumbles over the threshold of the room; he is without his cane. He limps across to where Elizabeth is kneeling. 'Lizzie,' his voice is slurred as though he has been drinking, 'did you know my boys are gone, did you know their grandmother took them . . .' He collapses onto the floor, his legs folding beneath him, slow and awkward like a camel. His features are smudged, he looks at Elizabeth, pushing back his wet hair, putting all his effort into focusing. 'I killed her. But you know that, don't you Lizzie. You know everything about us, our family. You always did.'

Elizabeth can hardly speak. 'Who?' she says, whispering. 'Who did you kill?'

Graeme swings his big head down and up. 'Karen. My wife.' He clutches his hair and drags in a breath, gasping. 'My wife,' he says loudly. 'Karen. It's my fault.' He looks into the fire. 'Right here in this room,' he adds. 'The boys know,' he says, ragged and tearful, 'the boys know everything.'

Agnes and Robert cross the room at the same time. Agnes sits down on the sofa, tucking her legs up and taking a sip from her drink as though she is watching television. She looks on as Robert stands next to Elizabeth. He puts his hand on his brother's head, stroking once, twice.

'Robert,' Graeme says, looking up. 'I didn't kill Jenny.'

Robert lifts his hand away quickly. 'I know that.'

'No,' he insists, 'I didn't kill Jenny.' He looks around the room, Elizabeth knows he is looking for Agnes. He twists around on his knees awkwardly. 'She did.' He points at Agnes. 'Agnes killed Jenny. That bitch. I never touched her. She did it.'

Graeme hauls himself up off the floor using Robert's arm for leverage. Once standing he doesn't let go of his brother; they are locked together head-to-head. At this moment they look terribly alike, almost mirror-image. Elizabeth stares, fascinated. Then she looks around to see what Agnes is doing. She is sitting on the settee, drink in hand.

Elizabeth screams.

The two men separate.

'She's gone,' says Elizabeth, 'where is Agnes?' One instant she was there, Elizabeth staring, the next she had disappeared. Elizabeth did not blink, she did not glance away. Agnes vanished.

Graeme pulls his gun from the back of his waistband and heads for the door.

Moments pass. Robert looks from the fire to the glass of whisky on the table and back at the fire again. He stares at Elizabeth as though he is trying to think of something to say. Then he gives a shudder and it clicks in to place.

'Have I told you, Lizzie,' his voice is quiet, controlled, 'how very much I love my wife?'

His face changes again. 'Graeme will kill her,' he says. 'He'll try to kill Agnes. I've got to stop him – I –'

A bright light comes up in the far corner of the sitting room. They both turn. Agnes is standing in the door to the kitchen, the light from behind rendering her silhouette black. She walks forward, now they can see she is smiling, she draws Robert toward her. 'Robert,' she says, 'let's go upstairs. Let's –'

'For god's sake Robert,' Elizabeth shouts, 'you've got to listen to me.' With surprising force she grabs Robert by the arm and pulls him through the sitting room, the foyer, out the front door, into the pouring rain. They grapple. Robert is reluctant to use his full strength. Elizabeth pulls him down into a puddle that has collected in the drive. 'There's a book,' she repeats, 'it's about Agnes, witchcraft, it's about Agnes Samuel –'

Now Robert is very angry. He pushes Elizabeth into the mud, and stands up. She grabs his trouser leg. He shakes his foot, trying not to hurt her, kicking until he is free.

Robert runs into the house calling Agnes's name. There is no reply. He travels from room to room, leaving muddy handprints on the walls, dripping onto the carpets. From their bedroom he looks out over the field. He sees a figure running away from the house; he flies down the stairs and through the kitchen, outside.

Martin acts

In the sitting room, by the fire, Martin stirs. He is alone. Everyone has rushed away. Gripping the black vinyl arms of the wheelchair, he stands up, and sits down again. Pushes himself up, sits down heavily. Stands up one more time, and then, unable to move his legs, falls forward onto the floor.

He lies there, staring at the carpet, for a long time.

It is dark and there is chaos

Elizabeth is looking for Agnes. She wants to find Agnes, to confront her, to find out the truth. If she finds Agnes, she can protect Robert. Elizabeth knows Robert needs to be protected.

It is a moonless night. The rain is light but piercingly cold, it burns as it lands on her face. Elizabeth stands in the garden and looks back at the house. Upstairs the rooms are dark and, for a moment, she sees a face. Jenny. Now she is gone. Elizabeth shakes her head, I'm seeing things. There is no point in becoming too afraid.

The grass is slick, slippery, the earth is soft and muddy. Elizabeth makes her way across the garden as fast as she can, toward the rose arbour at the bottom. There is a low stone bench next to an old brick wall. It is empty. Elizabeth blinks. Agnes is sitting on it.

'Come and sit beside me,' she says pleasantly.

Elizabeth obeys. She feels very cold and searches her pocket, hoping for gloves that aren't there. The stone bench sends a chill up her spine. Agnes isn't wearing her coat either, she sits as calm and relaxed as earlier.

'These Throckmorton men,' she says with a laugh, 'so dramatic.'

'It hasn't always been that way.'

'No?' Agnes raises her eyebrows. 'Do you mean to say that Robert and Graeme got along before I showed up?'

Elizabeth considers. 'No.'

'And Graeme and Karen had the perfect marriage?'

'No.'

'And Jenny wasn't a fucked up depressed motherless teenager?'

'No, I –'

'See what I mean? I haven't done anything. They were already doing it to themselves.'

'So what are you doing?' Elizabeth asks.

'What do you think?'

'You came to Warboys to –'

Agnes interrupts. 'Oh look,' she says, pointing across the field, 'there goes Robert. I'm sure I saw Graeme heading that way a few minutes ago. Let's follow, shall we?' Agnes tries to stand, Elizabeth grabs her wrist and pulls her back down to the bench. She is surprised by her own audacity.

'I want to know why you are here.' She speaks quickly, as if she hopes her very tone will make Agnes respond.

Agnes looks at Elizabeth unmoved, as though it is natural to be sitting on this bench in the night, in the rain. 'Does anyone know the answer to that question?' She smiles.

Elizabeth persists. 'Do you love Robert? Did you ever love Robert?'

Agnes gives her a pitying look. She tries to stand, Elizabeth pulls her down again. She can see that Agnes is getting angry.

'I'm not here to answer your questions. That's one thing you can be sure of.'

'I want you to tell me if you love him. He deserves your love. He's got nothing to do with that other Robert Throckmorton, all those years ago.'

Agnes twists her arm away abruptly. She catches Elizabeth off balance and sends her hurtling off the bench, into the roses. By the time Elizabeth recovers, Agnes is gone. But her voice returns through the dark: 'You don't know anything about love Elizabeth; you don't know anything.'

'You're wrong Agnes Samuel,' Elizabeth answers. 'You're wrong. You wait. You'll see.'

Graeme loves Agnes

Graeme lurches through the grounds of the estate. He does not have his cane, and the metal of the gunbarrel rubs against his tailbone where he has shoved it into his trousers. He sees Agnes ahead of him flickering through the trees. She enters one of the holiday cottages. He labours in that direction, too aware of how heavily he is breathing, his feet uncertain on the wet and treacherous ground. Without his cane his leg may betray him.

She has left the door of the cottage ajar. Graeme stands on the threshold, swaying. This is the cottage in which he has been living and it smells bad. There are dirty dishes, open boxes of cereal, cans of drink, piled on the floor around the heap of clothes in which he has been sleeping.

She is sitting on the bare stripped bed, composed, seductive. She smiles and he feels as though her smile is melting him, melting his hard heart. At that moment he knows he could love her again. She speaks. 'Have you come to kill me?' and she laughs. She pats the bed, uncrossing her legs. She knows he wants to kill her and fuck her, he wants both these things. 'You know Graeme, you're not bad-looking,' she says, 'for a cripple.'

Graeme dives toward her, pushing her down on the bed. He pulls his gun out of his trousers and when she sees it Agnes laughs once again. He throws himself on top of her and they grapple. She's right, he thinks, I do want to kill her. I do want to fuck her.

Agnes stops struggling. 'We don't have to do this,' she says. 'We don't have to fight.'

She reaches up and gives him a kiss on the lips. He responds to her, he can't help it.

'Kiss me again,' he says.

She reaches up as though to embrace him and then knocks his arm away. He loses his balance. The gun spins out of his hand and drops to the floor, skittering out of sight. They both roll off the bed, searching for the weapon on their hands and knees. Graeme sees his chance, he pushes the television off the table; it misses Agnes narrowly, knocking over a lamp. The lamp smashes, wires fuse, sparks discharge, and the lights in the cottage fail. At the power point an electrical fire ignites, it runs up the power leads and leaps on to the curtains. Agnes lies on the floor laughing. Graeme crawls toward her.

Robert is crossing the field, drawing near to the cottage. He knows Graeme and Agnes are there, he can hear shouting, crashing. He's got to get to Agnes, he can't think of anything else. He's got to get to her, he's got to save her. Without her his life is worth nothing; without her he can't live.

Robert flings himself through the door. He jumps onto Graeme's back, flattening him to the floor. Agnes rolls under the bed, she retrieves the gun. The cottage is burning, flames running up the wallpaper, along the carpet. Agnes stands over the men, pointing the gun, laughing as Graeme attempts to get out from under Robert. The brothers haul themselves to their feet. She hands the gun to Robert as Graeme screams and lunges at her, grabbing at her throat.

'I'll kill you,' he shouts, 'I'll kill you,' and he squeezes hard, his hands closing around her neck.

Agnes can not breathe. Her face is pink and her eyes bulge slightly. She can not make a sound. She stares past Graeme, into Robert's eyes.

'Let her go,' says Robert.

Graeme tightens his grip.

'Let her go Graeme.'

Graeme looks at Robert, shaking his head. 'I'll kill her,' he says.

Agnes makes a little sound, her pupils dilate.

'Let her go, Graeme,' Robert says slowly.
'No,' replies Graeme.
Robert shoots his brother in the head.

Robert shoots his brother in the head

Robert shoots his brother in the head. The bullet enters his left temple and exits through the other side, spewing gore. Neither Agnes nor Robert makes a sound. Graeme lets forth a kind of whistle, a tiny squeak, then slumps forward into Robert's arms. Agnes steps back. Robert drops the gun.

The cottage explodes into flames, roaring.

Out on the lawn, Elizabeth arrives. She is unable to get close enough to do anything, driven back by the heat.

Inside the cottage, Robert is frantic, looking for Agnes. He can't find her. He can't see her through the smoke and the flames. He has got to get out of the cottage.

Robert bursts through the front door and rolls on the ground, his clothes on fire. Elizabeth throws herself onto him, smothering the flames with her body.

'She's inside,' he screams, 'she's inside there.'

'There's nothing you can do,' Elizabeth shouts. 'Nothing.'

The cottage burns for a long time.

Robert can't leave

Elizabeth helps Robert up off the ground. His face is blackened with soot. He stands in front of the burning building. He thinks everything he loves is inside that cottage. Elizabeth tries to pull him away. No, he says, he can't leave. She should go and ring the fire brigade. She tries to get him to come with her, he needs to keep warm. But he won't go. He'll stand guard over the pyre. It's like Bonfire Night, he thinks. He needs to stand guard over the fire.

In the end, when it is clear that there will be nothing left except a smoking watery hole, no survivors, it is the Fire Chief who persuades Robert to come away. An ambulance transports him over the field. He takes one look at the big house, unchanged, unscathed, and begins to weep.

Elizabeth

I knew she was gone for good. As I held Robert in my arms I knew it was over. I felt a cheap sense of victory. Robert looked up at me, bewildered and frightened, but also, I think, relieved.

The cottage burned to the ground. They found Graeme in the charcoal and debris. Robert told me he had shot him, he whispered it to me in the kitchen while the doctor and the firemen milled around making cups of tea. For a few days I was worried that they would find out, but Graeme's body was so charred that the coroner did not determine that he had been shot before he was consumed by flames.

When I got to the house to ring the fire brigade, I found Martin lying on the floor. God knows how he got there, I can only assume Agnes pushed him. He was cold and bruised but, as far as the doctor could tell, basically all right. Like me, like Robert; I knew then we would be all right.

It's a cliché of village life to think that every family who lives there has been there for centuries, a cliché that no longer holds much truth; Agnes's presence in Warboys demonstrated that. In our village there were very few people whose families had been resident for more than one generation. The Throckmortons, of course. I think Geoff Henderson's lot had been around for quite a while, and Geraldine Andley, the woman Jim Drury liked to refer to as the village tart. The rest of us, Jim and Lolita included, were transplants. Old and established transplants in most cases, but incomers all the same. I'm sure there were other old families in the region, the fens are known for their isolation, their flat wet ancientness, their inbreeding. But it was the character of Warboys to be characterless. It was part of the reason why we had no collective memory. Why Agnes Samuel moved among us, unrecognized. And I think that we had no memory precisely because of what happened; our past was too shameful to look on and that was why so many people had drifted away. The guilt that lay buried beneath our cobbled streets made us easy prey.

I gave up working for the Trevelyans so I could take care of Andrew and Francis and Martin, full-time. With the insurance money and revenue raised from the sale of my parents' house, we rebuilt the cottage. Since then we have added three more cottages and expanded the estate's holiday facilities considerably. With the help and advice of the National Trust we have finished fixing up the house, including the magnificent carved plaster ceiling in the Elizabethan ballroom. It hangs over our heads like gorgeous sculpted ice cream. The public can make appointments to visit. And we offer accommodation in the old wing of the house, upmarket bed-and-breakfast. Occasionally we have guests who are interested in the strange history of the witches of Warboys, Mother Samuel, Father Samuel, and their daughter Agnes, but we do not encourage them.

The painting still hangs in the entrance hall. I've never told Robert that Agnes said the portrait is of his sixteenth-century namesake; as far as he's concerned it's some crusty old relative, of no relevance to today's Throckmorton family. There can't be too many people in this world who can say they are proud of the past, no matter how distant or recent. We all have secrets, we all have mysteries.

I think about that little book from time to time. The story it tells is grim, but if you read between the lines, it's much worse. The Samuels were beholden to their neighbours the Throckmortons, the power the wealthy family had over their lives was absolute. Disease and illness were feared, there was no cosy NHS surgery down the street. Infant mortality was very high; the Samuels had only one child, Agnes, in their old age – there must have been other children, what was their fate? Agnes's father, John Samuel, was a brutal man and he fought hard against the allegations of witchcraft, but he could not stop the Throckmortons from making their case. And those confessions came after years of sickness and blame and terror, and we all know how unreliable confessions can be. When you read between the lines that book tells a different story, one that's not hard to discern from the vantage point of our shiny new century.

I'm not ashamed to say that we are doing well. The boys are tall and straight-backed and thriving. Andrew excels in school. Francis has started school himself now, and he's very lively. Sometimes he tells little lies, but children do, don't they? One day he told me he saw Agnes at school, that she was outside the classroom looking in through the window. When I asked him to explain all he did was giggle. I'm sure he was making it up and I tried not to make an issue out of it; that's what the childcare books advise.

Robert and I are considering having our own child, before it's too late. He is a quiet man, he doesn't say much, but I think he is content.

We are cautious. We keep to ourselves. Agnes came to Warboys to destroy the Throckmortons and, although she went a long way toward succeeding, ultimately she failed. We don't want to tempt fate. We don't want to appear too good, too happy. I felt dead for a long time, and now I feel alive.

Robert

I murdered my brother. I killed my own brother. Graeme killed Karen. Jenny killed herself. And I shot Graeme. I have to live with it, I have to live with this fact. It breathes when I breathe, it sleeps where I sleep; it's not going to go away.

And I still don't believe that Agnes and Graeme were unfaithful to me. Even if I had seen it, seen them, together, I don't think I would have believed it was happening. I would have thought it was a trick, my eyes were deceiving me. Elizabeth tells me that it has to have been true, she reminds me that both Karen and Jenny made the same allegation. But I don't know, I still find it hard to register. And I suppose in a way it doesn't matter, I don't have to believe it, even if it is the truth. There are bigger truths out there, truths more difficult to face.

And Agnes disappeared. She left me behind. She left me to get on with my life.

I inherited the two little boys, if inheriting is the right word for it. Their welfare became my responsibility, mine alone. Graeme was dead, and so was Karen. Graeme and Karen and I had never discussed their guardianship, but it didn't require discussion. And in some ways the boys were lucky. Their parents were dead, there is no underestimating that loss, but they didn't have to leave their home. They were quite aware of what had happened. But they were used to me, and I to them, and we were better off because of that. I can't bear to think about what happens to other children in this situation; both parents dead and sent to live with strangers. New rules, new food, new house, new everything. I did what I could to make things easier for them and I had Elizabeth there to help me. Elizabeth was there beside me, right away. She held me in her arms while the cottage burned to the ground.

The boys don't call me Daddy. Despite the biological facts. Nor Elizabeth Mummy. They call me Robert, ever since they learned to speak they've called me Robert, not Uncle Robert. They call Elizabeth Lizzie. But they come to us as though we are their parents. They come to us in the night – I'm in what was Graeme and Karen's room, with Elizabeth. They get out of their beds, one at a time, and they trot down the hall to where we are sleeping. They stand at the foot of the bed and call our names until we wake up and invite them in. Most nights our bed is full of little boys by three or four a.m. They put their cold feet on our backs and snuggle down. Once in a while Francis wets the bed, either his own little bed or our bigger one. We don't make a fuss, we simply strip the sheets, change his clothes, stroke his head. A little bit of bed-wetting is a small price to pay after the trauma of what took place. The boys are very good, so good, quiet – too quiet. We can't begin to know how to help them get over what happened, so we let life continue. And life does continue.

There's so much talk about 'the family' these days. The disintegration of the extended family, the importance of the family unit. But families aren't so terrific. In fact most of the really sick stuff you hear about these days takes place within the family. I had a big family once, now I have a small, make-shift family. Roles shift and change. We make do, we get by. We take care of each other, we take care of my father. Agnes used to say it was one of the things she loved about me, how when she married me, she married my family. I loved her for that as much as anything.

Elizabeth and I got married in a private ceremony in Geoff and Marlene Henderson's garden. Geoff and Marlene were our only guests, our witnesses. The vicar performed the ceremony, he kept it brief. I wasn't that keen to be married by him again, I thought it would bring forth too many associations with my wedding to

Agnes. But Elizabeth pointed out that with anyone else we might have to do something about my first marriage, I might be asked to produce divorce papers or a death certificate or something like that. The vicar was in Warboys throughout, he saw what happened. People in the village went to him with their worries and, later, their fears about Agnes. He agreed to marry Elizabeth and me; I think he saw it as a way of putting the whole episode firmly in the past.

And it is in the past. But the past lives on inside me.

Elizabeth says that the arrival of Agnes coincided with everything going wrong – not coincided, Elizabeth says that it was *because* of Agnes that everything went wrong. But I'm not so sure. Graeme and Karen had been having problems for years, and Jenny, well, when she was born our mother died and that was a long time before Agnes arrived. So you see, I say to Elizabeth, the Throckmortons were already in difficulty.

'Well,' says Elizabeth, 'you only made her task easier. You helped her on her way.'

In the evenings Elizabeth and I watch telly. It fills the silences. It makes our evenings totally unlike the evenings I used to have at home with the red, orange and gold of the open fire, Agnes, and the whisky. Our evenings are cool blue and flickering, we like them that way. Occasionally one of us laughs at something that's been said and we turn and smile at each other. Elizabeth has a very sweet face and the sweetest thing of all is how familiar it is to me.

I know everything there is to know about Elizabeth. Our pasts are shared in many ways. There are no surprises, no gaps in our knowledge. I guess we resemble Graeme and Karen in that way. Reassuring for the boys, I suppose, a kind of continuity. And reassuring for me.

At night sometimes I creep into the old wing of the house. I sit on the floor outside what was once our bedroom. I think about what happened. I think about Agnes. I listen out for the voices.

Part of me left with Agnes. The better part perhaps, I don't know.

Elizabeth is happy, and that's a good thing. Our lives are dull. We are predictable. To see us now you'd never guess at what happened.

I've been to the library to look at the book. I haven't told Elizabeth. I was shocked by it, by the story it told. I think there is no escape from that story. 1593; the Samuels were hanged, my family was responsible. It's enough to turn anyone toward evil.

At night sometimes I hear the voices. Three voices moaning, singing through the house, through the eaves. I greet them silently. I'm happy to hear them. They're all that is left of Agnes for me.

Agnes. My best. My beloved. My girl.

And Agnes?

She isn't gone, is she? No body was found and – no matter how fierce the flames – they should have found some kind of remains. She slipped away through the trees. Did she? Robert wonders. Elizabeth wonders as well, although she won't admit it; it is, after all, her greatest fear. The villagers wonder: did she fight through the smoke and fling open the bathroom window and climb out? Did she gather her cashmere shawl around her shoulders and walk away from Warboys? Is she somewhere now, marshalling her strength, sharpening her charm on yet more eager strangers? And she will return, won't she? It might be ten years before that black taxi makes its way down the high street, it might be one hundred years. We might have to wait another four centuries before we see Agnes Samuel again. But she will return. She will come back to Warboys.

Robert wonders.

Robert hopes.